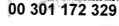
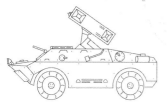

9K31 Strela-1

KT-167-707

AH-1 Cobra

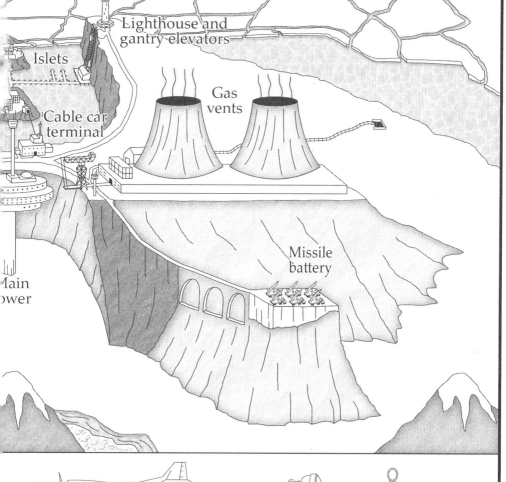

Lighthouse and
gantry elevators

Islets

Gas
vents

Cable car
terminal

Missile
battery

Main
Power

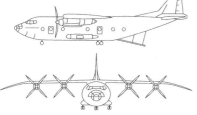

Antonov An-12

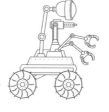

BRTE-500

MATTHEW REILLY

SCARECROW
AND THE ARMY OF THIEVES

MATTHEW REILLY

SCARECROW
AND THE ARMY OF THIEVES

First published in 2011 & 2012 by Orion Books,
an imprint of The Orion Publishing Group Ltd
Orion House, 5 Upper Saint Martin's Lane
London WC2H 9EA

An Hachette UK Company

1 3 5 7 9 10 8 6 4 2

A CIP catalogue record for this book is
available from the British Library.

Hardback ISBN: 978 1 4091 1096 5
Export HB ISBN: 978 1 4091 1097 2

Printed in Great Britain by Clays Ltd, St Ives plc

The Orion Publishing Group's policy is to use papers that are natural,
renewable and recyclable products and made from wood grown in sustainable
forests. The logging and manufacturing processes are expected to
conform to the environmental regulations of the country of origin.

www.orionbooks.co.uk

To my loyal readers,
this one's for you

SO ENERGETIC ARE THESE ACTIONS AND SO
STRANGELY DO SUCH POWERFUL DISCHARGES
BEHAVE THAT I HAVE OFTEN EXPERIENCED THE FEAR
THAT THE ATMOSPHERE MIGHT BE IGNITED . . .

Nikola Tesla, inventor

MORE: WHAT WOULD YOU DO? CUT A GREAT ROAD
THROUGH THE LAW TO GET AFTER THE DEVIL?
ROPER: I'D CUT DOWN EVERY LAW IN ENGLAND TO
DO THAT!
MORE: OH? AND WHEN THE LAST LAW WAS DOWN,
AND THE DEVIL TURNED ROUND ON YOU—WHERE
WOULD YOU HIDE?

Robert Bolt,
A Man for All Seasons

HISTORY IS MOVING PRETTY QUICKLY THESE DAYS
AND THE HEROES AND VILLAINS KEEP ON CHANGING
PARTS.

James Bond in *Casino Royale*,
written by Ian Fleming

BACKGROUND REPORT

CLASSIFICATION: TOP SECRET/EYES ONLY
AUTHOR: RETTER, MARIANNE (D-6)
SUBJECT: THE 'ARMY OF THIEVES'

INCIDENT 1: 9/9
THE CHILEAN PRISON BREAKOUT

The first incident occurred on September 9 and it involved the mass breakout of one hundred prisoners from a maximum-security military prison at Valparaiso, Chile.

Shortly before dawn, a small force of heavily armed men attacked the prison using military tactics and suppressed weapons. The operation took less than thirty minutes. All of the prison's guards were killed.

Among the prisoners released were twelve former high-ranking members of the Comando de Vengadores de Mártires, the 'Avengers of the Martyrs', a right-wing paramilitary group that performed abductions and assassinations for the Pinochet regime.

On their departure, the attackers left a message on the gates of the prison:

THE ARMY OF THIEVES IS RISING!

It had been painted in the dead guards' blood.

INCIDENT 2: 10/10
THE THEFT OF THE 'OKHOTSK'

One month and one day later, on October 10, a Russian cargo freighter, the OKHOTSK, was seized by persons unknown off the west coast of Africa.

According to its cargo manifest, the ship was carrying timber, fuel and building supplies des-tined for Zimbabwe and its seizure was initially believed to be the work of west African pirates. But then the Russians sent half of their Atlantic fleet to find the ship.

Our investigations have revealed that the OKHOTSK was actually carrying a large weapons shipment intended for sale to three embargoed African regimes. Its cargo was:

- 310 AK-47 ASSAULT RIFLES;
- 4.5 million rounds of 7.62mm AMMUNITION for those rifles;

- 90 RPG-7 GRENADE LAUNCHERS;
- 9 STRELA-1 AMPHIBIOUS ANTI-AIRCRAFT VEHICLES, each equipped with four 9M31 surface-to-air missiles;
- 12 ZALA-421-08 unmanned aerial surveillance DRONES;
- 18 machine-gun-mounted JEEPS;
- 9 SHIPBORNE TORPEDO LAUNCH PODS containing four APR-3E torpedoes each; and
- 2 MIR-4 DSRV (Deep Submergence Rescue Vehicle) mini-submarines.

The freighter was manned by a ten-man squad of Spetsnaz special forces troops.

This last fact makes it extremely unlikely that the OKHOTSK was taken by African pirates. African pirates are usually poor fishermen who attack commercial vessels for the purpose of securing ransoms; at the first sign of any military presence on a ship they invariably flee.

On the contrary, the force of men that took the OKHOTSK knew exactly what was on it and were skilled enough to defeat a team of crack Russian paratroopers to get it.

To this day, the OKHOTSK has not been found.

INCIDENT 3: 11/11
A ROBBERY OVER GREECE

In the early hours of November 11, an unmarked German Gulfstream jet carrying nine billion euros

from Germany to Greece disappeared from the skies above northern Greece.

The plane's cargo of hard currency was intended for use in the latest stage of Greece's financial bailout.

The wreckage of the plane was discovered the following morning. One crew member was missing, the other three had all been shot in the head at close range.

The money was gone.

Painted on the interior walls of the plane was the same symbol seen at the Chilean military jail: a circle with an 'A' inside it plus the taunt: 'THE ARMY OF THIEVES WAS HERE!'

INCIDENT 4: 12/12
ATTACK ON A MARINE BASE
Helmand Province, Afghanistan

In the early hours of December 12, a large and heavily armed force of over one hundred men attacked a remote United States Marine Corps staging and supply base in southern Afghanistan.

The force attacked with precision, skill and overwhelming violence, killing all of the twenty-two engineers and maintenance staff stationed at the isolated base.

The attackers' objective, it seems, was not the

murder of US service personnel. They were after
the aircraft kept at the base.

The attackers took four AH-1 Cobra attack helicopters plus two Marine Corps V-22 Osprey 'Warbird'
gunships (one of which contained eight crates of
brand-new USMC cold-weather Arctic/mountain warfare clothing intended for US forces fighting in
Afghanistan over the winter).

The attackers painted on the walls of a tent:
'SEASON'S GREETINGS, YANKEE SCUM! FROM THE ARMY
OF THIEVES!' plus the 'A' symbol.

INCIDENT 5: 1/1
A SECOND BREAKOUT
Darfur, Sudan

Soon after midnight on January 1, a temporary UN
prison camp in the Darfur region of Sudan was
raided by a force of armed and masked men.

102 prisoners variously described as 'rev-
olutionary fighters, Islamic militants and
narco-mercenaries' from several African nations
were freed from the prison and spirited away. All
but two of the camp's UN guards were killed.

The two surviving guards reported that the raid-
ing force used a variety of Russian-made assault
weapons and two American Cobra attack helicopters. The raiders departed with their large
number of escapees in two V-22 Osprey gunships
with US Marine Corps markings.

Before they left, they spray-painted a message on one of the prison's walls: 'THE ARMY OF THIEVES JUST GOT STRONGER ...'

INCIDENT 6: 2/2
APARTMENT BOMB IN MOSCOW

The spectacular destruction of a twenty-story luxury apartment building in Moscow on February 2 has been well documented in the media.

What was not revealed to the media was the graffiti found covering every wall of the destroyed building's adjoining parking lot: hundreds of A's in circles had been spray-painted there.

INCIDENT 7: 3/3
THE TORTURE OF AN AMERICAN OFFICIAL
Washington, D.C., USA

Shortly after midnight on March 3, a small group of unidentified men raided the Georgetown home of the former US Secretary of Defense, killed his two bodyguards and kidnapped the ageing Secretary.

The Secretary was found — alive — by two early-morning hikers in Rock Creek Park, bound to a torture device.

He had been waterboarded.

Carved into the skin of his chest was the following symbol:

During his subsequent debriefing, the Secretary exhibited symptoms of severe shock. He continually shouted: 'Beware the Army of Thieves! Beware the Army of Thieves!'

CONCLUSIONS

The seven incidents outlined above describe in somewhat grim detail the rise of a new non-state entity calling itself the 'Army of Thieves'.

Where it is based and who comprises it are not known.

What is known is this: it is a force of militarily-trained individuals that over the last seven months has obtained for itself a considerable supply of weapons, finance and manpower.

It does not, as yet, show any religious or cultural motivations for its aggressive acts. We do not yet know what is driving this rogue 'Army'.

But it wants us to notice it.

It has carried out one operation a month, every

month, for the last seven months, in accordance with a pattern where the number of the day and the month are the same. Clearly, it wants us to see this pattern, and we should be aware of it, because tomorrow is April 4 ...

SCARECROW

AND THE ARMY OF THIEVES

**DRAGON ISLAND BASE
AS SEEN FROM THE AIR
FACING NORTH**

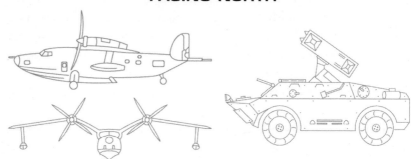

THE ISLAND OF THE DRAGON

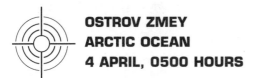

OSTROV ZMEY
ARCTIC OCEAN
4 APRIL, 0500 HOURS

The plane hurtled down the airstrip, chased by furious machine-gun fire, before it lifted off with a stomach-lurching swoop and soared out over the vast expanse of Arctic sea ice that stretched away to the north.

The plane's pilot, a sixty-year-old scientist named Dr Vasily Ivanov, knew he wouldn't get far. As he'd lifted off, he'd seen two Strela-1 anti-aircraft vehicles—amphibious jeep-like vehicles that were each mounted with four 9M31 surface-to-air missiles—speeding down the runway behind him, about to take up firing positions.

He had perhaps thirty seconds before they blasted him out of the sky.

Ivanov's plane was an ugly Beriev Be-12, a genuine 1960s Soviet clunker. Many years ago, as a young recruit in the Soviet Air Defence Force, Ivanov had flown this very kind of plane, before his talents as a physicist had been spotted and he had been reassigned to the Special Weapons Directorate. On one recent occasion when he had sat as a passenger in the freezing hold of this plane, he'd actually thought that the Beriev and he were very similar. They were both ageing workhorses from a bygone era still toiling away: the Beriev was an old forgotten plane used to shuttle old forgotten teams like his to old forgotten bases in the north; Ivanov was just

old, his bushy Zhivago-style moustache growing greyer every day.

He also never imagined he'd actually pilot a Beriev again, but his team's arrival at the island that morning had not gone according to plan.

Ten minutes earlier, after an overnight flight from the mainland, the Beriev had been making a slow circuit over Ostrov Zmey, a remote island in the Arctic Circle.

A medium-sized semi-mountainous island, Ostrov Zmey—'Dragon Island'—had once held the highest security classification in the Soviet Union alongside nuclear research bases like Arzamas-16 at Sarov and bioweapons centres like the Vektor Institute in Koltsovo. Now, its massive structures lay dormant, kept alive by rotating skeleton crews like Ivanov's from the Special Weapons Directorate. Ivanov and the twelve Spetsnaz troops on the Beriev with him had been arriving for their eight-week stint guarding the island.

When they'd arrived, everything had appeared normal.

As winter faded and the Arctic saw the sun for the first time in months, the sea ice around Dragon had started to break up. The vast frozen ocean stretching north to the pole looked like a pane of smoked glass that had been hit with a hammer—a thousand cracks snaked through it in every direction.

Yet the cold still lingered. The complex at Dragon remained covered in a thin layer of frost.

Despite that, it looked magnificent.

The base's striking central tower still looked futuristic thirty years after it had been built. As tall as a twenty-storey building, it looked like a flying saucer mounted on a single massive concrete pillar. Two slender high-spired mini-towers were perched atop the main disc, as was the base's squat glass-domed command centre.

The towering structure gazed out over the entire island like some kind of space-aged lighthouse. Looming to the east of it were the two mighty exhaust vents. Where the tower exuded grace and sophistication, the vents expressed nothing except brute strength and power. They were the same shape as the cooling towers one saw at a nuclear power plant but twice the size.

The once-great base bore the usual signs of a skeleton crew: pinpoints of light in various places—offices, guardhouses, on the disc-shaped tower itself.

It was also a fortress. Well defended by both its construction and the landscape, a small force like Ivanov's could protect it against any kind of attack. You'd need an army to take Dragon Island.

As his plane had arrived at the island and overflown it, from his seat in the hold Ivanov had seen a steady plume of shimmering gas issuing from the massive exhaust vents, rising into the sky before being blown south. This was odd but not alarming; probably just Kotsky's team venting excess steam from the geothermal piping.

Upon landing on the island's airstrip, Ivanov's team of Spetsnaz guards had disembarked the Beriev and made their way toward the hangar, where Kotsky himself had been standing, waving. Ivanov had lingered behind in the Beriev with a young private he'd ordered to help him carry the new Samovar-6 laser-optic communications gear he'd brought along.

That small delay had saved their lives.

Ivanov's Spetsnaz team had been halfway across the tarmac, totally exposed, when they had been cut down by a sudden burst of machine-gun fire from a force of unseen assailants who had evidently been lying in wait.

Ivanov had dived into the pilot's seat and calling on the skills of his past life, gunned the engines and got the hell out of there—which was how he came to be fleeing Dragon Island.

Ivanov keyed the plane's radio and shouted in Russian. 'Directorate Base! This is Watcher Two—!'

Electronic hash assaulted his ears.

They'd jammed the satellite.

He tried the terrestrial system. No good. Same thing.

Breathing fast, he reached around and grabbed the Samovar radio pack on the seat behind him, the new hardware he'd brought to Dragon Island. It was designed to make secure contact with its satellite not through radio waves but through a direct line-of-sight laser. It had been developed specifically to be immune to the usual jamming techniques.

Ivanov thunked the high-tech radio on the dashboard, pointed its laser sighter up at the sky and turned it on.

'Directorate Base, this is Watcher Two! Come in!' he yelled.

A few moments later, he got a reply.

'*Watcher Two, this is Directorate Base. Encryption protocols for the Samovar-6 system are not yet fully operational. This transmission could be detected—*'

'Never mind that! Someone's at Dragon! They were waiting for us and attacked my team as soon as they disembarked the plane! Shot them all to bits on the tarmac! I managed to take off and am now being fired upon—'

As he said this, Ivanov once again saw the gaseous plume rising from the island's massive vents and his blood went cold.

Mother of God, he thought.

'Base,' he said. 'Perform a UV-4 scan of the atmosphere above Dragon. I think whoever's there has started up the atmospheric device.'

'*They did what . . . ?*'

'I can see a vapour plume rising from the towers.'

'*Good Lord . . .*'

Ivanov made to say more but suddenly the Beriev was hit from behind by a 9M31 surface-to-air missile fired by one of the Strelas. The entire tail section of the old plane disintegrated in an instant and the plane plunged out of the sky.

A few seconds later, the Beriev hit the sea ice and nothing more was heard from Vasily Ivanov.

⏻

His distress call to the Russian Army's Signals Directorate, however, *was* heard by one other listener.

A KH-12 'Improved Crystal' spy satellite operated by the US National Reconnaissance Office.

The message was downloaded and decoded by an automated system according to standard protocols—intercepts of Russian military signals were picked up all the time—but when the keywords DRAGON, UV-4 SCAN and ATMOSPHERIC DEVICE were all found in the same transmission, the message was immediately forwarded to the highest levels of the Pentagon.

THE WHITE HOUSE SITUATION ROOM
WASHINGTON, D.C.
3 APRIL, 1645 HOURS (45 MINUTES LATER)
0545 HOURS (4 APRIL) AT DRAGON

'*Never mind that! Someone's at Dragon!*'

Vasily Ivanov's voice rang out in the wide subterranean room. As Ivanov spoke in Russian, a US Army linguist translated his words into English.

The President of the United States and his Crisis Response Team listened in cold silence.

'*They were waiting for us and attacked my team as soon as they disembarked the plane! Shot them all to bits on the tarmac!*'

The CRT was composed of generals and flag officers from the Army, Navy, Marines and Air Force, the President's National Security Advisor and senior personnel from the NRO, CIA and DIA. The only woman in the room was the representative of the DIA, Deputy Director Alicia Gordon.

'*I managed to take off and am now being fired upon—*'

Manning the digital playback console was a young analyst from the National Reconnaissance Office named Lucas Bowling.

'*Base. Perform a UV-4 scan of the atmosphere above Dragon. I think whoever's there has started up the atmospheric device.*'

Bowling turned off the recording.

'What's a UV-4 scan and have we done it yet?' asked the Army general.

The President's National Security Advisor, a former four-star Marine Corps general named Donald Harris answered. 'UV-4 is a region of the light spectrum invisible to the human eye, the fourth grade of the ultraviolet spectrum.'

'I've got the scan here, sir,' Bowling said, glancing at the President. 'But if I may, before I show it to you, it would be helpful to take you back a bit. After we received this intercept, the NRO rescanned all our satellite images of the upper Arctic over the past two months using UV-4 overlays. This is a composite image of scans taken by six multi-spectrum IMINT reconnaissance satellites depicting the upper northern hemisphere in the UV-4 spectrum as it appeared six weeks ago.'

A satellite scan appeared on the screen:

It showed the northern hemisphere as seen from above the North Pole. One could see the Arctic Ocean and the larger island chains of Svalbard, Franz Josef Land and Severnaya Zemlya; then Europe, Russia, China, Japan, the north Pacific and finally the United States and Canada.

It was only barely noticeable, but streaming out from a tiny island not far from the pole was a dense black plume of dark smoke-like matter. In reality the plume was transparent, but through a UV filter it appeared black.

The plume originated at a dot marked 'Dragon Island'.

Bowling narrated. 'As I said, this image is six weeks old. It depicts a small plume of gaseous matter emanating from an old Soviet weapons laboratory complex in the Arctic known as *Ostrov Zmey*, or Dragon Island.'

'Looks like that ash cloud that shut down air travel a while back, from that volcano in Iceland,' the Army man said.

Bowling said, 'The atmospheric dispersal is very similar, but not the cloud itself. That ash cloud was composed of dust-sized particles of volcanic rock. This cloud is an ultra-fine gas seeded into the lower and middle atmospheres.

'It's so fine that to the untrained observer looking at it with the naked eye, it would look like a shimmering heat haze. But, as you can see, it is clearly visible in the ultraviolet spectrum. This is because it is a compound derived from triethylborane, or TEB. Soviet scientists experimented extensively with TEB and its derivatives back in the 1970s and 1980s.'

'What is this TEB? It's not an airborne poison, is it?' the Navy admiral asked.

'No, it's not a poison. It's worse than that,' Air Force said. 'TEB is a highly combustible explosive mixture usually stored in a solid state. Basically, it's rocket fuel. We use it ourselves. TEB is a pyrophoric composition that has been employed as the solid-state fuel in ramjet engines like that on the SR-71 Blackbird. When mixed with triethylaluminum, it's used to ignite the engines of the Saturn-V rocket.'

'It's one of the most combustible substances known to man,' the National Security Advisor said to the President. 'It burns bright, hot and big.'

He turned to face the people from the DIA and CIA. 'But I understood that liquid-state TEB and its variants were stable when stored in hexane solution and I thought the Russians keep it in hexane tanks.'

'They do,' the DIA deputy director said. 'At bases just like Dragon. Only Dragon is different. It's special. If our intelligence is correct, during the 80s that place was a goddamn house of horrors—a classified facility where Soviet scientists were allowed to do whatever they wanted. And they got up to some seriously messed-up stuff. Experimental electromagnetic weapons, flesh-eating bugs, molecular acids, explosive plasmas, special nuclear weapons, hypertoxic poisons.

'During the last few years of the Cold War, among other things, Dragon was the epicentre of Soviet research into caustic Venusian atmospheric gases, gases which are highly toxic and which the Soviets brought back to Earth on two of their *Venera* probes. It's believed that they managed to mix some of the more deadly Venusian gases with TEB.

'Apparently, the Soviets wanted to create a skin-melting acid rain similar to that found in the atmosphere of Venus and loose it upon America. You create a gas cloud of TEB infused with an exotic Venusian gas, send the mixture up into the jetstream over the Pacific and, given the right weather conditions, a skin-searing superhot acid rain falls on America.

'Even the location of Dragon is no accident: it sits at the top of the world, at the start of the spiralling wind pattern we call the jetstream. Anything hoisted up into the air above Dragon is quickly whisked around Europe, southern Russia, then China, Japan and across the Pacific to America. It's the same jetstream that swept that volcanic ash cloud from Iceland across Europe. But the thing is—' the DIA deputy director paused.

The room was silent with anticipation.

'—the Soviets couldn't get it to work. The TEB-based acid rain project never got beyond the test phase. Instead, by accident, the Soviets created something much more dangerous.

'There are rumours in the scientific weapons community that they found another use for their TEB/Venusian gas compound: namely, sending a combustible gas cloud up into the atmosphere and *igniting* it with a powerful catalytic blast, creating an "atmospheric incineration event".'

'A what?'

'They set the atmosphere on fire. The science is fairly straight-forward: for a fire to burn, it requires oxygen. A device like this takes that principle to the ultimate extreme—technically it's called a thermobaric weapon, or a fuel-air bomb, because, once ignited, the explosive uses oxygen in the air as the main fuel for the blast. Weapons specialists call it a Tesla device, after the great Nikola Tesla who postulated a weapon that could ignite the entire atmosphere.

'But such a weapon would require a massive amount of gas in the atmosphere *and* an ignition device of extraordinary heat and power—a semi-nuclear weapon, essentially—and we don't believe the Soviets ever managed to build such a device.'

A cough.

It was the CIA's representative. He cleared his throat and spoke for the first time.

'That,' he said, 'may not be entirely correct.'

'Dragon Island,' the CIA man said, 'was indeed one of the crazy outliers of the Cold War.

'Let's not be delicate about it. What the Soviets did there was seriously fucked up. It was cutting-edge science, with no boundaries, ethical or otherwise—at Dragon, Russia's best physicists were allowed to work with the most exotic and dangerous substances known to man, including those Venus samples you mentioned, all to create new forms of death. Dragon Island was the crown jewel of the Soviet Army's Special Weapons Directorate. Its scientists not only pushed the envelope, occasionally they broke through it. Dragon was their Area 51, Los Alamos and Plum Island all rolled into one.

'But when the USSR collapsed in 1991, Dragon Island's program was terminated. Only thing was, the stuff they built there was *so* exotic, destroying it raised more questions than answers. And so the Russkies have been sending skeleton crews there ever since, just keeping the lights on, so to speak, making sure stable solids don't become unstable liquids and that compounds meant to be stored at absolute zero stay at absolute zero. Put simply, Dragon Island still *is* a house of horrors.'

He turned to the President. 'And it is my unfortunate duty to report to you, sir, that the Russians did in fact build a Tesla device and it is kept at Dragon.

'They call it the "Atmospheric Weapon" and it is a two-stage device: the first stage is the combustible gas which is belched up into the atmosphere via a pair of massive vents on Dragon; the second stage is the explosive catalyst that ignites the gas. This catalyst

is basically a quasi-nuclear explosive composed of a spherical inner core of corrupted uranium-238—so-called "blood uranium" or "red uranium", because of its deep maroon colour. Red uranium is not as potent or as radioactive as yellowcake but its corrupted atomic structure makes it react with TEB far more intensely than a regular thermonuclear blast would; indeed, a regular nuke wouldn't set off such a gas cloud.

'A red uranium sphere is small, roughly the size of a golf ball. You encase one in a standard beryllium bridgewire implosive detonator—the kind you find inside a regular nuclear weapon—and then fire the whole unit by missile into the gas cloud. The subsequent blast is hot enough to light the gas and set off the incineration— a rolling chain reaction of white-hot acid-fire follows, sweeping around the northern hemisphere, igniting the atmosphere itself. It's like lighting gasoline with a match, only this creates a firestorm of global proportions.'

The President shook his head in disbelief. 'Who builds something like this? If it destroys the northern hemisphere, it destroys them, too.'

'In fact, sir, that's *exactly* why it was built,' DIA deputy director Gordon said. 'A device like this is called a "scorched earth" weapon: it's the weapon you use when you've *lost* a war. When the Germans saw that they'd lost World War II, they retreated, burning farms as they went, scorching the earth. The idea was that if they were going to lose the war, then the victors would not gain anything by winning it.

'The Soviet atmospheric weapon is similar: in the event of the United States disabling or destroying their stockpile of ICBMs in some kind of hostile exchange, the Soviets, facing certain defeat, would set off the atmospheric weapon, leaving nothing behind but scorched earth for the victors.'

'Only this weapon doesn't just scorch *their* country, it wipes out the entire upper half of the Earth,' the President said.

'That's correct,' Gordon said. 'Mr President. If someone has taken Dragon Island and initiated its Tesla device, then, yes, we have a problem, but it appears we've caught it in time. Whoever is at Dragon Island would need to have spewed the combustible aerosol into the atmosphere for *weeks* for the weapon to be in any way effective.'

Relief fell over the Situation Room.

The NRO man, Bowling, however, swallowed deeply.

'Then you don't want to see this.' He hit a key on his laptop that projected a new image onto the screen. 'This image was taken four weeks ago:

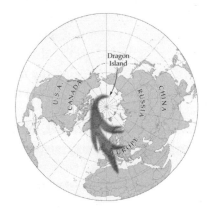

'And this one, two weeks ago:

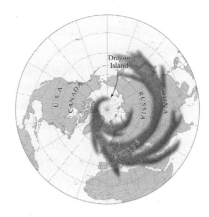

'And this last image was taken forty-five minutes ago, after we caught the distress signal.'

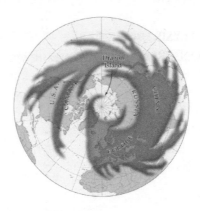

'Holy shit . . .' someone breathed.

'Jesus Christ . . .'

The murky cloud had swept around *the entire northern hemisphere* in an ugly elongated spiral, blanketing every major landmass in the top half of the world. It looked like an oil slick that had stained the planet, only this was in the atmosphere. The image of the befouled Earth loomed in front of the shocked faces of the Crisis Response Team.

'Whoever took Dragon Island has been belching out combustible gas for nearly six weeks,' Bowling said. 'They sent it up into the jetstream and the jetstream did the rest. The entire northern hemisphere is now covered by this gas cloud.'

At that moment, a young assistant ran into the room and handed a transcript to the DIA deputy director, Gordon.

The deputy director read it then looked up sharply. 'Mr President. This is from our Russian MASINT station. It just intercepted an emergency transmission from the head of the Russian Special Weapons Directorate in Sarov to the Russian President in Moscow. It reads:

SIR,

DRAGON ISLAND TAKEN BY AN UNKNOWN FORCE.

SATELLITE ANALYSIS HAS REVEALED THAT ATMOSPHERIC GAS DISPERSION FROM DRAGON HAS BEEN ACTIVATED FOR SOME TIME, PERHAPS AS LONG AS 41 DAYS.

REMOTE ANALYSIS HAS CONFIRMED THAT SIX URANIUM SPHERES AT DRAGON ARE BEING PRIMED FOR IMMINENT USE. PRIMING TAKES APPROXIMATELY TWELVE HOURS AND IT APPEARS THAT PRIMING BEGAN SEVEN HOURS AGO.

WE HAVE FIVE HOURS TO STOP THIS UNKNOWN FORCE INITIATING THE ATMOSPHERIC WEAPON.'

Gordon put down the transcript.
Silence gripped the room.
The President looked at a wall clock. It was now 5 p.m., or 6 a.m. at Dragon. 'Are you telling me that in five hours an unknown force is going to set off some kind of superweapon that will ignite the atmosphere of the northern hemisphere?'
'That's correct, sir,' Gordon said. 'We have five hours to save the world.'

The President stood up. 'Get the Russian President on the phone right now—'
The door to the Situation Room was flung open.
A young Air Force major charged in. 'Mr President! The Russians just launched an ICBM from Omsk in Siberia! It's bearing down on a target in the Arctic Ocean, a remote island base. They're firing a nuclear missile at one of their own islands!'

 **THE KREMLIN
MOSCOW, RUSSIA**

At that exact moment, in a similar underground room in Moscow, the Russian President and his own crisis response team were watching a live feed from a missile-tracking satellite.

A blinking dot indicated the nuclear-tipped intercontinental ballistic missile heading directly for Dragon Island.

'Impact in four minutes,' a console operator said.

The blip pulsed closer to Dragon.

The room was deathly silent.

Every eye was on the display.

'Three minutes to—*wait!* Missile is changing course. What the hell—?'

'What's going on?' the Russian President demanded.

'The missile. It's . . . it's turning around. It's coming back toward its launch silo . . .'

In the White House Situation Room, the President and his Crisis Response Team watched on a similar screen as the Russian missile retraced its flight path.

'It's going *back* toward its launch site?' the President asked. 'How?'

'They've hacked the missile's guidance system . . .' Alicia Gordon said ominously.

'Who has?'

'Whoever's at Dragon Island.'

'Is that even possible?'

'We can do it,' Gordon said simply. 'And it looks like whoever's taken Dragon can do it, too.'

The Russian President watched in horror as the blip on the screen sped back toward its original launch location.

The console operator beside him spoke urgently into his headset: 'Omsk Missile Control, listen to me! *It's coming back at you!*—No, we can see it! Issue self-destruct order—What do you mean, the missile is not responding—?'

A moment later, the blip hit the launch site in Omsk, Siberia, and Omsk went off the air.

The horrified silence that followed was broken by a second console operator.

He turned to the Russian President.

'Sir. I have an incoming signal from Dragon Island.'

'Put it on screen,' the Russian President said.

A viewscreen came to life. On it, facing the camera, was a man wearing gaudy Elvis sunglasses and a snow-camouflaged Arctic parka.

The parka's hood covered his head. Combined with the glasses, this meant that the only part of his face that was visible was from the nose to the chin, but even that small area was distinctive: a foul strip of horribly blistered, acid-scarred skin ran from his left ear down the length of his jawline. He looked more like a demented rock star than a terrorist.

'Mr President, good morning,' the man said calmly in perfect Russian. 'I could tell you my name, but why bother? Call me the Lord of Anarchy, the General of the Army of Thieves, the Emperor of Annihilation, the Duke of Destruction, call me whatever you want. My glorious, furious army—my Army of Thieves—an

alliance of the enraged, the starving, the disenfranchised and the poor, is rising. It is the dog starved at his master's gate that will starve no more. Now it is time for you, the masters, to be held to account. I am the instrument of that reckoning.

'My army of reprobates holds your nasty little island and we intend to use its terrible weapon. As you are clearly aware, I can detect and counteract any missile strike you send against me. Your missiles' guidance systems are crude and easily corrupted. Be assured that the next nuclear missile you fire at me will be redirected *not* at its launch silo but at the nearest major city. The same goes for any other nation that dares to fire a nuke at me. And don't even think about sending in a bomber or counter-terrorist force. I can see and will shoot down any aircraft that comes within five hundred miles of Dragon Island.

'Mr President, you and I both know the weapon I have at my disposal. Instead of wasting time firing missiles at me, call a priest and make peace with your god. It would be a better use of the precious few hours you have left. Let anarchy reign.'

The screen went black.

 THE WHITE HOUSE SITUATION ROOM

The President slammed down the phone. He'd just spoken with the Russian President.

'An air approach is out of the question,' he said, 'and the Russians don't have any units close enough to get to Dragon by sea within five hours. What about us? Do we have any assets in that area? Anyone who's close enough to get there—undetected, by sea or over the ice, within five hours—and stop that weapon from going off?'

'I'm sorry, sir. The Air Force has no such assets in that region,' Air Force said.

'Neither does the Army, sir,' Army said, shaking his head.

'We do, sir,' Navy said. 'Got a SEAL team in a sub about seventy nautical miles north-east of that island. Ira Barker and his boys. Doing Arctic training. They're tough, close and all geared up. They can get there in maybe three hours.'

'Call them,' the President ordered. 'Call them now and send them in. Tell them to sabotage, disable or destroy anything in order to stop that device going off. And while they're on their way to Dragon, dispatch a larger force that can get there later, just in case these SEALs do somehow succeed in delaying this.'

While all this was happening, the Marine Corps representative had moved off to a corner of the room where he spoke into a secure phone. He hung up and turned to the President. 'Sir. There's also . . . well . . .'

'What! *What?*'

'I've got a small equipment-testing team up there, camped on the sea ice about a hundred miles north of that island. Been there for the last seven weeks. A few Marines, a DARPA guy and some civilian contractors testing new gear in extreme weather conditions. It's not exactly an assault unit but it's somebody and they're up there.'

'Who's in command?' the President asked.

The Marine general said, 'A captain named Schofield, sir. Callsign, Scarecrow.'

'Scarecrow?' the President said, recognising the name. 'The one I spoke to the French President about a few months back? The *United States citizen* that the French military put a floating bounty on?'

'That's him, sir. That French business is the main reason he's up in the Arctic now. They sent hit teams to kill him twice when he was stationed at Parris Island. Both times, he survived. We wanted to get him out of harm's way so we sent him north with that test team.'

There were other reasons, too, the Marine general knew, but he didn't feel they needed to be mentioned right now.

The President's face set itself in a fixed grimace. 'I asked the

French President to cancel that bounty and you know what he said to me? He said, "Monsieur, I will accede to your demands on finance, trade, on Afghanistan, even on Iran, but I will not belay that order. That man killed French soldiers, destroyed a French submarine and sank a French aircraft carrier. The Republic of France will not rest until he is dead."'

The President shook his head. 'Call this Scarecrow. Send him in behind that SEAL team with the same orders: sabotage, disable, destroy. Tell him to do whatever he can to stop this madness.'

FIRST PHASE
THE CALL TO ARMS

((○)) Dragon Island

DRAGON ISLAND
4 APRIL, 0830 HOURS

The US–Soviet 'Cold War' will go down in history as the most prolonged period of military madness ever seen. Weapons of extraordinarily destructive capability were built, to the extent that if a war were ever fought, there would have been no world left for the winner to live in.

—Richard Wainwright
The Cold War
(Orion, London, 2001)

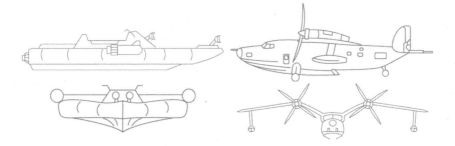

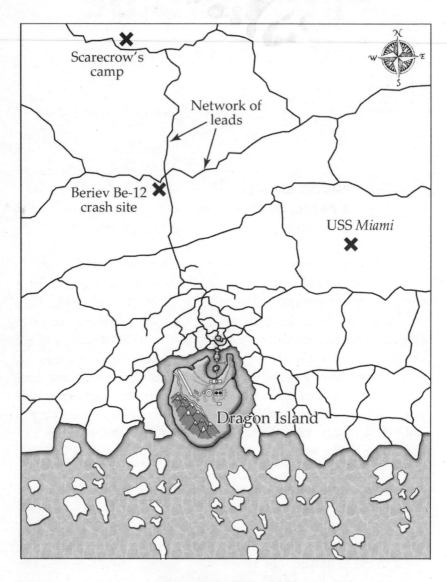

**DRAGON ISLAND
AND NORTHERN SURROUNDS**

ARCTIC ICE FIELD
4 APRIL, 0830 HOURS
2 HOURS 30 MINUTES TO DEADLINE

The two assault boats sped down the narrow ice-walled canal.

They skimmed along at fifty kilometres an hour, thanks to their state-of-the-art pumpjet engines and bullet-shaped hulls, both of which had been designed by the Defense Advanced Research Projects Agency. And while the lead boat tore a fierce wake through the still waters of the alleyway, its engine barely made a sound.

The boats were prototype AFDVs—Assault Force Delivery Vehicles—small and fast craft intended to deliver American troops to hostile shores quickly and silently. They looked a little like Zodiacs, only these boats were sleeker, with ultrathin inflatable rims that rode close to the waterline. Not yet in active service, they were still in the testing phase.

Seated on the motorcycle-like saddle of the first boat was Captain Shane M. Schofield, USMC.

In his mid-thirties, Schofield was about five-ten, with a rugged creased face and black hair. He usually wore his hair cut short and his chin clean-shaven, but after seven weeks in the Arctic, his hair was longer and he had a healthy stubble around his jaw. Schofield had striking blue eyes and would probably have been considered handsome were it not for the pair of hideous scars that cut down vertically over them, one for each eye. The scars were the source of his operational nickname: Scarecrow.

They were wounds from a previous mission-gone-wrong, from

a time when Schofield had been a pilot in the Marine Corps' Air Wing. Shot down over enemy territory, he'd been captured and tortured, during which his eyes had been slashed with a razor blade. Surgery had saved his sight, but he had not been allowed to fly again, so he had retrained as a line animal, ultimately rising through the officer ranks of the Corps to command an elite Force Reconnaissance unit.

Today, as usual, Schofield kept his damaged eyes concealed behind a pair of wraparound silver anti-flash glasses: military-grade Oakley Ballistics. The lower half of his face was wrapped in a scarf, Jesse James–style, to ward off the snow-flecked wind that assailed his face as he drove.

In the first assault boat's compact rear tray behind Schofield sat three passengers—one young Marine and two civilian members of his testing team.

The second boat was being driven by Schofield's second-in-command and loyal friend, Gunnery Sergeant Gena Newman, call-sign Mother.

At six-foot-two, with a fully-shaven head and a burly imposing physique, her call-sign was not indicative of any special maternal instincts. It was short for Motherfucker. Her assault boat held two passengers in its rear tray: another Marine and one more civilian contractor.

It had been just over two hours since Schofield and his test team had received an emergency transmission from Washington, informing them of the situation at Dragon Island. They had also received a bundle of digital documents over a secure data feed.

These included an mpeg of the Russian President's conversation with the mystery man holding the island and claiming to be the leader of a group calling itself the Army of Thieves; a DIA report by someone named Retter that mentioned seven incidents involving this Army of Thieves; a map of Dragon; and the co-ordinates of the downed Beriev that had called in the crisis.

They also received a brief document titled 'Operation of Atmospheric Weapon' outlining the component parts of the device on

Dragon Island: the two massive vents that spewed the gas, six small red uranium spheres, and the missiles that fired the spheres into the gas cloud. Broadly speaking, if they could destroy or sabotage any one of those three elements—before the spheres were primed to operating temperature—they could stop the operation of the weapon.

Scarecrow was unimpressed: given that the vents had been belching gas for six weeks, that really only left the last two options. Although as he thought about it some more, perhaps there was one other way—

But then he was informed that a SEAL team on a nearby Los Angeles–class submarine, the USS *Miami*, had already been dispatched to take the island by force.

Looking at his map of the island, Schofield didn't like their chances.

Dragon Island was a natural fortress. Its shores were made up almost entirely of three-hundred-foot-high cliffs, and in the only two places where the land came down to the water's edge—a long-abandoned 19th-century whaling village and a submarine dock—there were all manner of fences, walls, gun emplacements and watchtowers. There was a third access point: three small islets nestled in and around the bay on Dragon's northern coast, but that route was so easily guarded against as to be useless.

In short, Dragon Island was perfect for a defending force and hell for an offensive one. Even a relatively small garrison could hold out a large attacking army for weeks.

It was just as he was thinking about the SEAL incursion that a secure ULF signal came in from the USS *Miami*. It had already started powering toward Dragon and would get there a good hour before Schofield and his people could.

A short and very one-sided exchange followed with the SEAL commander, a gruff but experienced specialist named Ira 'Ironbark' Barker.

'Just sit back, Scarecrow. We'll take care of this,' Ironbark had said.

'If you just wait an hour, we can catch up and go in with you,' Schofield said. 'I mean, we don't even know how many men are on that isla—'

'I ain't waiting and my boys sure as hell don't need your help,' Ironbark said. 'I've seen this sort of shit before. No amount of gun-toting thugs can match a fully-trained SEAL team. So I'm gonna say this once and once only: *stay out of our way, Scarecrow*. We are going to that island and we are going to shoot everything in sight. I don't want you and your nerds stumbling in there afterward and getting in the way. Besides, who have you got with you anyway, a couple of Marines and some geeks from the science fair?'

'I have seven people. Four Marines, including me, and three civilians.'

'Which means you'll be about as helpful as a fart in an elevator. Jesus, *civilians*. Why don't you leave saving the world to the experts and stay in your heated tents.'

'What about the plane, then?' Schofield asked pointedly. 'The Beriev that started all this? Shouldn't you check that out before you go in? The pilot might still be alive, he might also have some better intel on disabling the device—'

'Fuck the plane and fuck the pilot. I already have the layout of the island and I know enough to disable the weapon. That pilot can't help me.'

'Well, I'm going to check him out.'

'Fine. Do that. I don't care. I've heard about you, Scarecrow. Heard you got *initiative*, which to me means you're unpredictable. And I don't like unpredictable. Do what you want, just stay out of my way or else you might get shot. Understand?'

'I understand.'

'Ironbark, out.' The line went dead.

And that was how Schofield and his little team came to be zooming south through a maze of ice-walled canals, heading for the site of Vasily Ivanov's crashed Beriev Be-12.

SEVEN WEEKS IN AN ARCTIC CAMP
MARCH–APRIL

How Shane Schofield—a former commander of a crack Force Reconnaissance Unit—came to be in the Arctic with a small team of scientists was a story all by itself.

Over the years, he and Mother had gone through a lot together: a mission in Antarctica during which they had defended a remote US ice station from French and British special forces units; that business concerning the former President at a secret base in the Utah desert called Area 7; and, of course, the bounty hunt in which a group called Majestic-12 had put an $18.6 million price on Schofield's head.

It was during that last incident that Schofield's girlfriend, Lieutenant Elizabeth 'Fox' Gant, had been captured and brutally executed, for no reason other than to taunt Schofield. And although Schofield had ultimately prevailed in that mission, it had been at tremendous cost.

Some people in authority believed that the matter had taken him to the limit of psychological endurance and even broken him. There were rumours that at one point in the mission he'd tried to take his own life. Even Mother had wondered if he'd ever be the same again.

But after four months of mourning that was labelled stress leave, he'd gone to his superiors at Marine Headquarters in the Naval Annexe Building in Arlington and announced that he was ready to get back to work.

Given the concerns about his mental state—and the wariness some Marines had about working with him—he was at first assigned to a teaching position at the Marine Corps' recruit training facility at Parris Island in South Carolina.

For such an experienced and decorated warrior, the appointment was seen by many as an insult, but it had actually been a good fit.

As the former commander of a Force Recon unit, the new recruits at Marine Corps Recruit Depot Parris Island had hung on his every word. And Schofield had turned out to be an excellent teacher: generous with his knowledge, uncommonly patient, and always willing to stay late to work with a recruit who wasn't quite getting it. His students adored him.

That said, everyone at Marine HQ knew it was bullshit. It was just that no-one wanted to rush Scarecrow back into active service. (Although there *were* rumours that as a damaged and therefore expendable leader, he had been sent on a particularly bloody mission to an island in the Pacific Ocean called Hell Island. But no-one could verify these rumours and Schofield himself would not be drawn on them.)

And then came the first French assassination attempt.

They were waiting for him one Sunday night outside a restaurant in Beaufort as he emerged from dinner with his grandfather: a pair of DGSE agents looking to bag the French military's five-million-euro floating bounty on the Scarecrow.

Schofield had spotted them lurking across the street, had seen them follow him and his grandfather to the nearby parking structure. Upon entering the parking lot's stairwell, he'd quickly doubled back, disarmed and disabled them both.

The two French agents were now in Leavenworth in a special section reserved for protected inmates. The prisoners at Leavenworth, despite their own crimes, were oddly patriotic when it came to foreigners who tried to kill United States Marines and had not given the two Frenchmen a pleasant welcome.

The second attempt had come six months later.

It had happened on a quiet country road a few miles from Parris

Island, as Schofield was driving back there late one night. Another pair of French agents had pulled up alongside his car and abruptly opened fire. A short running gun-battle had followed and it ended with Schofield firing back with his Desert Eagle pistol and killing the gun-toting passenger before ramming the rival car off a bridge, sending the second French assassin plunging into a swamp.

The driver had survived. He was next seen sitting slumped on the front steps of DGSE headquarters in Paris, still covered in mud, handcuffed, with a pink bow tied around his mouth. A message was written in permanent marker on his forehead: 'This belongs to you.'

Despite a face-to-face meeting between the new American President and his French counterpart on the subject, the French resolutely refused to remove the bounty on Schofield's head.

And then this assignment had come up.

The Corps needed experienced Marines to test new equipment in extreme climates. It would involve accompanying scientists from the Defense Advanced Research Projects Agency, the famous DARPA, and some private contractors to the ends of the Earth—baking deserts, steaming rainforests and the brutal cold of the Arctic—to test prototypes of new weapons, tents, armour and vehicles.

Naturally, it wasn't the kind of mission that the Corps wanted to waste on top talent, but as far as the brass were concerned it was perfect for Scarecrow: psychologically scarred, possibly unpredictable and the target of a vengeful foreign nation, it would keep him usefully occupied and out of harm's way.

Schofield didn't mind the Arctic.

It was quiet and peaceful and at this time of year it was actually quite beautiful. It was always a perfect dawn—the sun lurked just above the horizon, never setting but never rising either, bathing the ice plain in spectacular horizontal light. It was bitingly cold, sure, but still beautiful.

It also helped that he had a good team up there with him.

Eight people and one robot.

Over the last seven weeks, huddled in their camp of silver domed tents, Schofield's team had got along pretty well—as well as eight human beings living in close proximity in freezing conditions could get along, really.

Having Mother around helped.

She could silence anyone who bitched or moaned with a single withering look. And even then, the only member of the team who'd been even remotely problematic was the senior executive from ArmaCorp Systems, Jeff Hartigan, and getting 'the Look' from Mother usually shut him up.

Mother, of course, had insisted on coming along. Not even the Commandant of the Marines Corps dared say no to Mother Newman. After many years of loyal and distinguished service in the Corps, she had her choice of deployment and she went where Scarecrow went.

'Because I'm his Fairy Godmotherfucker,' she would say when asked why.

The other two Marines in the group were considerably younger: Corporal Billy 'the Kid' Thompson and Lance Corporal Vittorio Puzo, a hulking Italian-American who because of his famous surname quickly got the nickname 'Mario'.

Scarecrow had a soft spot for the Kid. While not academically gifted—he failed most written exams—what he lacked in smarts, he made up for in a desire to *be* smarter. He was also good-natured, a crack shot and a dab hand at field-stripping and rebuilding almost any kind of weapon.

Mario, on the other hand, was less easy to like.

He was a surly and dour guy from the Engineering Corps who kept largely to himself when they weren't working. A highly skilled mechanic, he was responsible for maintaining the various vehicles they were testing.

Like Schofield, however, both the Kid and Mario were in the Arctic doing field testing for a reason.

They were also broken.

The Kid had lost the hearing in one ear in a training accident, so he couldn't go on active deployment. And a little digging on Schofield's part had revealed that Mario had been implicated in the disappearance of some sidearms and over $20,000 worth of vehicle parts from a Marine lock-up; he hadn't been formally charged but a cloud had lingered over him and this assignment was seen by some as an unofficial punishment.

As for the four civilian members of the team, as far as Schofield was concerned, two of them were great and two less so.

Zack Weinberg was from DARPA and he was your typical geek genius: he was 29, gangly and thin, and he wore huge glasses that seemed three sizes too big for his head.

A physicist by training, he was at DARPA because of his work in robotics. Hopelessly devoted to *Call of Duty* video games and all things *Star Wars* and *Star Trek*, he was in the Arctic testing several new DARPA inventions, the main one being a small bomb-disposal robot called the BRTE-500, or, as Zack called it, 'Bertie'.

Bertie was DARPA's answer to existing battlefield robots like the PackBot, the Talon and the weapons-mounted variant of the Talon called SWORDS.

'Except Bertie comes with a few extra features,' Zack said the day he pulled the little robot from its crate. 'Unlike other bots that require human operators to control them remotely, Bertie is able to operate completely independently. Thanks to an artificial intelligence chip developed by my team at DARPA, he can follow spoken orders, learn, and even assess a situation and make tactical decisions.'

'He can make tactical decisions?' Schofield said. To him, the little robot—with its two spindly bomb-disposal arms and its curiously emotive single-lens 'eye' mounted on a stalk—looked like a cute toy. It scurried around on four rugged little tyres and, when necessary, extended a set of triangular treads that enabled it to climb up steps and over obstacles.

'He's a smart little bot,' Zack said, 'and for a weedy little fella, he packs a punch. He was initially designed for bomb disposal but I removed his IED water blaster and lightened his armour plating—replaced all the steel with ultralight titanium. Then I augmented him with some *offensive* capabilities.'

As he said this, Zack attached a gunbarrel to Bertie's weapons mount . . . and suddenly the little robot took on a wholly different appearance: he looked like Wall-E with a great big gun.

'Those capabilities include,' Zack explained, 'four internal rotator-fed ammunition clips which load a custom-modified lightweight short-barrelled internal-recoil-compensated 5.56mm M249 machine gun; a blowtorch for cutting through fences and razor wire; full digital sat-comms; a high-res camera that can send video images back to base; a first-aid pack, including a diagnostic scanner and defibrillator paddles, both of which Bertie can apply himself; oh, and four of our new MRE ration packs in case the human beings working with him get hungry. And all this in a package that weighs about thirty kilograms, so you can even pick him up and carry him if you really need to get out of Dodge in a hurry.'

Schofield couldn't help but like Bertie: the little robot followed Zack around the camp like a devoted puppy, albeit a puppy with a machine gun on its back.

Mother, however, was doubtful. 'I don't know. How can we know he won't short-circuit and open fire on us with that cannon?'

'Bertie can distinguish between friend and foe,' Zack said. 'I've scanned all our team's faces into his memory bank with instructions that we are never to be fired upon.'

'Hello? Didn't you see the ED-209 in *RoboCop*?'

'This is the big question about robotic weapons,' Zack said. 'But Bertie has operated for three hundred hours without hurting anybody he wasn't supposed to hurt. We have to trust him sometime. Hey, speaking of which, Bertie, scan Captain Schofield. Facial and infra-red, please.'

The robot scanned Schofield's face, then beeped.

Its robotic voice said, '*Scan complete. Individual identified as Captain Shane M. Schofield, United States Marine Corps. Service identification number 256-3569.*'

Zack said, 'Store as secondary buddy, please.'

'*Captain Shane M. Schofield stored as secondary buddy.*'

'What does that mean?' Schofield asked.

'Bertie needs someone to follow. I'm his primary buddy, which is why he follows me, but if something were to happen to me, he needs a secondary buddy which I think should be you.'

'I'm honoured.'

Schofield liked Zack. On quiet evenings, they played chess and during those matches Zack would happily explain things like space-time, the speed of light and the Big Bang Theory—the TV show *and* the universe-creating event.

On a few occasions, Schofield even played chess against Bertie, with the little robot moving the pieces with its long spindly arm.

Bertie won every time.

The second civilian Schofield got along well with was Emma Dawson, a young meteorologist from the National Oceanic and Atmospheric Administration.

In her late twenties, Emma was pretty, articulate and tremendously hardworking—she was almost always reading a chart or working away on her laptop. She was in the Arctic measuring the rate at which the sea ice was melting.

Her beauty had not gone unnoticed by the young males in the team. Schofield had seen the Kid and Mario—and young Zack— staring absently at Emma on various occasions. But she rarely

looked up from her work, and Schofield wondered if it was the practised skill of an attractive young woman: bury yourself in your work so you don't have to fend off unwanted advances.

The final two civilian members of the field team kept mainly to themselves.

Jeff Hartigan was a senior executive for ArmaCorp Systems, a weapons maker that produced assault and sniper rifles. ArmaCorp was trying to convince the Marines to buy its latest assault rifle, the MX-18 carbine, but the Corps had insisted on cold-weather testing before they committed.

At 48, Hartigan was the oldest member of the group. He was also perhaps the only one who occupied a position of status back in the real world. As such, he was haughty and aloof and didn't care about anyone he deemed beneath him, which was pretty much everyone else in the camp—so long as they recorded the results of the carbine's tests, he didn't seem to care what they thought of him. Except during testing, he mostly stayed in his tent, well apart from the others, even going so far as to send his personal assistant—an equally aloof junior executive named Chad—to collect his food for him at mealtimes.

Their testing had generally gone well.

The ArmaCorp rifle had performed flawlessly in the ice-cold conditions—making Hartigan even more unbearable—and Bertie whizzed about impervious to all kinds of frost and snow, variously disarming explosives and blowing blocks of ice to pieces with his small but very powerful M249 machine gun.

A new anti-explosive paint-gel made by an Australian company, DSS, worked perfectly in the cold—after the gooey gel was painted onto a large crate, that crate could withstand the most powerful explosive blast, even one from some potent PET plastic explosive, brought along precisely for those tests. Longer-lasting scuba rebreathers and drysuits for cold-water insertions had performed excellently, as had the new Assault Force Delivery Vehicles: some had wondered if the deflating valves on their rubber skirts might freeze in the cold, but they'd held up just fine.

Mother liked the new MREs—Meals Ready to Eat—that they'd been instructed to try. Each MRE came in a small plastic tube the size of a Magic Marker, so they were extremely portable. Each tube held some powdered jelly, a high-energy protein bar and three new water filtration pills which worked brilliantly.

'The jelly still tastes like shit,' Mother said, 'but the water pills are fucking brilliant. Best field water I ever tried and I haven't got diarrhoea once.'

Zack said, 'That's always been an issue with water filtration pills. These ones are chitosan-based and so far the results have been great. Chitosan is a natural polysaccharide that dissolves organically in the body. Did you know it's also the main ingredient of Celox, the bullet-wound gel?'

Mother held up a hand. 'Hey. Genius. You lost me at polysaccha-something. I get it. It's an amazing new substance that will change the way we live.'

'Something like that,' Zack said, deflating a little.

Mother was more interested, however, in another device that Zack had been trialling: a new high-tech armoured wristguard.

DARPA had been developing it in the hope that it would become standard issue in the Marines and Army Rangers. Made of light carbon-fibre, the wristguard covered its wearer's forearm and featured, among other things, a high-resolution LCD screen.

'This screen is designed to display real-time data—video signals, even satellite imagery—to a soldier in the field,' Zack explained to Mother as they stood outside their tents one day, testing it.

'Real-time satellite imagery?' Wearing the wristguard, Mother peered at its small rectangular screen. Zack leaned over and touched some icons on it. The screen came alive, showing two people in black-and-white seen from directly overhead, standing on a barren white plain beside some hexagonal objects.

'Okay, now wave,' Zack said.

Mother waved her left arm.

On the screen, one of the figures waved its left arm.

'Oh, that is way cool . . .' Mother said.

'The wristguard operates like a satellite phone,' Zack explained. 'Encrypted, of course. But so long as you can make a connection with the satellite, you can get real-time imagery, data, even voice signals. Don't tell anyone, but I've configured it so you can even surf the net.'

Mother threw Zack a grin. 'You know, Science Boy, you and I are gonna get along just fine.'

Zack beamed.

A few items had been unable to be tested, like an acid-based aerosol 'anti-ursine agent'—or as Mother called it, 'polar bear repellent'. While Zack had studiously sprayed it on all their tents, armour and drysuits, it had defied testing since no polar bears had come near their camp during the entire trip (prompting Mother to conclude, 'Then I guess it works, doesn't it?').

And some things hadn't worked well at all.

A new version of the Predator RPG launcher froze up, while the older version worked just fine. And a portable proximity sensor on the armoured wristguard seemed to work okay at first, but toward the end of their tour, it started sensing a large moving object— a three-hundred-foot-long object—within half a mile of their camp.

But there was nothing near the camp. The endless ice plain, split by ever-widening cracks, stretched away to the horizon, starkly and obviously empty.

'It might be picking up killer whales swimming under the ice,' Schofield suggested. 'Or even a submarine.'

'No, it's a *lateral* rangefinder. It scans the landscape in a sideways direction, not downward. It's a glitch,' Zack said sadly. 'Shame. But then, that's exactly why we're here, to test these things out.'

Naturally, over the course of seven weeks in a remote Arctic camp, they had good and bad days, occasional clashes and the odd petty argument.

Like the time Mother accidentally picked up Zack's iPhone, thinking it was hers, and listened to some music.

'Goddamn hip-hop *shit*,' she said, yanking the earphones from her ears. 'How can you listen to this? It's elevator music.'

'What music do *you* like, then?' Zack challenged.

'Music peaked in the eighties, my young friend. Huey Lewis and the News. Feargal Sharkey. Ozzy Osbourne biting the head off a fucking bat *live on stage*. It's the same for movies. Seriously, there hasn't been a decent balls-to-the-wall action flick since *Predator*. Arnie doing the business and, oh my, Jesse "The Body" Ventura. God broke the mould after he made Jesse Ventura. Hollywood actors today are all fucking nancy boys. Can you think of any leading man today who could say the line, "I ain't got time to bleed"?'

Zack had to concede that he couldn't.

But he did manage to convince Mother to listen to some other modern songs and she had to admit that she quite liked Lady Gaga. 'Although, I'm not a "free bitch" like she is. I'm just a bitch,' she said after hearing one song.

On another occasion, as they gathered around the small gas fire in the mess tent, the Kid had said, 'Hey Mother, I saw a killer whale pop up for air through an ice hole the other day. You seen one yet?'

Mother stumped her left boot up on the table and rolled up her trouser leg, revealing that her left leg from the knee down was a prosthetic, all silver plating, hinges and hydraulics.

Zack leaned forward. 'What is that, stainless steel?'

'Titanium,' Mother said. 'Got it thanks to a killer whale I met in Antarctica.'

'What happened to the whale?' the Kid asked.

'It died,' Mother said, deadpan.

'Mother shot it in the head,' Schofield explained.

'You shot a killer whale *in the head*?' the Kid said in disbelief.

'Fuckin' fish had my leg in its mouth. What else was I supposed to do?'

Zack said, 'You know, whales aren't fish, they're—'

'I know they're mammals!' Mother snapped. 'Christ, everyone tells me that. But when one of them's got you by the foot and is pulling you under, trust me, you don't care whether it's a goddamn fucking mammal, all right!'

Schofield grinned.

During a long expedition, people will talk about many things over the campfire and this group was no different.

They discussed politics, sports, the killing of Osama bin Laden, all kinds of subjects.

One night they talked about the rise of China. It was one of the rare nights when Jeff Hartigan dined with the group and he spoke animatedly on the subject.

'It's hard to believe that only thirty years ago China was the laughing stock of the world, a rural shithole,' he said. 'Now, it's a genuine global powerhouse: 1.3 *billion* people, the bulk of whom work in factories for a few bucks a day, building the world's fridges, toys and DVD players. But now in China there's this huge new middle class that wants everything we have in the West: cars, iPhones, the latest fashions. China is the future for every business in the world, in both supply *and* demand.'

Mother looked doubtful. 'But as China rises, does that mean other countries have to fall? My husband, Ralph, is a trucker. Over the past few years, we've seen a lot of his buddies who work in factories get laid off—they're honest, hardworking, blue-collar workers who just can't compete with cheap Chinese labour. The work they do just keeps going overseas.'

Hartigan shrugged. 'Way of the world. A new power rises and an old one falls. America did exactly the same thing to England in the 1800s—outstripped it with industry, land and sheer human capital. Now China is doing it to us. And short of launching an all-out war, you can't stop this kind of thing.'

'Then what does the average American worker do? How do they pay their mortgage, keep a roof over their family's head?' Mother asked. She wasn't trying to make a point. She genuinely wanted to know the answer.

Hartigan said, 'There's nothing they can do. In things like this, *some* poor bastard has to be the loser. It's just that the average American has never been the loser before. Now he is. And he'd better get used to it because nothing can stop China now.'

On another occasion, a particularly spirited discussion arose when Zack—a very Jewish New York Jew—raised the classic campfire conundrum, 'The Nazi Dilemma'.

'You're a Jew in Germany during World War II,' he said, 'hiding in a ditch beside a country road at night with a group of twenty other Jews. A Nazi regiment marches by. You all duck for cover and lie very still. But in your group is a baby. It starts crying. If the Nazis hear it, they'll kill all of you. Someone suggests smothering the baby, killing it in order to save the larger group. What do you do? Do you let the baby live and condemn everyone else, including you, to death? Or do you kill one baby so that twenty other people may live?'

'You find a machine gun and kill the Nazis,' Mother said.

'Seriously,' Zack said.

'The choice is easy, kill the baby,' Jeff Hartigan said. 'The good of the majority must take precedence over the life of one person, even a child.'

'I disagree,' Emma said. 'If you kill the baby, you become as bad as the Nazis.'

The Kid said, 'I could never kill an innocent person to save my own skin, least of all a baby. Couldn't live with myself.'

'What about you, Captain Schofield?' Zack asked.

Schofield looked at them all, before settling his gaze on Hartigan. 'For me, the choice is also easy. Either we all survive together or we all die together. I don't leave any man behind. And I'd never sacrifice anyone in my charge who was slow or tired or just a little weaker than everyone else. A civilisation is judged by how it treats the vulnerable.'

'You'd give your life for a crying baby?' Hartigan asked, incredulous. 'And you'd give *my* life as well?'

'Absolutely and absolutely. But I'd also put up one hell of a fight to save you both before it came to that.'

Mother clapped him on the shoulder and gave him a big kiss on the cheek. 'And that, folks, is why I love serving with the Scarecrow!'

There were also, thankfully, some lighter conversations.

'Well, with one week to go,' Mother said, 'I have to say that this trip has really let me down. My horoscope in *Cosmo* a couple of months ago said that'—she pulled out a page ripped from a magazine—'"You will meet your mirror image in the next few months, a member of the opposite sex who is your natural partner. The chemistry will be irresistible. Sparks will fly."'

'You read *Cosmo*?' the Kid asked.

'When I'm in the waiting room at the dentist, yeah.' Mother tossed the page into the air and gazed pointedly at the men in the tent: Schofield, the Kid, Mario and Zack. 'I mean, look at you lot. Except for the ever-handsome Scarecrow, who's like a brother to me and therefore off-limits in that department, the rest of you are a pretty fucking sorry sample of masculinity. No alpha males here.'

'Hey!' the Kid said. 'I'm—'

'You, young man, are a boy. A whole-lotta-woman like me needs a whole-lotta-*man*,' Mother said. 'Oh, well, it's probably a good thing I didn't meet my male mirror. My Ralphy might get jealous.'

Ralph was all tattoos, sleeveless checked shirts and Popeye forearms, a real salt-of-the-Earth type. He and Mother had been married for years and as Schofield knew, Mother loved him dearly.

Although one night she'd made an odd comment that had surprised him: 'I don't know, Scarecrow, sometimes I worry about Ralphy and me. We got married young and now we're both nearly forty and we know each other so well, maybe *too* well. There's no mystery anymore. When I'm home, every night it's the same old routine—eat dinner, feed the dogs, watch some TV and then finish off with *The Daily Show*. Ralph's sweet but sometimes . . . I don't know . . . we've even been having stupid fights lately and we never used to do that.'

'Ralph's a legend,' Schofield said, 'and you're lucky to have him. You two were made for each other.'

And of course there were times when you had to get away from the group and be by yourself.

Often Schofield would retire to his tent to read a book, while some nights he'd sit down with the DARPA wristguard and correspond with a friend of his at the Defense Intelligence Agency, David Fairfax.

A T-shirt-and-sneakers-wearing cryptanalyst, Fairfax had helped Schofield on a couple of missions and they'd kept in touch.

The night before he got the call from the White House Situation Room, Schofield turned on the wristguard to find a message from Fairfax waiting for him:

FFAX: GOT AN UPDATE ON YOUR FRENCH PROBLEM.

Soon after, they were corresponding via live encrypted messaging:

SCRW: WHAT'S UP?

FFAX: LATEST TAPS ON DGSE REVEAL THAT LAST MONTH AN AGENT KNOWN AS 'RENARD' REQUESTED TO TAKE THE LEAD ON YOUR CASE.

SCRW: REQUESTED?

FFAX: YEAH. I DID SOME CHECKING. FROM WHAT I CAN FIND, RENARD IS AN AGENT FROM 'M' UNIT IN THE DGSE'S ACTION DIVISION. 'M' UNIT IS FRANCE'S EQUIVALENT OF THE CIA'S SPECIAL ACTIVITIES DIVISION. THEY PERFORM PARAMILITARY OPS, SPECIALISING IN EXTRAJUDICIAL KILLINGS AND ASSASSINATIONS. RENARD HAS NEVER WORKED WITH THE U.S. SO WE HAVE NO FILE ON HIM. IDENTIFYING MARKS: A TATTOO ON THE INSIDE OF HIS RIGHT WRIST SHOWING A TALLY OF PAST KILLS, CURRENTLY AT THIRTEEN.

SCRW: THANKS FOR THE HEADS-UP.

FFAX: ANY TIME. WATCH YOUR BACK.

Schofield stared at the screen. No matter who you were, living with a price on your head was a constant source of anxiety and stress. And this French business just wasn't going away.

He gazed at the screen for a long time before signing off.

For her part, Mother had spent the last seven weeks watching Shane Schofield very closely.

More than anyone else, she knew what he had been through during that Majestic-12 bounty hunt and the months after.

She had been there on a rainswept cliff on the French coast when he had put his own gun to his chin and almost pulled the trigger. She'd been the one who stopped him going through with it.

He appeared to be doing okay. He was actually smiling again, not much but a little. That said, he did admit that he still didn't sleep well and some days she saw deep bags under his eyes.

Mother knew the Corps had sent him to see a bunch of high-priced shrinks. The psychiatrists had offered him anti-depression drugs but he'd refused. He'd do any therapy they suggested—CBT, couch sessions, even a few sessions of hypnotherapy—but he wouldn't take drugs. He hadn't thought very highly of the shrinks, except for one, a lady in Baltimore he'd found separately; he said she was exceptional. But in any case it seemed like he was now more or less back to normal.

More or less.

For Mother knew he wasn't completely whole again.

And she knew why he wasn't sleeping. Her tent was next to his and on several occasions she'd heard him talking in his sleep, yelling plaintive cries of: 'Fox . . . no . . . not in the . . . guillotine . . . no . . . *NO!*'

Then Mother would hear him wake with a gasp and breathe very heavily for a minute or two.

And then came the morning when the call came from the White House Situation Room.

At 6:30 that morning Schofield called the group together, all eight of them, four Marines, four civilians.

He told them what he knew: that a group calling itself the Army of Thieves had taken Dragon Island and would be ready to set off some kind of atmospheric weapon at 11:00 a.m. local time. A missile attack had failed and aerial assaults would be likewise ineffective, which was why they were being sent in. They were one of only two groups close enough to get to Dragon in time by sea.

'The Army of Thieves?' Mother said. 'Never heard of 'em.'

Schofield said, 'Doesn't sound like anybody has—at least until recently. The White House is sending through whatever intel they can find. Apparently, the DIA has something and the CIA is checking.'

The Kid said, 'Why the delay in setting off the weapon?'

'It takes time to prime the weapon's principal element, some small uranium spheres, and they're not fully primed yet. That's why we have this window.'

'Cutting it a little close, aren't we?'

'Closer than you think,' Schofield said. 'We need to prep all our gear. After that, it'll take us nearly three hours just to get there. And the island itself is seriously fortified. Even if they open the front door for us, we'll have maybe an hour to get in and *get to* the weapon in time, then disable or destroy it. And somehow I don't think they'll be opening the front door for us.'

He turned to the four civilians: Zack, Emma, Hartigan and Chad.

'But four Marines is not enough to do this. We need as many bodies as we can get and if you're willing to come along and help us, I will gladly take you. However, let me say this very clearly from the outset: *this is not compulsory.* None of you has to come. We'll be a secondary team—I repeat, a secondary, back-up team—but if the primary SEAL unit fails to resolve this, we will be going in. And that will be ugly.

'So none of you has any illusions about what "ugly" means, let me tell you now: it means shooting to kill, bloody wounds, broken bones and dead bodies right in your face. So, if you don't want to go, you don't have to and no-one will hold it against you.

'But . . .' he held up a finger, 'if you do come, then I ask only one thing of you: that you obey my orders. However crazy or bizarre they seem, there will always be some logic to them. In return, I promise that I will not leave you. If you are captured or caught, while I still have breath in my body, I will come for you. Got that? Good. All right then. Who's in and who's out? Speak now or for-ever hold your peace.'

The group fell silent.

The civilians variously stared at the flickering gas flame or at their feet, deciding what to do.

Zack spoke first, swallowing, then nodding. 'I'm in.'

'Me, too,' Emma Dawson said uncertainly. 'Although I'm not much with a gun. I fired one once at my uncle's ranch.'

'Don't worry, honey babe,' Mother said gently. 'Give me a couple of minutes with you and you'll be a kick-ass bitch from Hell, just like me.'

Jeff Hartigan snorted. 'This is ridiculous. What chance have you got—four Marines and some untrained civilians—against a dug-in military force? Like hell I'm going. I'm staying here and so is Chad.'

'No, I'm not,' Chad said quietly. 'I'll go.'

'What?' His boss whirled.

Schofield turned, too. He hadn't expected this.

'I said I'm going.'

'You will do no such thing,' Hartigan said. 'You'll stay here with me while these others go off and get themselves killed.'

The assistant shook his head. Schofield wondered if he'd ever stood up to his boss before.

'I'm sorry, Mr Hartigan, but I think we have to do something—'

'You think we have to do something,' Hartigan mimicked. 'Please. Chad, I thought you were smarter than this.'

Chad bowed his head. 'I'm sorry, sir.'

Schofield said, 'I'm not. It's good to have you aboard, Chad.' He turned to Hartigan. 'Sir, if everyone else is going, staying here on your own does present certain dangers. Perhaps you'd like to reconsider—'

'I'll be perfectly fine, thank you very much, Captain,' Hartigan said. 'You are the ones who should rethink your positions. Idiots.'

Schofield just nodded and said no more.

They spent the next half-hour hurriedly preparing for the mission: the Marines field-stripped their weapons, checked their mags; Zack loaded up Bertie with ammunition; and Mother even gave Emma and Chad a quick lesson in marksmanship.

When Schofield saw that Zack was bringing the experimental wristguard, he grabbed it and sent off a message to Dave Fairfax:

SCRW: SOMETHING'S COME UP. GEARING UP FOR BATTLE. CAN YOU LOOK UP A TERRORIST GROUP CALLED THE 'ARMY OF THIEVES' FOR ME, PLUS AN OLD SOVIET ARCTIC BASE CALLED 'DRAGON ISLAND'. ANY INFO WOULD BE APPRECIATED. GOTTA RUN. OUT.

He then ordered everyone, civilians included, to put on drysuits in case they fell into the freezing water. Schofield and his Marines wore new snow-camouflaged drysuits—they looked like regular battle fatigues, only they were made of ultralight watertight material that retained body heat—with their gunbelts and holsters on the outside. On their backs, as always, all the Marines carried their signature weapon, the Armalite MH-12 Maghook, a magnetic grappling hook.

The civilians wore simple grey drysuits with hooded parkas on top for extra warmth; and since they didn't have combat boots, they just wore their cold-weather Arctic boots, a mixture of heavy-duty Nikes and Salomons.

When everyone was ready, the seven members of the departing team boarded the two assault boats and set off on the long journey south to Dragon Island.

Jeff Hartigan watched them go, remaining at the camp, alone. His last words to Schofield were, 'You're a fool, Captain. You must realise that you cannot win this.'

Schofield didn't reply. He just started his boat and pulled away.

ARCTIC ICE FIELD
4 APRIL, 0840 HOURS
2 HOURS 20 MINUTES TO DEADLINE

Killer whales and extreme cold are two things that the Arctic and the Antarctic have in common, but in many other respects they are actually quite different.

While Antarctica is a vast landmass covered in snow and ice, the Arctic is simply a giant frozen sea. Even the North Pole itself is situated on floating ice. In 1953, a submarine called the USS *Nautilus* sailed under the Pole; six years later, the USS *Skate* surfaced at the Pole, bursting up through the ice itself.

Around March every year, as the sun rises for the first time in months, the sea ice begins to melt, creating long cracks called 'leads'. As the region warms, these leads get wider and wider, forming a labyrinthine network of canals and alleyways in the sea ice, some a few feet deep, others over thirty feet deep. Polar bears hunt in leads because seals and small whales surface in them to breathe.

The leads were also useful for an insertion team, as any land-based radar system could only scan the surface of the sea ice: anything down in the sunken network of leads would not be detectable to such devices. The leads could really only be monitored by human eyes looking down from a surveillance aircraft, and as Scarecrow's little assault boats raced down a major lead to the site of the crashed Beriev, no such aircraft could be seen.

Ⓞ

At 8:40 a.m., Schofield's boats came to a small pancake-shaped ice floe floating out in the middle of their lead.

A large white shape lay slumped on it, unmoving.

'*What is that . . . ?*' Mother said over the radio.

Schofield slowed his boat, bringing it in close to the little ice floe. The white shape became clearer.

'It's a polar bear,' he said.

'*Great, now we can test that stupid bear repellent,*' Mother said. '*Hey Kid, go on. Go over and pat the nice widdle bear.*'

'Not this time, Mother,' Schofield said as his boat came further around the ice floe and he saw the other side of the unmoving bear. 'This bear's deader than disco.'

It certainly was. The bear's throat was ripped open, its belly a grisly mess of blood, flesh and sprawling intestines. This polar bear had practically been disembowelled.

The Kid said, 'Jesus . . . the thing's been gutted.'

'But not eaten,' Schofield observed. 'That's not right.'

Emma said, 'No, it's not right at all. The polar bear is an apex predator. The only other animal in these parts that could do something like this is *another* polar bear. You're correct: another bear might attack a fellow bear out of starvation or for territorial reasons, but it would almost always eat its fallen rival. Polar bears are the most dangerous bear in the world primarily because they are opportunists; they'll eat anything they can find, including humans and other bears. But this bear has been slaughtered *and then abandoned*. Polar bears just don't do that.'

'*Are there any gunshot wounds?*' Mother asked.

'Not that I can see.' Schofield stared at the dead bear for a long moment. It was absolutely huge, and its snow-white coat was matted with blood. Who or what could have done this?

It didn't escape his notice that they were now only about thirty miles from Dragon Island.

'Come on,' he said, turning. 'We've got a plane to find.'

He gunned the engine and his sleek assault boat powered away from the remains of the dead polar bear.

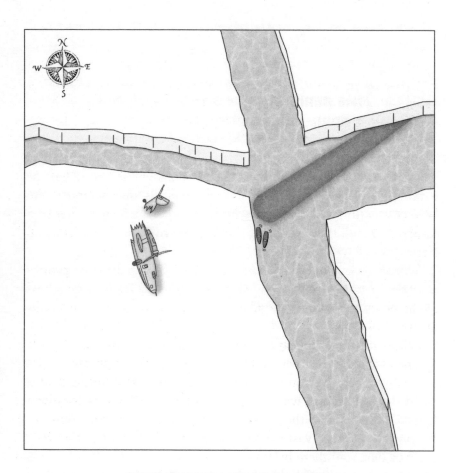

THE BERIEV CRASH SITE

THE BERIEV CRASH SITE
4 APRIL, 0900 HOURS
2 HOURS TO DEADLINE

Twenty minutes later, the two assault boats pulled to a halt at a junction of two major leads. The ice walls that bounded the watery junction rose about twenty feet above the boats. After two hours of travel, they were close to the co-ordinates of the crashed Beriev.

Scarecrow extended a ladder, hooked its curved upper prongs over the lip of the ice wall and started climbing. His team remained in the boats below him, huddled in their drysuits and parkas, looking very anxious.

Schofield's head appeared above the flat edge of the ice plain.

The crashed Beriev was right there, barely fifty yards away.

It was tipped over on its left-hand side, its nose pointing southward. Its tail section was completely destroyed, and its left wing had snapped under the weight of the fuselage rolling onto it. Beyond the plane, a vast expanse of ice stretched away to the west, cracked here and there by leads.

Far to the south, Schofield saw Dragon Island for the first time.

It loomed on the horizon, small but visible, a jagged upthrust of mountains on the otherwise perfectly flat horizon. Low clouds hovered above it. It looked dangerous, even from here.

Scarecrow peered warily up at the sky, scanning for surveillance aircraft.

Nothing. Only the purple dawn-like sky and some high-altitude

clouds, although to the south, around Dragon, the sky did seem to shimmer somewhat.

He saw something.

A tiny object, circling lazily high above him. It wasn't a surveillance plane; it was too small. It looked like a large Arctic bird, gliding on the thermals.

Schofield swore. He was completely unprepared for a combat mission and he knew it. He was working with untrained civilians just to make up the numbers and he had almost zero surveillance equipment. He wished he had a simple waveguide radar or even just a parabolic dish to scan the immediate airspace. But he didn't even have that. Right now, all he had were his eyes and they just weren't good enough.

'Mother, come on up. Bring Bertie with you. Everyone else, stay in the boats for now.'

He stepped up onto the flat surface of the ice plain, MP-7 sub-machine gun poised and ready.

A few moments later, Mother joined him. She plonked Bertie on the ground between them and the little robot beeped and spun on his chunky tyres.

Mother stood beside Scarecrow, clasping a menacing Heckler & Koch G36A2 assault rifle in her hands.

Most Force Recon NCOs used the standard-issue M4, but Mother preferred the venerable German assault gun, and hers came with all the optional extras: it had a 100-round C-Mag drum magazine, underslung AG36 grenade launcher with the new anti-tank zinc-tipped incendiary grenades, a Zeiss RSA reflex sight and Oerlikon Contraves LLM01 laser light module. With all the additions, it looked like something out of a science fiction movie.

Scarecrow glanced from his compact MP-7 to her G36. 'Could you have attached anything else to that thing?' he asked.

'Quiet, you,' she said. 'Weapons options are like good commanders: you love 'em when you've got 'em, and you wish you had 'em when you don't.'

'I'll take that as a compliment.'

Mother scanned the area. 'It's too quiet here.'

'Yeah, it is. Bertie, acquire and identify that object up in the sky, please.'

'*Yes, Captain Schofield.*' Bertie's optical lens tilted skyward.

As the robot did this, Scarecrow and Mother approached the crashed plane, guns raised.

Standing before the Beriev, Schofield pulled down the thermal-vision scope on his helmet.

He saw the crumpled plane in infra-red, saw the strong residual warmth of its intact wing-mounted engine plus two man-shaped blobs in the cockpit, dim but pulsing.

'I got two human signatures,' he said. 'Looks like they're still alive in there—'

Suddenly, Schofield's earpiece crackled to life.

Ironbark Barker's voice growled: '*SEAL team in position off the north-east corner of Dragon Island. Commencing underwater insertion via the old submarine dock.*'

Ironbark and his team were going in.

Scarecrow returned his attention to the plane and stepping cautiously forward, arrived at its cracked cockpit windshield. Since the Beriev was rolled on its side, he couldn't get in via its side doors, so he smashed one of the cockpit windows while Mother covered him, her G36 ready to fire.

Schofield saw two figures slumped in the plane's flight seats. Still strapped into the pilot's seat was an older man with a bushy grey moustache and 'IVANOV' stencilled onto his parka. He groaned as Schofield reached in and touched his carotid artery.

'This must be the guy who sent out the distress call. He's alive.' Schofield pulled out a heat-pack from his first-aid pouch and pressed it against Ivanov's chest. Ivanov immediately started breathing more deeply.

Mother crawled in and checked the other man, a young Russian private by all appearances. He was pale and pasty-faced, but after a few slaps, he came to with a grunt.

Beside him, Vasily Ivanov regained his senses. He blurted

something in Russian before, seeing the US flags on Schofield's and Mother's shoulders, he switched to English: 'Who are you?!'

Schofield said, 'We're United States Marines. Our people picked up your distress signal and we're here to—'

Gunfire.

Schofield spun. Mother did, too.

But it wasn't *here*. It was in their ears, in their earpieces.

Then Schofield heard Ironbark's voice again and it was shouting desperately.

Cut into the cliffs on the north-eastern flank of Dragon Island was a Soviet-era submarine dock. It was essentially a rectangular concrete cave that had been carved into the rocky cliff face, and like all such edifices of the once mighty Soviet Union, it was enormous.

It featured two berths that could hold—at the same time, completely sheltered from the elements—a nuclear ballistic missile submarine and a 30,000-ton bulk carrier. The tracks of an oversized railway system ended at the edge of the two docks. In the old days, Soviet freighters had unloaded their cargoes—weapons, weapons-grade nuclear material or just steel and concrete—directly onto the carriages of a waiting megasized train.

Today, one of those berths was occupied by a most unusual sight: a huge red-hulled Russian freighter lay half-sunk beside the dock, deliberately scuttled. It was tilted dramatically forward, its bow fully under the surface while its stern remained afloat. The stricken vessel's name blared out from that stern in massive white letters: **OKHOTSK.**

It was the mysterious Russian freighter that had gone missing with an army's worth of weapons and ordnance on board: AK-47s, RPGs, Strela anti-aircraft vehicles, ZALA aerial drones, APR torpedoes and even two MIR mini-submarines. One of those compact glass-domed submersibles could be seen tilted on its side on the half-submerged foredeck of the freighter.

Apart from the *Okhotsk* lying alongside the dock, the rest of the vast concrete cavern lay empty, long unused, its many ladders, catwalks and chains doing nothing but gathering dust and frost.

The first of Ironbark's Navy SEALs emerged silently from the ice-strewn water, leading with a silenced MP-5N. He was quickly followed by a second man, then Ironbark himself.

It was a textbook entry. They never made a sound.

There was only one problem.

The force of a hundred armed men stationed at various positions around the dock, using the ageing debris and the half-sunk wreck of the *Okhotsk* as firing positions. They formed a perfect ring around the water containing the SEALs.

And as soon as all twelve of the SEALs had breached the surface, they opened fire.

What followed was nothing less than a shooting gallery. The SEALs were annihilated in perfectly executed interlocking patterns of fire.

Schofield heard Ironbark's voice shouting above the rain of gunfire: '*Fuck! Go under! Go under!—Jesus, there must be a hundred of them!—Base, this is Ironbark! SEAL assault is negative! I repeat, SEAL assault is fucked! They were waiting in the submarine dock! We're being slaughtered!* Miami, *we have to get back to you.* Miami, *come in—*'

Ten miles away, the Los Angeles–class attack submarine, the USS *Miami*, hovered in the blue void beneath the Arctic sea ice.

Inside its communications centre, a radio operator keyed his mike: 'Ironbark, this is *Miami*. We read you—'

'What the hell . . .' the sonar operator beside him said suddenly before shouting: 'Torpedo in the water! *Torpedo in the water!* Signature is of an APR-3E Russian-made torpedo. Bearing 235! It's coming from Dragon and it's coming in fast!'

☼

'*Launch countermeasures!*'

'*It's locked on to us—*'

Schofield listened in horror to the frantic commands being given on the *Miami*.

'*—Take evasive action—*'

'*—can't, it's too close!*'

'*—too late! Brace for impact! Fuck! No!—*'

The signal from the *Miami* cut to hash.

Schofield heard Ironbark yell: '*Miami? Come in. USS* Miami, *respond!*'

There was no reply from the *Miami*.

Mother looked at Schofield in utter shock.

Schofield kept listening.

'*Ah! Fuck!*' Ironbark shouted in pain before, in a hail of louder gunfire, his signal also went dead and the airwaves went completely silent.

Schofield and Mother listened for more, but nothing came.

'Holy shit . . .' Mother whispered. 'A hundred men waiting? A force that can take out a SEAL team and a fucking Los Angeles–class attack sub? Who in God's name is this Army of Thieves?'

Schofield was thinking exactly the same thing.

'Whoever they are,' he said, staring out the cockpit's shattered windshield at Dragon Island on the southern horizon, 'our little team just became the last people on Earth capable of stopping them.'

Back in the assault boats, the rest of Schofield's team waited tensely.

The Kid and Mario manned the controls of the boats, in case a swift departure was required.

Emma and Chad stared up at the ladder rising out of the lead, waiting for Schofield and Mother to return.

Zack, however, was busying himself with the wristguard. The high-tech device was one of his pet projects at DARPA and its failure frustrated him. There was no reason it shouldn't be working fine. Also, tinkering with it took his mind off the mission at hand.

He had the wristguard's upper panel flipped open and was peering at its internal workings.

He flicked it on—and suddenly the wristguard started pinging urgently, a red light blinking.

Zack frowned. 'It's saying there's a three-hundred-foot-long object alongside us again.'

'The sea ice?' the Kid said, glancing at the ice walls around them.

'No, it's a metallic signature. The wristguard's sensors can distinguish between ice and steel.' Zack shook his head. '*Why?* Why is it doing that—ah-ha . . .'

He spotted something deep inside the wristguard's internal wiring. 'The emitter mirror's been bent sideways. It must've got bumped somewhere. The emitter's been pointing *down* the whole time.'

Now it was the Kid who frowned.

'Wait a second. Are you saying that, right now, your wrist gizmo is picking up a three-hundred-foot-long metal object *underneath* us?'

Zack said, 'Well, yes, I suppose so . . .'

'How far away is it?' the Kid asked.

'Two hundred yards . . . no wait, one-ninety . . . one-eighty. Whatever it is, it's getting closer.'

The Kid's face fell. He looked up in the direction of the Beriev. 'This is not good.'

A beep from just outside the Beriev's smashed windshield made Schofield turn.

'*Captain Schofield,*' Bertie said. '*Object identified.*'

'Let me see.' Schofield was still inside the Beriev with Ivanov. Bertie came over, stopping next to the side-turned windows of the cockpit. Schofield looked at the display screen on the little robot's back.

When he saw what was on the screen, he said, 'Oh, *shit . . .*'

Bertie narrated: '*Object is a Russian-made ZALA-421-08 unmanned aerial vehicle. Vehicle is designed for reconnaissance and surveillance purposes. It carries no weapons payload. Electric engine, wingspan of eighty centimetres; maximum flight duration: ninety minutes. Standard payload: one 550 TVL infra-red-capable video camera, one 12-megapixel digital still camera.*'

Schofield was moving quickly now. He scrambled out of the Beriev, got to his feet and scanned the sky.

And found it: the high-flying, bird-like object he'd seen earlier.

Only it wasn't a bird.

It was a drone.

A small, lightweight surveillance drone.

'They know we're here,' he said aloud.

As if in answer, four dark aircraft appeared above the southern horizon, two big ones hovering in between two smaller ones, coming from Dragon Island.

They grew larger by the second.

They were approaching. Fast.

His earpiece came alive again.

'*Scarecrow!*' It was the Kid. '*Zack's got the wristguard's proximity sensor working. I think he's picked up a submarine lurking out here and it's closing in on us!*'

Schofield's mind spun.

Drones, incoming aircraft, the loss of Ironbark's team and the *Miami*, and now *another* submarine here . . .

Damn.

This was all happening too fast, way too fast for a commander out in the middle of nowhere with no support, few combat troops and nothing in the way of serious hardware.

His brain tried to put it all together, to somehow order it all.

You can't figure it out now. You can only stay alive and figure it out as you run.

'Kid!' he yelled, diving back inside the Beriev. 'Keep those engines running! Mother! Get these two out of the cockpit! Things are about to get hairy!'

The four aircraft were two V-22 Ospreys and two AH-1 Cobra attack helicopters, all of which had been stolen from the Marine Corps staging base in Helmand Province, Afghanistan, four months earlier.

The Ospreys were, quite simply, aerial beasts. With tiltable rotors, they were capable of both swift aeroplane-like flight and helicopter-like hovering. And these Ospreys were the variant known as the 'Warbird': they were armed to the teeth. They each had not one but two 20mm six-barrelled M61 Vulcan cannons, door-mounted .50 calibre AN/M2 machine guns, and missile pods slung under both wings. The Warbird was the mother of all gunships—big and strong, yet also fast and manoeuvrable—and the Army of Thieves had two of them.

The two Cobras weren't shy either: they carried slightly smaller M134 six-barrelled miniguns underneath their sharply-pointed noses.

The two Ospreys thundered over the ice plain, flanked by the Cobras, sweeping over the network of watery leads, rushing toward the crashed Beriev.

A short distance from the crash site, one of the big Ospreys broke away from the other three aircraft and zoomed off to the north-west. The remaining three attack aircraft kept coming straight for the Beriev.

'Base, this is Hammerhead,' the pilot of the Osprey that had stayed on course said into his mike.

While he wore a Marine Corps tactical flight helmet and a Marine Corps winter warfare parka, he was not a United States Marine.

Flowing tattoos lined his neck and lower jaw—images of snakes, skulls and thorny vines. In addition to the Marine parka, he wore Uzbek gloves and Russian boots. The eight armed and similarly tattooed men sitting in the hold behind him had the broad faces, dark eyes and olive skin of native Chileans. They, too, wore a hodgepodge of Arctic gear, including Marine Corps parkas, and they held AK-47 assault rifles in their laps with easy familiarity.

'We're coming up on Ivanov's plane,' Hammerhead said. 'The drone spotted two people approaching it. They must've come by boat through the leads, so the tower radars on Dragon couldn't spot them.'

A calm voice replied in the pilot's ear.

'*Just as we suspected. It's the American testing team.*' The speaker grunted a short, cruel laugh. '*The Pentagon must be desperate if it's sending product testers against us. Take out Ivanov's plane with missiles, then find this test team and kill them all.*'

Inside the Beriev's cockpit, Schofield and Mother were moving frantically now.

Mother released the young Russian private from his flight seat and they shimmied out the smashed cockpit windows.

Schofield slid to Vasily Ivanov's side and had just started to extract Ivanov from his flight seat when, through the lopsided cockpit windshield, he saw one of the Cobras loose a pair of heat-seeking missiles.

The two missiles looped through the air, zeroing in on the stricken plane.

Scarecrow yelled, '*Bertie!* Missile scrambler! Now!'

Outside the Beriev, Bertie replied, '*Missile scrambling initiated.*' He then emitted a powerful burst of short-range electronic jamming.

Almost immediately the two missiles peeled away and slammed into the ice plain a short distance from the Beriev in twin explosions of fire and ice.

Schofield struggled with Ivanov's seatbelt. It was jammed with frost.

'Mother!' he called. 'Get back to the boats! Before that Osprey lands and unloads ground troops!'

'What about you?' Mother shouted back.

'I gotta get this guy out! I'll catch up! Now, go!'

Mother bolted, hauling the dazed young Russian private with her. As they ran across the fifty yards of open ground between the Beriev and the lead containing their boats the second Cobra tried to loose another missile, but this one also went haywire and smashed into the ice.

'Cobras, forget it. They've got anti-missile countermeasures,' the pilot named Hammerhead said. 'I'm going to unload the ground team. You take care of those two runners.'

The Osprey powered ahead of the two Cobras, up-tilted its rotors and swung into a hover.

As it did so, its side doors were pulled open from within and drop ropes were tossed out. Within seconds, eight heavily armed men in black balaclavas and Marine Corps parkas were sliding down the ropes and hitting the ground one after the other.

They fanned out in perfect formation, AK-47s up, moving in on the crashed Beriev.

At the same time, one of the Cobras pivoted in the air and aimed its M134 at the fleeing figures of Mother and the Russian private.

The minigun whirred to life, barrels spinning, and unleashed a thunderous burst of hypermachine-gun fire.

The ice behind Mother's running feet leapt upward as bullets strafed it.

'Dive!' she yelled to the young private limping along beside her.

They dived forward, toward the ladder hooks looped over the edge of the ice, chased by bullets.

Mother hit the ice on her belly and slid forward like a batter trying to steal second, before she hit the edge and went flying off it into open space, falling suddenly as she felt a bullet slap against the sole of her left boot. She dropped in a clumsy heap onto the first boat waiting at the base of the ladder.

Behind her, the Russian private did the same, but he was a split second behind Mother and that made a world of difference to the result.

As he slid over the lip, he was literally ripped apart by the hail of bullets. Blood fountains spurted all over his body, but propelled by his own dive, his corpse continued off the edge and, like Mother, it also dropped into the first AFDV, right next to Emma Dawson, who screamed at the sight of the bullet-riddled body that thudded down next to her like a slab of meat on a butcher's block. It was no longer recognisable as a human being.

Mother gasped, out of breath. 'Mother*fucker*, that was close! Oh, Jesus, Scarecrow . . .'

The roar of the hovering Osprey was deafening. A tornado of ice and snow swirled around the Beriev.

Inside the crashed plane's cockpit, Schofield splashed some water from his canteen onto Ivanov's buckle and the frost melted and the seatbelt unjammed. Schofield yanked the Russian from his flight seat.

'Come on, buddy,' he said, peering outside and seeing the eight-man balaclava-and-parka-wearing force approaching the Beriev from the south. He glanced eastward.

'Mother, you okay?'

'*I'm clear, but my guy's toast. What about you?*'

'On my way—uh-oh . . .'

One of the balaclava-clad men dropped to a prone position, took aim down the sights of a very powerful bipod-mounted machine gun and squeezed the trigger—

—*braaaaaaaaaack!*

The gunman was himself thrown backwards by a terrible burst of machine-gun fire.

Schofield snapped up to see—of all things—Bertie's gunbarrel smoking.

'Oh, good robot,' he said. 'Good robot.'

Bertie lay down some more deadly fire and the other attackers variously dived for cover behind the Beriev itself or returned fire at Bertie. Bullets bounced off the little robot's metal flanks while Bertie just kept panning left and right, emitting short controlled bursts.

But then while Bertie was facing right, Schofield glimpsed another enemy commando to their left—appearing between the Beriev and the lead containing their escape boats—as he swung a Russian-made RPG-7 rocket-propelled grenade launcher onto his shoulder.

The man was only just in Scarecrow's field of vision. Schofield had to peer up through the cracked windshield of the Beriev just to see him. The angle was too narrow to fire at the man and in any case, Schofield didn't have anything to match the firepower of an RPG.

He looked about himself for options.

Wait a second . . .

The parka-clad commando peered down the sight of his rocket launcher, steadied it on his shoulder—as inside the cockpit of the Beriev, Shane Schofield pushed Ivanov backward and said, 'Cover your ears!'

Then Scarecrow yanked on the ejection lever of the Beriev's co-pilot's seat.

A gaseous *whoosh* filled the cockpit as a section of the plane's roof was jettisoned and the co-pilot's seat blasted out of the Beriev. Since the plane was lying on its side, the flight seat rocketed *laterally* through the air, shooting low over the ground on a flat horizontal trajectory before it struck the RPG-wielding commando with terrible force, square in the chest, cracking every one of his ribs before sending him flying backwards, all but breaking the man in two.

Vasily Ivanov's eyes boggled as he looked out through the

newly-opened hole in the roof of the cockpit and saw the dead commando on the ice plain.

'You see that?' Schofield yelled to Ivanov as the other parka-clad commandos opened fire again. ''Cause that's how we're getting out of here, too! Is that flightsuit you're wearing good in Arctic waters?'

'It is designed to survive in icy water for a short time, yes,' Ivanov stammered.

'Good enough.' Schofield reached out through the smashed cockpit windshield with one hand, yanked Bertie back inside, and handed him to Ivanov. 'Here, hold my robot!' Schofield then sat on the remaining pilot's seat and pulled Ivanov onto his own lap. 'Now hold on to your breakfast.'

Then, with all three of them sitting on the pilot's seat, Schofield pulled that seat's ejection lever.

The flight seat shot out of the Beriev—with Schofield, Ivanov and Bertie on it—blasting through the ring of enemy commandos surrounding the plane!

The seat flew—on its side—a foot above the ice plain, the world around it blurring with speed, the force of its screamingly-fast lateral flight pushing Schofield and Ivanov down into it.

After about forty yards of this kind of flight, the speeding pilot's seat hit the ground where it bounced twice like a skimming stone before shooting clear off the lip of the ice floe and out over the watery alleyway—out over the stunned faces of Mother and the others still in the two assault boats.

Having cleared the lip, the flight seat arced downward and speared into the freezing water of the lead, entering it with an almighty splash.

'What was that?' Chad asked, astonished.

'That was the Scarecrow,' Mother said, shoving the Kid out of the driver's saddle, taking the controls and gunning the engine. 'Hang on, people! We gotta grab him!'

Underwater silence.

As the flight seat shot under the water's surface, Scarecrow and Ivanov separated, floating apart in the ice-blue haze. Bertie's flotation balloons activated immediately on contact with the water and Schofield saw the little robot rise up and away to the surface.

Scarecrow felt the sting of the water against his face, the only part of his body not covered by his drysuit. It was outrageously cold, like daggers of ice.

The impact with the water had flipped his reflective glasses onto his forehead, and as he hovered there in the clear blue water of the Arctic, he was enveloped by eerie silence.

But not total silence. An odd *thrumming* could be heard.

It was then that Schofield realised that he was not alone.

There was something in front of him.

Something impossibly huge, black and enormous, hovering there in the void like a leviathan of the deep. Only it wasn't an animal of any sort. It was man-made, mechanical.

It was a submarine.

A screaming sense of déjà vu overcame Schofield.

This had happened to him once before, during that mission in Antarctica, when he had come face-to-face with a French nuclear ballistic missile submarine. On that occasion, he had managed to destroy the submarine in question. It was one of the events that had made him a marked man by the French.

No. It couldn't possibly be French—

And then Schofield saw the markings on the sub's dome-shaped bow, saw the distinct blue-white-and-red flag painted on it.

Yes, it could. This submarine was French.

In the meta-time in which the brain operates, Schofield's mind rapidly connected some dots.

The wristguard's proximity sensor had picked up this submarine only minutes ago—which meant the sensor might not have been broken earlier in their trip and may actually have picked up the *same* submarine back then—the sub had followed them here—which meant it was a good guess that the sub *wasn't* part of what was happening at Dragon Island—indeed, it was a better guess that this sub, this French sub which appeared to be following his team, *probably had no idea at all* what was going on at Dragon.

This French submarine, he realised with a shock, was up in the Arctic trying to find *him*.

Gazing at the gigantic submarine, Schofield suddenly noticed that there were three smaller submersibles mounted on its back, compact Swimmer Delivery Vehicles—similar to his AFDVs but smaller—carrying three frogmen apiece and which were at that very moment lifting off from the sub and coming toward Schofield.

It was an assassination squad.

A French hit team, coming for him, and yet totally unaware that they'd walked into a far more deadly firestorm.

Schofield swam for the surface.

Schofield burst up from the icy water and found himself treading water beside Ivanov and Bertie—the little robot was floating happily thanks to his flotation balloons, his fat tyres propelling him slowly but valiantly toward Schofield.

'*Captain Schofield, do you require assistance? My buoyancy features can keep you afloat till our colleagues arrive.*'

Just then, like a shark rising from the depths, the first French SDV breached the surface ten yards from Scarecrow, Ivanov and Bertie.

One frogman drove while two more held short-barrelled FA-MAS assault rifles, raised and ready to fire—

With a roar, something slammed into the first French SDV, sending all three of the frogmen on it flying into the water.

It was Mother's assault boat and it *crunched* over the top of the smaller French submersible, breaking it clean in two, before Mother swung her AFDV to a perfect halt beside Schofield.

'Haul them out!' she yelled to the Kid, Emma and Zack in the rear tray.

Schofield scooped up Bertie while the Kid and the two civilians grabbed him and within seconds he and the robot were in the boat. A moment later, Ivanov was, too.

'Go, *go!*' Schofield yelled. 'This place is about to get really crowded and this might be our one and only chance to get out of here in one piece!'

That was the understatement of the year.

For in the next moment, several things happened at once:

First, the other two French submersibles surfaced, revealing more armed frogmen on their backs.

But then a Cobra thundered by overhead from the direction of the crashed Beriev, rotors thumping, minigun blazing, strafing the world. The skinny attack chopper's wave of bullet-impacts traced a line across the water's surface—a line that cut right across one of the newly-surfaced French submersibles, ripping the three frogmen on it to shreds.

That first Cobra was quickly followed by the second AH-1, which swooped into a deadly hover low over the water, right in front of Mother's boat! It pivoted in the air, levelling its minigun at them.

'Fuck me . . .' Mother breathed.

The only weapon they had that possessed anywhere near enough firepower to threaten the Cobra was the grenade launcher on Mother's G36 which right now lay at her feet, out of reach, and—

Schofield didn't stop to think about it.

He quickly snatched up Bertie, held the little robot in front of him and instead of pulling a trigger—because Bertie didn't have one—yelled: 'Bertie! Fire! Fire! Fire!'

Bertie's M249 came to stunning life.

Each shot emitted a deep puncture-like whump—*whump!-whump!-whump!*—yet the recoil was largely contained by Bertie's internal compensator. The shots hit their mark. They erupted all over the Cobra's body: cracking its canopy, slamming into its engine housing where they ruptured something, causing a thick plume of black smoke to stream out from the Cobra's exhaust and the chopper banked wildly away, wounded but not defeated.

Mother yelled, 'Scarecrow! What now! Which way do we go?'

That was the question, Schofield thought. In the cacophony of clattering gunfire, booming robots and thumping choppers, he tried to think clearly.

We need to talk to this Russian guy, get some intel and make a decent plan. We don't have much time but—he recalled the old military maxim—*a good plan with less time is better than a bad plan with more time. Maybe we can double back north, regroup a little, and then head for Dragon*—

He turned to face the intersection that led back north when a monstrous *whooshing* noise filled the air and, right in his path, the giant black hull of the French submarine exploded up out of the water, breaching the surface spectacularly.

The bulbous nose of the sub rose a full thirty feet into the air before it slammed back down onto the surface with a colossal splash that sent huge waves rolling out in every direction, causing Schofield's two low-slung boats to rock wildly.

Schofield's face fell.

It was completely blocking their path. They couldn't go north.

Then, with a deafening roar, the V-22 Osprey shoomed overhead, cutting a beeline for the massive French submarine.

It's going for the more dangerous prey first, Schofield realised. *Once it takes out the sub, it can come after us at its leisure.*

With its rotors tilted upwards, the Osprey did a low banking pass over the sub, in the process dropping two Mark 46 Mod 5A anti-submarine torpedoes from its wing-mounts.

The torpedoes hit the water with twin splashes and immediately zeroed in on the submarine. The Mark 46 is a fine torpedo: reliable, accurate and deadly. Fired from this range, the French sub would have no time to launch any countermeasures and the Mark 46s wouldn't miss.

Sure enough, a few seconds later, they hit.

It sounded like the end of the universe: two terrific and immense explosions.

The massive French submarine was almost lifted completely out of the water by the blast. A geyser of whitewater sprayed a hundred feet into the air and rained down on the entire area. As the sub bucked skyward, its midsection cracked and folded, wrenched open like a beer can, and as the great sub lunged back down into the foaming water—fatally wounded, its innards literally ripped open—it immediately began to sink.

The rain of spray fell on Schofield's thunderstruck face.

The scene before him simply defied belief:

The French submarine—smoking and flaming, its bow tilting unnaturally upwards—was sinking. Cries and shouts rang out from inside it. And all the while the Osprey hovered over it, pummelling it with relentless gunfire, taking down the sailors who now scrambled out of the conning tower, fleeing one form of death only to step into the line of fire of another.

Then there were the two Cobra attack choppers: the wounded, smoking one had backed off a little but the unhurt one was hovering low over the ice-walled intersection, nailing the three frogmen on the third and last French submersible, strafing their defenceless bodies with minigun fire, flinging them into the water, turning the hapless frogmen—killers who had walked into a much bigger fire-fight—into convulsing fountains of bloody pulp.

'Captain!' a voice called from behind Schofield. '*Captain!*'

Schofield turned.

It was the Russian, Ivanov.

'We can go south from here without having to land on Dragon Island! There are a couple of small islets near the main island we can land on, if only briefly!'

'Good enough for me.' Schofield turned. 'Mother—!'

He stopped short.

He saw the wounded Cobra chopper pivoting in the air a short distance away, turning its brutal minigun on the last three French frogmen in the water—the frogmen from the submersible that Mother had run over as it had approached Schofield; only now they were treading water, totally exposed, at the mercy of the smoking Cobra.

And something inside Schofield clicked.

Whoever was flying these Cobras and the Osprey were cold bastards, and even if these French assholes had been coming to kill him, they didn't deserve to be shot like fish in a barrel. And in the back of his mind he thought that these French troops, if rescued, might even be of some help . . .

And so Schofield scooped up Mother's G36, shucked its under-slung grenade launcher and jammed down on the trigger.

A zinc-tipped anti-tank grenade zoomed out from the launcher and, trailing a dead-straight smoke tail behind it, rocketed inside the Cobra's already-smoking exhaust and detonated.

The Cobra exploded.

It simply burst outward in a flaming fireball, spraying fragments of metal before it just dropped out of the sky and splashed into the icy Arctic water in front of the stunned French frogmen.

Mother called, 'Oh, yeah, now you like those optional extras, don't you!'

'Quiet, you!' He turned to face Mario and Chad in the other AFDV. 'Mario! Chad! Get over here! Help us pick up these frogmen, then let's get the hell out of here!'

'What are you—?' Mother frowned but Schofield just yelled, 'Do it!'

The two American speedboats came to fast halts beside the three stunned frogmen. They were quickly yanked out of the water: two went into the rear tray of Mario and Chad's boat while the third, a big fellow, dropped into Schofield's rear tray, his wetsuit dripping.

'Bonjour,' Schofield said. 'Welcome to our nightmare. Mother! South, now! Zack!'

The bespectacled geek looked up, alarmed, clearly not expecting to be called upon. Schofield pointed at the wristguard on Zack's left forearm.

'You're gonna be our guide! Use the satellite imaging! Get us through this maze to the islets north of Dragon!'

Zack looked down at his wristguard: its display now showed a zoomed-out image of the labyrinth of ice-walled leads in which they found themselves.

'Me?'

'Yes, you. And you'll have to get it exactly right or we all die,' Schofield said, taking the handlebars from Mother and handing back her G36. 'You guide, I'll drive, Mother will shoot. Let's do it!'

He gunned the thrusters and the AFDV leapt off the mark, kicking up a tail of spray as it peeled out, closely followed by the second American assault boat.

They sped south, leaving the sinking French submarine behind them, and headed in the direction of Dragon Island.

It was a whole lot quieter back at Schofield's old camp.

Jeff Hartigan was in his tent revising some of his test notes when he heard the distant sound of an aircraft.

He stepped out of his dome-shaped tent and peered south.

A lone plane appeared above the horizon, approaching.

For a brief moment, Hartigan felt a stab of fear—and wondered if perhaps he'd made a mistake staying at the camp alone—but then the aircraft came closer and he saw that it was an American V-22 Osprey with 'MARINES' painted in large black letters on the side.

He relaxed. He'd been right and Schofield had been wrong. The Pentagon had found some Marines stationed somewhere nearby to come and get them.

Hartigan started waving. The Osprey brought itself into a hover and landed near the camp.

Smiling, he went out to meet it.

Schofield's two AFDVs shot like bullets through the narrow ice-walled leads.

Guided by Zack, Schofield swung the first low-slung inflatable speedboat left and right—dodging pancake-shaped ice floes and sweeping around corners—trying to put as much distance as possible between them and the Cobra and the Osprey, before the two deadly aircraft finished off the French submarine and came after them.

They'd come a good way south, maybe ten miles, since they'd seen the French sub get torpedoed by the Osprey.

Mother sat behind Schofield, eyes searching the sky, G36 at the ready. In the rear tray sat Emma, the Kid, Ivanov and the big French frogman, who still looked hopelessly confused.

'Take the next left!' Zack yelled over the wind. 'Then immediately go right!'

Schofield did so.

As he did, he glimpsed something up ahead between the walls of the lead.

Dragon Island.

The huge island looked completely out of place in the Arctic landscape. While the frozen sea around it was all white, flat and level, Dragon was dark, massive and jagged, a spiking upthrust of black rock that at some point in time millions of years ago had burst up through the pack ice and stayed. With its high snow-covered peaks and sheer cliffs looming over the ocean, it looked like an imposing natural citadel.

Schofield saw a light on one of the clifftops: the uppermost window of a watchtower or lighthouse; it seemed impossibly tiny compared to the scale of the island on which it stood.

In the foreground in front of the island, however, just as Ivanov had said, were a few small islets, low mounds of earth that rose above the ice field. They were covered in snow and mud and various oddly-shaped buildings.

'Nice work, Zack,' Schofield said when he saw them. 'You got us here.'

'Don't stop at the first islet! It's contaminated!' Ivanov said, coming alongside Schofield. 'Go to the second one. Are these boats submersible?'

'Yes, why?' Schofield was surprised that Ivanov might suspect that. The full capabilities of these AFDVs were classified.

'The second islet has a small loading dock that is accessible only by submersible,' Ivanov said. 'We might be able to land there unseen.'

Schofield frowned. 'Who builds a loading dock that's only accessible by submersible?'

'It wasn't built that way,' Ivanov said. 'The dock was intentionally destroyed, because of an . . . accident . . . there.'

'An acci—'

A line of minigun rounds cut across their path, ripping up the water in front of their boats and the remaining Cobra roared past overhead.

'They found us!' the Kid yelled.

'Mother!' Schofield called. 'Go cyclic!'

'On it!' Mother raised her G36 and returned fire on full auto as they sped down the ice-walled alleyway toward the islets.

She fired hard but her bullets pinged off the Cobra's armoured flanks. She tried firing her grenade launcher as Schofield had done before, but this Cobra's pilot was ready for that: he released a showering spray of firecracker-like chaff and Mother's grenades—confused into thinking that they had hit something solid—exploded too early and the Cobra remained unharmed.

It rained fire down on the fleeing, banking speedboats.

Schofield swung left and right, trying to put the ice walls between him and the chopper. He swept around a corner just as it was torn apart by minigun fire.

'Kid!' he yelled. 'Keep an eye out for the Osprey! They probably split up to search for us and that Cobra will have told him where we are by now—'

With a deafening boom, the Osprey arrived, roaring low above them, its two six-barrelled Vulcan cannons blazing.

Chunks of ice and fountains of water kicked up all around the two speedboats as they shot behind another corner.

'Goddamn it!' Mother was still firing her G36 for all she was worth. The Kid joined her, firing with his much smaller MP-7. Even working together, they were nothing near a match for the firepower of the Osprey and the Cobra.

Schofield looked ahead: they were still about a mile away from the first—contaminated—islet.

Too far. They'd be dead in a quarter of a mile.

'Scarecrow . . . !' Mother yelled urgently.

'I know!' They were out of time and he knew it.

Unless . . .

'Mario! Deflate skirts and prepare to submerge! Mother! I need one minute!'

'I can give you maybe thirty seconds, honey buns!'

'Give me whatever you can!'

He started flicking switches as Mother ejected one C-Mag and inserted another and prepared to fire again.

The Osprey swung around behind them. The Cobra dropped into the long alleyway in front of them, guns up, rotor blades blurring, cutting them off.

Shit! Schofield's mind screamed. *Caught in the middle.*

Mother saw it, too. 'Game over, dudes . . .'

'*Mais non*,' a gruff voice said from behind her, followed by a loud *shuck-shuck*.

Both Mother and Schofield turned to see the big French frogman—in fact, he was huge, easily six-feet-four—heft an absolutely *gigantic* gun that had been slung across his back, a gun that was nearly eight times heavier than Mother's G36. It was a Russian-made 6P49 Kord, a brutish belt-fed heavy machine gun that was usually mounted on a tank turret and which fired 12.7mm ammunition. This Kord had been adapted for individual use and hung from two straps over the Frenchman's impressively broad shoulders.

The burly frogman ripped off his scuba hood, revealing a wild tangle of brown hair and an equally wild beard that reached down to his collarbone. He hoisted the Kord into a firing position and let fucking rip.

A blazing three-foot-long tongue of fire roared out from the big gun's muzzle, releasing an unimaginable torrent of heavy-bore bullets at the Cobra.

The chopper's armoured flanks and windshield might have been able to resist Mother's G36 fire but they were no match for the Kord.

The Frenchman's bullets literally *chewed up* the helicopter.

Its windshield collapsed in a shower of spraying glass that quickly became intermixed with blood as the pilot behind it was chewed up, too. Then the chopper's engine was hit and it flashed for a moment before the whole thing exploded under the awesome barrage of fire.

The chopper dropped into the water, a broken shell of an aircraft. Even the Osprey peeled away when the Frenchman turned his monstrous gun on it.

Schofield spun to see the big-bearded French frogman release his trigger with a satisfied grunt of 'Hmph.' He nodded to Schofield, 'Allez! *Go!*'

Mother just stared at the Frenchman, stunned. She looked down at her G36 as if it were a peashooter.

As for Schofield, he didn't need to be told twice.

He flicked more switches. 'Mario! You ready? Let's do this before that Osprey comes back!'

'*Ready for dive, sir,*' came Mario's voice in his earpiece.

Schofield turned to the passengers on his boat. 'Mother, open the

regulator panel. Everybody, grab a mouthpiece, loop your wrists through a wrist cord, and slot your feet in the stirrups on the deck so you don't float away. Zack, make sure Bertie doesn't float or sink or whatever.'

Mother opened a small panel under the boat's central saddle, revealing eight scuba regulators attached by hoses to a single compressed-air tank. Some extendable rubber cords with loops on their ends also popped out.

Schofield said, 'Okay, Mario, follow me.'

As everyone scrambled for the regulators and wrist cords, Schofield deflated the AFDV's outer rubber skirt, transforming the sleek black assault boat into a sleek black submersible. He threw his glasses into a pouch on his belt and reached for a scuba mask under the saddle and slipped it over his eyes. He then jammed a regulator into his mouth.

A moment later, their 'boat' slid under the surface and disappeared beneath the pack ice. Beside it, Mario's AFDV—with Chad and the other two Frenchmen on it—did the same.

Ten seconds later, the Osprey came back for another pass, all guns blazing, but it hit nothing for by then the two Marine Corps assault boats were gone.

The two submersibles glided through the eerie underwater world of the Arctic.

It was a ghostly world of pale blue water and the white undersides of the pack ice. Everyone clung to the AFDVs by virtue of the wrist cords and foot stirrups.

As the two submersibles moved further through the haze, the ocean floor gradually rose up to meet them.

They'd reached the first islet.

Wearing a scuba mask and breathing through a regulator, Ivanov pointed to the right. Schofield skirted the edge of the islet, following its shoreline while still staying under the sea ice. A few minutes later, the two submersibles crossed another short channel, after which they saw the ocean floor rise up again to meet the pack ice: they'd come to the second islet.

Ivanov directed Schofield around the base of this islet until they arrived at a square concrete-walled entrance about the width of a train tunnel boring into the rocky landmass.

It was the loading dock Ivanov had mentioned.

Large chunks of broken concrete formed an ungainly roof above the entrance; bent and broken iron rebars protruded from it. At some time in the past, presumably during the 'accident' Ivanov had mentioned, the dock's roof had caved in, blocking access to boats, but there was still room for a submersible to gain entry.

Beyond the tangle of concrete, there was only darkness.

Schofield hit the lights and two sharp beams lanced out into the murky tunnel.

Followed by Mario's submersible, he carefully guided his Assault Force Delivery Vehicle into it.

About thirty yards in, he saw the surface. The water was so calm, it looked like a rectangular pane of glass.

Schofield signalled to Mother and the big French frogman to ready their weapons. They did so. Then Schofield brought their AFDV upward and broke the surface.

The AFDV breached inside a small concrete dock, its harsh white lights illuminating the space.

Schofield removed his mask. Shocking images greeted him.

Bloody smears on the concrete walls.

Cracked glass also stained with blood.

The half-eaten skeleton of what appeared to have once been a polar bear.

And the smell. Jesus. It smelt like an abattoir: a nauseating mix of blood and flesh.

A thick reinforced glass door with an illuminated keypad lock led further into the islet's structure. Mercifully, the door was intact, but its other, inner, side looked like someone had thrown a bucket-load of blood onto it. Its wire-framed glass was etched with many deep animal scratch-marks.

'What the hell is this place?' Schofield stepped cautiously off the AFDV onto the concrete dock. Before anyone could answer him, something rushed at him from the shadows.

It was huge and white and it moved with shocking speed, launching itself at Schofield with a roar.

Scarecrow had no time at all to react. He spun to see a blur of bared jaws, shaggy white fur and outstretched claws—

A burst of gunfire echoed in the close confines of the dock and the thing's head snapped backwards, hit by a volley of tightly clustered rounds.

A second burst followed and the polar bear's chest—for indeed it *was* a polar bear, though unlike any polar bear Schofield had seen—was ripped open, hit in the heart, and it toppled to the floor, dead.

Holy fucking shit . . .

Schofield turned to see who had saved him, expecting to see Mother or the big French frogman holding a gun.

But it hadn't been either of them.

It had been one of the other two French frogmen. Indeed, this time it had been the smallest of the three French troops. He held a smoking Steyr TMP machine pistol—an Austrian-made weapon that looked like a teched-up Uzi—in a perfect firing position.

Then the frogman turned and aimed the TMP at Schofield. As he did so, Schofield glimpsed the assassin's right wrist. Tattooed onto it were a series of tally marks: thirteen of them.

This was Renard.

The assassin from France's external intelligence agency, the DGSE, who had *requested* to kill Shane Schofield.

Gun extended, the frogman yanked back his scuba hood . . . to reveal that he wasn't a man at all.

A dark-haired woman stared at Schofield with deadly eyes.

''Allo, Captain Schofield,' she said evenly, her French accent strong. 'My name is Veronique Champion of the Direction Géné-rale de la Sécurité Extérieure. Call-sign: Renard. As you are probably aware, I am here to kill you, but before I do, would you be so kind as to tell me what on Earth is going on here?'

Schofield stared down the barrel of Veronique Champion's Steyr.

His team stood behind him—Mother, the Kid and Mario, plus the three civilians, Zack, Emma and Chad.

Champion's two French companions stood behind her, their weapons raised. The big one's Kord looked like a Howitzer in the tight confined space.

And off to the side stood the Russian, Vasily Ivanov.

An uneasy stand-off.

Champion—Renard—stared intently at Schofield, evaluating him. She was tall, as tall as he was, and in other circumstances, she would have been striking: she had an athletic figure, slender and lithe, a short bob of black hair pulled back off her angular face, flawless pale skin and eyes that were as black as pitch and which did not waver.

As far as weapons were concerned, in addition to the state-of-the-art Steyr, she wore a weapons belt with various smoke and stun grenades on it, a couple of five-minute scuba breathing bottles the size of energy drink cans, two knives, a silver SIG Sauer P226 pistol and in a small holster across her chest, a Ruger LCP, a pocket pistol of last resort.

Schofield cocked his head to one side.

'Veronique *Champion*?' he said.

'You recognise the name?'

'I once encountered a French scientist named Luc Champion at an ice station in Antarctica,' he said carefully.

The woman did not blink. 'I am aware of this.'

'Luc Champion was related to you? Your brother?'

'My cousin. I had known him since childhood.'

In his mind's eye, Schofield could see Luc Champion as if it were yesterday: he had been the French scientist from Dumont d'Urville Station who had led a team of disguised French paratroopers into Wilkes Ice Station to kill everyone there.

'He was a civilian, a scientist—' Veronique Champion said.

'—who intended to kill all the civilian American scientists at that station so that he could be the first man to study an alien spaceship which turned out not to be an alien spaceship,' Schofield hit back.

Champion's face went cold. 'Did you kill him yourself?'

'He was complicit in a murderous plan—'

'*Did you kill him?*'

'No. Barnaby had him killed.' In the face of an overwhelming incoming force of British SAS troops, Schofield had fled Wilkes Ice Station with his people on some hovercrafts. He'd left Luc Champion behind, handcuffed to a pole. The SAS commander, Trevor Barnaby, had had Champion shot in the head. They'd found the body later.

Veronique Champion still had her gun pointed at Schofield.

Her dark eyes scanned him closely—for a long, tense moment— before abruptly she tilted her head, frowning in genuine confusion, and Schofield realised why.

She'd been searching for a lie but hadn't found one. This had surprised her and Schofield imagined she wasn't used to being surprised. She had come to kill a killer but had instead found—

'Captain Schofield. As you are no doubt aware, the Republic of France wants you dead. For what you did at Wilkes Ice Station and for other actions elsewhere, including the destruction of the aircraft carrier, *Richelieu.* I also want you dead, for my own reasons. Yet a short while ago, you plucked me and my men from hostile waters *knowing* that we had been sent to kill you. Why would you do this?'

Schofield said simply, 'I'm facing an almost impossible task here, something much bigger than your country's vendetta against me. I figured if I rescued you and you were someone who would stop

and listen for a moment, you might help me on my mission. You just lost an entire submarine and I need as many soldiers as I can get. I took the risk that you might hear me out.'

Champion didn't move.

Her gun stayed level.

Then, very slowly, she lowered it.

'All right, Captain. I'm listening . . . for now. But know this: if we choose to help you and we emerge from this alive, the old score must be settled.' She waved at her men. 'This is Master Sergeant Huguenot and Sergeant Dubois. Now, tell us what is going on.'

Schofield quickly told Champion and her men what he knew about the situation at Dragon Island, the Army of Thieves, and the atmospheric weapon they had initiated. It was, he added, the Army of Thieves that had destroyed her submarine when the French had inadvertently intruded upon their skirmish.

Schofield took the wristguard from Zack and used it to show Champion the video clip of the leader of the Army of Thieves addressing the Russian President. While he did this, Mother sidled up to the big French commando.

'Hey,' she said.

''Allo.'

'Nice gun. A Kord.'

'Merci beaucoup,' he said with a quick nod. He glanced at her rifle. 'G36. A fine weapon, too.'

Mother extended her hand. 'Gunnery Sergeant Gena Newman, USMC, but everyone calls me Mother.'

'I am Master Sergeant Jean-Claude François Michel Huguenot, on secondment to the DGSE from the First Parachute Regiment. I am known as *Le Barbarian*.'

With his shaggy hair and beard, Mother could see why. 'Barbarian. Nice.'

'Trust me, it is a title well earned. I eat like a bear, drink like a Viking, kill like a lion and make love like a silverback gorilla! Bah!

My friends call me Baba and I have just decided that *you*, Gunnery Sergeant Mother Newman, with your impressive G36, may call me Baba.'

Mother eyed him sideways. *Who was this guy?* With his big physique, big gun, big hair, big beard and big mouth, he was—

'Oh, God. You're my mirror,' she said aloud.

'What?'

'Nothing.'

Fortunately, at that moment she heard the French woman mention the Army of Thieves and she and Baba joined that conversation.

'The Army of Thieves . . .' Veronique Champion said, having just finished watching the mpeg of its leader addressing the Russian President.

'You've heard of them?' Schofield said.

'The tracking of terrorist organisations is not the primary occupation of my division within the DGSE but, yes, I have been to briefings in recent months where this organisation has been mentioned.'

'And?'

Champion said, 'DGSE has been monitoring a series of incidents perpetrated by this group over the last year, one incident per month, in accordance with a crude pattern. The CIA and the DIA know all this.'

'We were sent this summary.' Schofield showed Champion the DIA report by the agent named Retter on the wristguard's screen. She scanned it quickly.

'I have seen a similar report.'

'So who are they and why are they doing this?'

'Who are they?' Champion shrugged. 'A new terrorist group? A franchise of al-Qaeda? A renegade army with no allegiance to any nation? No-one knows.'

'What about their leader? The guy who taunted the Russian President? Any idea who he is?'

'The man who leads them is unknown to us. In the few pieces of CCTV footage that exist of the Army's actions, he always wears large sunglasses plus a hood or helmet of some sort to conceal his identity. But he makes no effort to hide the acid scars on the left side of his face: the DGSE searched every military database we have for soldiers or specialists with such a distinctive facial feature but found nothing.

'Having said that, some of his lieutenants have also been caught on closed-circuit cameras during those incidents and some of them *are* known. I recall that his right-hand man, for instance, is an ex-Chilean torturer named Typhoon or Typhon or something like that.'

Champion paused, thinking.

'By all appearances, the Army of Thieves is an army of rogue soldiers led by a small cadre of very capable veterans. Its members are volatile but they are no rabble. On the contrary, it is a very effective and disciplined fighting force. It has successfully attacked Russian military vessels and United States Marine Corps bases.'

'But what do they *want*?' Schofield asked. 'Groups like this always *want* something: recognition of a new state, the freeing of prisoners, the removal of American troops from their land. In that video clip, their leader told the Russian President that his Army was an alliance of the angry and enraged, the disenfranchised and the poor, the "dog starved at his master's gate". That last phrase, by the way, is a quote from William Blake, from a poem called *Auguries of Innocence*.'

'Nice poetry reference, boss,' Mother whispered. 'Classy.'

'Is he some kind of demented Robin Hood?' Schofield said. 'Bringing down rich nations on behalf of poor ones?'

'I do not know,' Champion said. '*We* do not know.'

Schofield bit his lip in thought. 'The first breakout in Chile released approximately one hundred prisoners. The second in the Sudan released another hundred or so. Add to that an inner sanctum of commanders and we're looking at two hundred, perhaps two hundred and twenty men.'

'And only ten of us,' Mario said sadly. 'Good fucking luck . . .'

'Hey, I count for ten,' Mother said.

'And I, twenty,' Baba said.

'Ironbark's team said they encountered *a hundred* men waiting for them at that submarine dock,' Mario said despairingly. 'Look at what happened to them, and they were SEALs!'

Schofield checked his watch.

It was 9:35 a.m.

'We still have an hour and twenty-five minutes.'

Mario stood up. 'Are you *listening*? Even if we had *fifty* fully trained men, we couldn't storm that island in a week! Look at us: stuck in a stinking hole with nowhere to go. If they decide to send anyone in after us, we're screwed. This has officially become a suicide mission.'

Schofield gave Mario a long hard look but said nothing, because in all honesty, the young Marine was right.

While Schofield and the others were assessing their situation in the dock, the V-22 Osprey that had attacked them flew south to Dragon Island.

The gunship soared over the three little islets to the north of Dragon before rising swiftly to clear the cliffs of the island's northern coast, cliffs that formed a U-shaped bay around the closest islet. The winter pack ice had melted substantially here and the bay was unfrozen, dotted here and there with ice floes the size of cars.

The Osprey swept up and over an old cable car terminal that connected the closest islet to Dragon Island. Upon clearing the terminal, an astonishing view met the plane's pilot, the man known as Hammerhead.

Off to his left were the two colossal vents, belching the shimmering TEB mixture into the sky. At some time during the morning, some wag had spray-painted a huge A-in-a-circle on the flank of one of them—the mark of the Army of Thieves—as a kind of 'fuck you' to the various reconnaissance satellites that, no doubt, would now be watching the island.

Directly in front of the Osprey was the main tower, the huge three-storey disc-shaped structure mounted atop a single two-hundred-foot-high concrete pillar. The whole structure was nestled in a circular concrete pit and access to it could be obtained only via one of two crane-operated bridges on either side of the pit. From each crane's long extended arm hung a bridge that could be lowered to span the gap between the rim and the disc.

On top of the disc itself was a helipad, the two tall spires, and the large glass dome that enclosed the complex's command centre.

From the base of the great pillar to the tip of the highest antenna on top of the taller spire, the whole structure was at least four hundred feet tall and it dwarfed the approaching Osprey; it also made the many men stationed at the base's various guardhouses and watchtowers, the members of the Army of Thieves, look like ants.

Hammerhead brought the Osprey into a hover above the helipad, landed softly and with his four-man crew behind him, marched into the command centre.

Hammerhead and his crew stood before their leader.

The clear glass dome that covered the command centre was easily seventy feet across. Beneath it lay several levels of consoles, computers and communications desks, all surrounding a raised platform from which a commander could look out over Dragon Island in every direction.

Seated in the command chair was the leader of the Army of Thieves.

He no longer wore his gaudy Elvis sunglasses. Instead, his eyes were visible for all to see. They were quite unnerving: pale grey eyes that rarely blinked. The discoloured acid-melted skin on his left cheek and throat was also clearly visible, as were the many guns in the many holsters he wore on his thighs, under his shoulders and on his back. A series of small tattoos ran in an ordered line down his neck: among them an image of a Russian cargo ship, a crude 'USMC', and an apartment building with 'Moskva' written over it.

To his men, he had no name other than 'the Lord of Anarchy, General of the Army of Thieves'. They addressed him as 'my Lord', 'Lord', or 'sir'.

He was Caucasian but had deeply tanned skin. Where he hailed from, no-one knew.

He spoke English with an American accent but then he was also fluent in Russian, Spanish and Farsi.

All anyone in the Army of Thieves knew for sure was that they had all been recruited by him at some time or another. None knew how

his inner circle had come together: the Lord of Anarchy and his tight gang of five men who had known each other before they formed the Army—the four senior officers with shark nicknames: Hammerhead, Thresher, White Tip and Mako; and of course Typhon.

Naturally, there were rumours among the men: some said they were ex–Turkish Army officers who had tried to join al-Qaeda but had been turned away because they were too aggressive; others claimed they were a mix of ex-Chilean and ex-Egyptian torturers who had performed enhanced interrogation on terrorist suspects on behalf of the United States; others still claimed they were American mercenaries who just loved the sight of blood.

Beside the Lord of Anarchy stood his XO, Colonel Typhon. Named after the most feared creature in Greek mythology—of immense size, it had fiery eyes and even the gods quailed before it—he was an exceedingly tall, blank-eyed killer whom the men feared greatly.

Upon acceptance into the Army's ranks, every member of the Army of Thieves met Typhon.

It was he who bestowed the insignia of promotion—a red-hot branding iron to the skin of the forearm which was then infused with tattooist's ink, creating raised chevrons on the skin. Your rank in the Army was not stitched onto your sleeve, it was seared onto your very skin.

It was also Typhon who performed the initiation ceremony—a drug-hazed beating of horrific proportions while you viewed four television screens at once, screens that bombarded you with clips of gore and grotesquery, snuff killings and beheadings, rape and bestiality, drowning and torture.

The men obeyed the Lord of Anarchy because he was their leader. They obeyed Typhon out of pure terror.

'Report,' the Lord of Anarchy said.

'My Lord,' Hammerhead said, 'we found the wreckage of Ivanov's plane. By the time we arrived, the American testing team was there. We engaged them but then a French submarine surfaced nearby.'

The Lord of Anarchy raised an eyebrow. 'A French submarine? Go on.'

'The sub did not appear to be acting in concert with the Americans but we torpedoed it anyway. While we were engaged with the sub, the American team knocked out one of our Cobras and then fled in their assault boats. My second Cobra reacquired them a short while later not far from the islets near here, but the Americans brought down that chopper as well and by the time I got there, they were gone.'

'Gone?'

'Their boats, they must have been a new type of subskimmer, sir.'

'They *are* a testing team, Captain. I fear, however, that you have neglected something in your report.'

Hammerhead froze, confused. 'Wh . . . what was that, sir?'

'How you failed in your mission. You were ordered to go out and kill the Americans. You did not. Ergo, you failed.'

'They put up a hell of a figh—'

'I cannot tolerate failure, Captain. Not during this mission. This army expects only one thing: that each of its members performs his duties to the letter. You have not done this, thus you endanger us all. Who is your immediate junior officer?'

Hammerhead nodded to the younger man beside him. 'Flight Lieutenant Santos, sir. From Chile.'

The Lord of Anarchy turned his gaze upon the younger man, looked him quickly up and down. Then he turned to Typhon and nodded.

The dead-eyed XO pulled a gleaming meat cleaver from behind his back and placed it on a table in front of Hammerhead and the young lieutenant.

The Lord of Anarchy said, 'Lieutenant Santos, I need to teach your captain a lesson, one that he will not soon forget. Now, I could punish *him*, but in my experience I have found that the only truly effective way to motivate someone—or, for that matter, to

extract information from an enemy—is to hurt someone close to them or in their charge. So, if you would be so kind, Lieutenant Santos, would you cut off your own left hand, please.'

A few of the communications operators who had been surreptitiously watching this exchange looked up suddenly.

Santos's eyes went wide. He threw a look at Hammerhead, but his captain just stared resolutely forward, not meeting his eye.

The Lord of Anarchy waited patiently. He said nothing.

Then, to all the spectators' surprise, the young lieutenant stepped forward and picked up the steel-bladed cleaver.

Many of them had heard about this sort of thing before, but none of them had ever seen it: tales of the Lord of Anarchy ordering disobedient or disgraced members of the Army to hack off parts of their own body. Fingers, toes, and in one famous case—according to rumour—the Lord had ordered a man who had raped an African nun to sever his own penis . . . and the man had done it.

How he could make this happen, no-one knew. Those members from African and South American countries called it black magic or voodoo, while those from Western nations suspected it was some kind of subliminal process that had been implanted into their minds during the sadistic initiation ceremony. Whatever it was, it made an impact. It ensured total obedience.

As the audience watched, Santos tested the weight of the cleaver in his right hand. Then he placed his left wrist flat on the wooden table.

And raised the cleaver.

The communications men held their breath . . .

The Osprey crew watched in horror . . .

Hammerhead kept staring forward . . .

The Lord of Anarchy gave away nothing . . .

Typhon smiled . . .

The meat cleaver came down hard and the lieutenant's scream cut through the air.

⏻

The Lord of Anarchy turned to Hammerhead.

'Do not fail me again, Captain. This Army is depending on you. Dismissed.'

As Hammerhead left with his remaining crew members, the Lord of Anarchy directed his personal guards to the now-kneeling figure of Santos. The young lieutenant clutched the bloody stump of his left arm to his body.

'Put him to work in the gasworks beneath the main vents,' the Lord of Anarchy said, 'in a place where he can be seen by all the men. Let word of this spread.'

Santos was dragged away.

When he was gone, the Lord of Anarchy turned to his XO.

'Colonel Typhon, how long till the uranium spheres are ready?'

'One hour and twenty minutes, sir.'

'This American testing team bothers me. While small, its members are worryingly determined. They might be more trouble than they appear.'

'Mako is on his way back from their camp now. He found one person still there, a military contractor named Hartigan. Mako's bringing him back now in the second Osprey.'

'Take Mr Hartigan to the gasworks, too, and torture him. I want to know everything he knows about that test team. He may also provide some *entertainment* for the men later.' The Lord of Anarchy nodded at his surveillance screens. 'Where are they now?'

'They're on Bear Islet.'

'Do we have visuals?'

'Yes, sir. CCTV feed.'

'Get stills of all of them and run the images through the military databases. In the meantime, send in Bad Willy and his boys, plus a few berserkers, from behind, and Thresher's team from in front. We've come too far for some rogue group of wannabe heroes to stop us now. Squeeze them and kill them.'

BEAR ISLET LOADING DOCK
4 APRIL, 0940 HOURS
1 HOUR 20 MINUTES TO DEADLINE

In the dark concrete loading dock on Bear Islet, Zack Weinberg and Emma Dawson were checking the corpse of the polar bear that had come bursting out of the shadows upon their arrival. As always, Bertie trailed along behind Zack.

'I've never seen a polar bear like this,' Emma said. 'Look at its coat: it's shaggy and matted and filthy. Polar bears usually have short coats which they keep fastidiously clean.'

Zack winced at the sight of the dead bear. It was indeed filthy. It was also stained all over with its own blood from the gunshot wounds.

'It's smaller than other polar bears I've seen,' he said.

'Yes, it is.' Emma stepped around the corpse, eyeing it analytically, scientifically. 'I'd say it's an adolescent, the bear equivalent of a teenager; moody, aggressive and impetuous.'

She gazed through the reinforced glass door that led into the islet's laboratory structure. In there she saw a wide octagonal space with a sunken section in the middle. On the elevated walkways ringing that sunken section, four larger polar bears padded around, pacing. One of them came over to the glass door and peered through it at her and Zack.

'Do you think this bear was *living* in this dock?' Zack asked.

Emma shrugged. 'It's a good home for a polar bear. A fully enclosed cave with a single underwater entrance.'

'But why would it be living apart from the others?'

'Adolescent bears of all species—grizzlies, Kodiaks, polars—often overstep their bounds and fall foul of the older bears. I'd guess this bad boy crossed one of the older males and got chased out. He was living here in exile—'

Smack!

The large bear on the other side of the door punched the glass.

The door shuddered, but held.

Schofield turned at the noise, took in the bear on the other side of the door. 'You guys okay over there?'

Zack and Emma nodded.

'How about you, Chad?' Schofield said.

The young executive was sitting with his back against the wall and his head bowed. He looked up, clearly shaken by their recent experiences, but nodded gamely.

Schofield glanced at the stalking bear. 'I think it's time we learned more about this place from Mr Ivanov.'

The group gathered around the Russian scientist.

'All right, Mr Ivanov, or is it "Doctor" or maybe "Colonel"?' Schofield asked.

'It is "Doctor".'

'Okay, Dr Ivanov. We know the big picture stuff about Dragon Island, now I want the details from someone who knows them: I want to know everything about that island, from the layout to the atmospheric weapon and what we can do in the next eighty minutes to stop it going off.'

Ivanov shook his head. 'Ostrov Zmey is a rock, a fortress. With enough men stationed at its watchtowers, it is very difficult to take by force.'

'If it's so impregnable, how could this group take it so easily?' Mother asked.

Ivanov sighed. 'I suspect they bribed one of the members of the skeleton team I was coming to replace. Specifically, a man named

Dr Igor Kotsky. In the new Russia, we men of science are not well paid and I know Kotsky was in considerable debt. He could have been easily bought. We all could have been bought. When my relief plane arrived at Dragon, Kotsky was there at the hangar, waving us in, calling us over . . . into a waiting field of fire.'

'Okay, then,' Schofield said, 'tell us about the weapon. We've been told we can disrupt its use by stealing or destroying some red uranium spheres or destroying the missiles that will fire them into the gas cloud. Is that correct?'

'That is right,' Ivanov said. 'In theory, you could also disrupt the creation of the gas cloud itself, but it is far too late for that. If you destroyed the vents now, you might create a gap in the gas cloud, but any gap you created would not be wide enough. The atmospheric flame, once ignited, is incredibly potent. It would be able to leap any such void. You would need a gap created by at least ninety minutes of zero gas production to create a large enough gap and that is not possible anymore.'

'So it comes down to the spheres and the missiles?'

'Yes.'

'So where are these spheres kept?'

'They are stored in a sealed laboratory atop the shorter of the two spires mounted upon the main tower. They are the reason for our enemy's delay—due to their substantial potency, the red uranium spheres are kept at a temperature close to zero Kelvin, or –273 degrees Celsius. So they must be primed before use: priming involves reheating them to ambient temperature at a very precise incremental rate or else their molecular structure will break down and their ability to light the gas will be lost.'

'How many of these spheres are there?' Champion asked.

'Well, there are six in *that* lab . . .' Ivanov said, a little hesitantly. Schofield saw it.

'Are there more spheres elsewhere on Dragon Island?' he asked.

Ivanov grimaced. 'There is a secret laboratory built directly underneath the main tower, beneath the great pillar. This laboratory is only accessible by a security-coded elevator and is equipped with a reheating unit of its own and one red uranium sphere. It is a fallback, a last retreat in the event of nuclear conflict, but . . .'

'But what?'

'But Kotsky does not know about it. Its existence is beyond his level of clearance. And if Kotsky does not know about it, then neither can this army.'

'Hmmm.' Schofield bit his lip in thought. 'Still, if we can get to that shorter spire and disrupt the priming process, we can render the spheres useless.'

'Yes, *if* you get there in time,' Ivanov said.

Champion asked, 'Can we destroy the spheres with a grenade blast?'

'No, they are too dense for a conventional explosive to do any damage to them. Such an explosive would not even crack a red uranium sphere. It requires a large, carefully timed and even more carefully calibrated *implosive* blast to break one.'

'How much do they weigh?' Schofield asked.

Ivanov shrugged. 'They are heavy for their small size, as one would expect of a semi-nuclear substance. Perhaps three kilograms each. Why?'

'Because a three-kilogram sphere the size of a golf ball will sink like a stone,' Schofield said. 'If we can steal those spheres and get them to the coast and hurl them into the ocean, finding them would be all but impossible.'

'This is true,' Ivanov said.

'Wait a second,' Mother said. 'Aren't we talking about radioactive material here? You can't just pick up a nuclear substance and *run off* with it.'

Ivanov said, 'No, this is the advantage of red uranium. While its explosive energy is great, its passive radioactive decay is minimal. You can carry it in a suitcase or even create a hand grenade with a tiny amount of it—'

'Hold on. There are *other* devices made from this stuff?'

'Why, yes. Our weapons scientists fell in love with red uranium. It is an almost perfect thermobaric explosive. Smaller devices were

fashioned, including hand grenades with red uranium cores the size of ball bearings that could blow apart a T-72 tank.'

'You assholes built *nuclear* hand grenades?' Mother said.

Ivanov bowed his head. 'This island is a product of a different time. We were given leave to create whatever weapons science would allow and so we did. On occasion, we may have gone too far—'

'No shit,' Mother said.

'Hey! I have a family, too!' Ivanov said indignantly. 'Two sons. Six grandchildren. They live in Odessa, in southern Ukraine. If the weapon is ignited, the firestorm will kill them, too. I have as much to lose in all this as you do. I may have helped build this terrible thing, but I most assuredly do not wish to see it set off.'

'Okay, everyone, settle down.' Schofield got back on topic. 'What about the missiles that are used to fire the spheres into the gas cloud? Where are they located?'

Ivanov nodded. 'Our enemy will have readied the battery of intermediate-range ballistic missiles on the launch pad to the south of the main tower. Sabotaging those missiles is a possibility, but as one would expect, the missile site is very well protected—one can only get to it via a high, single-lane bridge. If our enemies have men guarding the missile site, it will be exceedingly difficult to get to.'

Schofield was silent for a moment, deep in thought.

'There might be one other thing we can do,' he said. 'It occurred to me before, but it comes with . . . complications.'

'What's that?' Mother asked.

'The reason we're here is because this Army of Thieves is able to detect incoming missiles and bombers from long range, right? They even managed to turn a Russian ICBM around and have it strike its own launch site.'

Mother shrugged. 'They're teched up. We know this.'

Schofield said, 'But it goes deeper than that. To possess this kind of early-warning capability—which lets them see an incoming missile or plane from thousands of miles away—they must be patched into some kind of early-warning satellite. Which means somewhere on this island there's a satellite uplink connecting them to that satellite.'

'Oh, I see, I see . . .' Veronique Champion nodded. 'But, yes, as you say, such a plan brings with it substantial complications.'

Mother didn't get it. 'Wait, wait. What complications? I don't see it.'

Schofield said, 'If we take out the Army of Thieves' satellite uplink—destroy it or disable it—then the Army of Thieves will be blinded and we can open the way for a nuclear strike on this island.'

'Once that uplink is destroyed,' Champion added, 'a nuclear missile launched from, say, Alaska or a site in central Russia could strike this island inside twenty minutes. The complication is—'

'Us,' Schofield said. 'We won't have time to get away before any nuclear missile hits. If we can find and knock out their uplink, we can save the world . . . but in doing so, we kill ourselves.'

'Oh,' Mother said. 'Right. I see.'

There was a short silence.

'We have to keep it as an option,' Schofield said seriously. 'Maybe not our first option, but if all else fails, we might have to consider it.'

He turned to the group.

'All right, people, here's how we're going to do this. If we can somehow get in, I say we make this a split-op: one team goes for the spheres while a smaller second team tries to disable the missile battery. I'll lead the first team: if we can disrupt the reheating of those spheres before eleven o'clock, we stop this thing cold; if not, we steal the spheres and get them to the coast and toss them into the ocean. At the same time, the second team—I'm thinking of the Kid and Mario here—tries to knock out the missiles, thus preventing the bad guys from firing the spheres into the gas cloud should the first team fail.'

'Sounds like a plan,' Mother said.

'If we can get in there by eleven o'clock,' Champion said. 'That in itself will be extremely difficult.'

Schofield nodded. 'While we're doing all this, Dr Ivanov is going to try and spot any recently-added satellite uplink dishes around the complex. In the event of everything going to Hell, our last

resort will be blowing the uplink and calling in a nuclear airstrike on ourselves. Any questions?'

No-one said a word. They were all taking in exactly what the final option meant.

'I have a question,' Mother said. 'For him.' She jerked her chin at Ivanov. 'Who *the fuck* designs and builds a global-killing weapon like this?'

Ivanov smiled tightly. 'You may not like the answer. You see, we stole the plans for the atmospheric device, indeed for this whole complex, from a top secret laboratory at Nellis Air Force Base in the United States of America. Your country designed this terrible weapon. We just built it.'

Schofield nodded at the reinforced glass door, at the shaggy polar bears on the other side.

'What about them? What's the story with the bears?'

'They were another experiment,' Ivanov said. 'An experiment gone wrong.'

'Oh, come on. What did you do to the bears?' the Kid asked.

'It was not one of my projects,' Ivanov said, 'and not one I agreed with. The idea was not unlike the infamous US tests with dolphins: we tried to train the bears to carry out certain military tasks. Laying mines, attaching explosives to submarines. One group, however, was given advanced mood-altering drugs, to heighten their aggressive instincts, the goal being to turn them into hyper-aggressive frontline troops that would strike fear into the hearts of an enemy force as they rampaged toward them.'

Emma Dawson was shocked. 'You tried to make polar bears *more* aggressive? And *obedient*? Were you out of your minds?'

Ivanov shrugged. 'There was a similar American project only recently, involving gorillas, based on an island in the Pacific Ocean known as Hell Island.'

At his words, Mother glanced at Schofield but he just shook his head imperceptibly.

'But it didn't work, did it?' he said.

'No. The drugs wreaked havoc with the bears' primitive brains and they became demented, enraged, deranged with fury. They started attacking their handlers and the other bears. They also became very resourceful and continually broke out of their cages.'

'They attacked the other bears.' Schofield recalled the dead polar bear they'd seen on the ice floe earlier that morning, the one that had been torn to pieces by something. 'And they're cage-breakers. Wait, are you saying that those bears in that lab are *not* trapped in there?'

'Oh, no,' Ivanov said. 'There are other exits to that laboratory: cracks in the roof dome, fire exits. When Dragon Island was decommissioned in 1991 and reduced to a skeleton staff, we just left the bears to their fate. They come and go as they please. These ones choose to stay here.'

Emma shook her head. 'You just left them. You guys are something else.'

Schofield gazed through the reinforced glass door at the pacing bears. 'Deranged polar bears. Just what I need—'

'Er, Captain . . .' Zack said, looking the other way, down into the pool of water behind them. He was crouched at its edge with Bertie beside him. 'What is that?'

Schofield turned . . .

. . . and saw it.

An eerie green glow coming from deep within the pool.

It was moving, growing, coming closer.

Schofield hurried to the edge of the pool, where he grabbed Bertie, flipped him upside-down, and plunged the little robot's stalk-mounted lens under the surface while keeping his display screen above the waterline.

'Shit!'

On the display Schofield saw six small sea-sleds rising quickly through the haze—each sled bearing two armed men wearing scuba gear. They were zooming quickly through the tunnel toward the dock, their forward lights emitting sharp green beams.

'They sent a dive team in behind us . . .'

He yanked Bertie out of the water and spun, taking in all the available options. The enclosed concrete dock had only two possible escapes: the pool of water and the reinforced glass door that led into the lab containing the polar bears.

'Between a rock and a hard place.' Schofield quickly put his battle glasses back on and drew his Desert Eagle pistol . . .

. . . and aimed it at the reinforced glass door. 'Only one option. Marines, ready your weapons!'

Then he fired repeatedly into the door and eventually its glass shattered and the world went completely mad.

SECOND PHASE
ENTRY INTO HELL

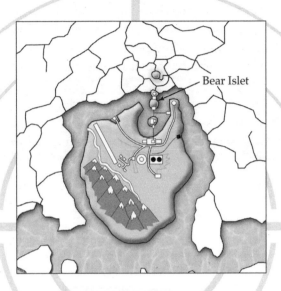

Bear Islet

BEAR ISLET
4 APRIL, 1000 HOURS
T-MINUS 1:00 HOUR TO DEADLINE

A dove house filled with doves and Pigeons
Shudders Hell thro all its regions.
A dog starved at his Master's Gate
Predicts the ruin of the State.

—William Blake
Auguries of Innocence

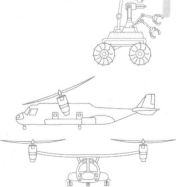

SIDE VIEW

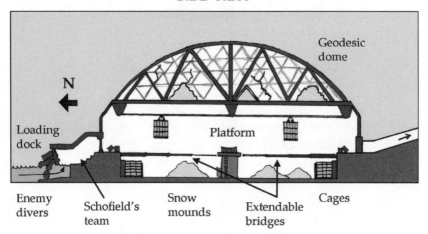

Geodesic dome

N

Loading dock

Platform

Enemy divers

Schofield's team

Snow mounds

Extendable bridges

Cages

OVERHEAD VIEW

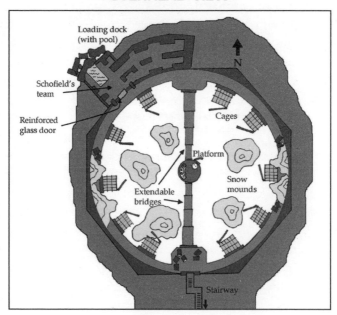

Loading dock (with pool)

N

Schofield's team

Reinforced glass door

Cages

Platform

Extendable bridges

Snow mounds

Stairway

THE BEAR LAB

Gun up and moving fast, Schofield led his people into the realm of the polar bears.

It was a huge laboratory, easily seventy metres across, with a circular upper level that ringed a twenty-foot-deep pit. Schofield and his team were now on that upper level and, looking down into the pit, Schofield saw ten large (and open) cages embedded in its outer walls: cages, he presumed, that had once held the polar bears. The whole lab was covered by a translucent geodesic dome—made of many triangular panels and girders—that sprang across the wide space without the aid of a single support pillar.

Two narrow and rail-less retractable bridges extended from opposite rims of the wide pit to an elevated platform in its middle. The platform had a waist-high console on it and a hatch in its floor. Schofield noticed that the platform's curved cylindrical wall was made of thick reinforced glass and that it encased a ladder within it; where the ladder met the floor of the pit, a curved glass door gave access to the pit itself. That was how the Soviet scientists had once entered the pit safely: via the platform and its internal ladder.

And the whole place was absolutely filthy.

It stank of bear shit, urine and rotting flesh—the smell of a carnivore's lair. Some of the panels of the geodesic dome had been shattered, allowing snow to penetrate the lab and form high

mounds all around the pit. Through some of the holes in the roof, Schofield could see the sky.

What had once been a shining state-of-the-art laboratory was now the picture of neglect; a frost-covered, rusting, stinking, freezing dump.

The only apparent exit, Schofield saw, was a door on the far southern side of the lab, but thanks to high mounds of snow on both the eastern and western rims of the pit, the only way to get to that door was via the two retractable bridges that extended across the pit.

The four mangy polar bears turned as one as Schofield's gunfire shattered the glass door. Gathered by the snow mound on the western side of the pit, they watched with great interest as eleven human beings stepped out into the foul lab.

The alpha male rose onto its hind legs and bellowed loudly, issuing a challenge. A younger adolescent bounded toward them, teeth bared.

'Go! Onto the bridges! Get to that door on the other side!' Schofield pushed everyone past him as he eyed the approaching bear. He raised his Desert Eagle and fired it twice above the bear's head.

The big pistol's booming shots rang out in the wide space. The bear slowed a little but kept advancing.

As he took off after the others, Schofield glanced back inside the dock behind them—

—in time to see a small cylindrical object pop up out of the rectangular pool, tossed up by someone underneath the surface. It hovered in the air for the briefest of moments and at the zenith of its arc, Schofield saw it clearly.

It looked like a standard M67 frag grenade, only it had an odd silver band painted around it. Whatever kind of grenade it was, it had been thrown up by the incoming force to open the way for a sub-surface entry.

'Grenade!' he yelled. 'Take cover!'

Everyone dived behind something: the doorframe, a crate, a

barrel. Schofield himself ducked behind the doorway next to the Kid.

The only thing that didn't take cover was the unfortunate adolescent bear.

The grenade went off.

The grenade's deafening blast was followed by a wave of superheated silver liquid that came spraying out through the dock's doorway.

The adolescent bear was hit full-on by the liquid blast and it started wailing immediately, clutching at its eyes, the shaggy fur on its limbs, face and belly splattered with the hot viscous silver goo.

As the bear shrieked, a sizzling sound caught Schofield's attention.

The doorframe beside his head was *melting*. A dollop of silver acid slid slowly down the steel frame, *dissolving* the frame as it went.

'An acid grenade,' he said to the Kid. 'It's like a frag, only worse. It's not designed to kill, just to maim and incapacitate, so that we stop to help the wounded—'

It was then that the bear *really* started wailing, and it was perhaps the most horrific cry Schofield had ever heard.

The silver acid had started eating through the bear's skin and the poor animal was in absolute agony. Its pelt was peeling off its flesh. Then its belly melted all the way through and its intestines began to ooze out of it, spilling onto the floor with a foul slopping noise.

Terrified and confused, the shrieking bear scratched at its face with its claws, only to scratch *off* the skin, revealing bone, tendons and flesh. It was a sickening sight.

The bear fell to its knees.

Boom!

It dropped dead, shot through the head by Shane Schofield. A mercy killing.

'Move, people!' he yelled. 'The bad guys will be here in approximately three seconds!'

They arrived in four.

They rose out of the pool like deadly wraiths.

They wore body-hugging grey-and-white wire-heated wetsuits and looked down the barrels of compact MP-5N machine pistols held pressed against their shoulders in expert firing positions.

Schofield couldn't tell how many of them there were—ten, twelve, maybe fourteen—but having paved the way with the acid grenade, they came up fast and firing.

Bullets shredded the walls.

Schofield and the Kid returned fire, loosing wild shots behind them as they dashed across the first extendable bridge after the others.

'Mother! Give us cover!' Schofield yelled.

Leading the group, Mother stopped on the central platform and raised her G36.

'Baba! Help her!' Veronique Champion called, and the big French commando joined Mother, aiming his massive Kord at the shattered reinforced door behind them.

The first attacker came through the doorway—*braaack!*—to be torn apart by the combined brutal fire of Mother and Baba. One second the wetsuit-clad attacker was there, the next he was simply gone.

The civilians hurried past Mother, Baba and Champion, racing out across the second extendable bridge, led by Mario. As they came to the door on the far side—it was surrounded by discarded crates and barrels—the attacking force launched their own machine-gun salvo.

A burst of fire even more powerful than Baba's and Mother's came lancing out of the dock's doorway: heavy machine-gun fire laced with tracers.

It was so strong it compelled everyone—Mother, Baba, Champion, Schofield and the Kid—to take cover. Mother and Baba ducked behind the console on the platform while Champion stumbled and fell through the hatch in the platform's floor, dropping down within its reinforced glass walls—while bullets smacked off the curved walls, leaving scratch-marks and cracks—before landing clumsily at the base of the platform structure—

—just in time to see another shaggy polar bear come roaring out of one of the darkened cells and leap at her, jaws bared, aiming for the open door in the base of the glass-walled platform—

—Champion quickly slid forward and kicked the glass door in front of her shut, an instant before the bear *slammed* into the outside of it, causing the transparent door to shudder violently and the bear to fall back onto its ass, dazed and groaning.

Schofield and the Kid had been halfway across the first bridge when the tracer fire had started.

They both dived forward, joining Mother and Baba behind the console on the central platform.

A shout came from Mario over at the southern door:

'Kid! Look out! *Above* you!'

The Kid looked up—

—just as a blurry white shape dropped from the network of girders supporting the geodesic dome and landed on the second bridge right in front of him.

It was another deranged bear.

During the mayhem, it had clambered across the girders and now dropped right in their path. It roared at them an instant before its head exploded like a punctured soccer ball and Schofield and the Kid turned to see Baba holding a massive .44 Magnum pistol extended in his hand.

The headless bear dropped off the bridge and thudded down onto the floor of the pit, blood oozing from its open neck.

'Fucking Hell . . .' the Kid gasped.

Mother snapped round at the bearded Frenchman's shot. 'God-damn, you are good!'

'Oui,' Baba replied.

Schofield quickly took in the situation.

Veronique Champion was ascending the ladder below him.

Mario and the three civilians—Chad, Emma and Zack, plus Bertie—as well as Ivanov and the third French agent, Dubois, were safely in the far doorway, taking cover there behind some crates and barrels.

On the other side of the wide octagonal space, in the doorway to the dock, Schofield saw eight wetsuit-clad attackers gathering in a four-on-four fanning formation—coolly preparing to attack. At their feet, lying just inside the doorway, were two men manning bipod-mounted heavy automatic weapons.

These guys aren't common thugs, Schofield thought. *They're trained. And they're planning somethi—*

Suddenly, two dark-skinned men firing AK-47s from the hip came charging out from behind the eight others, emerging from the dock at a mad run, guns blazing in every direction.

Even from where he stood, Schofield could see they had the crazed yellow-red eyes of ganja weed users. But these two Africans were *totally* out there: they wore torn wetsuits and bore many tat-toos on their necks; their hair was half-shaved and their faces were literally covered in piercings: eyebrow rings, nose rings, lip studs. They shrieked an ululating war cry as they ran in a crazed ducking-and-weaving kind of way.

Schofield's eyes went wide.

It was a suicide run, designed to take out as many of his people as possible before the two berserk runners were inevitably shot down. It was the exact opposite of the cool calculation Schofield had thought he was seeing. It was also a disconcerting tactic, designed to shock and confuse, and for a moment, it had indeed shocked him.

The two 'berserkers' sprayed the whole laboratory with AK-47 fire as they dashed for the first bridge, bobbing, weaving and screaming.

As they raced out onto the bridge, Schofield raised his pistol and shot the first one in the chest, but he just kept on coming—still shrieking and firing—and it took four more shots until he snapped backwards and dropped off the bridge, his gun *still* spraying bullets. Mother took five shots to drop the other one.

'Mother*fucking* crazy bastards . . .' she breathed.

'Retract that first bridge!' Schofield yelled.

Baba scanned the console for the correct switch and punched it.

The first bridge began to retract into the outer wall of the circular pit, creating a fifty-foot-wide chasm between Schofield's position on the central platform and the dock's doorway.

'Mother! Take the Kid and your new French friend and go!' He glanced downward. Veronique Champion was almost up the ladder. 'I'll cover you guys, then you cover us when I come over with Ms Champion!'

With those words, he stood suddenly and laid down a shitload of fire—causing his attackers to take cover—while Mother, the Kid and Baba hustled across the second bridge, firing as they went, and joined the others at the far door.

Champion rejoined Schofield on the central platform, rising up through its hatch.

'Mother! You ready to return the favour?' he called.

'*Gotcha, boss,*' Mother's voice replied in his earpiece.

'Okay, let's go—' Schofield said to Champion as he broke cover and ran, just as three things happened at once:

First, his enemy's machine-gunners unleashed a new burst of tracer fire that pinged off the second bridge, sending sparks flying up all around Schofield's feet.

Second, that volley of sizzling tracer bullets sliced through the air *between* Schofield and Champion, separating them, forcing Veronique Champion to dive *back* to the platform.

And third, the second bridge began retreating into the far wall

of the pit as Schofield ran across it—it was retracting, its segments reverse-telescoping into each other inches behind his running boots. One of his opponents had found a control panel by the dock's doorway and had retracted the bridge, isolating the central platform, leaving Champion stranded out on it.

Covered by Mother's fire and running at full speed, Schofield dived over a crate and tumbled to a halt beside the others at the far door.

'Sexy French Chick is still out there!' Mother shouted above the gunfire.

Schofield spun to see Champion huddled behind the console out on the island-like platform, hopelessly pinned down.

'Leave her!' Mario yelled. 'She wanted to kill us before!'

'We don't leave anybody,' Schofield said. 'Dr Ivanov, what's behind this door?'

Ivanov said, 'A stairway leading up to a structure we called the Stadium.'

'Does it take us toward Dragon Island?'

'There's a pontoon bridge on the other side of the Stadium that connects this islet to Dragon Island, yes.'

'Then we keep going that way,' Schofield said. 'Kid! Mario! You two take the lead, get everyone out of here! Get to this Stadium! Mother, stay with me.'

The others all started up the stairs with the Kid and Mario—except for Baba and Dubois. They stood their ground.

'I will not leave Renard,' Baba said simply.

'I wasn't going to leave her, either. I'm gonna try to get her out of there right now,' Schofield said.

With Baba and Dubois hovering behind them, Schofield and Mother watched the attacking force pummel the central platform on which Veronique Champion was stranded.

'Mario does have a point,' Mother said to Schofield softly. 'She did want to kill us before . . .'

'We need every able-bodied soldier we can get,' Schofield whispered, unholstering his Maghook.

'Oh, here we go . . .' Mother said.

'Just cover me, please.'

Mother sprang up and opened fire as Schofield stood suddenly and aimed his Maghook up at the girders supporting the huge domed roof—

But he caught himself in mid-action and didn't fire.

For at the exact moment that he rose, Veronique Champion did something similar. In fact, she did exactly the same thing.

She sprang up from her crouched position, and aimed a device very similar to Schofield's Maghook and fired it up at the overhead girders. Schofield only caught a glimpse of it, but her Maghook-like device was larger than his, bulkier, and the tip of its grappling hook was sharper, like an arrowhead.

It shot upwards, its pointed silver tip slicing through the air, a cable wobbling behind it like a tail. With a crisp *whack*, the sharp hook lodged, three inches deep, right *into* one of the metal girders and held.

Schofield stared as Champion then sprinted into the open, gripping her device's gun-like launcher, and leapt out over the pit, into open space, and swung . . . just as he would have done.

She swooped out over the bear-infested pit, a graceful sixty-foot swing—covered by Mother's fire—before her swing-arc brought her perfectly to the outer platform, where she landed deftly right in front of Schofield.

'Nice move . . .' he said.

'Thank you,' Champion said. With the flick of a switch, she reeled in her 'Maghook' and within seconds, they were away, dashing through the doorway after the others.

As they fled, neither Schofield nor Champion noticed the closed-circuit TV cameras surveying the lab from above.

Those cameras had caught everything, including clear shots of both their faces.

From his position inside the loading dock, the commander of the small enemy force also watched them go.

His name was Wilhelm Mauser, but everyone who knew him called him 'Bad Willy'. Technically, he was a German citizen and once upon a time he had been a sergeant in the German Army. But an unhealthy taste for young girls that became apparent during a multinational peacekeeping mission in Africa had seen him dishonourably discharged. It was also the source of his nickname.

Bad Willy smiled.

'Thresher Team, this is Bad Willy,' he said into his throat-mike. 'Just flushed them out of the Bear Lab. They're coming right to you.'

'*Copy that, Willy. We're ready and waiting in the Stadium.*'

OVERHEAD VIEW

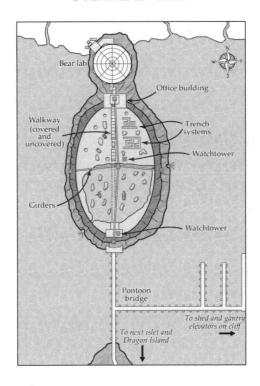

Bear lab

Office building

Walkway
(covered
and
uncovered)

Trench
systems

Watchtower

Girders

Watchtower

Pontoon
bridge

*To shed and gantry
elevators on cliff*

*To next islet and
Dragon Island*

SIDE VIEW

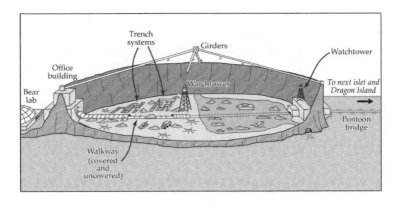

Trench
systems

Girders

Watchtower

Office
building

Watchtower

*To next islet and
Dragon Island*

Bear
lab

Pontoon
bridge

Walkway
(covered
and
uncovered)

THE 'STADIUM' ON BEAR ISLET

'Everybody got all their fingers and toes?' Schofield asked as he hurried up a long dark flight of stairs, moving past the members of his little team.

They all nodded.

'What do we do now?' the Kid asked.

'No choice,' Schofield said. 'Either we keep going forward or we die trying—'

Gunfire cut him off. A volley of bullets slammed into the stairs at the bottom of the passageway.

'Come on.'

He led them onward.

Schofield emerged from the stairway inside a squat, cube-shaped building that seemed to burrow into Bear Islet's mountainous core. It contained a few drab offices and a wider open-plan space, long abandoned.

'These were the offices for the scientists who worked on this islet,' Ivanov said.

Schofield's eyes never stopped roving.

The building seemed to straddle a narrow waist-like section of the islet. Schofield saw daylight through a bank of windows at the far, southern, end. Their only option was to keep going that way.

'Mother, Kid. I need you two to hold the stairway behind us for as long as you can. We're going south.'

'Roger that, Scarecrow.'

He ran southward, came to the bank of windows and looked out through them.

'Good God . . .' he breathed.

Beside him, Veronique Champion also stopped short. 'What is this place?'

They were looking out over a vast oval-shaped crater bounded by sheer hundred-foot-high rocky walls. There was a network of trenches cut into the near half, a watchtower in the middle and a semi-frozen lake at the far end. A covered walkway extended out across the space, half-buried in the earth before it delved *below* the lake to finally emerge at another cube-shaped building at the opposite end of the crater, a twin of the one they were standing in. Atop that building stood a second watchtower, gazing out over the crater.

Over the top of it all, four massive girders reached skyward, joining above the first watchtower in a t-shaped junction 150 feet above the floor of the crater. From those girders hung floodlights that presumably illuminated the great space at night. It really did look like a football stadium, or perhaps a gladiatorial arena.

'This,' Ivanov said, 'is the Stadium. This is where my colleagues tested the bears in combat.'

'Scarecrow!' Mother called from the top of the stairway leading back to the Bear Lab. 'They've got too much firepower back here! Do some of that officer shit and make a decision!'

A steep flight of stairs covered by a clear glass awning led down to the Stadium's floor, where it met the half-buried walkway that ran down the length of the enormous crater. A section of the glass awning over these stairs was shattered, leaving a thirty-foot segment of the stairway open to the sky.

Something inside Schofield's brain baulked.

He didn't like this. Something about it was wrong. But then, they had no choice.

'Everybody! Down the stairs! Get to that walkway!'

They took off down the awning-covered stairs, bounding down them, with Mother and the Kid as the rearguard, firing at the wetsuit-clad members of the Army of Thieves now emerging from the other stairway behind them.

As Schofield and the others hurried down the stairs toward the Stadium, they suddenly burst out into the segment where the overhead awning was broken and they could see the sky—

A withering burst of gunfire cut through the air all around them, bullets raking the exposed segment of stairway.

Chad dived away, covering his head, as beside him the third Frenchman, Dubois, was hit several times and fell. He was still alive but badly wounded, and Champion scooped him up, pulling him out of the line of fire.

Emma Dawson shrieked as a stray round clipped her left leg. She stumbled and Zack dived to her side, dragging her back up the stairs to safety.

Everybody else fell back, too.

A hailstorm of enemy rounds hammered the stairs. Some hit the glass awning, but its reinforced glass deflected the long-range shots. Sparks exploded everywhere.

'Goddamn it!' Mario shouted, ducking his head.

Zack shielded Emma with his body while Schofield and Champion frantically scanned the Stadium for the shooters and found them right where they expected them to be: on the second watchtower atop the far building, with a perfect line-of-sight looking straight down the central walkway.

They'd been waiting for Schofield's people to appear.

Schofield swore. He'd walked right into a fucking trap.

He opened fire with his MP-7—a useless spray that wouldn't hit anything from this range, but it would make the shooters at the other end of the crater duck. Mario, Champion and Baba did the same and the enemy's fire stopped for a moment.

'We can't stay here!' Schofield yelled. 'Military people! Rolling cover fire! *We must not stop firing or else we are dead!*'

He then looped Dubois's arm over his shoulder and helped the wounded Frenchman as they all hurried down the stairs, the military people firing as they ran.

Zack helped Emma and she limped along as fast as she could as they entered the flat covered walkway that ran down the length of the Stadium. Rounds from the enemy shooters peppered the glass awning but bounced away.

As he hurried along under Dubois's weight, Schofield yelled, 'I should've seen it! They weren't even *trying* to kill us back in that lab. They were flushing us out here, into this Stadium. It's a turkey shoot.'

'So how do we get out?' Zack shouted with Emma draped over one shoulder and Bertie gripped in his spare hand.

Schofield peered at the area around them. From the crashed Beriev to the exploding submarine to the race through the leads to the Bear Lab to this, he hadn't had a chance to get his bearings at all.

'Right now, I have no idea,' he answered truthfully. 'We'll just have to keep running and firing till I get one.'

They kept running and firing, hustling down the covered walkway.

A short distance ahead, the reinforced glass awning of the walkway had been shattered, leaving a long stretch of the trench open to the sky. Here a large mound of snow had fallen into the sunken path, filling it, blocking the way.

Schofield peered back down the walkway, searching for the original enemy force that would soon arrive behind them.

He tried to calm his mind. He only had a few seconds, but if they were going to get out of this, he needed to think clearly and make the right decision.

Okay. What do you have to do?

I need to get to Dragon Island to stop the ignition of the atmospheric weapon inside the hour.

But my enemies are outmanoeuvring me at every turn. They're carrying out a co-ordinated plan while I'm improvising as I go.

They know the terrain. I don't. I only know where I am when I look around the next corner.

And now they're both in front of and behind us and about to rip us apart.

I am seriously about to lose this battle . . .

So what do you need to do to stop that happening?

I need to alter the conditions of battle.

Okay. How are you going to do that?

I need to disrupt their plan. I need to get out of this walkway and make them play a game of my choosing—

His eyes scanned the area around them: the high rocky rim of the crater, the t-shaped girder structure above the whole space, the watchtower in the middle of the Stadium—

The watchtower . . .

That was it. That was how you changed the state of this battle.

If I can just buy a little time . . .

He recalled seeing a network of military-style trenches cut into the floor of the Stadium; trenches in which the Soviets had tested their polar bears in combat scenarios.

That might work . . .

'People!' he called. 'We can't stay in this walkway! When you get to that open section up ahead, climb up the snow mound and go left into the trenches! They'll give us some cover!'

A bullet whistled past his ear.

It had come from behind.

Their pursuers had arrived at the start of the walkway.

With Dubois still on his shoulder, Schofield whirled and opened fire with his spare hand. So did the Kid, Mario and Mother, forcing the attackers back up the stairs.

Leading the way, Zack and the limping Emma arrived at the open section of the walkway. The snow mound rose before them, white and huge, blocking the way—and the sightlines of the snipers on the far tower—but also providing an ungainly slope up which they could climb out of the sunken walkway.

Suddenly, more enemy rounds sizzled past their heads, smacking into the walls of the walkway. These rounds had come from the *side*, from more shooters stationed up on the rim of the crater, on both the eastern and western sides—these shooters were huddled beside the large steel buttresses from which the mighty girders that straddled the immense Stadium sprang.

Baba and Champion stepped up alongside Zack and Emma and returned fire.

'Go!' Champion yelled. 'Get to the trenches!'

Zack—still carrying Bertie like a suitcase in his free hand—pushed Emma up the snow mound before joining her. They scrambled on their hands and knees across some open muddy ground, bullets impacting all around them, before they dropped into the safety of the nearest trench.

The two civilians landed inside the six-foot-deep trench. Its dark earthen walls were covered in frost. The trench stretched away from them, tight and narrow, branching off into several other trenches: a mini-maze of right-angled twists and turns.

From somewhere in those passageways, Zack heard a low growl.

'I don't think these trenches are empty . . .' he said.

In the walkway, Schofield was still firing back at the pursuing force with Dubois hanging from his shoulder.

He jerked his chin southward. 'Mother! I want that watchtower! Get to it via the trenches! Kid, Mario: protect Dr Ivanov and Chad, and catch up with Zack and Emma!'

'Whatever you say, Scarecrow!' Mother hurried up and out of the walkway, firing in every direction as she went. Mario and Chad went next, followed by the Kid who reached back down to grab Ivanov.

Veronique Champion came alongside Schofield, still firing nonstop.

'Captain!' she shouted. 'We can't continue like this! We need to change the conditions of this battle or we won't last much longer!'

'I know! I know!'

'Do you have a plan?'

'Yeah! We get into the trenches and work our way over to that watchtower!'

'And then?'

'From there, I'm going to—' Gunfire cut him off.

'Never mind! That is good enough for me for now!' Veronique threw an arm underneath Dubois and, covered by Baba, helped Schofield drag the wounded French soldier up the snow mound.

They had almost made it up the mound when suddenly Schofield realised that the gunfire from *behind* them had stopped.

He frowned, peered back down the walkway.

There was now no-one at the base of the stairs at that end. No shadowy figures, nobody.

That wasn't good. It meant they were up to somethi—

Clink, clink, clink.

A small metal cylinder bounced down the stairs and rolled to a halt at that end of the walkway.

It looked to Schofield like a smoke grenade, only smaller. At first he thought it might be another acid grenade but this cylinder wasn't painted silver. Rather, it was painted bright red with yellow bands at either end.

Up above Schofield, Ivanov had stopped and turned, too, and he saw the grenade.

His eyes went wide. 'Captain! Get out of the trench now! It's a red uranium grenade!'

Baba and Champion were already out of the trench. Champion was reaching back down, pulling Schofield—with Dubois on his shoulder—up the snow mound, when suddenly Dubois' boots slipped and as he scrabbled for a purchase, Dubois—almost unconscious from loss of blood—lost his grip on Schofield's hand and fell back down the mound, tumbling back into the walkway.

Schofield made to dive after him but before he could, he heard Ivanov yell to Champion: 'No! It's too late! Get the captain out!' and Schofield felt Champion yank him up and out of the walkway and he fell face-first onto cold hardpacked mud a split second before the red-and-yellow grenade spectacularly went off.

A five-foot-high horizontal finger of yellow-red fire whooshed past Schofield, completely filling the walkway as it rushed by him: a blasting, rushing, rampaging stream of liquid fire.

Dubois never stood a chance.

The fire lanced right *through* him, liquefying his body in an instant. An entire human being just melted in the blink of an eye.

Schofield's eyes boggled.

It looked like the elongated tongue of fire sent forth by a flame-thrower, only bigger, much bigger: this was a tongue of fire eight feet wide by five feet high, contained only by the walls of the walkway. It was as if the walkway had suddenly been flooded not with water but with *fire*: blazing yellow liquid fire.

Before it destroyed Dubois, the finger of flame had rocketed down the roofed section of the sunken passageway, its intense heat shattering the reinforced glass awning, sending successive sections of the awning exploding skyward.

Then, after liquefying the Frenchman, the river of fire slammed into the snow mound and obliterated it, too, slicing through it like a hot knife through butter and sending an explosion of steam shooting a hundred feet into the air, engulfing the area around the walkway in a dense cloud of fog.

Schofield fell back from the blazing, glowing walkway.

When he regathered himself—wild bullets were still impacting all around him—he saw that the finger of fire had burned itself out, the snow mound was simply gone and the grey concrete walls and floor of the half-buried walkway glowed incandescent orange, like

embers in a fireplace, the outer layer of the concrete having been melted by the intense heat.

Covered by the newly created fog, Schofield rolled backwards with Champion and dropped into the nearest trench, landing next to Mother, the Kid, Baba and Ivanov. Mario and Chad hovered nearby, both looking very anxious. Zack and Emma were nowhere to be seen.

'What the hell was that!' Schofield gasped.

'That,' Ivanov said, 'was a grenade with a thermobaric core.'

'But it was tiny . . .' Mario said.

'Its red uranium core would have been the size of a grain of rice,' Ivanov said, 'and its explosion was small because it only fed off the ambient oxygen in the air. An explosion that uses an incendiary gas cloud is far more potent.'

'That was a *small* explosion?' Mother said.

'Doesn't matter now.' Schofield stood, gazing up at the watchtower looming above the mist-enshrouded trench system. 'Unless we get out of this Stadium fast, we're not going to be any use to anyone. We're heading for that tower, people.'

As they hurried off, the Kid came alongside Schofield. 'Sir, I can't find Zack and Emma, and neither of them are wearing headsets.'

Schofield frowned for a second in thought, before he touched his throat-mike and said, 'Bertie? Do you read me?'

'*I read you, Captain Schofield,*' Bertie's voice replied.

'Put me on speaker, please.'

'*You are on speaker.*'

'Zack? You hear me?'

Zack's voice came in. It sounded distant, like someone on a speakerphone. '*I hear you, Captain.*'

'Where are you? Is Emma with you?'

Zack was hurrying through a misty trench with Bertie whizzing along beside him and Emma draped over his shoulder, limping.

'We're in the trench system, but we must've taken a wrong turn somewhere. We're lost.'

'*Can you see the watchtower in the middle of the Stadium?*' Schofield's voice said through Bertie's speaker.

Zack peered out over the rim of the trench he was standing in. At first he saw nothing but the rocky inner wall of the crater and the office building that they had come through.

'No . . .' He turned and jumped. 'Oh, wait, I see it. Damn, we went the wrong way. I took us back toward the northern end of the crater.'

'*Never mind. You did good. You stayed alive. Just head for that watchtower. We'll meet you there.*'

'Got it.'

Zack and Emma hurried off, unaware of the distinctive footprints Zack's cold-weather Nike boots left in the mud behind them.

Schofield strode quickly through the trench-maze, moving fast and low, taking every turn decisively. Ahead of him, rising above the fog layer, was the watchtower, coming closer with every step.

'So what's your brilliant plan, Captain?' Champion said.

'Down here, we're rats in a maze.' He never stopped moving. 'They have men all around us—three sniper positions to the south, east and west, plus the flushing team behind us to the north. If we stay here, it's only a matter of time till they take us out. We need to turn the tables. We need to take some higher ground, take *them* out, and then roll on to Dragon Island without losing any more time. That watchtower is the key to it all.'

A stray bullet whistled down through the fog and lodged in the mud wall beside Schofield's head. He barely noticed it, kept moving.

Champion said, 'If they see you up in that watchtower, they'll hit it with an RPG within thirty seconds . . .'

'I know,' Schofield said. 'That gives me thirty seconds to do what I have to do.'

Schofield and his group came to the edge of the trench system, to the point where it was closest to the watchtower.

'Okay, folks,' Schofield readied his MP-7, 'this little operation will have two phases. First phase, I'm the bait. I make a break for the watchtower . . . their snipers up on the eastern and western rims fire on me . . . you take them out. Got it?'

'Oui,' Baba said.

'So long as you're happy being bait,' Mother said.

'And the second phase?' Champion asked.

'I take out their other sniper position over on that southern watchtower.'

'Which will of course depend on whether you survive the first phase,' Champion said.

'Yeah.' He took a deep breath. 'Okay, let's roll.'

And with those words, he broke cover and sprinted for the base of the watchtower.

Muzzle flashes erupted immediately from the eastern and western rims of the crater and a line of bullets chewed up the dirt inches behind Schofield's running feet.

The strafing was about to catch up with him when Mother, Mario, the Kid, Champion and Baba all rose together—Mother, Mario and the Kid pointing east, the French pair pointing west—and opened fire on the enemy positions.

The two sniper posts were ripped apart by their fire and in each position, three figures were hurled backwards. The muzzle flashes from up there ceased.

Schofield hit the base of the watchtower at a run as a new volley of gunfire pinged against its criss-crossing struts.

This gunfire came from the *other* watchtower, the one that stood on top of the office building at the distant southern end of the Stadium.

His heart pounding, Schofield clambered up his watchtower's internal ladder.

'Mother! That other watchtower!'

Bullets sizzled past him as he climbed, ricocheting off the tower's struts, whizzing past his head. One round made a popping sound as it broke the sound barrier millimetres in front of his face and cut a slit-like mark on the lens of his glasses. Another hit his left hand, smashing into his little finger. Schofield grimaced with pain but kept climbing.

The others offered what cover fire they could, but the south-facing angle wasn't as good as the eastern and western ones, and the fire from the southern watchtower was only minorly inhibited.

Schofield reached the cupola of the watchtower and he saw the whole massive crater spread out around him, a perfect 360-degree view.

But he didn't stop to enjoy it. His thirty seconds were almost up.

For right then he saw a small figure on the southern watchtower hoist a long-barrelled object onto his shoulder: an RPG launcher.

Schofield kept moving.

He yanked his Maghook from his back-holster, aimed it skyward and fired—

—at the exact moment the figure in the southern watchtower fired his rocket-propelled grenade.

The Maghook flew up into the sky, trailing its cable—while the RPG lanced across the Stadium at blinding speed, a tail of smoke extending out behind it.

The Maghook's magnetic head thunked against the underside of the t-shaped girder-junction above the massive crater and Schofield hit 'SPOOL' on his handgrip and he was suddenly whisked up into the air, shooting skyward on the Maghook's cable . . .

. . . a millisecond before the entire watchtower beneath him was hit by the RPG and exploded, instantly transformed into a multitude of metal shards that showered outward in a star-shaped spray of fire and smoke. A gigantic fireball expanded beneath the fast-rising figure of Shane Schofield.

Reeled upward by the Maghook's internal spooler, Schofield came to the underside of the girder-junction and for a moment he hung suspended a dizzying 150 feet above the floor of the Stadium.

He didn't care. He quickly climbed up on top of the four-pronged girder-junction, reholstered his Maghook, and then did what he'd come up here to do.

He lay down on his belly, pressing his chest armour flat against the superlong metal girder that stretched away from him southward, shooting down at a wickedly steep angle over that half of the Stadium: over the lake and the office building and even the watchtower at the far end.

The girder was about three feet wide; Schofield reached out with his arms and hooked them over each side, gripping his MP-7 in his right hand and his Desert Eagle in his left.

Then he pushed himself off.

Head-first, Schofield skimmed down the length of the massive girder, sliding on his chest armour, gaining speed as he went, arms and legs bent on either side, pressing against the outer edges of the girder, keeping him steady and controlling his speed as he rocketed down the steep slope.

The floodlights suspended from the girder rushed by beneath him. He saw the lake go by and then the southern office building came closer, then the watchtower mounted on it.

At which point, Schofield opened fire with both his guns—withering fire, deadly fire. He pummelled the watchtower all over and saw all the men on it convulse under the weight of his crushing gunfire. Five of them dropped, dead.

Then he arrived at the southern rim of the crater, arresting his slide by pressing his boots against the outside of the girder and he came to an abrupt, lurching halt.

He saw three more enemy soldiers in parkas gathered at the base of the watchtower and he slid on his butt down the rocky inner wall of the crater behind them, firing as he did so. They all fell as, finally, he came to a halt at the bottom of the crater wall, guns smoking and empty, his enemy's position silent and devoid of movement.

He still held his guns levelled even though he was out of ammo. If anyone had survived his attack, he was screwed, but it appeared that no-one had.

Within moments, Schofield was up in the cupola of the second watchtower, reloaded and rearmed and looking through the gun-sights of one of his enemy's sniper rifles.

'Mother,' he said into his throat-mike. 'The way is clear. Bring everybody through the underwater walkway. I'll cover you from here.'

Veronique Champion and Baba just stared open-mouthed at what they had just seen.

Champion said nothing.

Baba nodded. 'I *like* this man, Scarecrow!'

The Kid, Mario, Chad, Ivanov, Champion and Baba dashed for the walkway again—only this time, instead of being fired upon from the far watchtower, they were covered by it, by Schofield.

The original Army of Thieves unit that had hounded them out of the Bear Lab—Bad Willy's unit—was now pinned down on the stairs at the northern end of the Stadium by Schofield's sniper fire.

'Zack,' Schofield said into his throat-mike as he peered through the scope of the sniper rifle. 'Where are you?'

'*We're still lost in the trenches,*' Zack's voice replied.

'Well, get out of there and get to the walkway again. I have it covered now.'

'*Copy that,*' Zack said. '*We're coming.*'

Zack hustled through the trenches with Emma hanging off his shoulder and Bertie rolling along beside him. He panted as he ran, breathless and afraid.

He rounded a mud-walled, frost-covered corner and saw another mud-walled, frost-covered trench.

He was hopelessly, hopelessly lost.

'How you doing?' he asked Emma.

'It hurts like hell.' Emma winced as she limped along. She looked at him. 'Please don't leave me, Zack.'

Zack stopped, turned and looked her square in the eye. 'Emma. Hey. Look at me. No matter how bad it gets, I will not leave you, okay? I will not leave you. Either we get out of this together or we go down together.'

She nodded weakly. 'Thanks.'

Zack looked up at the rim of the trench above them. 'We gotta get topside. I don't know which way we're going anymore—'

'How sweet,' a nasty voice said from somewhere very near.

The dense foggy air made it sound uncomfortably close. '"Either we get out of this together or we go down together." Brave words . . . Zack.'

Zack spun, searching for the owner of the voice, but he saw nothing except the empty trench reaching away into the fog.

Emma's eyes went wide. 'They're in these trenches . . .'

'The name's Willy,' the voice said. 'Bad Willy. Because I have a very bad willy. See, I just love to get acquainted with the ladies even when they don't want to get acquainted with me. And I must say,' he cooed menacingly, 'I just *love* the sound of your voice . . . Emma.'

Zack and Emma exchanged horrified glances.

'Come out, come out, wherever you are . . .' Bad Willy's voice sang a moment before Zack heard—very close—the *chk-chk* of a safety being unlocked.

Zack picked up Bertie by his carry handle. In the thick silence, he worried that the whirring of Bertie's electric motor might give their position away.

'This way!' Zack whispered as he pulled Emma around another corner, just as a terrifying roar shook the air and a gigantic shaggy polar bear filled the muddy alleyway in front of them.

It reared on its hind legs, rising to its full fourteen-foot height, opening its jaws to reveal a set of fearsome fangs as it bellowed in pure animal rage.

Like the bears in the lab, this bear's coat was shaggy and matted and filthy. Its eyes were wild, deranged, infuriated.

Zack pushed Emma backwards, putting himself between her and the bear. But it was no use. With startling speed, the massive white creature dropped onto all fours and launched itself at them and Zack could only shut his eyes and wait for the end—

—only nothing happened.

He opened his eyes, to find himself looking into the rapidly dilating nostrils of the bear from a distance of five centimetres.

Its foul hot breath washed over his face.

Only then did Zack realise that the animal's nose was twitching, sniffing: sniffing him.

With a rude grunt, the bear jerked away from Zack, all interest in him abruptly and inexplicably lost.

'Why is it—?' Emma said in a hushed voice.

'I don't—' Zack whispered, but then he realised that he *did* know why.

It was the bear repellent. The bizarre spray-on aerosol that he'd been forced to bring with him on their trip. He'd sprayed it onto all his clothes out of pure scientific obligation, in the event that he encountered a polar bear, but until now no such encounter had occurred.

'Score one for the polar bear repellent,' he said softly.

But then the bear roared again, louder than before and it lunged at them again and Zack had a terrifying thought that he'd been wrong and that the stupid bear repellent didn't work at all but before he knew what was happening, the bear leapt clear over him and Emma, launching itself at the four armed men who had just rounded the corner behind them!

Bad Willy and three of his men.

The bear did not pause as it fell upon Willy's point man: it thumped him to the ground and had already ripped out his throat by the time Bad Willy recovered his wits and opened fire, blowing the bear away in a storm of bullets. The bear dropped to the ground with a heavy thud.

But the distraction had been enough for Zack and Emma to glimpse Bad Willy—he was a short man with wiry, sinewy muscles, a bald head and a bony, hollow face. A silver chain hung suspended between a piercing in his left eyebrow and a ring in his left nostril.

For a brief, fleeting moment, Zack and Bad Willy locked eyes.

Zack froze.

Willy grinned.

And raised his gun.

'Bertie, *fire!*' Zack said, still gripping Bertie in his hand like a suitcase.

The little robot opened fire with its machine gun. Zack hadn't aimed at all and the spray of gunfire was totally wild.

Willy's men dived for cover, but not before Zack's blaze of robot gunfire had taken out the man standing beside Willy. He went flying backwards, convulsing horribly. The roving burst then found Bad Willy and the right side of his head exploded with blood and Bad Willy screamed before falling to the ground.

Zack's eyes went wide at the sight, and the thought, of what he had just done.

He yelled, 'Bertie! Cease fire!' and started running again, hauling Emma along.

Rounding the next corner, they saw Mother kneeling atop a trench wall, waving to them and reaching down with her hand.

A minute later, as Mother lifted them out of the trench, Zack heard a familiar nasal voice call out:

'Zacky-boy! Oh, Zacky-boy! You shot off my fucking ear, you little piece of no-good ratshit! I am going to hunt you down, you candy-ass fuck, and the tasty Emma, too, and when I do, I am going to tie you up, rip your eyelids off, and make you watch me fuck her to death! You hear me, Zacky!'

A cruel cackle echoed out from the fog-enshrouded trenches.

'You're just making new friends everywhere you go, aren't you, Science Boy?' Mother said. 'Come on.'

Then they were off, racing through the underwater section of the walkway, covered by Schofield's sniper fire.

The three of them joined the others inside the cube-shaped building at the southern end of the Stadium.

Like the office building at the northern end, it bored through Bear Islet's high volcanic cone, its cracked, frost-covered windows looking north over the Stadium and south at the one remaining islet that lay between them and Dragon Island.

Once Mother, Zack and Emma were safely at his side, Schofield looked southward.

Beneath him, a decrepit pontoon bridge connected Bear Islet to the next islet—the final islet bore a warehouse-sized building on its back; beyond the warehouse, on higher ground, Schofield saw a cable car station whose long swooping cable stretched up to reach Dragon Island.

It was one way to get to Dragon Island, but there was another one nearby: halfway along the pontoon bridge that joined the two islets was a second and longer pontoon bridge that branched away at right angles from the main one. This second bridge stretched eastward, where it met a large, rust-covered, corrugated-iron shed that had been built into the base of the nearest cliff, on the edge of the bay, *on* Dragon Island itself. Two towering industrial-sized gantry elevators ran up and down the face of the cliff, having once serviced the shed.

'Dr Ivanov,' Schofield said, 'the pontoon bridge or the cable car?'

'We call that last islet "Acid Islet",' Ivanov said, 'as it houses a substantial acid research laboratory. Its cable car, however, is very old; it was built when this facility was originally constructed back in 1985. It works but it is rarely used these days. The extreme cold has always made it quite unreliable, which is why the pontoon bridge was built in 1990. The bridge is newer and would definitely be faster.'

'Faster is better,' Schofield said, eyeing the elevators at the end of the pontoon bridge.

He checked his watch: 10:26 a.m. God, had it only been twenty-six minutes since they'd blasted into the Bear Lab?

At his feet lay the bodies of five members of the Army of Thieves, dressed in their stolen Marine Corps parkas. Crouching beside one of the corpses, Schofield pulled off the man's helmet and goggles. An ordered series of tattoos ran down the side of his throat: images of a Russian ship, the letters 'USMC', a building with 'Moskva' written over it.

The other Thieves, Schofield saw, bore similar tattoos on their throats, although some had more than others.

'What do they mean?' Chad asked.

Schofield was silent for a moment. Then he got it. 'They're medals. Markers of participation in certain military engagements.'

'Holy shit. What kind of army is this?' Chad said distastefully.

Schofield stood and turned back to face his team. They were variously breathless, dirty and bloodstained—Chad looked particularly pale, and the older Ivanov was sweating profusely. Only the big Frenchman named Baba seemed okay: he looked like he was out at a picnic, fresh as a daisy.

Having lost Dubois, they were down to ten now, and in a dark corner of his mind Schofield wondered how many more of them would be lost on this mission.

'So what's the plan now, boss?' Mother said, coming alongside him and peering out at the last remaining islet.

'Now we get across to those gantry elevators.'

'How?' Champion asked.

Schofield stared out at the pontoon bridge that angled toward the supply shed and the gantry elevators.

'By going backwards,' he said.

Inside the command centre on Dragon Island's high disc-shaped tower, the Lord of Anarchy gazed at a freeze-frame of Shane Schofield, caught on a surveillance camera inside the Bear Lab.

'So who is he?' he said.

'He's a Marine, sir. Captain Shane Michael Schofield. Call-sign Scarecrow,' Typhon said. 'He's got a history.'

The Lord of Anarchy stared intently at the headshot of Schofield on the screen.

Then he read the accompanying bio . . . and grinned meanly. 'How *very* interesting.'

He looked up. 'What about the others?'

Typhon said, 'We counted eleven of them in the Bear Lab, including the Russian, Ivanov, but it looks like one of their people was killed in the Stadium. Of those remaining, in addition to Schofield, I got hits on five in the military databases.'

'And?'

'Three more Marines and two French paratroopers who are now with the DGSE.'

'Let me see.' The Lord of Anarchy took a seat at the console and clicked through the service records of Mother, the Kid, Mario, Champion and Baba.

When he was done, he leaned back in his seat and smiled to himself.

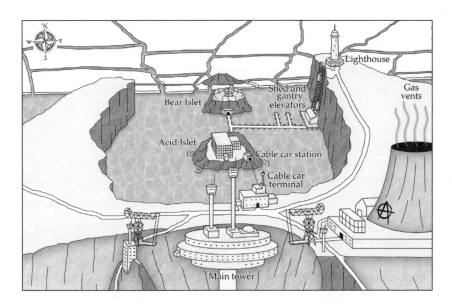

NORTHERN BAY AND SURROUNDS

The northern coast of Dragon Island was shaped like a gigantic U, in the middle of which lay the last islet.

Ivanov had called it 'Acid Islet'—after the enormous acid research laboratory that stood on it—and while it was actually quite large, the three-hundred-foot-high cliffs of Dragon Island that ringed it on three sides made it look tiny.

At the northern end of the islet was the pontoon bridge that joined Acid Islet to Bear Islet. Branching eastward from that bridge was its longer side-bridge that led to the shed and the gantry elevators on the eastern side of the bay.

Overlooking the whole bay from a commanding position on top of the eastern promontory was a lighthouse that also acted as a watchtower.

On that lighthouse, two sentries from the Army of Thieves looked out at the Stadium on Bear Islet with keen interest. They knew that Bad Willy had been sent in from behind to flush the intruders toward Thresher Team, which had crossed the pontoon bridge not long ago—

Suddenly, four parka-clad members of Thresher Team came dashing out across the bridge from the Stadium, running for their lives, heading *back* toward the shed. The first man helped the second who limped along as best he could; the third and fourth ones covered them, firing defensively back at Bear Islet as they fled.

They then stopped firing as four *more* Army of Thieves men followed, also running desperately, and also firing behind them as they ran. All around the fleeing figures, the wooden posts and floorboards of the bridge shattered and splintered under heavy-calibre gunfire.

The Army sentries on the lighthouse spotted two or three figures firing from an oversized doorway at the Bear Islet end of the pontoon bridge.

The intruders.

They were forcing Thresher back.

The retreating men from Thresher Team reached the halfway point of the bridge, the spot where it intersected with the longer side-bridge that would take them to the shed and the gantry elevators—when suddenly one man convulsed and fell, hit. He was scooped up by the man beside him.

As this happened, the junior of the two sentries keyed his radio. 'Base, this is Lighthouse. Intruders appear to have established a position at the south end of Bear Islet. They're forcing Thresher back across to the supply shed and the elevators.'

'*Copy that, Lighthou*—' came the reply.

'Wait!' the more senior man on the lighthouse said abruptly. He was a very large and very capable Chilean lieutenant known in the Army of Thieves as Big Jesus.

He was watching the retreating men on the pontoon bridge closely.

'That's not Thresher Team . . .' Big Jesus said slowly. 'Members of the Army of Thieves are trained to leave any wounded men behind. It's the intruders, wearing Thresher's uniforms. Cliff team: RPG that pontoon bridge now! Destroy it!'

Down on the pontoon bridge—sixty yards from the shed and the elevators—dressed in a bulky Marine Corps parka that he'd taken from a dead Army of Thieves man on Bear Islet, Shane Schofield started down the longer side-bridge, racing *backward* toward the shed.

In his ear was a very high-tech radio earpiece/mike he'd also stolen from the dead Army of Thieves man—it was small, earbud-sized, with a tiny 10mm-long filament microphone that he had switched off for the moment. But it could still receive, and through it he'd been listening to a conversation between his enemies that had sounded very promising: a sentry on the lighthouse high above him had bought his illusion, that he and the others were actually Army of Thieves men in retreat.

As he listened, Schofield fired back at Bear Islet—each shot, of course, going wildly high—while helping the 'wounded' Kid. Beside him, Baba did the same with a similarly 'wounded' Champion, who had done a stellar job imitating that she had been shot. Emma, Zack, Chad and Ivanov, also dressed in stolen parkas, ran along behind them.

At the Bear Islet end of the bridge, Mother and Mario—with Bertie—were crouched in a doorway, ostensibly firing at the fleeing team, but hitting only the timber of the bridge, completing the deception.

But then the radio conversation turned sour. Someone had figured out their plan, ordering: '*It's the intruders, wearing Thresher's uniforms. Cliff team: RPG that pontoon bridge now! Destroy it!*'

Gunfire came blazing out from the clifftop above Schofield, and out of it emerged an RPG, screaming downward. It slammed into the pontoon bridge right in front of Schofield and the bridge went flying up into the air, water spraying all around it. When the geyser settled, Schofield saw that his route to the shed was gone: a broad section of the pontoon bridge had been destroyed. There was no way across it now.

He called as he turned. 'We're made! Everybody! Go the other way! Get to the next islet! Mother and Mario! Haul ass!'

Their cover blown, Schofield, Champion and Baba opened fire on the clifftop, covering the others as they all turned and ran full-tilt across the shorter pontoon bridge toward Acid Islet. Mother and Mario scooped up Bertie and raced out into the open, also firing up at the clifftop as they went.

But Schofield's cover fire wasn't enough. As they all changed direction, the terrified Chad was hit in the back by a line of bullets and his chest burst with bloody exit wounds and he fell into the water beside the intersection of the two bridges. He was dead before he hit the surface.

Zack and Emma paused wide-eyed beside his body, but Champion pushed them on. 'He's dead! You can't help him! Allez! Allez!'

Schofield also glanced silently at Chad's floating corpse as he hurried past.

Mother came alongside him as he did so. 'These assholes aren't stupid, Scarecrow!'

'No, they're not.'

Once they were all across the shorter bridge and on the islet, huddled inside a small abandoned guardhouse there, Schofield tossed a grenade behind them onto the pontoon bridge and it detonated. The near end of the bridge blew apart, so that it now had a gaping void in it. No-one would be following them that way.

But they still hadn't made it to Dragon and now the Army of Thieves knew exactly where they were.

'What do we do now?' Mother said, breathless. Beside her, Emma had started sobbing and Zack looked horrified.

'Emma, Zack,' Schofield said sharply, making them look up. 'I'm sorry, but we can't grieve now. We knew this was going to be bad and we knew people might get shot. Trust me, Chad's in a better place. He doesn't have to go through any more of this.'

Schofield turned to gaze southward, across this new islet at Dragon Island. His eyes fell on the cable car station at the southern tip.

A steeply sloping cable rose up from the station, soaring out over the waters of the bay to meet a much larger terminal that hung off Dragon Island, off the summit of the nearest cliff. Made of grim grey concrete, the cable car terminal looked about as inviting as a World War II gun emplacement. But it was their only choice now.

'We just lost any element of surprise we ever had,' he said, 'and since we don't have the advantage of numbers, all we have left is speed. So we go in fast and we go in hard, and we absolutely do not stop.'

'Keep moving, keep moving,' Schofield urged, hustling everybody along a bitumen road that led up to the large warehouse-sized building that occupied the central section of Acid Islet.

They entered the building and a vast space met them: a huge hall the size of a football field.

A single grated super-catwalk suspended from the ceiling ran down the length of the space, hanging above two dozen menacing-looking industrial vats. Minor catwalks branched off the main one and from them ladders reached down to the floor where the vats lay.

Each vat was round with steel walls, about the size and shape of an above-ground backyard swimming pool. Some bore pressurised lids on them, while others were open to the air, revealing their strange contents: liquids of various putrid colours—off-green, off-brown, off-yellow—some frozen, others not. A couple of them bubbled. A tangle of pipes and valves linked some of the vats. Suspended from chains above one of the vats was a man-sized cage with semi-melted bars.

'The acid laboratory,' Ivanov said as they moved. 'We experimented with acids for use in chemical weapons, grenades and, well, torture.'

'Torture?' Mother asked.

'Trust me, when you are lowered into an acid bath and you start to see your own skin boil, you will tell your questioner everything he wants to know,' Ivanov said grimly.

'Charming,' Schofield said, pushing them along. 'Keep moving.'

He glanced downward as he said this and glimpsed a thick lead

door down on the lowest level, partially obscured by the minor catwalks. It looked like a walk-in safe at a bank, but the big nuclear symbol on it, accompanied by a warning in Russian, gave away its true character: radioactive material storage.

'Don't stop.' He pushed everyone along. 'We gotta get to that cable car.'

A few minutes later, they emerged from the acid warehouse and raced up a short road that ended at the cable car station.

Dragon Island loomed before them, impossibly huge, protected by its mighty cliffs, the only method of access: the long swooping cable that joined the cable car station to the terminal hanging off the cliff.

As Schofield arrived at the cable car station, he saw it waiting there, sitting by the platform, suspended from the cable: a long bus-sized cable car.

'It's very likely our enemy will have men waiting at the other end of this cable,' Champion said. 'Like those gantry elevators, this is an obvious entry point.'

'And easily defended,' Mother added.

'I know,' Schofield said, 'which is why I think we should go in all guns blazing.'

It took a few tries and some tinkering from Mario, but after a couple of minutes the cable car's engine came to life.

Shortly after that, with a laboured mechanical groan, it rumbled out from the station on Acid Islet and began its ascent to Dragon Island.

It took two minutes to make the three-hundred-metre climb— two tense interminable minutes. It moved upward at a steady pace.

And the whole time it was being observed.

By the ten Army of Thieves men waiting in the upper terminal.

'Thermal scan is in,' one of those Thieves said. He stood at the very end of the terminal's platform, practically at the edge of the cliff itself, holding an infra-red scanner pointed at the rising cable car. 'There's nobody in it . . .'

The commanding officer of this group of Thieves frowned darkly. His call-sign was White Tip.

'They might be using thermal blankets to hide their heat signatures. Gentlemen, ready your weapons. When it comes in, shoot the shit out of it.'

The cable car entered the upper terminal, its multi-wheeled overhead unit creeping along the cable.

White Tip and his terminal team were waiting for it, guns raised, safeties off. One man wore a flamethrowing unit clipped to a chest-harness. Its pilot flame flickered, ready.

Thunk!

The cable car shunted to a halt. Its doors began to slide open . . .

White Tip's unit prepared to fire . . .

The doors slid fully open . . .

And at first White Tip and his men saw no-one.

Because they were looking too high.

By the time they lowered their gazes, it was too late.

Bertie opened fire.

Bertie razed the terminal, firing on full auto in a perfect sixty-degree arc.

White Tip and his men didn't stand a chance. They were cut down where they stood, torn to pieces by the little robot's devastating fire. They dropped like marionettes that had had their strings cut.

Once all the Thieves in the terminal were down, Bertie rolled out of the cable car and took up a defensive position in the landward doorway of the terminal. As he stood guard there,

Schofield recalled the cable car and it headed back down to Acid Islet.

They now had four minutes—two for the cable car to return to Acid Islet and two for it to make the journey back up to the terminal on Dragon.

Alarms began to sound all over Dragon Island. Sirens came to life.

The two crane-operated drawbridges giving access to the main disc-shaped tower began to rise, sealing off the building. On the helipad, the crews of the two Ospreys ran for their aircraft.

Bertie's camera lens saw and heard it all, including the two Russian Army trucks filled with men that came speeding out from over by the eastern lighthouse, coming toward the cable car terminal.

While he waited for the cable car down on Acid Islet, Schofield had a look at Emma's leg wound: the bullet had taken a nick out of her thigh. Schofield patched it up. He also wrapped a gauze bandage around his own shot left little finger, splinting it to the finger next to it.

The cable car arrived.

Everyone boarded it and as they rode it for two seemingly endless minutes, Schofield eyed the Ospreys and the two trucks on his wristguard with concern.

Both Ospreys had been in the middle of refuelling when the alarm had sounded and the fuel hoses refilling their tanks were still connected, preventing them from lifting off. The trucks, however, were already halfway to the terminal. This was now a race to see who got to the terminal first—his cable car or the trucks. And the Ospreys wouldn't be far behind.

Schofield checked the time.

10:40 a.m.

'People, we've got twenty minutes till those uranium spheres are primed and ready to be fired into the gas cloud.'

'It's not enough time,' Mario said forlornly.

'While there's still a second to spare, we keep trying,' Schofield said firmly.

On his wristguard, he pulled up a plan of Dragon Island's main tower, nestled in its circular, almost moat-like, chasm:

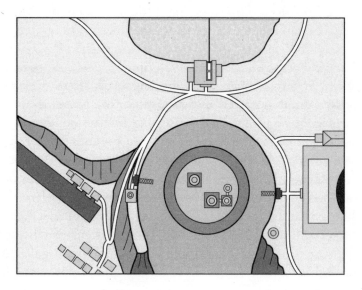

'Okay,' he said, 'they're going to be coming at us the moment we land on Dragon, so we can't waste a second once we're there. Dr Ivanov, you said the spheres are in the shorter spire on the main tower. How wide is that chasm surrounding the tower?'

Ivanov said, 'It is broad. Perhaps 250 feet.'

Schofield grimaced. 'Too wide for a Maghook.' He nodded at Champion's French-made Maghook-equivalent, the one she'd used to swing to safety in the Bear Lab. 'I didn't get to ask you before: what is that and how long is its cable?'

Champion said, 'It is a FA-MAS *Ligne Magnétique* Multi-Purpose Grappling Gun, but we just call it "Le Magneteux". While similar to the Armalite MH-12 Maghook, it is, with respect, superior to that device in almost every way.'

She offered the Magneteux to Schofield. It looked like his Maghook, only sleeker, more modern, and a little larger. It also bore not one but *two* high-tech silver grappling hooks sitting in parallel firing barrels.

'The Magneteux has two cables, each 200 feet long, plus two hooks which fire from two independently directable firing barrels. Each hook has fold-out claws, magnetic adhesion and a threaded drill bit that can lodge into solid surfaces like stone, concrete or, if fired from close enough, steel.'

Schofield examined the sharpened tip of the Magneteux's hook. It was indeed threaded like a self-tapping screw. 'It spins as it flies?' he asked. 'And that causes it to drill into a solid surface?'

'Correct.'

'Impressive.' His little Maghook certainly couldn't do that.

Baba cut in. 'Each cable of the Magneteux can hold a load of up to 1,000 kilograms. The American Maghook can barely hold two hundred.'

'What's this?' Schofield touched a compact detachable black unit clipped to the side of the Magneteux: it looked like a rubber suitcase grip with four small motorised clamp-wheels attached to it. 'An ascender?'

'Yes,' Champion said. 'A motorised ascender. It clips onto the cable and hauls you up it. Very fast. Beats climbing.'

Ivanov said, 'But if the cable is only 200 feet long, it's not going to be long enough. The moat is at least 250 feet wide.'

Schofield held the French Magneteux in his hands. 'A thousand kilograms, you say? For each cable.' He turned to Baba: 'You have one of these as well?'

'Oui.'

Schofield nodded, thinking quickly now. He glanced at the incoming trucks on the wristguard. 'If we can get hold of a— Dr Ivanov, do you keep any vehicles in the terminal at the top of this cable? Any jeeps maybe, or cars?'

Ivanov said, 'No jeeps or cars. But there is a garage attached to the western side of the terminal that houses some small fuel trucks. They are old but still in working order.'

'That'll do,' Schofield said. 'All right, folks. This is the plan.'

As the cable car rose, he quickly outlined his plan for getting to the uranium spheres on the shorter spire of the main tower and, if necessary, stealing them.

When he was finished, Baba swore, Champion gasped, Zack gulped and Mother just said, 'You're insane, you know that?'

'The only way for this to work,' Schofield said, 'is to do it *fast*. Nonstop. If we stop for even a moment, it's over. They'll move the spheres and we're screwed. Hopefully, they'll be caught off-guard and we'll need the hesitation that usually follows that. Having said all this, the plan *will* require two of you to take something of a leap of faith with me. Mother? Baba? You up for it?'

Mother said, 'Always.'

Baba looked closely at Schofield. His jaw twitched. Then he said: 'Qui veut vivre éternellement?'

'What's that mean?' the Kid asked.

'It means,' Baba said gruffly, 'who wants to live forever? The Barbarian is afraid of no man *or* mission. I will take this leap of faith with you.'

'Good,' Schofield said. 'Okay, everyone, take a look at this map and make sure you know where you have to go—'

But just then, as he passed round the wristguard with the map on it, a voice spoke in Schofield's ear.

'*Captain Schofield,*' it said pleasantly. '*Captain Shane Michael Schofield of the United States Marine Corps, call-sign: Scarecrow. I am the Lord of Anarchy, General of the Army of Thieves. You've managed to survive a lot longer than I thought you would and I see now that you are on the cusp of setting foot on my island.*'

It took Schofield a moment to realise that the voice was coming through the second earpiece he was wearing: the one he'd taken from the dead member of Thresher Team.

It took him another second to see the small surveillance camera in the top corner of the cable car, its pilot light on.

'*I'll take that glance at the camera as proof that you can hear me loud and clear. You have one of my radios in your ear.*'

Schofield checked his people. Mother and Veronique Champion

both looked back at him, eyes wide—they also wore Army of Thieves earpiece/mikes. But none of the others did, so as they all perused the map, they couldn't hear the Lord of Anarchy's words.

The cable car kept rising.

They were less than a minute out now.

The two troop trucks kept closing in.

'*My torturers have recently made the acquaintance of your campmate, Mr Hartigan, and he has been most forthcoming with information about you and your band of merry men—civilians tend to be forthcoming when they have a pair of electrodes attached to their skull,*' the Lord of Anarchy said.

'*And now I have your file in front of me, Captain. You're a genuine hero. A former Marine Corps pilot, shot down, tortured, rescued, then retrained as a ground officer. Served with distinction ever since, albeit to the considerable dismay of the French Government. They still have a price on your head.*'

Schofield said nothing.

'*Such service, I see, has not been without loss,*' the Lord said. '*Tell me, Captain, how did you feel when you were informed that Jonathan Killian had cut off your girlfriend's head?*'

Still Schofield said nothing. Mother and Champion listened in dumbstruck horror.

'*Never mind. I already know the answer,*' the Lord of Anarchy said. '*I can see from the file notes of the three psychiatrists who treated you that you did not take it well at all. It was practically a nervous breakdown. Must be hard for a hero to save every hamburger-munching moron in the world but not be able to save the woman he loves. Is it hard to walk through a shopping mall knowing that those fat idiots will never know what you did for them? What you sacrificed for them? Being a hero sure isn't what it's cracked up to be. Of course, I can't claim to know what it's like to die in a guillotine, but I would imagine Lieutenant Gant died with tears in her eyes and begging for her life.*'

Schofield touched his earpiece softly, enabling its microphone. 'You motherfucker,' he said softly.

'Ah-ha, he speaks,' the Lord of Anarchy said. 'A word of advice, Captain: be careful with your new French friends. Ms Champion is a most efficient killer. I can't imagine she will forget her orders, even in the unlikely event that you manage to overcome me. But then, Ms Champion—you can hear me, too, can't you?—are you still haunted by the face of your dead husband and those of your former colleagues? The ones Hannah Fatah killed after you brought her in? Captain Schofield, look closely at your new friend: she was once a hero like you and she is now an example of what heroes become after they lose everything.

'The clock is ticking, Captain, and in less than a minute, the real battle will begin. A battle between you and me. Me, with my army of brigands and bandits. You, with your team of damaged souls. Like your loyal Gunnery Sergeant, Ms Newman, the famous Mother. Did you know that her marriage is in tatters because of you? That her husband has threatened to leave her because of her concern for you? That she herself has been seeing a Marine Corps therapist?'

Schofield didn't know that.

He looked to Mother—and she turned away.

'Or that Corporal Puzo is not to be trusted. That the Marine Corps knows that he is more loyal to a criminal family in New Jersey than he is to the Corps? That he has been slipping sidearms and assault weapons to that Mob family for over a year? And yet still the Corps was happy to assign him to you.'

Schofield glanced at Mario. The Italian-American lance corporal was peering up at the terminal, blank-faced, oblivious to the fact that he was being talked about.

'Ask yourself, is he a man you can trust in the battle to come? Or what about young Corporal Billy Thompson? Were you aware that he was dropped from active service not because of some minor deafness in the left ear but because of a diagnosed mental disorder? A disorder found at the extreme end of the attention-deficit spectrum, a disorder that makes him highly susceptible to suggestion, peer pressure, that makes him easily led.'

The cable car rose ever higher.

Twenty seconds to go.

The two troop trucks kept coming.

Schofield checked his wristguard. On it, Bertie's view panned back to the main tower, to the helipad with the Ospreys on it—

The Ospreys were no longer there.

Schofield's heart stopped. The Ospreys must be in the air.

His eyes darted upward, searching the sky. His slow-moving cable car would be an easy target for a pair of gunships—

A savage hail of bullets slammed into the cable car, hitting it all over, shattering its windows and an Osprey shoomed by overhead.

Everyone ducked below the windowline, except for Baba, who hefted his Kord and loosed a violent burst in reply. The big gun's supersized rounds razed the entire left side of the Osprey, sending one of its gunners sailing down into the water far below. The Osprey's left-side engine was also hit and it flared with flames and started belching thick black smoke and peeled away as the second V-22 took its place and unleashed its own rain of gunfire, but at that moment the bullet-riddled and now windowless cable car entered the upper terminal, mercifully moving out of the line of fire.

Crouched below the windowline, Schofield's face was now set, his jaw clenched. The Lord of Anarchy had got inside his head but he wasn't going to let it show.

'You talk a good game, asshole,' he said softly into his Army of Thieves mike, 'and you're obviously connected to be able to get all this information. But now *I* know something about you: you wouldn't be saying all this if you weren't worried about me. And guess what?'

The cable car lurched to a halt beside the terminal's platform.

'I just landed on your island.'

Schofield clicked off the earpiece/mike and raced out of the cable car, guns up, setting foot for the first time on Dragon Island.

THIRD PHASE
INSIDE HELL

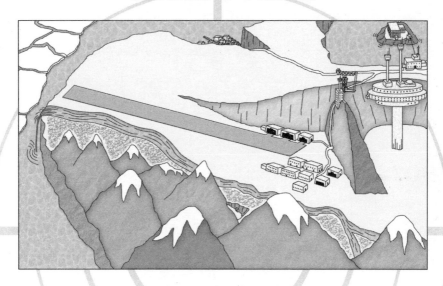

DRAGON ISLAND
4 APRIL, 1042 HOURS
T-MINUS 18 MINUTES TO DEADLINE

Into the jaws of Death,
Into the mouth of Hell
Rode the six hundred.

—Alfred, Lord Tennyson
The Charge of the Light Brigade

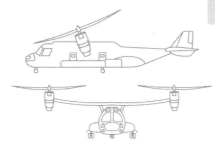

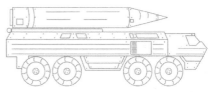

THIRD PHASE

THE PENTAGON
3 APRIL, 2142 HOURS
1042 HOURS (4 APRIL) AT DRAGON

At the same time as Shane Schofield was arriving at Dragon Island under fire and under pressure, David Fairfax was walking quickly down a deserted corridor in the Pentagon's B-Ring.

In the Pentagon, status radiates outwards: if you're in A-Ring, the centremost ring, you're somebody. D-Ring, on the other hand, is a backwater. If you're in D-Ring, you're nobody, an Oompa-Loompa in the vast military system. A mathematician by training, Dave worked in the DIA's Cipher and Cryptanalysis Department in a basement office buried deep beneath C-Ring, so he existed somewhere in the middle of it all.

Today, Fairfax wore his standard work attire: jeans, Converse sneakers, Zanerobe T-shirt plus a new red 'WristStrong' rubber bracelet of which he was immensely proud.

Even by the standards of the computer boffins who worked at the Pentagon, it was casual attire, but for Dave Fairfax it was tolerated, especially by the Marine Corps colonels who always nodded respectfully as they passed him by.

They knew that in his service file there was a most unusual notation: a classified Navy Cross that Fairfax had been awarded for acts of extraordinary bravery while engaged in action against an enemy of the United States. During the 'Majestic-12 Incident'—which Schofield had roped Fairfax into—Fairfax had found himself, shaking with nerves and wearing a helmet two sizes too

big for him, leading a team of twelve United States Marines into battle on a heavily guarded ballistic missile–equipped supertanker anchored off the west coast of America.

His actions had saved three US cities from annihilation but only a few very high-ranking people knew it. Fairfax was just pleased he could still wear jeans and sneakers to work.

It was going on 9:45 p.m. as he walked down the curving corridor of B-Ring. It was late and nearly all of the workers in this wing, mainly analysts working for the DIA, had gone home for the day.

After Schofield had asked him to look into Dragon Island and the Army of Thieves, Fairfax had discovered a few things about Dragon and not much about the Army. It had taken time; it had also required him to peek into some databases that he was technically not authorised to enter.

As far as Dragon Island was concerned, he'd found that it was mentioned several times on the JCIDD, the ultra-high security document database accessible only to the highest ranking military and intelligence officers . . . and computer jockeys like him.

Dave had a list of those documents in his hand now:

AGENCY	DOC TYPE	SUMMARY	AUTHOR	YEAR
USN	SOVIET SUB REPAIR BASES	List of Soviet Navy ballistic missile submarine repair facilities	Draper, A	1979–present
NWS	MACRO WEATHER SYSTEM ANALYSIS	Analysis of jetstream wind patterns	Corbett, L	1982
CIA	POSSIBLE LOCATIONS	Geographical options for Operation 'Dragonslayer'	Calderon, M	1984

CIA	SOVIET CHEM & BIO WEAPONS DVLPT SITES	List of known Soviet chemical and biological weapons development sites and facilities	Dockrill, W	1986
USAF	HIGH-VALUE TARGET LIST (USSR)	List of first-strike targets in the USSR in the event of a major conflict	Holman, G	1986, 1987, 1988, 1989, 1990, 1991
NRO/USAF	SATELLITE LOCATION LIST	Interagency swap of GPS data concerning Russian bases	Gaunt, K	2001 (updated 2006)
ARMY	SOVIET CHEMICAL & BIOLOGICAL WEAPONS SURVEY	List of known chemical and biological weapons kept by USSR/Russian Special Weapons Directorate	Gamble, N	1980–1991; 1992–present

Right now, Dave wanted to run that list by the person most knowledgeable about the Army of Thieves, the author of the DIA's background report on it, Marianne Retter.

Fairfax came to an office marked: B2209 RETTER, M. He could see a light under the door and raised his fist to knock—

—just as the door opened and an attractive woman in her mid-thirties appeared before him, wriggling into an overcoat.

She stopped short. 'Hi there . . . ?'

'Hi,' Fairfax said awkwardly. 'I'm Dave Fairfax, Cipher and Cryptanalysis.' He pointed dumbly at his security badge. 'You're Marianne Retter?'

'Yeah, and I'm kinda in a hurry.'

'I just have a few quick questions for you.'

'Can you talk as you walk?'
'Sure.'

Marianne Retter was a fast walker. Dave struggled to keep up with her as she strode toward the Pentagon's River Entrance.

'I want to ask you about a background report you wrote recently about a terrorist group called the Army of Thieves,' Dave said.

Retter glanced at him as she walked. 'I've been monitoring their activities for a couple of months now, but until today, nobody of note seemed to care too much. But *today*, well, now everybody wants to know about the Army of Thieves—right now, I've been summoned to the Situation Room at the White House.' She shrugged. 'I predicted that they were gonna do something and they musta done it.'

'You *don't* know what they've done?' Dave asked.

'Nope. Do you?'

'No, but I know someone who's close to it and that it's ongoing.'

Retter stopped so suddenly that Dave tripped as he stopped, too.

Her hazel eyes bored into his. 'It's *ongoing* and you know *where* it's happening?'

'Yes.'

'So where is it?'

Fairfax blinked. This was a classic exchange between intelligence folk: he had to show the strength of his knowledge, but not *too much* of it, at least not till he knew this woman better.

'My source is a Marine in the Arctic Circle. He's been ordered to take them down.'

Marianne Retter gave nothing away. She eyed Fairfax up and down, her brain visibly deciding whether or not she should share information with him.

'Fairfax. You were the analyst who stormed that fake supertanker with the nukes a while back with a team of Marines.'

'That's supposed to be classified . . .'

'I gather intelligence for a living,' Retter said with a cute smile. 'Plus, I also did a tour in ICI.'

ICI stood for Internal Counter Intelligence. The DIA's version of internal affairs.

'That's me,' Fairfax said.

'You have a Navy Cross,' Retter said. 'And they don't give those away for nothing.'

Fairfax said, 'All I know about you is that you're currently America's leading expert on the Army of Thieves and that your surname is a palindrome.'

'Palindrome,' Retter said. 'Most of the guys I meet these days can't even spell *palindrome* let alone use it in a sentence. You're smart, and kinda quirky, and that Navy Cross of yours means you aren't a total schmuck, so listen up: I'm on my way to the White House to brief the President on everything I know about the Army of Thieves. There's a car waiting for me right now at the River Entrance. Between here and there, I'll tell you what I know if you tell me what you know. Deal?'

'Deal.'

'That background report I wrote covers most of what we know about the Army of Thieves,' Retter said as she and Dave rode the elevator down to the River Entrance lobby. 'They basically came out of nowhere last year. They look like a gang of anarchists, but I don't know if I buy that; I couldn't say it in my report because it's far too speculative, but I think that's what they're *supposed* to look like. Taken individually, all of their acts look opportunistic, wild, random and violent. But taken together—with a pinch of imagina-tion—all those acts could be interpreted as, well, calculated and co-ordinated.'

'Try me,' Dave said. 'I like imagination.'

Retter counted each point off on her fingers:

'One, they break out a hundred assholes from a Chilean military prison in Valparaiso, including a dozen officers, most of whom *we* trained at the School of the Americas, a delightful Spanish-language training facility at Fort Benning. If you were a murderous Latin

American dictator in the 1980s and 90s, you sent your henchmen to the School of the Americas.'

'Really?' Fairfax said.

'Oh, yeah. Then they steal a Russian freighter *filled* with every assault rifle and RPG known to man; a Greek plane packed with hard currency; and then—and this is fucking ballsy—they steal those Ospreys and Cobras from a Marine base in Afghanistan. They break out another hundred fundamentalist foot soldiers from a UN prison in the Sudan, and hey presto, they've suddenly got a fully armed assault force the size of a small battalion, complete with officers and infantry, ready to do some serious damage.

'What I can't figure out, though,' Retter shook her head, 'are the last two incidents. The apartment bomb in Moscow on February 2 and the torture of the old Secretary of Defense here in D.C. last month.'

'What's wrong with them?' Dave asked as the elevator doors opened. They walked out into the lobby.

'They just don't . . . fit,' Retter said. 'All those men, weapons and gunships that the Army acquired over six months and *that*'s what they do? Blow up a building and cut up an old man? It doesn't make sense. They could do so much more. As I said, it just doesn't *fit*.

'The way I see it, this Army was building up to something much bigger. They were preparing for a fucking siege and those two incidents were small-time. Sure, the Moscow one got a lot of press, but still, they didn't have to break out two hundred men to blow up an apartment building in Moscow, did they?'

'When you put it that way, no,' Dave said. She was certainly direct, he thought, but her conclusions were sound.

'Maybe the Moscow explosion was designed to occupy the world's attention while the Army did something else,' he suggested. 'Perhaps both it and the SecDef incident were distractions to make us look the other way while they were preparing for today's activities up in the Arctic.'

Retter looked at him as she walked. 'That's a definite possibility.'

Dave said, 'Okay. I don't know nearly as much as you do, but I think what little I know can help you. My Marine up in the Arctic wanted me to look up both the Army of Thieves and some old Soviet Arctic base called Dragon Island. Maybe that's the siege you were looking for.'

'Dragon Island . . .' Retter said. 'Never heard of it.'

'It was built in 1985,' Dave said. 'Looks like it was a big Soviet experimental-weapons facility. In its heyday, it was a first-strike target. Just about every branch of our military, from the Air Force to the CIA, kept an eye on it.'

They came to the River Entrance.

Two unmarked Lincolns with flashing police lights mounted on their dashboards were waiting in the turnaround.

'This your first VIP trip to the White House?' Dave asked as he pushed open the door.

'My first with POTUS himself.'

'I got a VIP pick-up during that supertanker thing,' Dave said. 'Fast ride. No stopping for traffic lights. Certainly makes you feel important. My Marine escorts told me that whenever you get a VIP pick-up, look for four things about the car, the four things that make it a vehicle that the police will never stop: special DoD licence plates that start with a Z, an all-access ID tag affixed to the inside of the windshield, runflat tyres and, lastly, alloy wheels. If you get into a high-speed pursuit, you want some heavy-duty rims on your car.'

'What is it with boys and cars?' Retter said. 'When someone's on their way to brief the President, I don't think they look too closely at the car they're travelling in.'

Two burly men in suits waited by the Lincolns. Both were bald which only seemed to accentuate their sizeable frames. As Dave and Marianne approached the cars, one of the men stepped forward. 'Marianne Retter? Dwight Thornton, Special Transit.'

He held up his ID.

She held up hers.

Thornton nodded and opened the rear door of the first car for her.

Retter stopped and turned to Dave. 'It was nice meeting you, Mr Fairfax. Maybe we can meet again under less urgent circumstances.'

'I hope so—' Dave cut himself off. 'Those aren't alloy wheels,' he said, eyeing the first car's wheels. It was the same with the second car—it had the right plates and ID tags and even runflat tyres, but inside those tyres, it just had standard rims.

Dave turned to see two more big men materialise from the darkness behind them, subtly blocking the way back to the River Entrance.

'These men aren't here to take you to the White House,' he whispered. 'They're here to kidnap you.'

Retter glanced from Dave to the man who'd said his name was Thornton.

And, just slightly, ever so slightly, his eyes flickered. 'Is there a problem, ma'am?'

'You see it now?' Dave asked.

'Yep,' Retter said.

'Run.'

They broke into a run, dashing suddenly right, heading for the entrance to the Metro system twenty metres away.

The two men by the cars took off after them. So did the two blocking the way back into the Pentagon, all four drawing silenced Glock pistols as they did so.

Fairfax and Retter bolted down the stairs to the subway station, hurdling the turnstiles and arriving on the platform just as a train pulled to a halt and opened its doors.

They dived into it, melding in with the members of the evening commuter crowd, just as the train's doors shut and it moved off, a moment before their pursuers arrived on the platform, flushed and out of breath, their pistols now concealed beneath their coats and their faces furious at the fact that their quarry had got away.

No sooner had the cable car stopped beside the platform of the upper terminal on Dragon Island than Schofield was racing out of it at full speed.

He joined Bertie in the doorway, arriving there in time to see the two enemy trucks skid to simultaneous halts twenty yards away. The main tower soared skyward before him. With its white exterior, it looked futuristic, imposing and impenetrable.

'Bertie, cover us,' he said. 'Hold this doorway for as long as you still have bullets.'

'*Yes, Captain Schofield.*'

Army of Thieves troops began pouring out of the two trucks. Bertie started firing at them and they dived for cover.

As the little robot held the main doorway, Schofield led the others westward, toward the garage Ivanov had said was on that side. Schofield threw open a door to reveal a darkened garage with two small trucks parked inside it. The first was a medium-sized fuel truck with a rusty cylindrical aluminium gasoline tank on its back. A steel rung-ladder ran up the back of the tank and along the length of its upper side. The second truck, parked behind the tanker, was a compact cement mixer with a rotatable barrel mounted on its back.

Schofield pointed at the tanker as he moved. 'Mother, Baba. Onto the tanker. Mother, start her up. Everyone else, when we

drive out of here and get their attention, go as fast as you can to your assigned positions.'

The others—Champion, Ivanov, the Kid, Mario, Zack and Emma—all nodded at him in reply.

Schofield gave them a look. 'If this doesn't work, Mother, Baba and I won't get out of it alive. Then it'll be up to the Kid and Mario. Good luck. I'll either see you all later or see you on the other side.'

Behind him, the engine of the tanker truck came alive.

'Captain.' Baba was peering at a gauge on the side of the tanker truck. 'This tank still has fuel in it. Given the plan, it might be wise to empty it. It'll make it lighter.'

'Do it.'

Baba turned a spigot on the back of the truck's cylindrical tank. Diesel fuel started pouring out of it, splashing to the ground.

Schofield then climbed into the driver's seat, while Mother and Baba clambered up the steel rung-ladder on top of the truck's tank, weapons ready.

'Open the door,' Schofield said.

Ivanov hit a switch and the garage's roller door slid upward. Daylight flooded into the garage.

Schofield gunned the truck and it roared outside, into battle.

As Schofield's tanker truck sped out of the garage, Zack turned to check on Bertie back in the terminal's doorway.

He saw the little robot firing out through the open door, saw enemy rounds ping harmlessly off his flanks.

'Come on, Zack.' Emma pulled him away. 'We have to get into position. Bertie'll be okay.'

Just as she said those words, however, a rocket-propelled grenade hit the doorway in which Bertie stood.

A fireball erupted all around the little robot, consuming him, and a split second later Bertie came flying out of it, hurled backwards through the air at alarming speed.

Bertie sailed back across the terminal and slammed into the

opposite wall—a few feet from the gaping aperture through which the cable car had entered the terminal; a sweeping view of the northern bay and the islets lay beyond that aperture, as well as a three-hundred-foot sheer drop.

Bertie lay on his side, looking dazed and confused, if a robot could look that way. His fat rubber tyres spun but got no traction.

Zack shouted, 'No!' but then Bertie righted himself, rolling back up onto his tyres and seemed okay—

—just as the first Army of Thieves man, moving low and fast, entered the terminal with another RPG on his shoulder, crouched and fired it at Bertie.

This time the robot stood no chance.

The RPG lanced across the space toward him and detonated.

This blast sent Bertie sailing *out through* the aperture in the northern wall of the terminal into nothing but air.

With a squealing whistle, Bertie disappeared from Zack's view and fell a full three hundred feet down the face of the cliff before disappearing into the freezing waters of the bay with a tiny splash, his part in this battle now well and truly over.

The sudden emergence of Schofield's tanker truck from the garage attached to the western side of the terminal caught the other Army of Thieves troops assailing the terminal's main entrance by surprise.

The tanker truck, with Mother and Baba crouched on top of it and a gushing trail of diesel spilling out behind it, thundered out of the garage and sped toward the circular chasm containing the main tower.

The Army men raised their guns, but Mother and Baba sprayed them with a deadly burst and half of them fell. The others took cover—and so didn't see some of Schofield's other people scamper out of the garage on foot.

It didn't matter. The tanker truck had seized the Army men's attention completely.

Chiefly, this was because its path was very unusual.

For it wasn't heading toward either of the two crane-bridges that granted access across the moat to the tower.

No.

It was speeding in a dead-straight line—not on any road, but over open ground—a line that ran directly from the cable car terminal to the tower, a line that would end at the sharp concrete edge of the moat.

'What the hell are they doing?' one of the Army men breathed.

The Lord of Anarchy was watching the speeding tanker truck from his command centre on the tower.

'What the hell is he doing?' he said.

The tanker truck picked up speed as it rushed toward the edge of the moat.

It was only twenty metres from the moat and still accelerating when the remaining Osprey thundered by overhead, cannons blazing.

Sizzling rounds strafed the ground all around the speeding truck, raking the dirt behind it, *igniting* the leaking trail of diesel fuel there.

The line of diesel fuel burst to life, erupting as an elongated wall of flames behind the speeding truck!

Schofield saw it in his side mirror. 'As if this wasn't crazy enough,' he muttered as he kept driving toward the edge of the moat. 'Mother! Baba! You ready?'

'Ready up front!' Mother called back.

'Ready at rear!' Baba shouted.

'Please God, this better work . . .' Schofield whispered before he floored it completely and the tanker truck rushed toward the edge of the moat and flew off it into empty, open air.

Wheels spinning, the tanker truck shot off the outer edge of the circular chasm and soared out into space; a small concrete gutter on the rim of the moat kicked its nose upward as it did so.

As the truck's tyres left the ground, Baba fired both of his Magneteux's two grappling hooks *back at* the concrete rim of the moat. With loud twin *thunks!* the two drill bit–tipped hooks plunged deep into the concrete and held. Their cables—unspooling rapidly—stretched back to Baba on the truck and he quickly looped the Magneteux's launcher under the tanker truck's steel ladder.

At the same time, crouched at the forward end of the truck's roof, Mother waited. Waited . . . waited . . . and waited . . . for the truck's flight to get them as far out into the void as possible. Then, as the truck's nose dropped, she fired the two hooks from the Magneteux that she held—Champion's—only Mother fired her pair of hooks at the disc-shaped tower *in front of* the flying truck.

Her French-made grappling hooks soared out into the air, trailing their cables, and slammed into the thick concrete flank of the disc, just above the windows of the disc's middle level. Then, just as Baba had done, Mother looped her launcher around the steel rung-ladder that ran along the top of the truck's tank and held on as tightly as she could, waiting for the jolt.

When it came, it was stomach-dropping.

The truck, sailing out through the air, came to a sudden, lurching, swinging halt.

The combined effect of the two co-ordinated launchings was remarkable: the truck didn't fall into the great moat.

Instead, as it began to drop in its natural arc, the four cables—two

in front, two at the rear—went taut, and like a rope bridge hanging across a mountain gorge, the truck now hung suspended from the four cables *out in the middle of the chasm!*

It looked totally bizarre.

A one-and-a-half-ton fuel truck hanging in the middle of the void, like a fly caught in a spider's web, suspended by the four cables between the outer rim of the moat and the colossal tower, hanging a dizzying two hundred feet above the concrete base of the moat, with the tiny figures of Baba and Mother on its back and . . .

. . . without missing a beat, Shane Schofield emerged from the cab of the truck and, moving fast, attached Champion's motorised ascender to one of the cables stretching up to the disc-shaped tower.

The ascender whizzed him up the cable at tremendous speed, and in a few seconds he arrived at the windows of the second level of the disc—where with his spare hand he raised his Desert Eagle pistol and blasted the windows to shit.

They shattered and he used the momentum of the motorised ascender to swing in through them.

And suddenly he was inside.

He checked his watch.

10:57.

Three minutes to go.

He dashed into the tower.

In an attempt to cut off access to the tower structure, the Lord of Anarchy had raised his two crane-bridges—but now, as Schofield had hoped, that order would work against him.

Now the bulk of the Lord's men would not be able to get across onto the tower until those bridges were lowered back into place again; for most of his Army was on the outer rim of the moat in a conventional defensive deployment.

Lowering the two bridges would take time—maybe a minute—

and that meant sixty precious seconds that Schofield could use to get past the much smaller force of Army men on the tower itself, and get to the shorter spire and the lab inside it containing the spheres.

He sprinted as fast as he could.

The interior of the disc-shaped tower was like a 1980s office: beige carpet and brown faux-wood desks, but unlike the other areas of the island Schofield had seen, it was clean and well kept. It was also empty, a ghost town.

Schofield raced through it, firing his Desert Eagle left and right as he did so, not at any enemy troops but at the surveillance cameras he saw mounted near the ceiling. They exploded in sprays of sparks as he rushed by.

He dashed past abandoned desks and workbenches before he came to an elevator situated—he guessed—directly underneath the shorter spire. He crouched by the elevator doors and lay something on the floor beside them, flicking switches.

Time check.

10:59 became 11:00.

The spheres were ready for use.

He was now officially operating on borrowed time.

Gripping his Desert Eagle in one hand, he drew his MP-7 with the other. Then he hit the call button and raised both guns.

The Lord of Anarchy stared at the tanker truck hanging from the four cables, bridging the moat.

'Now that's inventive,' he said.

Beside him, Typhon was less controlled. He yelled into a radio: 'Tower Team! We have an intruder in the building and he's coming toward you! He's going for the spheres! Get out of there and take the spheres with you!'

A surprised voice replied: '*Sir, the spheres only just reached operating temperature a few seconds ago. We're opening the reheater unit now and it'll take at least a couple of min—*'

Typhon scowled. 'Then tell your guards to cover the elevator. I'm sending reinforcements.'

He turned to a small six-man Army team stationed inside the command centre. 'Get to that tower now!'

As Typhon raged, the Lord of Anarchy called up a CCTV screen that displayed the interior of the elevator that serviced the shorter spire's lab.

On that screen, in silent black-and-white, he saw the elevator's doors open and saw Shane Schofield enter it. Then he saw Schofield aim his MP-7 directly up at him and fire.

The image cut to hash.

The laboratory at the summit of the shorter spire was a circular space with windows facing every direction. It had a commanding view of Dragon Island, blocked only by the grey concrete column of the taller spire that stood a short way to the east. In the lab's centre was a compact structure that contained a kitchen, a toilet, a closet, a little bunkroom with two cots and the elevator: the only point of access to the lab.

Inside the lab were two Army of Thieves technicians—men who had been selected for this task because of their engineering backgrounds—and the Russian scientist who had allowed the Army of Thieves onto Dragon Island, Igor Kotsky.

Kotsky was a big lump of a man, overweight and pear-shaped, with a hunched, stooping stance, combed-over thinning hair and venal eyes. He often perspired greatly, as he did now.

The three men stood before a large incubating chamber. The chamber housed the six uranium spheres and had just completed its twelve-hour priming cycle.

With the techs was a small guard team of three Army troops. These men were regular Army of Thieves men who had thought

guarding the lab was an easy assignment. They'd spent the last few hours lounging around, smoking.

Now, at Typhon's command, they leapt to their feet and aimed their guns at the elevator as it arrived with an ominous *ping!*

In the tower's command centre, the Lord of Anarchy gazed at Shane Schofield's military record. It appeared on a screen beside a CCTV image of the men gathered in the sphere lab, waiting tensely.

The Lord of Anarchy spoke to the picture of Schofield on the screen: 'Captain. Even if you get the spheres, how will you get them off this tower, let alone off this island?'

In the shorter spire's lab, the elevator doors opened.

The waiting Army guards opened fire. The walls of the little elevator were shredded with bullet holes, a wave of fire that no human being could possibly survive.

They stopped firing.

The smoke cleared. The elevator was empty.

There was no-one in it—

Then a floor hatch in the elevator popped open and Shane Schofield emerged from it, MP-7 firing.

The three guards fell and within seconds Schofield was standing in the doorway of the elevator with the dead men at his feet and his guns pointed at the horrified figures of Igor Kotsky and the two Army of Thieves technicians.

'Step away from the priming unit,' he commanded.

Schofield hurried to the incubating chamber, holstering one of his guns. It opened with a hiss and he beheld the six gleaming spheres, sitting in two neat rows of three. They were deep maroon in colour, the colour of blood, with gleaming polished sides; and they really were small, the size of golf balls.

They looked perfect. Perfect and potent.

Schofield didn't care for that. He just started grabbing them and stuffing them into three small purpose-built Samsonite cases sitting nearby; cases that the two Army of Thieves technicians had themselves been about to place the spheres into. The cases were specially designed to carry two spheres each in snug velvet-lined recesses.

Schofield clipped two of the small cases to his weapons belt and carried the third in his spare hand.

He looked at Kotsky and the terrified technicians as he raised a small handheld remote.

'You might want to hold on to something.' He thumbed the switch on the remote.

There was movement all around the tower now.

The two crane-bridges that gave access to it touched down and Army men hurried across them in large numbers, racing toward the shorter spire.

One Osprey banked around the mighty tower, sweeping in toward the tanker truck that hung suspended across the moat, while the other one—the one Baba had hammered with his Kord earlier—had limped back to the helipad where it now sat, its wounded engine still belching thick black smoke.

On the tanker truck, Mother and Baba were making their own hurried escape plans.

Baba attached his ascender to one of the cables leading back up to the outer rim just as gunfire from the Osprey started raining down on them.

'Do you think your man made it?' he shouted to Mother.

She glanced up at the shorter spire. 'We'll find out in a couple of seconds! Go!'

Gripping the ascender, Baba whizzed up the cable, while Mother opened fire on the Osprey with her G36.

Admirable as her effort was, her bullets sparked ineffectually off the gunship and the big Osprey swooped into a hover right in front of her, its cannons rotating into position to return fire.

Mother's jaw dropped. 'Oh, fuck me, I'm dead . . .'

Baba reached the rim of the massive moat, where Zack and Emma met him, driving the second truck from the garage, the cement mixer. Veronique Champion arrived a few seconds later, skidding to a halt in a newly-stolen jeep.

They saw the Osprey facing off against Mother down below them.

Baba said, 'Do not watch. This will not be pretty.'

Without warning there came a mighty explosion.

At first it was difficult to tell where it had come from. It hadn't come from the summit of the shorter spire. Nor had it come from anywhere near the Osprey and Mother, the crane-bridges or the rim of the moat.

No, it erupted—a sudden powerful blast—from the *base* of the short spire, from the point where it rose from the disc-shaped body of the tower, from the point where Schofield had planted a wad of PET plastic explosive beside the elevator earlier.

The fireball sent a cloud of concrete blasting out from the northern side of the spire's base, carving a great chunk out of it . . .

. . . causing *the whole short spire* to topple like a slow-falling tree.

It was an absolutely incredible sight.

The spire—with the glass-enclosed lab at its summit—seemed to fall in horrifying slow motion, tipping from its destroyed base, falling northward.

It finished its terrible fall with a bone-crunching, earth-shuddering impact, a colossal crash of concrete on concrete: the spire's long slender body crashing down against the flat upper surface of the main disc.

The spire's glass-enclosed lab smashed down against the very edge of the disc—not far from the cables holding up Mother's tanker truck—every single one of its windows shattering with the mighty impact, sending glass spraying out in every direction.

A cloud of concrete dust flew up around the whole mess and when it cleared, the spire could be seen lying on its side, looking like a dead snake: its once straight and vertical column now broken and horizontal; its glass lab was wrecked beyond repair, resting crumpled on its side.

As he gazed out at it through the dome of his command centre, the Lord of Anarchy found it hard to believe that anyone inside the lab could have survived such a fall.

Unless they had been prepared for it, he thought.

And there he was.

A tiny figure came hurrying out of the shattered side-turned lab, carrying some small black cases, and running for the cables holding up the tanker truck.

Shane Schofield.

Of course, it hadn't exactly been easy for Schofield.

After depositing the six spheres into the three little Samsonite cases, Schofield had raced round to the *southern* side of the lab, to the elevator's doors. On the way, he'd grabbed the two mattresses from the cots in the bunkroom and laid them vertically against the elevator's door. Then he'd pressed himself against the mattresses and held on tight as the cluster of PET explosives he'd placed at the base of the spire went off.

The explosives detonated and the spire fell northward and he rode it all the way down on its southern side. When the lab hit the disc and every window in it shattered as one, Schofield's body slammed against the two mattresses which lay flat against the now-horizontal elevator door, softening the blow, sort of. Shards of glass had rained down all over his body but luckily nothing bigger than that hit him.

He was shaken and dazed, which was more than the two techs could say. They'd been crushed under the falling lab. The fate of the Russian traitor, Kotsky, had been worse. He'd been flung by the force of the fall clear out of the lab and Schofield had last seen him flying through the windows, screaming all the way to his death at the bottom of the concrete moat.

Schofield didn't care.

He couldn't stop. He had to keep moving.

He hustled out of the destroyed lab, covered in concrete dust, heading out into the Arctic chill once again.

As for Mother, the spectacular fall of the shorter spire had saved her life.

It came crashing down just above the hovering Osprey, causing the Osprey's pilot, Hammerhead, to take evasive action and bank away from it. Concrete dust billowed out all around Mother and the Osprey, obscuring the air around both of them for a few precious moments.

Mother heard the Osprey's rotors roaring as it banked around her. It would be back in a few seconds—

A sudden thump made her turn and she saw Scarecrow standing on the roof beside her, with two Samsonite cases clipped to his gun-belt and a third in his hand. He'd just whizzed down a cable from the edge of the disc using his ascender as a descender.

Mother yelled, 'Christ, this is the craziest snatch'n'grab I've ever seen!'

'It's desperation over style, Mother.' He hurried over to the tail end of the suspended tanker truck, to the two cables that rose up from it to the rim of the massive moat.

'But did you have to destroy everything?' she shouted.

'I haven't destroyed *everything* yet. Hurry up, this isn't over! This way!'

He reached for the Magneteux at the rear of the truck.

'But you didn't bring the ascender!' Mother shouted.

'We're not using the ascender this time! Hold on to me!'

Mother knew not to argue. She just looped her arms around Scarecrow's waist and held tight. As she did so, the dust cloud parted and she saw the Osprey materialise behind them, hovering in the void, guns poised.

'Scarecrow!'

'Just hang on!' With his other hand, Schofield grabbed the French Magneteux that Baba had looped around the rung-ladder of the truck and—

—pressed the unspool switch.

The French Maghook unspooled a fraction and the result was instantaneous: it came free of the tanker's rear ladder.

Which meant the tanker truck was now no longer suspended between the rim and the tower, and Schofield and Mother swooped away from the tower, swinging *northward* on that Magneteux's cables—while the tanker truck, still dangling from the other pair of cables attached to the main tower, swung *southward*, where it smashed into the right wing of the hovering Osprey!

The Osprey rocked in mid-air, like a boxer recoiling from a punch. The swinging truck had shattered its starboard wing, and it dropped out of the sky, wheeling out of control before crashing down against the bottom of the moat, where it exploded spectacularly.

For their part, Schofield and Mother's swing ended with them slamming at speed into the outer wall of the concrete moat. They bounced off the wall, but somehow managed to hang on.

Schofield then reeled in the Magneteux and they whizzed up the side of the chasm, where Zack, Emma, Champion and Baba awaited them in the cement mixer and the stolen jeep.

'Alors!' Baba exclaimed. 'This is my kind of mission!'

'Holy fucking shit, dude,' Zack said, surveying the destruction all around them.

Schofield didn't stop moving. He climbed into the back of the jeep with Baba and threw the Magneteux to Champion, saying: 'Drive! We're not out of this yet. We have to get to the coast and throw these spheres into the sea.'

'Why can't we just throw them into the bay from the cable car terminal?' Zack asked.

'Water's too shallow there. They could find the spheres easily with divers. We need to dispose of them in deeper water—'

Gunfire cut him off.

Four troop trucks filled with Army men were hurtling toward them from both crane-bridges.

Schofield yelled, 'Mother! Take the wheel of that cement mixer and lead the way! You're our blocker! Get us to the airstrip! Hopefully Ivanov has found us a plane!'

They sped off the mark, heading for the runway.

Dragon Island's airstrip was situated on a plain of lower ground to the west of the main complex.

Getting to it meant driving down a steep bitumen road that swept around the north-western side of the crater containing the main tower.

With four Army trucks behind them, Schofield's two vehicles—the cement mixer and the jeep—raced down the steep slope at reckless speed. Gunmen on the various towers they passed fired at them, their bullets strafing the road all around the fleeing vehicles. A couple of the mixer's tyres were hit and punctured and it began to slip and slide wildly as it sped down the narrow cliff-side road.

A couple of Army of Thieves men in jeeps tried to cut them off by parking their jeeps across the roadway, but Mother drove the cement mixer like a rampaging NFL blocker: she just ploughed straight through the roadblocks, the heavy cement mixer smashing the jeeps out of the way, sending one flying off the edge of the road and crunching the other one against the rocky cliff on the inner side.

More Army of Thieves troops joined the chase. Five, six, then seven trucks containing armed men now pursued the two fleeing vehicles. Schofield and Baba fired back at them while Champion drove hard. Bullets flew every which way. A stray one hit a jerry can full of gasoline mounted on the back of the jeep and it caught fire.

Schofield ducked away from the spraying blaze and keyed his radio. 'Dr Ivanov! We've got the spheres but we also have an entire army on our tail! Our vehicles have taken heavy fire and I don't think they'll make it to the coast! Do you have a plane ready?'

'*Yes, Captain!*' Ivanov's voice replied. '*I am in an Antonov-12 in the first hangar.*'

'Get it out onto the runway!' Schofield yelled.

'*What about the Strelas? They shot me down the last time I tried to flee this place!*'

'We don't need to get away! We just need to get to the end of the runway so we can dispose of these spheres and you *did* manage to do that last time! And if we're in a plane, we might just escape, too!'

'*Okay . . .*'

Thirty seconds later, the shot-up cement mixer and the flaming jeep swept off the steep cliff-side road and sped out onto the runway, just as a huge prop-driven cargo plane rumbled out of the first hangar there, propellers whirring.

It was an Antonov An-12, a medium-sized transport plane capable of carrying 20,000 kilograms of payload in its rear hold, either vehicles or ninety fully armed troops. Born in the 1950s, it was a dependable warhorse, the Soviet equivalent of the C-130 Hercules, and it was known for its distinctive nose: the An-12 had a glass nose cone from which a spotter could look out.

The big plane pivoted, pointing its glass nose westward. The long black runway stretched away from it for a mile in that direction, ending at some high cliffs. Running along the runway's left-hand side, parallel to it, was a wide free-flowing river fed by snowmelt from the mountains of Dragon Island. It, too, ended at the high cliffs, tipping over them in a spectacular three-hundred-foot waterfall.

Also at the end of the runway, however, speeding full tilt in an effort to get into a position to fire on the plane before it lifted off, were the same two Strela-1 amphibious anti-aircraft vehicles that had shot down Ivanov's Beriev six hours earlier. And they still had their deadly surface-to-air missile pods on their backs.

As the Antonov came fully around, its rear ramp lowered and Schofield's two vehicles sped into it, Mother's cement mixer first and then the flaming jeep.

'We're in!' Schofield yelled into his radio as he kicked the flaming jerry can off the back of his jeep. 'Go! Go!'

The plane immediately powered up, its four turboprops blurring ever faster and with a shrill whine, it slowly began to accelerate.

Schofield leapt out of the jeep and raced forward, up a short flight of steel stairs and into the cockpit, where he found Ivanov at the controls.

The Antonov picked up speed—

The two Strelas skidded to twin halts at the end of the runway—

All we have to do is get in the air, Schofield thought. *Even if they hit us and we crash, I can send these spheres to the bottom of the ocean, never to be found again.*

The Antonov was halfway down the runway and almost at take-off speed—

The Strelas' missile pods began to lower, taking aim—

'We're gonna make it . . .' Schofield breathed, an instant before he caught sight of a lone Army of Thieves trooper off to the right of the runway, holding a Predator RPG launcher on his shoulder. The lone man fired the Predator and Schofield watched in horror as it zeroed in on the accelerating Antonov and disappeared under its nose.

A colossal thump shook the Antonov.

A second later, the entire cockpit lurched downward, throwing Schofield and Ivanov forward in their seats, and an ear-piercing shriek of metal-on-bitumen assailed their ears as the big plane's nose slammed down against the runway and started grinding terribly, kicking up sparks.

The Antonov's forward wheels had been completely destroyed by the Predator and all of its forward momentum was lost. It peeled away to the left, turning sideways as it slowed, fatally wounded, a little more than halfway down the runway.

And as the big plane ground to a halt, Schofield saw *all* of the Army of Thieves' pursuit vehicles converge on it like hyenas closing in on a wounded water buffalo: the two Strelas from in front, the many trucks from behind.

His mission—a desperate and daring snatch-and-grab—was over.

In record time, he had island-hopped across bear-infested islets, penetrated Dragon Island by cable car, got across the moat, taken the lab at the summit of the spire, grabbed the spheres, got out of there by toppling the spire *while he was in it* and now he had failed within sight of the coast.

He bowed his head. 'Fuck.'

The situation on the runway quickly became a stand-off.

The Army of Thieves' vehicles formed a wide circle around the halted Antonov, which was parked at right angles across the snow-rimmed runway, its forward landing gear destroyed, its nose pointed down.

'Cover the entrances!' Mother called as she and Baba quickly took up positions in the Antonov's two side doors, while Schofield rushed to its still-open rear ramp and hit 'CLOSE'.

The ramp didn't close.

A bullet from the surrounding Army of Thieves force smacked off a steel strut beside his head and he ducked back inside.

'The ramp won't close!' he called.

Ivanov came back from the cockpit. 'Many things in my country do not work. Ramps, doors. This is a very old plane.'

Suddenly, a familiar voice came alive in Schofield's ear: '*Oh, Captain, so close!*' the Lord of Anarchy said. '*My, that was exciting! You came so very close to getting away. I bet you can see the ocean from where you are.*'

'Screw you.'

The Lord of Anarchy chuckled.

'I still have your spheres,' Schofield said.

'*You do indeed, but that doesn't concern me greatly. You see, while it may look like one, this is not a stand-off. It is a woefully one-sided siege. Because you are isolated with a finite amount of ammunition, while my men surrounding you have all the time and firepower in the world. No, Captain, now it is time for me to screw you. Mako, send in three berserkers, as an example to Captain Schofield.*'

Schofield frowned. *What*—

Suddenly three men burst forth from the surrounding force: they were Africans, each holding two AK-47s and firing madly as they ran toward the stricken Antonov. They had the same excessive facial piercings that the two suicidal maniacs in the Bear Lab had had.

Their bullets hammered the plane. Some rounds whizzed in through the open rear ramp and Schofield had to dive behind the jeep parked there before he could raise his MP-7 and return fire. Mother and Champion joined him, blasting away with their guns.

The first mad runner convulsed as he ran, but he must have been juiced up on ganja weed or some kind of hyper-stimulant because he took at least ten hits to his body before he finally stopped moving forward; then Mother shot him in the face and his whole head popped in a spray of red and he flopped to the ground, still.

But the other two berserkers kept coming, their rain of gunfire undisturbed.

Schofield, Champion and Mother fired and fired, using an inordinate amount of ammo to bring them down. The second madman fell, then finally so did the third—he skidded hard onto his face at the base of the ramp, having almost made it inside the plane.

Silence.

Gunsmoke.

Schofield was completely fucking shocked. If the Lord of Anarchy had more of these crazy suicide runners, then it was only a matter of—

'*Captain, I'm sure that by now the mathematics of your situation is becoming clear: if I keep sending in my berserkers, eventually you will run out of bullets. And I have many such men, who will gladly run to their deaths for me, if only to use up your ammunition. Mako, three more, please.*'

There came another battle cry and three more crazed, multi-pierced runners came charging across the open runway firing wildly at the Antonov and Schofield and his team were forced to cut them down, too.

Mother shook her head. 'This is fucking nuts! It's like a shooting gallery where the targets fire at you! Who the hell does suicide runs like this?'

'And how does their leader get them to do it?' Champion asked.

'Addictive drugs, conditioning, torture, I don't know,' Schofield said.

'However the fuck he does it,' Mother said, 'I can't keep this up much longer. I'm down to my last clip.'

Baba said grimly, 'Me, too.'

Schofield bit his lip in thought. There was only one way this could end—and that was very ugly. Out of ammo and with nowhere to go, they'd be at the mercy of the Army of Thieves. Death at their hands would not be quick and—if only for a fleeting instant—Schofield actually considered putting a bullet through each of his people's brains; it might be the most humane thing to do in this—

'How are you feeling in there, Captain? Getting low on ammo now, aren't you? Feeling desperate? Thinking of cutting a deal? I mean, how will you feel when your people are completely defenceless and my men storm that plane? My men, I fear, are not the kind of boys you bring home to meet mother. They are very zealous in their fanaticism, sometimes a little overzealous. They truly are the children of anarchy and I am their lord and master.

'Of course, you could nobly kill your own people: line them up, smile kindly and then put a bullet in each of their heads, so that their deaths are quick. Let me assure you that such a death will be better than the one I will provide them.'

Champion shot a look at Schofield as she heard this, too.

Schofield returned her worried glance. It also didn't escape his notice that the Lord of Anarchy had practically read his mind. He looked around himself for options, but there were none. They were screwed.

'Captain, go to the cockpit of your plane. Switch on the video communication screen.'

Schofield went into the cockpit where he found a video screen attached to the instrument panel—a modern addition to an old plane—and flicked it on. It was like a laptop screen, with a small camera on its upper rim.

The Lord of Anarchy's face appeared on the screen, smiling.

'*Hello, Captain. I thought we should do this face to face.*'

'Do what?'

'*I want to show you something. This.*'

On the screen, the Lord of Anarchy lifted something up into the frame.

Schofield's blood turned to ice.

It was a red uranium sphere, another one, a seventh one. The Lord of Anarchy held it between his thumb and forefinger.

Schofield's face fell. The Lord of Anarchy saw this and he grinned malevolently.

'*You see, Captain. I don't need your spheres at all.*'

Schofield's mind was racing, trying to put all this into some kind of order, and suddenly it all made sense: that extra sphere had come from the emergency bunker Ivanov had mentioned before, the one buried deep beneath the main tower, the bunker that the Russian traitor, Kotsky, *couldn't* know about . . . but which the Lord of Anarchy evidently did know of.

On the screen, the Lord seemed to peer intently at Schofield, trying to read his reaction to this.

'*It occurs to me, Captain, that you and I are very much alike. We will do anything to achieve our goals. You will risk your life to save the world, while I will do the same to destroy it. We are both passionate about what we desire. It's just that we each desire the opposite of what the other does. Which is why I will take so much pleasure in letting you see this. I will see the world go up in flames. You will see your own failure.*'

With those words, the Lord of Anarchy stepped away from his camera . . .

. . . to reveal that he was not inside his command centre anymore but rather *outside*, standing in front of a sixteen-wheeled missile launcher: a classic snub-nosed semi-trailer-sized 'transporter

erector launcher' that bore a single Russian SS-23 intermediate-range ballistic missile on its back.

The Lord of Anarchy handed his red uranium sphere to a pair of subordinates who placed it into an insertion capsule which was then slotted inside a waiting warhead. The warhead was attached to the missile and the missile was slowly aimed skyward.

Schofield could only watch helplessly as all this happened. There was nothing he could do—

Wait.

He keyed his own radio: 'Kid? Mario? You anywhere near the missile battery yet?'

The Kid's voice came in. '*We just arrived at the bridge leading to it, as ordered. But that bridge is guarded like Fort Knox. They got men all over it. We can't get to the battery. Why?*'

'Because they're already there and they're about to launch,' Schofield said sadly. 'They have an extra sphere and they're going to fire it right now.'

He bowed his head.

Now there really was nothing he could do but watch the end of the world.

'*Oh, Captain,*' the Lord of Anarchy said suddenly in his ear, '*keep an eye out for berserkers.*'

A sudden spray of bullets pummelled the outside of the Antonov. Down in the hold, Baba and Mother fired back, cutting down another three berserkers.

Champion came alongside Schofield in the cockpit, stared at the screen. 'SS-23,' she said. 'Medium-range ballistic missile, capable of striking a target perhaps 250 to 300 miles away. The Soviets claimed they discontinued building them under the INF Treaty of 1987.'

They could see at least four more transporter erector launchers parked behind the one on the screen, each with an SS-23 on its back.

'Looks like they ended up here,' Schofield said. 'This island is the graveyard of the Cold War.'

The missile's slow rise stopped.

It was vertical.

Ready for launch.

Ready to ignite the atmosphere and there was not a damn thing Schofield could do about it.

The Lord of Anarchy turned to the camera. '*Witness your failure, Captain. Witness the end of the world as we know it. Launch the missile.*'

A switch was thrown and the SS-23's thrusters burst to life, spewing flames and a billowing cloud of smoke. It rose into the air.

Schofield looked away from the screen and up into the southern sky.

Lancing up into the atmosphere, a tail of thick smoke extending out behind it, was the missile carrying the uranium sphere.

It rose rapidly and in a few moments it was a tiny speck high above the southern horizon, a speck that in a few seconds would change the face of the planet.

Schofield stared at it helplessly as the Lord of Anarchy said in his ear, '*Detonate.*'

A blinding flash lit up the southern sky.

What followed was a sight the likes of which neither Schofield nor Champion had ever seen in their lives.

A dazzling, incandescent, white-hot body of air expanded laterally from the point where they had last seen the SS-23 missile. The blast flame expanded with shocking speed, at an exponential rate. And in a single, horrifying instant, the entire sky to the south of Dragon Island went from pale blue to flaming yellow-white.

The atmosphere had been ignited.

The Earth was on fire.

THE WHITE HOUSE SITUATION ROOM
WASHINGTON, D.C.
SAME TIME

In the Situation Room, an Army tech manning a satellite console turned sharply.

'Sir!' he called to the Army general in the Crisis Response Team, 'I have a missile launch from Dragon Island!'

The President strode over and saw a real-time overhead satellite image of Dragon Island and the Arctic Ocean surrounding it.

'They're igniting the gas cloud,' DIA deputy director Gordon said. 'Our efforts have failed . . .'

No sooner had she said this than, on the monitor, a section of the ocean to the south of Dragon Island flared suddenly with blazing white light.

The tech said, 'Missile detonation detected . . .'

The President stared at the image, horrorstruck. 'God help us.'

FOURTH PHASE
INCINERATION

DRAGON ISLAND
4 APRIL, 1120 HOURS
T-PLUS 20 MINUTES AFTER DEADLINE

Every Harlot was a Virgin once.

—William Blake
'To the Accuser who is the God of this World'

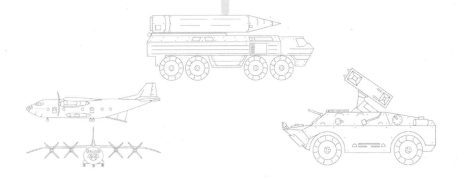

If someone were looking down on the Earth from space, Schofield figured, they would have seen a blinding flash from up near the North Pole, and then they would have seen the extending yellow-white inferno advancing around the globe in a spiral of fiery devastation.

At that thought, Schofield whipped up his wristguard and flicked on its satellite imagery, bringing up his own real-time overhead view of Dragon Island and the Arctic Circle.

On the black-and-white screen, he saw the atmospheric inferno.

It reached outward from Dragon Island like the claw of some mythical creature, reaching southward before curving eastward, following the course of the jetstream.

Schofield felt ill. He was literally watching the end of the—

And then suddenly the expanding wave of devastation and destruction stopped.

Abruptly and without warning, as if it had come up against an invisible wall in the atmosphere.

Schofield frowned. 'What the hell . . . ?'

By his crude reckoning, the roaring atmospheric fire had only gone about six hundred miles before it hit the invisible wall and stopped.

Then he heard the Lord of Anarchy's voice, only it wasn't directed at him: '*What the fuck just happened!*'

Another voice: '*Sir! We just caught an intruder in the gasworks under the main vents! He cut the TEB pipes feeding the vents! By the look of the oxidisation around the valves, he must've cut them two hours ago! We've been pumping useless gas up into the sky for the last two hours!*'

'*What? Who is he?*' the Lord of Anarchy demanded.

'*Says his name is Barker. Navy SEAL. Musta slipped past us when we killed the others in the submarine dock.*'

Schofield's mind raced.

It was Ira Barker.

Ironbark.

Somehow, Ironbark had survived the clusterfuck in the submarine dock and while Schofield and his people had been islet-hopping to Dragon Island and stealing the spheres, Ironbark had penetrated Dragon, got to the gas vents and, unknown to anyone, sabotaged them.

The SS-23 missile had detonated its quasi-nuclear payload but thanks to Ironbark, the gas cloud close to Dragon was *not* combustible, so the missile had ignited nothing—or perhaps it had just ignited some leftover trace particles of the gas, causing the 'smaller' incandescent flash in the sky that he had just seen.

At that exact moment something *else* became clear to Schofield . . . at exactly the same time as it appeared to dawn on the Lord of Anarchy.

'Thanks to Ironbark's sabotage,' Schofield said aloud, 'the sky for a few hundred miles is safe, but the atmosphere over the *rest* of the northern hemisphere is still contaminated with combustible gas. This isn't over. If the Army of Thieves gets another sphere, they'll fire the next missile *past* the safe zone and detonate it inside the infused atmosphere. Which means . . .'

He snapped to look outside.

'. . . they need our spheres again. They're not going to toy with us anymore. They're going to attack this plane with overwhelming force *right now.*'

No sooner had he said it than twelve berserkers burst forth from the ring of vehicles surrounding the plane, AK-47s blazing, followed by the rest of the Army force on the runway.

The Army of Thieves had just declared war on Shane Schofield and his plane.

Mother and Baba started firing straight away and managed to take down the first rank of berserkers, but this attack was far larger than any of the previous ones. It was simply too big to repel.

'We have ten seconds to do something!' Champion said urgently to Schofield.

Beside them, Ivanov said, 'But we have nowhere to go—'

'There's always *somewhere* to go . . .' Schofield said, his eyes searching as the sound of gunfire increased.

His gaze landed on the broad river right in front of their plane, the one that flowed parallel to the runway, ending at the high western cliffs of Dragon Island in a mighty waterfall.

'Why not?' he said as he reached past Ivanov and jammed forward on all four of the Antonov's throttles and—just as the next rank of berserkers reached it—the big cargo plane suddenly lunged forward, engines surging, tyres squealing, its destroyed forward landing gear shrieking as it scraped across the runway.

The plane shot forward *and charged straight off the side of the runway* and down a short embankment, rumbling toward the river.

Back in the hold, both Mother and Baba were thrown off their feet by the abrupt surge of power and the ensuing plunge down the embankment.

As she scrabbled for a handhold, Mother called, 'Scarecrow! What are you doing!'

'Keeping us alive!'

The Antonov picked up speed, bouncing wildly as it rumbled down the embankment and then—suddenly, crazily—shot off the

edge of the riverbank and plunged nose-first into the fast-flowing waters of the river!

The Antonov sent up a massive splash as its belly hit the water. Like most planes it was designed for a water landing, and even with its rear ramp open, it immediately began to float, bobbing like a child's bath toy.

Then, a few seconds after the great splash settled, the plane began to move, slowly at first, then more quickly. It pivoted on the surface of the river so that now it travelled forward, nose-first, carried downstream by the steady current toward the powerful waterfall that tumbled over the cliffs only six hundred metres away.

In the right-side doorway of the plane, Mother keyed her radio: 'Remind me how this course of action helps us, boss?'

'*They need our spheres,*' Schofield's voice replied in her earpiece. '*We get to the waterfall and hurl them into the ocean.*'

'And what're the bad guys gonna do about that?'

The answer to her question came a second later: the two Strela amphibious anti-aircraft vehicles came speeding along the airstrip, racing parallel to the floating Antonov before they veered off the runway, sped down the embankment, and without any loss of speed, leapt off the riverbank and plunged into the water alongside the free-floating plane. Their propellers kicked in and the two amphibious cars started moving in toward the Antonov!

'Oh, this is just a new level of crazy,' Mother breathed as she turned and, to her great surprise, found herself looking into the bloodshot eyes of a berserker rushing at her from the rear of the hold, brandishing a knife!

The crazy bastard was gunless—as the Antonov had accelerated off the runway, he and four other berserkers had been close enough to dive onto its rear ramp, some with their AK-47s, some without. This guy had discarded his AK as he'd leapt for the ramp, which was why he now rushed at Mother with a serrated knife and a cry of rage.

Mother parried his knife-hand away, but the madman tumbled into her, throwing her off balance, and he headbutted her hard and she fell backwards, toppling out through the open side doorway—she had to release her G-36 to clutch the doorframe and suddenly she was dangling out the door of the Antonov, dazed and reeling, just above the waves of the river, holding on with one hand.

Her attacker lunged forward, intent on pushing her out, just as Mother swung herself up, drawing her thigh-holstered Beretta M9, and jammed it into the berserker's mouth and fired.

The man's head exploded, spraying blood and brains, and he dropped, headless, to the floor while Mother hauled herself back inside.

On the other side of the hold, Baba spun to see Mother get attacked by her berserker—a split second before the walls all around him were hammered with impact sparks: two more berserkers were rushing down his side of the hold, firing their AK-47s as they skirted the jeep and the cement mixer to get to him. Baba fired back with his Kord.

Beside him, Zack and Emma cowered behind the cab of the cement mixer. Bullets whizzed past their faces, impacted against the walls above their heads.

Baba pushed Zack and Emma up onto the cement mixer's running board. 'Get inside!' he yelled.

Zack and Emma didn't argue. As Baba covered them, they clambered into the cement mixer's cab, disappearing inside it just as its tub was hit all over by a burst of machine-gun fire, but the tub's thick walls held and saved their lives.

As for Baba, he kept firing at the two berserkers, his Kord booming loudly. While clearly crazy, these berserkers weren't totally mindless: in fact, they were cunning little bastards. They mocked him, popping up and firing from behind the jeep, while cackling with high-pitched laughter. It was like doing battle with a pair of demented jesters.

'Merde!' Baba growled as one of the berserkers leapt onto

the rear seat of the jeep and levelled his AK-47 at him, but Baba adjusted his aim and fired his Kord at one of the rear wheels of the jeep, blasting the handbrake clamp to pieces and the car lurched suddenly, released, and rolled quickly backwards *out the open rear ramp of the Antonov, with the berserker on it!*

The jeep vanished out the back of the floating plane, dropping into the water rear-first with a great splash and Baba was facing one less enemy.

While all this was happening in the hold, Schofield peered out through the cockpit's starboard-side windows. Beside him, Champion and Ivanov were still coming to grips with their unusual predicament.

Schofield saw the two amphibious Strelas enter the water to his right, saw them powering alongside the floating Antonov. Disturbingly, he saw one man on each Strela heft an RPG-7 rocket-propelled grenade launcher onto his shoulder . . .

'This is about to get very bad. Here, take this.' He handed Champion one of the three small Samsonite cases containing the spheres. 'When we get to the cliffs, throw it as far as you can out to sea.'

'If we get that far—' she began to say just as all the forward cockpit windows shattered under heavy gunfire from an unknown direction.

Champion ducked instinctively but then—*whump! whump!*—the boots of the last two berserkers who had boarded the Antonov thumped down onto the bonnet of the plane.

Schofield quickly realised what had happened: after somehow boarding the plane, these two had climbed *up and over* the top of it to take the cockpit.

'Out! Now!' he yelled, pushing Champion back through the cockpit door and pulling Ivanov from his flight seat a nanosecond before the whole cockpit was raked with gunfire.

The cockpit's walls and seats were ripped to shreds.

Unfortunately, so too was Dr Vasily Ivanov.

The Russian scientist had moved a second too late and, still being pulled by Schofield, he was torn apart by the vicious storm of bullets. He exploded all over with bloody wounds and Schofield dived out the door an instant before the storm could sweep over him, too. In a distant corner of his mind, Scarecrow felt a pang of sadness for the Russian scientist: his help had been invaluable but he wouldn't be seeing his children and grandchildren in Odessa again.

With bullets sizzling all around them, Schofield and Champion came tumbling out of the cockpit into the rear hold.

One round took a chunk out of Schofield's left shoulder, while another plunged into Champion's lower back, emerging from her stomach in a gout of blood.

She yelled in pain, doubled over and stumbled.

Schofield caught her as he quickly took in the scene in the hold: the cement mixer; Baba beside it, near the open port-side door, firing at the last nimble berserker, who was peeking around the mixer's tub; various cables, folded seats and netting; the open rear ramp with daylight and the river beyond it, and lastly, Mother, crouched by the starboard-side door—

—through which an RPG suddenly rocketed in from outside, shooming low over her head before slamming into the cement mixer and exploding!

The cement mixer was thrown through the air . . . straight at Baba.

Baba had nowhere to go—and no time at all to get out of the way. The flying cement mixer cut across Schofield's view of the big Frenchman and with a deafening crash, smashed into the steel wall where moments before, he had been standing.

'Jesus Christ . . .' Schofield breathed.

He and Champion struggled to stay on their feet as the plane rocked with the explosion, when a second RPG fired from the other Strela hit one of the turboprop engines on the Antonov's right wing and that engine burst apart.

The plane lurched dramatically.

Having lost the weight of one engine on its right side, it tilted sharply to the left, and now with its balance seriously disturbed, water started rushing in through the open rear ramp. It quickly rose to a foot in depth.

'They're trying to sink us before we reach the waterfall!' Schofield called, gripping a handrail as the hold lurched wildly.

The wounded Champion, however, had not been able to find a handhold.

The plane's dramatic tilt threw her completely off the steps at the fore end of the hold. She landed awkwardly and lost her grip on the Samsonite case in her hand. It went tumbling away into the foot-deep water . . .

. . . where it splashed to a halt right in front of the nimble berserker who had been harrying Baba.

The berserker saw it, immediately recognised its importance, and scooped it up.

Then, right on cue, as if this whole situation wasn't already outrageous enough, an amphibious Strela came *roaring* in through the rear opening, kicking up a bow wave as it deliberately ran aground in the shallow water now covering the floor of the hold.

With Mother cut off by the Strela, Baba gone and Schofield too far away, the nimble berserker hopped, skipped and jumped his way down the semi-flooded hold and leapt onto the Strela's bow-deck, yelling to its driver words to the effect of 'We have them! Go!'

The driver didn't waste any time. The Strela's engines whined as it reversed out of the hold, dropping back into the swirling waters of the river, about to get away when—

Roooaaaar!

Schofield heard it before he saw it.

Heard the roar of the cement mixer's engine firing up before he saw the big truck, with its heavy mixing tub on its back, reverse— at speed—toward the rear of the semi-flooded hold.

The truck, driven by Zack, carved through the knee-deep water and went flying out the rear opening, where it crunched down *onto* the bow of the retreating Strela. Such was the weight of the cement mixer that its rear bumper drove *right into* the Strela's driver's compartment, horrifically denting it, crushing the hapless driver and gunner inside.

It had been a last-ditch ploy by Zack: he'd seen the berserker grab the case and done all he could do to stop his escape.

But it wasn't over yet.

For it was then that the bizarre cement-mixer-embedded-in-the-Strela hybrid began to float away from the plane!

It separated from the plane quickly—a few feet suddenly became twenty, and it drifted southward across the river's surface, heading for the bank opposite the runway.

But it still had a bad guy aboard it: the berserker who had leapt onto the Strela with the sphere case. He started firing crazily at the cab of the cement mixer that had thwarted his triumphant escape.

The cement-mixing tub prevented him from getting a clear shot but his angry rounds still managed to impact all around Zack and Emma in the cab. They ducked their heads as glass showered over them.

Zack risked a glance in the rear-view mirror and saw their nimble attacker coming toward the cab, gun raised, a second before the mirror itself exploded under the crazed man's gunfire.

Zack and Emma ducked away from the mirror's exploding shards but when they looked up again, it was to see the berserker standing in the cab's doorway, the sphere case in one hand, his AK-47 in the other, levelled at their faces.

He cackled crazily. 'Bye-bye, birdies!' he squealed with glee as he pulled the trigger.

The berserker's head snapped grotesquely backward, hit in the nose by a single bullet from Mother, appearing from the other side of the cement mixer, her M9 pistol aimed across the cabin.

Unseen by anyone, after Zack had reversed his cement mixer into the Strela, she'd dived after it and caught hold of the cement mixer's side-rail.

The berserker swayed for a moment, just long enough for Emma to reach out and grab his Samsonite case before he fell off the running board and disappeared into the fast-flowing river.

'Thanks, Mother—!' Zack called, but he was cut off by a jarring jolt as their cement-mixer-Strela hybrid ran aground against an outcropping of boulders on the south bank of the river.

They were ashore.

Mother looked westward, in the direction of the waterfall: it was barely a hundred metres away—

—when suddenly her view was blocked by the second Strela, bursting up and out of the river ahead of her, wheels turning, surging out of the water onto the shore.

'Fuck me,' Mother said.

She glanced over at the Antonov—it was now almost at the waterfall.

'Scarecrow!' she said into her radio. 'I got Zack and Emma and one sphere case, but we're cut off from the cliffs!'

'*I'm up to my neck in bad guys here, Mother*,' came the reply. '*I'm afraid you're on your own this time*—'

The signal cut off.

Mother pursed her lips.

'Shit. Shit. Shit. Come on, kids, if we can't get to the cliffs, we gotta find another way to dispose of these spheres before those bastards catch us.'

They leapt off their shipwrecked cement mixer and dashed across the shore, heading south into the rugged mountainous interior of Dragon Island.

Schofield was still stuck on the Antonov, rushing toward the water-fall with two Samsonite cases—four spheres—still to get rid of.

Things had got completely out of control.

The waterfall was fast approaching. Mother was gone, along with Zack and Emma. Baba had been flattened against the wall by the cement mixer. Champion was slumped on the floor at his feet, on the edge of consciousness. He'd been shot and he still had two berserkers up in the cockpit about to—

The cockpit door flew open. The two berserkers came rushing out of it, their gunfire raking the hold.

But their fire went high, and just as the berserkers caught sight of Schofield at the base of the steps beneath them and re-aimed their weapons, the entire plane suddenly tipped precariously forward, *outrageously* forward—

The plane had reached the waterfall.

And was going over.

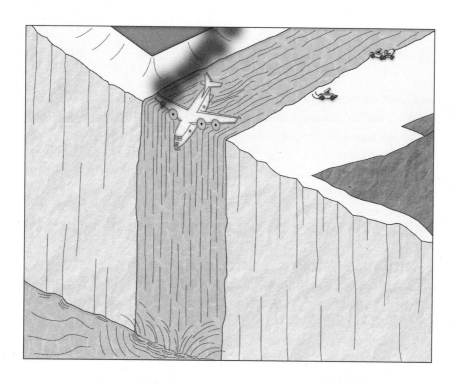

THE ANTONOV AND THE WATERFALL

But then abruptly the Antonov lurched to a shuddering stop.

With an ear-piercing shriek of metal on rock, the big plane came to an unexpected halt right on the lip of the waterfall!

It was an incredible sight: the big cargo plane, with its right wing belching fire and smoke, perched on the edge of the mighty Arctic waterfall, its nose tilted dizzyingly downward, its outstretched wings hanging low over the surging waves of the river, waves that rushed past it before launching themselves out into the void and falling three hundred feet into the ocean far below.

On the nearby runway, the pursuing force of Army of Thieves vehicles skidded to a halt while on the opposite bank, one could see the two Strelas: Mother's still with the cement mixer embedded in its bow, the other guarding the cliffs.

Everyone inside the plane was thrown forward by the sudden lurch.

Gripping Champion, Schofield was hurled forward and slammed against the wall, while the two berserkers—milliseconds away from killing him—were both flung by the inertia back into the down-turned cockpit.

It took Schofield a second to figure out what had happened.

The landing gear.

The Antonov's rear landing wheels must have caught on the lip of the waterfall and were now preventing the plane from going over.

This wasn't how I planned this at all, Schofield's mind screamed. *We were supposed to get across the river, then I'd get to the cliffs where I would throw the spheres into the sea. Now I'm hanging off the edge of a waterfall in a plane with two insane attackers who in about two seconds are going to try and kill me again.*

His searching eyes found the side door, only eight feet above and behind him. Did he have time to clamber up there and toss the spheres out—

Movement in the cockpit. The berserkers had regathered themselves. They'd be coming in seconds.

'Fuck it,' he said aloud, aiming his pistol through the cockpit doorway.

Only it wasn't aimed at either of the berserkers.

It was aimed at the landing gear retractor lever that hung from the ceiling above the pilot's seat.

Blam!

He fired and a spark pinged off the landing gear lever and the lever swung forward.

The result was instantaneous.

With its landing gear retracted, the plane went over the waterfall.

If the sight of the Antonov perched on the lip of the waterfall was incredible, the sight of it falling down the face of the waterfall was just astonishing.

It fell nose-first in an almost perfect swan dive, falling at exactly the same speed as the water falling around it, and for a moment, one might have been convinced it would swoop upward at the last second and soar to safety. But that didn't happen.

The Antonov hit the churning whitewater at the base of the mighty waterfall with a great splash.

The plane's glass nose shot underwater, its pointed tip penetrating the surface like an Olympic diver, shooting downward in a rush of bubbles.

It was only the wings of the plane—or more specifically, the engines on them—that brought it to a halt: a bone-jarring, deadly halt. The plane's cockpit had travelled about twenty feet under the surface when the wing-mounted engines hit the surface and the plane's downward journey stopped instantly.

The experience of the two berserkers in the cockpit was utterly unique: as the plane hit the ocean's surface, seawater rushed up at them through the shattered forward windows, a great foaming rush of it; but their downward inertia took them the other way and they were flung with terrible force down *into* the surging water.

In the hold behind them, Schofield sat with his back to the plane's steel forward wall, flat against a flight seat, with the groaning Champion gripped tightly in his arms.

After firing into the landing gear lever, he had leapt into the seat and quickly buckled the seatbelt.

The shuddering impact of the plane against the ocean's surface jolted him sharply, but the seat absorbed much of the shock and the belt held him tight. Champion was almost shaken from his grip, but somehow he managed to hold her.

But it wasn't over yet.

The worst was still to come, for the Antonov around him was now vertical, bobbing in the water.

Then, with horrifying speed, it began to sink.

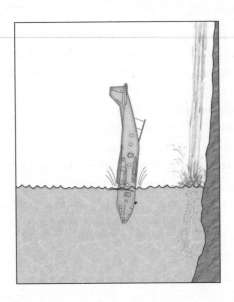

Water rushed up into the Antonov through its shattered cockpit windows, swarming up into the plane in a great roiling, bubbling rush, as if it were a sentient creature trying to swallow the plane from the inside out.

Schofield's world was turned vertical—the plane was sinking nose-first, so his forward end of the hold was now the *bottom* end—and it was filling fast. Water swelled all around him.

He scrambled to unlatch his seatbelt, still holding the barely conscious Champion.

As he did so, a mini-waterfall of seawater started flowing in through the open side door directly above him, raining down in an unbroken stream.

He looked upward, at the wide square opening at the very top of the hold: the plane's rear ramp was still open and through the opening it created, Schofield saw the grey Arctic sky.

He took in the situation quickly:

The wings of the plane were currently providing some buoyancy, slowing its descent a fraction, but the plane's fate was sealed: in a few moments, as it sank further, ocean water would come gushing en masse through that upper opening. At that point, the Antonov would become little more than a metal tube in the ocean, open at both ends, and it would sink to the bottom like a stone.

Schofield clenched his teeth. He still had a job to do: he had to dispose of the spheres.

With Champion draped over his shoulder, he sloshed over to the netting on the port side of the hold and started climbing it, heading for the open port-side door eight feet above him.

With every foot he climbed, the churning water at his boots chased him, rising higher, moving faster.

The water overtook his boots, then his knees, then his waist.

Schofield reached the door, and positioned himself to the side of its little waterfall. He looped some netting around Champion's left arm to hold her in place, which freed up both his hands, and he opened one of his small Samsonite cases to reveal its two gleaming red uranium spheres. He couldn't just throw the case out; like many such containers, it was very likely buoyant.

He grabbed one of the spheres—it was small and heavy, a deep polished maroon—and tossed it out the doorway. It fell away into the ocean, sinking quickly.

He did the same with the second sphere. It disappeared forever, too.

Two down. Two to go.

Schofield discarded the first Samsonite case and lifted the second one.

Beside him, Champion groaned something that sounded like a warning and he turned and found himself looking at point blank range into the demented face of a berserker!

The man had come from the cockpit, having somehow survived the fall, and he came bursting across the foaming water screaming with rage, his teeth bared, his hands clawing at Schofield.

Schofield hit him with the second case.

The blow broke the berserker's nose and the crazed attacker's face sprayed blood and he went flying backwards, out into the water.

Schofield gripped the netting by the door, tensing himself for a

second attack but it didn't come because right then the wide square opening at the upper end of the hold went under the surface of the ocean and his whole world went to shit.

An unimaginable *torrent* of seawater came gushing into the hold from above.

Several thousand gallons dropped on top of Schofield, Champion and the berserker in an instant.

Schofield managed to cling to the hold's side netting, and he pressed his body over Champion's so she wasn't ripped away from it. The berserker was less fortunate: out in the centre of the hold, he was forced under by the torrent of downward-rushing seawater.

The hold filled with water in an instant and the *whole* plane now went under—the Antonov had became the hollow tube of metal that Schofield had foreseen.

The plane soared down through the underwater haze, seemingly gliding on its outstretched wings, heading for the bottom a thousand feet below.

Inside its hold, the curved walls groaned loudly as the pressure from outside increased. Long before it hit the bottom, the plane's fuselage would crumple catastrophically inwards, its ribbed metal skeleton unable to resist the pressure of the ocean.

Holding his breath, Schofield grabbed something from Champion's weapons belt: one of her compact scuba rebreathers that offered five minutes of air and jammed it in his mouth.

When he had air in his own lungs, he grabbed a second mini-rebreather and stuck it in Champion's mouth, enabling her to breathe underwater, too.

Then he set about finishing what he had to do: hovering in the now totally flooded hold, he opened the second Samsonite case and tossed its two uranium spheres out the open side door. They sank into the void, disappearing forever.

Once that was done, he reached up and untied something tethered to the hold's wall beside Champion's head.

He grabbed Champion and gripping her tightly, made to pull the ripcord on the object, only for someone to suddenly grab his boot!

It was the berserker. The fucker just wouldn't die! And now he was stopping Schofield getting out of here.

The walls groaned. The skeleton of the plane creaked.

In seconds, the whole thing would implode and this maniac was stopping them getting out!

Schofield kicked at the berserker, but couldn't get him to release his grip.

Fuck it, Schofield thought. *This might do it.*

He yanked on the ripcord of the object he'd taken from the wall.

That object was a life raft.

As soon as Schofield pulled its ripcord, it inflated and shot up out of the hold like a bullet, wrenching Schofield free of the berserker's grip and he and Champion went whipping up out of the opening at the rear end of the sinking Antonov, yanked upward by the air in the fast-inflating raft.

The raft shoomed upward, trailing bubbles, with Schofield hanging from it by one outstretched arm, gripping Champion in his spare hand.

Seconds after they blasted out of the plane, it crumpled like a tin can, surrendering to the ocean's brutal pressure and the berserker inside it was crushed to nothing. The tangled wreck kept sinking, disappearing into the haze.

Aware of the effects of rising too fast through water, Schofield and Champion exhaled all the way up, until at last, the raft broke the surface.

The waterfall and Dragon's cliffs rose behind them. Sheer and covered in snow and ice, they would be impossible to scale.

In the other direction, to the west, was an expanse of sea ice, shot through with ten-foot-deep leads.

Schofield quickly pushed Champion up into the raft—she tried as best she could to help but the wound reaching through her back

to her stomach was clearly very painful. He climbed in after her and started paddling for the shelter of the nearest lead before any of their enemies arrived at the cliffs and saw them.

Within moments, they were in the shelter of the leads, and once there, Champion spat out her mouthpiece, fell back against the bow and closed her eyes, drifting out of consciousness.

Above her, Schofield swore.

His team was in complete disarray: Ivanov was dead, Baba too; the Kid and Mario were still at large, but now totally on their own; Mother, Zack and Emma had got away with the last two spheres, but Schofield knew that the Army of Thieves would already be hunting them. And lastly there was Champion and him: she had a gut-wound—if it didn't kill her, it would at least immobilise her— while his left hand and shoulder bore bullet wounds.

He had lived to fight another day, only now—battered, bruised and wounded—he was a long, long way from the fight.

CRYSTAL CITY, VIRGINIA
3 APRIL, 2230 HOURS
1130 HOURS (4 APRIL) AT DRAGON

Dave Fairfax ushered Marianne Retter into his apartment in Crystal City and slammed the door shut behind them, breathless.

They'd come straight here by train from the Pentagon, where they had just escaped from a group of men posing as a VIP transport team. Dave's place in Crystal City was pretty close to the Pentagon, just one Metro stop and a short walk away.

'Okay, you are now officially a very important person,' Dave gasped. 'That was just brazen. A straight-out kidnapping at the Pentagon's front doors.'

'Who *were* those guys?' Marianne asked.

'Don't know,' Dave said. 'But they knew who you were and where you were going and they didn't want you to get there. We gotta hurry. If they can identify me, we can't stay here for long. But if we're gonna keep investigating this matter, I need a computer with some serious software on it . . .'

Dave unlocked a drawer and pulled his home laptop from it. He flipped the computer open, threw on an earpiece and started typing quickly.

'They didn't look foreign,' Retter said to herself, her voice analytical. 'And their accents were flawless; outfits, too. Could they have been *American*? And while brazen, sure, they made a small mistake that most people wouldn't have picked up. But it was a mistake of speed—they could fake everything else, ID tags, cars, but they had to

get to me before they could source a car with the right wheels, which means the decision to snatch me was made in a hurry—'

'Wait.' Dave held up a hand, touched his earpiece. 'I'm tapping into encrypted radio airspace around D.C.—military, intelligence and police channels—using our names as keywords. Something like this goes wrong, people start calling their superiors over cell phones and radios . . .'

Text scrolled out on his screen.

'Oh, shit . . .' Dave said.

'What?' Retter leaned forward.

Dave nodded at the text scrolling out on the screen:

TRACK V–DATA SYSTEM

ECHELON SUBSYSTEM REGION: E-4 WASHINGTON, D.C. AND
                                    SURROUNDS

FREQUENCY RANGE: 462.741–464.85 MHZ

KEYWORDS: RETTER, MARIANNE, FAIRFAX, DAVID

KEYWORDS FOUND.

FROM USER: A9 (CENTRAL INTELLIGENCE AGENCY)

VOICE 1: THE <u>RETTER</u> SNATCH AT THE PENTAGON WAS BLOWN.
           WHAT HAPPENED?

VOICE 2: SHE IDENTIFIED US AND GOT AWAY WITH SOME GUY.

VOICE 3: WE HAVE HIS NAME. <u>DAVID FAIRFAX</u>. HE'S ALSO DIA. GOT
           A HOME ADDRESS IN CRYSTAL CITY.

VOICE 1: GET THERE NOW.

Dave looked at Marianne. 'And there you have it. You almost just got kidnapped by the CIA and we have to run *right now*.'

They fled from Dave's apartment, taking his laptop with them, and dashed to a nearby mall that stayed open till midnight. There they hid in a bookstore, in the coffee shop by the magazine racks, with a good view of the entrance.

'Okay,' Dave said. 'I think it's time for some more information sharing between you and me.'

'That assumes I can trust you,' Retter said.

'Navy Cross . . .' Dave said. 'On the run, too.'

'Oh, yeah, right.'

Dave put his laptop on the table and typed as he spoke. 'Okay, me first, here's what I know: my Marine contact is up in the Arctic Circle. He said he was about to go into battle and asked me to look up two things for him: the Army of Thieves and Dragon Island, an old and very nasty ex-Soviet base up there.

'My investigations into the Army of Thieves led me to you. My investigations into Dragon Island led me to *this*, which was why I was coming to see you. This is a list of American military and intelligence organisations who have made mention of or shown some interest in Dragon Island over the last thirty years.'

Retter's eyes went wide when she saw the screen. 'That's the JCIDD. It's only accessible to the Joint Chiefs and the highest ranking—'

'Did I mention that I'm a code-cracker?'

'Oh, right.'

'Any names you recognise?' he asked.

She scanned the list on Dave's screen:

AGENCY	DOC TYPE	SUMMARY	AUTHOR	YEAR
USN	SOVIET SUB REPAIR BASES	List of Soviet Navy ballistic missile submarine repair facilities	Draper, A	1979–present
NWS	MACRO WEATHER SYSTEM ANALYSIS	Analysis of jetstream wind patterns	Corbett, L	1982

CIA	POSSIBLE LOCATIONS	Geographical options for Operation 'Dragonslayer'	Calderon, M	1984
CIA	SOVIET CHEM & BIO WEAPONS DVLPT SITES	List of known Soviet chemical and biological weapons development sites and facilities	Dockrill, W	1986
USAF	HIGH-VALUE TARGET LIST (USSR)	List of first-strike targets in the USSR in the event of a major conflict	Holman, G	1986, 1987, 1988, 1989, 1990, 1991
NRO/USAF	SATELLITE LOCATION LIST	Interagency swap of GPS data concerning Russian bases	Gaunt, K	2001 (updated 2006)
ARMY	SOVIET CHEMICAL & BIOLOGICAL WEAPONS SURVEY	List of known chemical and biological weapons kept by USSR/Russian Special Weapons Directorate	Gamble, N	1980–1991; 1992–present

Retter bit her lip as she peered at the list.

'The usual suspects,' she said, 'Army, Air Force, Navy, CIA, even the National Weather Service analysing the jetstream. But if you look closely at it, this gives you a sort of rough history of Dragon Island.'

'How so?' Dave asked.

'Well, look. It starts with Dragon coming to the US Navy's attention in 1979 as a run-of-the-mill northern repair facility for the Soviet ballistic missile fleet. Then the Weather Service found it, due to its position under the Arctic jetstream. But then it gets interesting.

'Now, you told me earlier that the weapons base on Dragon was built in 1985. Look here: in 1986, Dragon appeared immediately on a CIA list of Soviet chemical and biological weapons sites *and* the Air Force's list of high-value Soviet targets. It actually stayed on that second list until the USSR's fall in 1991, but after that, it fell off it, no longer a high-value site. The other documents look like standard crap, like the 1984 CIA report titled POSSIBLE LOCATIONS by—wait a goddamn second—by "Calderon, M".'

'What?' Dave asked. 'Who's that?'

'Calderon, M is Marius Calderon,' Retter said thoughtfully. 'No way . . . this is one of *his* schemes. Fuck me, this could be the link you're looking for, Mr Fairfax.'

'What? Why? You know this guy?'

'Do I ever. I've come across his name a few times in my research into the Army of Thieves. This could explain a lot.'

Now it was Dave who leaned forward. 'So who is he and why is he writing about Dragon Island in 1984, a year *before* the base there was even built?'

A siren wailed outside the store, and they both spun, but it was just an ambulance, speeding away. They exhaled.

'Marius Calderon,' Retter said, 'is a hotshot at the CIA, been there since 1980 when they recruited him straight out of Army Ranger training.

'His original area of expertise was China: Calderon was assigned to observe and analyse China following its program of economic reforms that had commenced in 1978. But he's served in almost every corner of the CIA since: from the Activity to the special-ops division. Importantly for our purposes, in the late 1980s, he was an instructor at the School of the Americas, that military training academy I was telling you about that the US Army ran out of Fort Benning, at which . . .'

'. . . at which several Chilean members of the Army of Thieves learnt how to be really bad dudes,' Dave said.

'Right. The only reason I found out about this Calderon guy was when I was looking into those twelve Chilean officers broken out of that prison at Valparaiso. They all attended the School of the Americas *at the time Calderon was a teacher there*. All twelve were his students.'

'No shit . . .'

'So I looked up his record,' Retter said. 'In addition to all that other stuff, Calderon has spent the bulk of his career in the Agency's Psychological Warfare division. He's an expert in, and I quote from his file: "the retrieval of mission-critical information from unwilling enemy combatants through unrestrained psychological interrogation".'

'Torture,' Dave said.

'*Psychological* torture. For the last twenty-odd years, Marius Calderon has been the CIA's foremost expert in psy-ops and non-invasive torture, and these days non-invasive torture is back in fashion. Calderon's methods are standard practice at Gitmo and other rendition sites.

'His theory is that you can get a man to *do* anything or *reveal* anything by ruthlessly attacking his mind.

'It's said that in Afghanistan in 2005, he "turned" three captured Taliban troops using subliminal methods—he stapled their eyes open and bombarded them for six days straight with videos of violence, sadism, live amputations and bestiality, while beating them relentlessly and overwhelming them with loud music and the cries of other people being tortured. Those Taliban troops were then released and sent back to their villages, where they became ticking psychological time bombs, ready to explode when Calderon gave the word. After the CIA broadcast a certain radio message, all three of them went on shooting rampages in their home villages, killing over thirty people before turning their guns on themselves.'

'Jesus.'

'Back in the early 1980s, Calderon was the wunderkind of the CIA, the boy genius. In 1983, at the age of 27, he conceived and co-ordinated the little-known *Able Archer 83* exercise—a simulation of a NATO nuclear attack on the USSR that involved the participation of *real* heads of state. The Soviets, as Calderon had predicted they would, thought it was real and readied their nuclear arsenal . . . while every American military and intelligence agency observed them closely. For the rest of the 1980s, we knew *all* the Soviets' moves before they did. Reagan loved it. He gave Calderon the Intelligence Medal for it.

'Impressed by his work on *Able Archer 83*, the CIA used Calderon for all sorts of geopolitical analyses—Russia, China, Central and South America. But most of all, they used him as a *predictor*, an analyst of enemy intent, a forecaster of how America's enemies would react in certain scenarios, just like in *Able Archer*.

'Calderon was such a good reader of people and their motivations, their emotions and their intentions, that he was often able to predict what they would do. For instance, Calderon predicted every one of Mikhail Gorbachev's internal stratagems, from his rise to General Secretary of the Politburo in 1985 to glasnost and perestroika. Anytime Reagan met Gorbachev, the President was briefed personally by Calderon beforehand. Reagan would say it was like seeing all of Gorbachev's cards before playing poker with him.'

Retter said, 'I actually found one old report that Calderon wrote about China back in 1982, with some predictions he made back then.'

Retter still had her briefcase with her, filled with the files and notes she'd been taking to the White House. She opened it, pulled out a printed document and handed it to Dave.

It was titled:

THE COMING RISE OF CHINA
AND THE ENSUING FALL OF AMERICA
ANALYSIS BY
MARIUS CALDERON
JULY 2, 1982

'Nice title,' Dave said. 'Very alarmist.'

Retter said, 'The Communist Party called China's economic reforms "Socialism with Chinese Characteristics" but we would just call it free-market capitalism with a brutal government. The reforms began in 1978 and were slow to take hold. It wasn't until the late 1990s and 2000s that China's economy became the power-house we know it to be today. But in 1982, it was still a dump, an agrarian economy with collective farms and useless state-owned industries. Nobody took China seriously back then . . . except Marius Calderon. Read some of the highlighted paragraphs and remember that Calderon wrote them *back in 1982*.'

Dave scanned the document, glancing at the paragraphs Retter had marked with highlighter. They included:

THE 21ST-CENTURY SUPERPOWER: CHINA

Make no mistake, the Communist Party's sweeping economic reforms will create a new China, a China that by the year 2010 will challenge America as the dominant player in the world's economy.

As China's economy opens and expands, its industry will devour the globe's supplies of iron ore and aluminum, and its middle class will grow wealthier. *A billion Chinese consumers* will demand TVs, cars, refrigerators, plus all the other consumer goods that Americans have taken for granted since the 1950s, our golden age.

America is in decline. We don't manufacture anything anymore. The dream years from 1945 to 1970 (when we had no industrial com-petition from the countries we defeated in the Second World War, Germany and Japan) are over. Now in the 1980s, both Germany and Japan build better cars, whitegoods and consumer electronics than we do. American blue-collar workers can't compete with cheap labour from countries like Japan and Taiwan.

But all this is nothing compared to the industrial behemoth that China will become.

It was *industrial might* that allowed the North to win the Civil War; it was *industrial might* that allowed America to prevail on two fronts in World War II. *China's industrial might* is of a scale not seen before on this planet. And its recent economic reforms are designed for one purpose and one purpose only: to rouse the sleeping dragon and awaken that industrial might.

If implemented correctly, I foresee China's economy growing at double-digit annual rates every year for much of the 1990s and 2000s—

'Jesus,' Dave said. 'This guy foresaw China's double-digit growth back in 1982.'

'Read on,' Retter said.

Dave found the next highlighted passage:

FORESEEABLE CONSEQUENCES OF THE RISE OF CHINA

The first casualty of the rise of China will be the average American's standard of living. Our dollar will become worthless alongside the Chinese yuan (which the Chinese will be reluctant to float). Americans will not be able to travel while the Chinese will grow ever richer. Large deficits will follow and our government will start borrowing money from the Chinese.

American unemployment will reach unsustainable levels as low-skilled work (especially factory and manufacturing labor) will be done by cheaper workers in China.

And with economic strength goes political strength. As China grows wealthier, it will give aid to poorer countries and ultimately develop greater global influence than the United States—

Dave looked up from the document. 'This guy was good.'

'You don't know the half of it,' Retter said. 'He goes on to predict that China will bid for and win the Olympic Games in the first

decade of the 21st century and use the Games to showcase China to the world.'

'Okay. So where is he now?' Dave asked.

Retter raised her palms. 'I asked around at both DIA and CIA, but either no-one knows or they aren't telling. He's still with the Agency. He did some deep black stuff in its special forces paramilitary unit in 2002—did you know that the Agency owns and operates three Sturgeon-class submarines for clandestine insertions? Then he did some time at US "rendition stations" in Egypt and Turkey from 2003 to 2004. As for where he's been stationed for the last year or so, and what he's been doing, no-one's saying.'

'You think Calderon is connected with the Army of Thieves?' Dave asked.

'He personally trained the twelve Chileans who were sprung from the Valparaiso prison. They know him and they know his methods; they'd be a perfect officer corps for a renegade army. And there's something else: I mentioned that Calderon worked at the CIA's rendition stations in Egypt and Turkey—nasty remote compounds where we tortured prisoners from Afghanistan and Iraq. But at the rendition centre in Egypt, the CIA helped certain African governments extract information from *their* captured enemies, and one of our customers was the rather unpleasant government of the Sudan that was later brought down.'

Dave said, 'The second breakout was of a hundred Sudanese soldiers from a UN prison in the Sudan. Wait. Are you saying that this Calderon guy, a CIA agent, *put together* the Army of Thieves? Got the officers from Chile and the infantry from the Sudan?'

'Yes. I have another theory, too, but you'll think it's nuts.'

'Try me.'

Retter hesitated. 'I can't prove it but . . . well . . .' She took a quick breath. 'The leader of the Army of Thieves is smart, bold and totally brazen, yet he always covers his face. Why would you do that if you were an anarchist? I think he does it *because he doesn't want anyone to recognise him.* He *needs* to keep his identity a secret. I think it's entirely possible that Marius Calderon, a top CIA agent, is the *leader* of the Army of Thieves.'

'But why would this Calderon guy want to create a rogue army?' Dave said.

'That, Mr Fairfax, is not the question. Calderon is old-school CIA. The real question is: why would *the CIA* want to create a rogue army?'

'Maybe asking that question is the reason why they just tried to abduct you outside the Pentagon.'

'Indeed.' Retter nodded at the screen. 'So what's *this* document, then, this one Calderon wrote about Dragon Island in 1984 called "POSSIBLE LOCATIONS: Geographical options for Operation 'Dragon-slayer'"? I haven't seen it.' She gave Dave a look. 'I didn't have the clearance. What's Operation "Dragonslayer"?'

'Let's find out.' Dave clicked on it and typed in a few very illegal passwords.

A warning screen appeared, declaring: 'THE DOCUMENT YOU ARE ABOUT TO OPEN IS LOCATION PROTECTED.'

'What's that mean?' Retter said.

'It means, once we open it, this computer and its location will be digitally tagged by the owner of the document. They'll know we opened it and they'll know where from. If we want to read this, we have to read it fast and then move. You still game?'

'I want to know. You?'

'Hell yeah,' Dave said. He clicked 'OPEN DOCUMENT'.

A new window opened. Immediately, a blinking timecoded box appeared in the top right corner of the screen, warning: 'DOCUMENT OPENING RECORDED. SENDING USER IDENTIFICATION.'

Dave ignored it. He scanned the document quickly.

It was a PDF of an old typewritten document, date-stamped August 1984 and headed:

OPERATION 'DRAGONSLAYER'
ANALYSIS AND OPERATION CONCEPT BY
MARIUS CALDERON
AUGUST 1, 1984

It was short, just three pages long.

And in the café of that bookstore in suburban Virginia, with their computer's digital signature being sent who-knew-where, Dave Fairfax and Marianne Retter read it.

When they were done, they both looked at each other in horror.

'Oh, fuck . . .' Dave breathed. 'Fuck, fuck, fuck. No wonder the CIA tried to snatch you. We are in so much trouble.'

Dave went to switch off his laptop's wi-fi link—he could keep the computer, he could just never link it to the Internet again, otherwise they could keep following him from place to place.

But he stopped himself short.

There was one more thing he needed to do.

So he did it: he sent the document he had just read off into cyberspace.

'Cut the connection, flyboy. We have to go,' Retter said.

Dave cut it and they bolted from the bookstore.

 **DRAGON ISLAND**
4 APRIL, 1135 HOURS

The Lord of Anarchy—a man known in other circles as Marius Calderon—arrived at the end of the runway, where he was met by Typhon and Big Jesus.

Surrounded by the men of the Army of Thieves, the three of them looked down at the spot where the Antonov had disappeared under the ocean's surface.

'Schofield took four of the spheres over the waterfall with him,' Typhon reported. 'But before the plane went over the waterfall, three of his people were spotted leaving the plane with a case containing two spheres—they landed on the southern side of the river but one of our Strelas blocked them from reaching the cliffs.'

'They're on foot?'

'They are now, yes.'

'And they still have the spheres?'

'So far as we can tell. I just sent Bad Willy and his team across the river in a couple of Strelas to pursue them.'

The Lord of Anarchy gazed at the river: it snaked back up into the mountainous southern half of Dragon. There was a small quarry-mine in there, some dirt roads, but otherwise few places where someone could hide.

'Hunt them down, kill them, and bring me those spheres,' he said. 'We have time but not an endless amount of it.'

'We also found this,' Big Jesus said, stepping aside as two of his

men threw a limp figure to the ground at the Lord of Anarchy's feet.

The big, bearded and soaking wet form of Baba lay before the Lord of Anarchy.

His captors couldn't know it, but when the cement mixing truck had been hurled across the hold toward him, Baba had thrown himself out the side door of the Antonov an instant before the cement mixer had slammed against the wall.

'He washed up on the shore a few minutes ago,' Big Jesus said. 'A French commando, in league with the others.'

The Lord of Anarchy stared at the slumped figure of Baba.

'This is most fortuitous,' he said. 'He will be of use to us in our hunt for his companions. We will torture him and broadcast his cries to his companions on the island. Few can tolerate the wails of a friend being tortured and as you are well aware, Big Jesus, I have forgotten more about torture than most men will ever know. Take him to the gasworks.'

Mother charged through the undergrowth at the base of the mountain, pushing ice-encrusted branches out of the way, hustling across the slope. Zack and Emma hurried along behind her, Zack carrying the compact Samsonite case with the spheres in it.

'Mother!' he called forward as he ran. 'What do we do!'

Mother was trying to figure that out.

'I'm working on it!' she said between panting breaths. 'Usually I got the Scarecrow around to think for me! He does the thinking and I do the shooting. It's not often I have to think for myself.'

She kept running, her mind whirring. She kept hearing Schofield's last words to her: '*You're on your own this time.*'

So she asked herself, *What would Scarecrow do?*

'Okay,' she said. 'First, we gotta stay off the road. They can't drive a truck through brushland. Second, we either find a way to the coast—which doesn't look likely—or we find somewhere to hide these spheres.'

'You can't hide them on land,' Zack said. 'They might be small and their radioactivity minor, but they *are* still radioactive. Even if you buried them in the dirt, they could still be found with a Geiger counter.'

Mother said, 'Then we hide *with* them, while staying as mobile as possible. If we can stay out of sight for long enough, maybe the cavalry will arrive before these bastards find us.'

Emma said, 'When we were looking at the map before, I remember seeing a quarry or a mine in this part of the island. Some kind of rare granite—'

As she said this, they crested a low rise and beheld a wide

open-cut quarry before them, its sheer, square walls carved deep into the base of a small mountain.

Sloping ramps of hardpacked earth zigzagged their way into the great pit, while a network of steel ladders provided access from ramp to ramp; long-abandoned mining trucks stood like ghostly mechanical statues at various places on the ramps, rusted solid. Two very basic buildings provided a pair of entrances to the mine system.

Mother stopped for a moment, her eyes narrowing. She whispered to herself: 'All right, you stupid grunt, *think*. What would Scarecrow do?'

And it hit her. 'I know what he'd do. Okay, lovebirds. Listen up.'

Minutes later, a pursuing Strela from the Army of Thieves pulled to a halt on the crest overlooking the quarry—just in time to see Mother, moving backward, gun up, disappear inside one of the entrances to the mine.

'They're going inside the mine,' the pursuit group's leader, the Caucasian officer known as Mako, said into his radio.

Typhon's voice came over the line. '*There are only two entrances. Secure them, then go in and kill them all.*'

'Roger that,' Mako said. 'This won't take long.'

It didn't take long.

Mako's team moved with speed and precision. They sealed off the mine and then went in hard, leapfrogging each other in a co-ordinated rolling formation.

The mine system wasn't that complicated—it was just a basic rock mine from which granite was extracted—and within a few minutes, they were fired upon from a shadowy corner.

Mother.

That stand-off didn't last long, either, maybe ten, fifteen minutes. Mother fought bravely, but she was woefully outnumbered and outgunned, and eventually, she ran dry. Mako's men steadily flanked her until she stopped firing and stood up, arms raised in surrender.

Mako's team swarmed all over her position . . .

. . . to discover that she was alone.

Zack and Emma weren't there, and neither was the all-important case.

Mother had done what Scarecrow would've done: she'd lured her pursuers into the mine and kept them occupied for as long as she could, giving Zack and Emma time to escape with the spheres.

Mother stepped out from her position, arms raised, her face illuminated by half a dozen barrel-mounted flashlights.

Mako keyed his radio: 'Sir, this is Mako. We got one of the Marines, but she was a decoy. The other two are gone and they have the case. They're somewhere else on the island.'

The Lord of Anarchy said: '*One of the Marines, you say? Is it the woman, the big one? Newman?*'

Mako jabbed Mother with his gun. 'Are you Newman?'

'Yeah.'

'Yes, it's her.'

'*Bring her to me, alive,*' the Lord of Anarchy said. '*Do not harm her. I intend to enjoy that pleasure myself.*'

Elsewhere, Zack and Emma hurried through scrub, icy branches lashing their faces, running as fast as they could, away from the quarry-mine.

They knew full well that Mother would eventually be caught—that her fake last stand was designed to give them valuable time to get away and hide—and they didn't want her sacrifice to be in vain.

Staying on the south side of the island, however, was not an option. While mountainous, it was too barren and treeless, too exposed. There was nowhere to hide. Nor was there any way to

get in touch with anyone back home—to tell them that the Army of Thieves was being prevented from effecting their plan.

That meant venturing back north into the sprawling main complex of Dragon Island—to both hide and find some communications gear, and maybe even link up with the Kid and Mario.

Zack and Emma dashed across a shallow rocky ford in the river and headed back north, toward the main complex.

A mile or so behind them, two Army of Thieves Strelas stopped on the road overlooking the quarry-mine. The tattooed men on it glared at Mother—and offered a few lewd obscenities—as she was led away by Mako and his men.

One man ambled a short distance away from the main group, where he crouched on one knee and peered at the muddy ground.

It was Bad Willy. His left ear was now bandaged, but the gauze had leaked and an ugly splotch of blood stained it.

Bad Willy gazed long and hard at the muddy ground . . .

. . . at the fresh shoeprints in it, including one kind of print that was not often found on secret Soviet bases.

Nike hiking-boot prints.

'Oh, Zacky-boy . . .' Bad Willy said. 'I told you I'd find you.'

Calling his men to follow—on foot, since it was quieter, better for hunting—Bad Willy set off after Zack and Emma.

ICE FIELD TO THE WEST OF DRAGON ISLAND
4 APRIL, 1155 HOURS

Veronique Champion woke with a start.

She coughed a few times, blinking back to her senses and then looked around: to find herself sitting in an orange inflatable life raft, moving slowly through a tranquil Arctic lead, paddled by Shane Schofield. High walls of ice rose on either side of her.

A thick waterproof field dressing was wrapped tightly around her belly and lower back, staunching the flow of blood from her gunshot wound.

'What—how did we get here?' she asked. 'The last thing I remember is . . .'

Her voice trailed off as she peered upward, in the direction of Dragon Island. She could just see the peaks of Dragon's southern mountains over the top of the lead's walls.

Schofield smiled grimly. 'You passed out. I dressed your wound and gave you a shot of AP-6.' AP-6 was a field drug developed by SEAL Team Six. It was both a painkiller and a stimulant; it dulled any pain but also jacked up a wounded soldier long enough to allow them to get to a field hospital.

'You won't be doing any somersaults or jumps,' Schofield said, 'but you'll be mobile enough. I managed to dispose of four of the spheres, but there are still two out there: Zack and Emma have them, back on the island, and Mother's with them. We're going back in now.'

'Going back? How?'

'I'm taking us through these leads toward the north of Dragon Island, to the old whaling village. I figure the cable car and gantry elevators will be more closely watched now and the submarine station is way over on the other side of the island, so the village is our only choice, the only place where we can land.'

'That'll take a while.' Champion tried to sit up in the life raft but fell back, grimacing. 'Ah . . .'

Schofield glanced at her. 'You'll live but you won't be doing any more fighting today. The bullet missed your spleen by millimetres and, luckily for you, went right through.'

Champion groaned, blinking away the pain, and lay back against the inflatable bow of the raft. It was unusually peaceful here: the air silent, the water perfectly calm and the ice walls white as snow. It was like floating among the clouds.

'I figure it'll take us about ten more minutes,' Schofield said, paddling slowly but firmly.

'Un moment, s'il vous plaît. You saved me from that sinking plane?'

'Yes.'

'Why? Why would you do this? I was sent to kill you. I even told you that when all this is over, I would have to carry out my original mission.'

Schofield stopped paddling for a moment. The boat drifted. He looked at Champion long and hard.

'I saved you because this situation is bigger than your country's vendetta against me and I think you're smart enough to know that.'

Champion returned his gaze. 'You . . . *trust* me? Why?'

'Because you didn't come to kill me just for France. You came because of your cousin. You thought he was wronged, an innocent civilian murdered by a professional soldier: me. Your premise was wrong but the motive wasn't. It shows you have a sense of justice, of right and wrong, and I figure if you have that, you're a decent person, and decent people can be reasoned with. They also deserve to be saved if it's possible and it was possible.'

Champion cast her eyes downward. She seemed to be looking deep within herself. But when she looked up again, her gaze was hard.

'You're wrong. I once had a sense of justice. I was once decent. Now I am an assassin. When this is over, wounded or not, I must carry out my orders. I must make sure you are dead.'

Schofield didn't flinch.

'But you weren't always an assassin, were you?' he said. 'Sorry, but you're not the type. You're too thoughtful. Most assassins are cold-blooded for two reasons: one, they can't empathise, and two, they're stupid and any idiot can pull a trigger and feel powerful that way. But you're neither of those things. Something happened to you.'

'You want to psychoanalyse me?'

'Got nothing else to do right now.'

'All right.' Champion lay her head back and gazed skyward, gripping her stomach. 'I shall tell you about me, but only if you tell me about you, in particular: how a Marine recovers from the execution of his girlfriend by a psychopath.'

Now it was Schofield who looked down, but only briefly. 'Okay, fine. You first.'

Champion said, 'Before I was in the Action Division, I was in the DGSE's Directorate of Intelligence. I monitored Islamic extremist groups in Algeria, Morocco and Yemen. In particular, their increasing enlistment of women. I befriended a Yemeni mother of five, named Hannah Fatah. She fed me excellent information for three years, information that prevented two attacks on Paris—one on the Eiffel Tower and another at Charles de Gaulle Airport.

'Then one day, Hannah asked to be brought in. She was pregnant again and she feared that her superiors had discovered that she was a leak. I brought her in, took her back to the DGSE field office in Marseilles. When she walked into the debriefing room, with my boss—my husband at the time—and his boss watching through a two-way mirror, she set off a small wad of Semtex that had been surgically implanted into her uterus.

'I never suspected anything—Hannah already had a scar on her stomach from the caesarean birth of her last child, and the explosive was concealed from our X-ray and cathode ray scanners by a wrapping material made of human bone, designed to appear as a foetus. She passed through four security scanners before she got into that room and killed two very senior DGSE agents, one of them my husband, and three of my other colleagues. I alone survived. She had waited three years to do it.'

Schofield was silent.

Champion said, 'My empathy for Hannah Fatah got my husband killed. My closest colleagues, too. So I decided that I would no longer live with empathy. I became cold. I transferred to Action Division, and made my first kill within a month. I've been doing it ever since.'

She paused. 'Strange. In my research on you, Scarecrow, I struggled to find a defining reason why *you* became such an efficient killer of men.'

'Your research on me?'

'When you set out to assassinate someone, it is wise to know as much as you can about them. Pressure points, loved ones, weaknesses that can be exploited.'

'Why don't you tell me about myself then,' Schofield said. 'Let's see what you know and I'll tell you how accurate it is.'

'Okay,' Champion began.

As they glided through the network of narrow leads, Champion spoke slowly:

'Shane Michael Schofield is the son of John Schofield, a successful businessman, and the grandson of Michael Schofield, a highly decorated Marine, call-sign Mustang.

'Michael Schofield's actions during World War II are legendary in the Marine Corps. Indeed, several of them are *still* classified more than sixty years later, including one fabled mission known only as BLACK WOLF HUNT. Your grandfather is revered in the Corps, a most admired man. You and he are close, and you dine together at least once a month.'

Schofield nodded. 'So far, all correct.'

'But your father—John Schofield—was *not* a Marine, and you and he were not close, all the way to his death . . .'

Champion surveyed Schofield's face as she said this. His distant look gave her the answer she was after. It was true.

'Your father was a businessman and a very good one,' she said. 'He could never match your grandfather's military accomplishments so he chose to outdo him in the acquisition of money and he became a very wealthy man.'

Schofield said nothing.

It went further than that.

His father had *hated* his grandfather, despised him, despised the respect he received everywhere he went. And even though Michael Schofield had never put any pressure on John Schofield to do anything other than what his heart desired, John had been haunted by

the long shadow cast by his legendary father. It was, sadly, a torment that found expression in other ways.

Champion said, 'Your father regularly beat both you and your mother: I found hospital records from your youth detailing several broken noses and cigarette burns on your forearms.'

Schofield said nothing. It was either the bastard beat his mother or beat him, and that was a no-brainer. His beatings had started at the age of twelve. He still bore small circular scars on his forearms from the cigarette burns.

Champion went on. 'So when you turned eighteen, you joined the Marines and there you thrived. You became a pilot in the Air Wing, where you served with distinction until you were shot down over Bosnia, where a local warlord mutilated your eyes, leaving the distinctive scars that are the origin of your call-sign.

'After your rescue, you became a regular Marine rifleman, rising quickly to Force Recon level. You commanded Force Reconnaissance Unit 16 on that mission to Antarctica which brought you into contact with my cousin. You survived that—a delicate affair involving allies at war and even American forces fighting American forces—but it displeased some in high places and you were subsequently assigned to the President's helicopter, Marine One. It was an ornamental position and thus an insult for one so skilled and experienced, but you did it anyway.

'That assignment brought you into another incident that the US has successfully hidden from the world: Colonel Caesar Russell's coup attempt. The hunting of a President within the confines of his most secret base. Your acts there won you a classified Medal of Honor.'

Champion paused.

'Shortly after that, your father died, by his own hand.'

Schofield nodded silently. The bastard had got the death he'd deserved: bitter and alone, sitting in his wood-panelled office, he'd shot himself through the mouth.

Champion said, 'Your mother had already passed away several years earlier. Yet, despite your father's awful treatment of you as a child, he left you everything in his will. Twelve million dollars. Making you, a humble United States Marine, *a very rich young man.*'

Schofield said nothing.

This was all true, but few knew it. Champion's sources were excellent. Mother knew about the money and Gant had, too. And they had both approved of what he had done next.

Champion said, 'You donated it all to the Walter Reed Army Medical Center in Washington, D.C. Every penny. An act of principle?'

'You could call it that.' Schofield shrugged.

'It was *twelve million dollars.* You wouldn't have had to work again. Do you ever regret it?'

'Not for a second. It was a cruel man's money and I didn't want it. I sent it somewhere worthwhile.'

He looked away, kept paddling. Champion gazed at him for a long moment before going on.

'And then came the Majestic-12 bounty hunt during which the missile-builder, Jonathan Killian, had your girlfriend, Elizabeth Gant, call-sign Fox, cruelly beheaded in a guillotine. This was a pivotal event in your life. You retreated from military activity for four months. Your superiors thought it had broken you. You can't imagine how surprised they were when you turned up one day and said that you were ready to get back to work. Yet what did they do with you? They made you a teacher, and then they hid you away up here in a lowly equipment-testing unit. Another insulting assignment.'

Champion waited for him to respond.

'Fox's death *did* break me,' Schofield said. 'But ultimately I . . . I figured out a way to cope.'

'How?' Champion said. 'I am genuinely curious. How did you cope? Like I did, by becoming immune to emotion?'

Schofield thought for a moment.

'No. No, I didn't do that. In those first few months after the Majestic-12 thing, the Corps sent me to a bunch of psychiatrists, top-of-the-range shrinks, all with Top Secret clearance, the best

money can buy. Hell, one of them charged a thousand bucks an hour.

'But none of them worked. I kept thinking about Fox, picturing her death. I kept thinking about what I could have done. I felt powerless. I retreated into myself.'

'So what changed?' Champion asked.

'I found a new shrink, not a psychiatrist, but a psychologist, a simple therapist. And not through the Corps. Mother found her, saw her flyer tacked to the noticeboard at her husband's office and gave it to me—Ralph's a trucker and the company he drives for was offering free therapy to its long-haul drivers because of rising divorce rates.

'Anyway, that psychologist's name was Dr Brooke Ulacco and she wasn't some old white male Ivy Leaguer. She was a mother of two boys and she worked part-time out of the basement of her townhouse in Baltimore. I started doing therapy with her.'

In his mind's eye, Schofield could see it as if it were yesterday.

Arriving at the old townhouse, with its formstone walls, being met at the door by Brooke Ulacco, a tawny-haired woman in her forties with wide hips, a gentle smile and a razor-sharp mind.

He recalled sitting in her basement office—valiantly decorated with pot plants and some framed photos, but nothing could hide the pipes and water heaters—hearing the kids playing upstairs. He even remembered once when Dr Ulacco called out: 'Kids! I've got a client down here! Keep it down, will ya!'

Schofield liked that atmosphere.

Others might have found it distracting, but to him it was normal and that made it wonderful. It was the real world. Real kids playing in a real way and a real mom telling them to play quietly. That was who he fought for and that was why he did what he did, why he fought terrible missions against terrible people in terrible places.

Ulacco also didn't beat around the bush. She spoke plainly and honestly, sometimes brutally so. If she felt Schofield was skirting around an issue or an emotion, she called him on it, often cutting in with, 'Now, come on, Marine, that's not true . . .'

But she could also be extraordinarily kind. For instance, when he spoke of Gant, of her thousand-watt smile, of the wonderful person she had been, Ulacco would just sit back and let him talk. On those occasions, she never interrupted.

A problem arose early on: Ulacco didn't have the same high-level clearance that the other shrinks did, so at first Schofield couldn't tell her the details of what had happened on that fateful mission, just his feelings about them. After a time, though, when he felt he could trust her, he asked his superiors in the Marine Corps if Ulacco could be background-checked for the appropriate level of clearance, so he could tell her more. It took a few months, many checks (including two sweeps of her office for bugs) and three polygraph tests, all of which Ulacco endured without so much as a blink—she had a brother named Bryce fighting in Afghanistan, so she understood. But eventually clearance was given: 'TS/SCI' or 'Top Secret/Sensitive Compartmented Information', which allowed her to be told the details of those missions relevant to Schofield's treatment, and that made things much easier.

But while Ulacco's straight-talking manner and humble base-ment office made Schofield comfortable, it was her unusual brand of therapy that had made him well again.

'So what could this part-time suburban psychologist teach you that the best minds in mental health could not?' Champion asked.

Schofield shook his head. 'It'll sound weird, but she taught me about memory techniques, including one particular technique called the *method of loci*. Some people call it a memory palace or memory cathedral. You order your memories into a visual location of some sort—a cathedral, a town, a house, whatever, so long as it's a structure that you know very well and can thus picture easily. Then when you want to remember something, you travel through that memory location and find the memory you're after. What

Dr Ulacco taught me was more than that: she taught me how to use a memory location to *forget*.'

Champion said, 'Go on.'

'I needed to function, to be able to keep going,' Schofield said. 'I didn't want to forget Fox, but I needed to be able to . . . *compartmentalise* . . . the memory of her so I could move on and function and continue to be the person I am.'

'And what is your memory location?' Champion asked.

'It's stupid. You'll think it's silly.'

'I'll probably be dead within the hour, so what can it hurt to tell me?'

Schofield took a deep breath. He'd never actually told anyone about this, not even Mother.

'It's a submarine,' he said.

Despite herself, Champion snuffed a brief laugh. 'I'm sorry.'

'I told you it was stup—'

'No, it's clever. It's very clever. Submarines have strong walls, and compartments that you can close off with airtight steel doors. It strikes me as an excellent location to store memories, especially painful ones.'

'It was Ulacco's idea,' Schofield said. 'She suggested a spaceship or an aircraft carrier but I liked a sub the best. I've been on many, so I know the layout well and can conjure it up easily. I seal off the most painful memories in the farthest reaches of my imaginary submarine, behind many watertight doors. They're still with me, but I only access them when I really want to, when I'm ready to. Getting to them requires substantial mental effort. There's also another reason why a submarine is good.'

'Why is that?'

'Because you can *purge* a submarine,' Schofield said flatly. 'Eject the trash, so to speak.'

'You mean jettison memories for good?' Champion frowned. 'Forget things *forever*?'

'If you're disciplined enough, yes.'

At that, Champion made a strange face, a sorrowful one.

She said, 'This Fox, this Gant, she sounds like an impressive woman. So impressive that she captured your heart—a heart, I imagine, that is not often or easily caught. I can understand how damaged you were by her death. But to try to forget someone *entirely*'—Champion shook her head—'this is a very sad thing. Not even I did that. Is that what you did to keep going? Did you jettison her entirely from your memory?'

Schofield looked away again, kept paddling.

'I don't—'

At that moment, his wristguard vibrated.

Schofield looked down at it.

A message had come in, from David Fairfax.

'This conversation is to be continued,' he said, looking down at the message.

The message read:

FFAX: THANKS FOR GETTING ME INTO HUGE TROUBLE.
ON THE RUN FROM SOME CIA THUGS THANKS
TO YOU. READ THIS AND ALL WILL BE REVEALED.
I THINK THIS CALDERON GUY IS LEADING YOUR
ARMY OF THIEVES. GOTTA RUN NOW.

Schofield frowned. *The CIA?*

Attached to the message was a document in PDF form, titled OPERATION 'DRAGONSLAYER'. He opened it and, sitting down beside Champion so she could look on, started reading:

OPERATION 'DRAGONSLAYER'
ANALYSIS AND OPERATION CONCEPT BY
MARIUS CALDERON
AUGUST 1, 1984

Pursuant to my report of July 2, 1982 titled THE COMING RISE OF CHINA AND THE ENSUING FALL OF AMERICA, I have been tasked by the Agency's Director (Operations) with formulating a plan by which the United States can avoid the fate described therein. The plan I propose is this:

We use Russia to kill China.

Schofield glanced at Champion. 'Use Russia to kill China? This is about *China*?'

They kept reading:

EXECUTIVE SUMMARY
I have been looking into some of our recent prototype weapons programs and found one—an atmospheric or 'Tesla' device that uses the global jetstream to send a flammable plume of gas around the northern hemisphere. Weather models have shown that if placed in certain Arctic locations—including one Soviet fleet maintenance station in the Arctic Circle called Dragon Island—the chief victim of such a device will not be Russia but rather China.

Soviet spy agencies love nothing more than stealing our secrets. They thrive on it. The only thing that gives them greater pleasure than stealing an American military secret is subsequently constructing one of our own superweapons for use against us.

I propose we *allow* the KGB to steal the plans to this Tesla device— but we include with the device's plans some *fake* data showing optimal locations for such a device. In that data will be a note that, if built at Dragon Island, the device will destroy much of America.

Schofield looked over at Dragon Island, looming above the network of leads.
'No way . . .' he said aloud.

If the Soviets build the device—which I am quite certain they will do—the next step is setting it off at a time of our choosing, at a time when China is assuming global dominance, but in a way that cannot be connected to America.

For this I propose—

Schofield looked up.
'Oh, you have got to be kidding me. Those CIA sons of bitches . . .'

For this I propose that we create a fake terrorist army, perhaps two hundred men strong. We could call it the Army of Terror or some similar name—and use it to seize and set off the Tesla device on Dragon Island.

A crucial note: it is important that the members of this terrorist army *do not know* that their army is a sham.

Regular infantrymen are poor actors, mercenaries can never truly be trusted, and private contractors are worse than mercenaries. Only *true believers* can pull off this mission. We must also account for the possibility that members of our army might be captured and interrogated by a friendly nation (indeed, if they are unaware of the true nature of their army, having one or two members captured will actually be advantageous to us).

To that end, I propose we recruit genuinely disaffected militarily-trained individuals and we indoctrinate them to a cause of global chaos and anarchy. Under the leadership of a small inner core of trusted men, including myself, this army will then carry out a series of terrorist acts to establish the group in the global consciousness. After that, we take Dragon Island and set off the Russian device. Of course, when the mission is over, the members of our counterfeit army will need to be liquidated.

Schofield skimmed to the document's concluding paragraphs:

The predicted outcomes of the proposed operation are as follows:

China is completely destroyed, its population and cities incinerated by a firestorm of never-before-seen proportions. Ninety per cent of India, our next rising low-cost industrial competitor, is also wiped out. A few small slivers at the edges of the continental United States are lost (a necessary loss; we cannot be totally unharmed as that would arouse suspicion). And the Russians are blamed. The story is familiar—once again, Russia's notoriously poor safety protocols have failed and China's innocent population has suffered for it. A terrorist group is to blame and America rises again, the income of its working class population secured for the foreseeable future.

The American way of life survives.

Schofield stared at the screen in silence. '"The American way of life survives." Goddamn.'

He'd seen some messed-up plans in his time—he'd even done battle with an ultra-patriotic American agency called the ICG once before—but this took the cake.

He quickly brought up another screen on his wristguard, one he'd seen at the start of all this, showing a map of the world and the spiralling gas plume contaminating it:

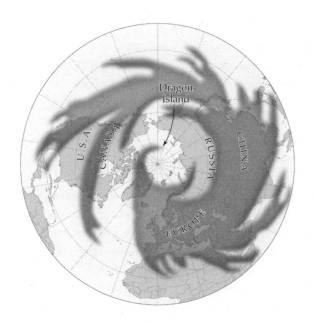

And there it was.
The plume completely covered China.

He hadn't really noticed that before. Like everyone else, he had been concerned about his own country; but even now that took on a new perspective: compared to China, Asia, Europe and India, America would only suffer a glancing blow at the hands of this atmospheric weapon.

Champion frowned. 'So the Army of Thieves is a CIA creation? A fake terrorist army?'

'One hundred per cent made in America,' Schofield said sourly.

Looking again at the Dragonslayer document, he even saw that Calderon had accounted for something else: the fall of the Soviet Union.

It has been suggested to me that this plan might be hindered by the potential fall of the Soviet regime (an event which this analyst believes will occur around the end of this decade). I do not believe that such a fall will adversely affect the plan. In fact, I think it will strengthen it.

Any new confederation that follows the fall of the Soviet regime will still have to safeguard all of the Soviet Union's many weapons of mass destruction, in particular its nuclear arsenal and weapons like the Tesla device. High-value 'exotic matter' weapons installations like Dragon Island will require upkeep by skeleton crews of military staff, who will be very easily bought off—

Schofield shook his head. 'And there you have it. A plan that was hatched back in 1984 comes to fruition now—now that China has become the world's 800-pound gorilla. There were only two things this Calderon guy didn't predict: that Vasily Ivanov would manage to get away for long enough to send out a distress signal . . .'

'And the second thing?'

'That my little test team would be in the area when he did.'

With those words, Schofield brought their life raft to a halt, just short of the end of the lead they were in.

A hundred metres beyond the end of the lead rose Dragon Island, or more particularly the long-abandoned frost-covered whaling village situated on the north-west coast of Dragon.

Schofield gazed at the village.

'There was a third thing he didn't anticipate,' he said. 'How determined I'd be to stop him.'

Mario and the Kid crouched behind a low concrete wall near the main vents, at a spot overlooking Dragon Island's missile battery. They were tense and alert, careful to stay out of sight.

Earlier, they'd watched and listened in astonishment as Schofield had rampaged through the complex, ultimately fleeing with the spheres to the runway.

But now things had changed.

Schofield had failed and now they had to step up. Their mission: destroy the Army of Thieves' missile battery and thus prevent the Army from firing any remaining spheres into the contaminated sky.

The Kid was also mindful of their last-ditch option: finding and destroying the Army of Thieves' uplink, the satellite dish that was connecting them to a missile-spotting satellite up in orbit and thus protecting them from a nuclear strike.

This was a tougher ask. An uplink dish didn't have to be that big, which meant it could be anywhere with a line of sight to the sky. If the Army of Thieves were smart—and by all accounts they were—it wouldn't be easy to spot, and sure enough, neither the Kid nor Mario had seen anything resembling such a dish.

And so, while Schofield had gone on his rampage, Mario and the Kid—still dressed in their Army of Thieves parkas—had carefully made their way toward the missile battery on the south side of the gas vents.

As they'd arrived at this vantage point overlooking the battery, however, a missile had been launched and the southern sky had lit up with blazing white light—and they thought they'd failed completely, that the Army of Thieves had succeeded. But then they heard frantic voices and saw Army men frantically running in all directions.

During this mayhem, a lone Army sentry caught sight of them, but Mario put him down with a single, silenced shot. As they hid the body, Mario had quickly grabbed the man's earpiece.

The two of them crowded around the single earpiece and listened in on the Army of Thieves' commentary of Shane Schofield's escape down the river:

'—*just drove the fucking plane into the river!*—'

'—*Get the Strelas in there!*—'

'—*Something just came out the back*—'

'—*Three of them are on that cement mixer. Get them! They've got two spheres!*—'

'—*Get those fucking spheres*—'

Shortly after, the plane had gone over the waterfall and after that, they heard a few transmissions about something happening over at the quarry and then nothing; radio silence.

And so now here they were, alone, Mario and the Kid, looking out over Dragon Island's missile battery. They might have been too late to stop the first launch, but they wouldn't let another one happen.

The battery was basically a high, flat-topped rocky mount attached to the rest of the base by a long thin bridge that spanned a gorge. The top of the rocky mount had been levelled and on it sat half a dozen semi-trailer-like transporter erector launchers with missiles on their backs.

The Kid gazed at the missile battery. 'I think we can get there unnoticed if we rope down this side of the bridge, hopscotch along the base of the gorge and then use Maghooks to get up the other side.'

Mario shook his head. 'Jesus Christ, don't you see? We're fucked. Scarecrow's dead and soon the others will be, too.'

'We keep fighting anyway,' the Kid said firmly. 'We have to. Now, come on. We got a battery to blow up.'

He scurried off.

Mario scowled. 'Not everybody's a hero, Kid,' he muttered.

They made it across just as the Kid had planned, traversing the gorge and then slithering up onto the flat top of the rocky mount via their Maghooks, before rolling under one of the transporter erector launchers unseen.

Almost unseen.

A lone surveillance camera had caught them in its sights.

Returning to his command centre, the Lord of Anarchy watched silently as the two Marines crab-crawled onto the mount.

He picked up his microphone.

The Kid lay tensed underneath the launcher, panting.

'Okay. Gimme your grenades,' he said to Mario.

Not very enthusiastically, Mario reached for a pouch on his webbing containing some grenades when a voice spoke in his ear: '*Hello, Lance Corporal Puzo. Lance Corporal Vittorio Puzo from the state of New Jersey. I see you there on the missile battery, lying on the ground underneath one of my launchers.*'

Mario started. He glanced at the Kid, who showed no sign of hearing anything. Then he realised: the voice had come through his Army of Thieves earpiece.

'*He can't hear me, Vittorio. Only you can. And it's probably better that way, given the offer I'm about to make to you.*'

Mario froze.

'Dude, give me the grenades,' the Kid urged.

Mario held up his hand, as if he was afraid of a sentry nearby, when he was actually listening to the voice in his ear.

'*I am the Lord of Anarchy, Vittorio, the commander of the Army of Thieves. I am your enemy, but this needn't be so.*'

'Mario . . .' the Kid hissed.

Mario handed him four grenades—but kept listening.

'Go on,' he said aloud.

'Huh?' the Kid said, but let it slide.

'*I can see what you have been ordered to do, Vittorio: destroy my missiles, thereby preventing me from launching the spheres into the gas cloud. Come now, Vittorio. You know the world. Seriously. Do you think these are the only missile launchers I have at my disposal?*'

Mario frowned. This had occurred to him. As soon as they blew up these launchers, they'd become hunted men straight away. And that would be a useless suicidal gesture if there were other launchers elsewhere.

'*Vittorio. Look at the situation. If you blow those launchers, my men will come over there in large numbers and kill you.*'

The Kid frowned at Mario, saw that he was mentally far away, listening to something. 'Hey, man, what the hell are you doing?'

Mario waved him off.

'*Of course, I have other launchers, Vittorio. So your death will be a futile and stupid sacrifice, a sad waste of your life. But I know you, Vittorio. I've got your file here in front of me. You aren't stupid. Your Uncle Salvatore in Jersey would tell you that this is the time to cut a deal.*'

'What are you offering?' Mario said roughly.

The Kid came over. 'I said, what the hell—'

The Lord of Anarchy said, '*If you kill young Corporal Thompson right now and refrain from destroying my launchers, not only will I let you live, I will give you safe passage from this island when this is all over, a mansion in Chile, as many women as you desire, and four million US dollars to live out the rest of your days in substantial luxury.*'

Close enough now, the Kid realised what Mario was doing and he looked at Mario in shock.

'What the fuck, man—?'

Mario answered him by drawing his Marine-issued M9 pistol and firing it at point blank range into the Kid's forehead.

Blam!

The Kid snapped violently backwards and dropped to the ground.

Mario stood up and walked away, not even trying to conceal himself from the nearby Army of Thieves men.

The old whaling village sat in a canyon that delved into the cliffs of the north-western coast of Dragon Island. There was only one way to get to it from the island's main complex: a fenceless single-lane road that ran steeply down one wall of the triangular canyon.

The village itself was a cluster of 19th-century shacks, slaughterhouses, water tanks, gangways and jetties. Chains, hooks and pulleys hung everywhere. The dry cold of the Arctic had preserved it all perfectly, although every piece of wood was pale and faded and every surface was covered in an undisturbed layer of frost.

Schofield and Champion swam, SEAL style, across the hundred metres of flat open sea from the ice field to the cliffs, careful not to cause ripples that a sentry might see; to assist the wounded Champion, Schofield had clipped his combat webbing to her weapons belt, so that he pulled her along as he swam.

They reached the base of the cliffs about two hundred metres west of the deserted village. From there, they clung to the base of the cliffs and came to the first jetty.

Of course there would be sentries here, Schofield figured. It was one of only a few points of land access to the island. The question was where they would be.

Neither Schofield nor Champion saw any such sentry and as they slid out of the water and up onto a frost-covered boat ramp, they thought they had arrived undetected.

But that wasn't the case. From the moment they had reached the base of the cliffs, they had been watched the entire time.

Only not by human eyes.

⏻

Unaware of this, Schofield and Champion crept through the snow-covered village, slipping quickly from corner to corner.

As they arrived at the inland edge of the village, Schofield saw the sentry team.

They'd taken the easy option.

They'd set themselves up as a roadblock a short way up the steep one-lane road that led out of the canyon. Someone might penetrate the village from the ocean side—and hide within its collection of structures—but if those intruders were to get onto the island proper, they had to negotiate the bottleneck that was the road.

Two jeeps and one motorcycle with a sidecar were parked across the road, blocking it. On them, six Army of Thieves men in bulky Marine parkas variously smoked, talked or paced, AK-47s slung loosely over their shoulders.

'Okay,' Champion whispered, 'how do you propose to get past them?'

'You still got your smoke grenades?'

Champion did.

'Give me two.'

She pulled two grenades from her weapons belt and handed them to Schofield.

'Here's the plan,' he said. 'I get up close to their roadblock, toss these, and in the smoke that follows, you take down the men on the right, I take down the ones on the left.'

'That's it? That's your plan?'

'You got anything better?'

'I suppose not,' Champion said. 'Wait. How are you going to get to the roadblock? There's at least fifty metres of open ground between us and them and those grenades won't work over that distance.'

Schofield nodded. 'I have a plan for that.'

'And that is?'

'Surrender.'

⏻

A moment later, Schofield emerged from cover, walking toward the roadblock across the short section of open ground, his hands held high.

The Army of Thieves team immediately whipped up their weapons, alert and wary.

Schofield's heart was beating loudly in his head. He just needed to get close enough—maybe ten metres—and then grab and throw the two smoke grenades now clipped behind his shoulders, out of his enemies' view.

He came closer. Thirty metres away.

'I want to give myself up!' he called as he walked.

They did not fire.

'Keep your hands where we can see 'em!' one of the Army men yelled nervously.

Closer still. Twenty metres . . . fifteen . . . ten . . .

Now, he thought as his hands tensed to reach back and grab the grenades—

'*Freeze*, Captain! And keep those fucking hands away from those grenades,' a deep voice said from down to Schofield's right.

Schofield froze and shut his eyes.

He swore inwardly. He hadn't seen the little corrugated-iron shed just below the edge of the roadway.

Nor had he seen the man who had been hiding behind it: a tall Army of Thieves man with a modern assault rifle held expertly in his hands and 'TYPHON' stencilled in Magic Marker on his parka.

The man named Typhon stepped up onto the road, his gun trained on Schofield. He yanked the two grenades off Schofield's webbing and tossed them to the roadway.

'Wouldn't want you using those now, would we?' Typhon said. The other members of the roadblock team now surrounded Schofield. Typhon took his guns. 'Hands behind your head, Captain Schofield.'

Schofield clasped his hands behind his head.

He thought of Champion and that maybe she could save him, but while she could manage simple tasks like swimming, she was

in no state to launch a rescue. And right now, the only weapons she had were her Steyr TMP and her two pistols—the SIG Sauer P226 and her little Ruger—and they would be no match against this many men.

Typhon stepped in front of Schofield, stood nose-to-nose with him, filling his field of vision.

The man's eyes were frightening. Black and hard, they were lifeless, pitiless. Schofield knew that kind of stare. The cold gaze of a sociopath.

'The boss thought you might come back,' Typhon said. 'You have a reputation for it.'

Schofield said, 'If you're going to kill me, kill me. Cut the pompous speeches.'

'Oh, we plan to kill you, Captain, of that you can be certain. But the short life left to you still has some worth to us. The boss would like to speak with you.'

Schofield saw the nod Typhon gave to one of the men standing behind him and he turned in time to see the man's rifle-butt come rushing at his face and Schofield's world went black.

FIFTH PHASE

THE TORTURE AND DEATH
OF THE SCARECROW

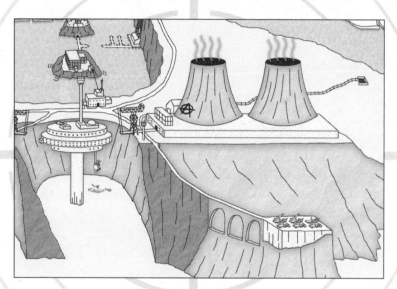

DRAGON ISLAND
4 APRIL, 1230 HOURS
T-PLUS 1:30 HOURS AFTER DEADLINE

The only truly effective form of torture involves inflicting severe pain on a friend or loved one of the person you seek information from. Everything else is a waste of time.

—'The Torture Memo' [unredacted]
Obtained under FOI Act,
US Department of Justice, April 2004

 **DRAGON ISLAND**
4 APRIL, 1230 HOURS

Schofield was slapped in the face and he awoke.

To find himself handcuffed to a steel bedframe that stood upright. His hands were spread-eagled, cuffed to the upper corners of the old bedframe. His feet were tied to the lower edge of the frame by a rope. He looked like a warped version of Christ on the cross.

Typhon stood before him. 'Wakey, wakey, Scarecrow . . .'

Schofield took in his predicament with not a little horror.

He was bare-chested. The upper half of his one-piece snow-camouflaged drysuit had been slipped off his shoulders and rolled down to his waist in the same way a car mechanic might roll down the upper part of his overalls.

Schofield shivered in the cold.

His parka, weapons belt and combat webbing had all been removed. Curiously, his boots and socks had also been taken, leaving his feet bare. His high-tech wristguard was also missing but his old Casio digital watch, clearly so crappy it was unworthy of taking, remained on his wrist. His weapons and Maghook were gone, but not his reflective glasses: they had been perched comically on top of his head.

He looked around.

He was in a small room with ceramic tile walls, drains in the floor and shower heads on the walls: a shower room of some sort.

Suddenly, the roar of a crowd came in through the only door to the room. Schofield couldn't quite get his head around the sound. *Cheering?*

Typhon slapped him again. Harder. 'He's awake.'

A second man stepped into Schofield's field of vision.

Schofield recognised him instantly. It was the man who had taunted the Russian President on the videolink, the one who called himself the 'Lord of Anarchy'.

He was older than Typhon, in his mid-fifties maybe, but he was fit, strong, still in shape. The acid scar on his left jawline was very prominent when seen up close. And his eyes: they were a strange pale grey, oddly hypnotic.

And they *weren't* like Typhon's. They were not psychotic; not empty of pity or care. In fact, they were the opposite of that: this man's eyes seemed designed solely to *detect* emotion, feelings, pain. They gleamed with intelligence and they saw right through you. Typhon was an enforcer. This man was something else, something more.

The Lord of Anarchy gazed at Schofield—crucified half-naked on the vertical bedframe—analysing him, evaluating him.

'So this is the famous Scarecrow,' he said. 'It's a pleasure to meet you. My name is—'

'I'm guessing you're Calderon,' Schofield said. 'Marius Calderon. From the CIA.'

Calderon smiled sadly. 'That, I fear, is a sliver of knowledge that means you cannot, ever, leave this island alive.'

'You like that piece of knowledge?' Schofield said. 'How about this one then: that this whole thing was a CIA set-up. You assholes at the Agency *let* the Russians steal the plans for this facility, knowing that they would build it. That's how you knew there was an extra sphere down in the bunker, because our people designed this whole complex in the first place. And now that China is an economic powerhouse threatening America's dominance, you created this fake terrorist army to set off the atmospheric weapon.'

Calderon smiled wanly. 'This terrorist army isn't fake. Its foot soldiers are real, or at least *they* think they are part of a real terrorist army.'

'What about you? The "Lord of Anarchy"? Let me guess, that acid scarring on your face isn't real, is it?'

Calderon touched the foul scarring on his left jaw. 'A good bit of plastic surgery, no? It's like your eyes: it's all anyone notices. When I go home, my skin will be repaired and my tattoos removed. So, too, these striking grey contact lenses. One does have to be something of a chameleon in this line of work.'

Calderon leaned in close to Schofield, pinned to the bedframe. 'In the end, Captain, I do all this, including changing my face, only for the betterment of the United States of America. A newly rich China threatens the livelihood of three hundred million Americans. The Communist Party of China is a brutal and corrupt regime. Do you really want *it* ruling the world? There are many things wrong with America but as a world leader, we are a much better option than China. But it seems you would prefer to see China as the leading superpower in the world. I thought you were supposed to be fighting for America.'

'I do fight for America,' Schofield said, 'but when it comes to the leadership of the world, that's not for me to decide. If America can't maintain its dominant status fairly, it doesn't deserve to be the world's leader. If America has to annihilate any country that threatens its dominant position, then we're as bad as the Chinese.'

Calderon nodded. 'Then it would seem that you and I are at an ideological impasse. A shame, really. You're bright and determined. If our goals were aligned, you and I would make a powerful team.'

And right then, quite abruptly, Schofield realised something.

'You haven't found the spheres yet,' he said. He glanced at Typhon. 'That's why your boy here didn't kill me on the spot.'

Calderon nodded philosophically. 'My men are scouring the island as we speak for your civilian colleagues, Mr Weinberg of DARPA and Ms Dawson from the National Oceanic and Atmospheric Administration.'

Schofield was surprised that Calderon might know Zack's and

Emma's names. While his own details could be found quite easily on a military database, theirs would have been harder to come by. His surprise must have shown.

'You're wondering how I know their names,' Calderon said. 'You notice details, Captain, even in your current circumstances. I'm impressed. Here is how I know. Lance Corporal?'

At that moment, at Calderon's call, into the shower room—uncuffed and totally free—walked Mario.

'Mario,' Schofield breathed. 'You didn't . . .'

'He did,' Calderon said. 'Shot your other young Marine in the head from point blank range. Lance Corporal Puzo and I speak the same language. I made him an offer he couldn't refuse.'

'Mario . . .' Schofield said again.

Mario eyed him indifferently. 'Sorry, *sir*. Had to choose a side and I chose the one I thought would win.'

'And the Kid?'

Mario shrugged. 'He died quick.'

'You fucking piece of shit,' Schofield said.

'Captain,' Calderon said, 'I know Mr Weinberg and Ms Dawson are somewhere on this island—on this base, no less—and my men *will* find them. But I am hoping that you will assist us in speeding up that process.'

'I can't see myself doing that.'

'Captain, please,' Calderon chuckled. 'You may know my name but you clearly do not know *who I am*. While you may deplore my methods, over the last nine years, I have personally prevented six 9/11-scale acts of terror on American soil by extracting information from captured terrorists. I am that worst of things: a necessary evil. I am the dark side of America's psyche.

'And for nearly thirty years now, in my quest to keep America safe, I have been a student of the human mind and the effects of torture on it—how to motivate a captive, how to hurt him, how to give him hope, and in some cases, how to break him. Right now, you need not concern yourself with *doing* anything to help me. Because what you are about to experience is not about what you will do. It's what we will do *to* you in order to get Mr Weinberg and Ms Dawson to reveal themselves.'

Calderon nodded to Typhon. The tall XO stretched some duct tape roughly over Schofield's mouth.

'And solely for my own amusement,' Calderon said as Typhon slid a rolling hand-truck under the vertical bedframe, 'I intend to break your mind while I torture you.'

Then, led by Marius Calderon—now once again in his role as the Lord of Anarchy—and trailed by the treacherous Mario, Typhon wheeled Schofield's bedframe out of the shower room, where it was greeted by an enormous cheer from the crowd massed outside.

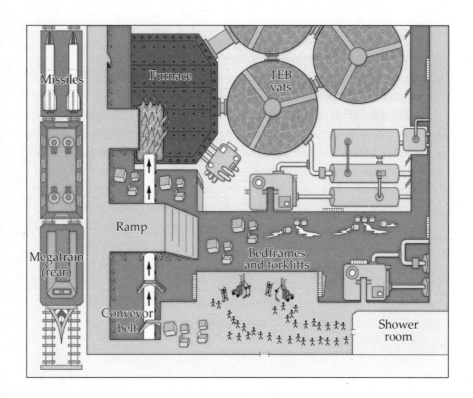

THE GASWORKS

Schofield was wheeled out into an enormous hall-sized space, where a crowd of forty members of the Army of Thieves was waiting for him.

He realised immediately that he was inside the gargantuan gasworks beneath Dragon Island's mighty vents. He was on the highest of three levels, on a large balcony overlooking a massive, *massive* space. Immediately below him was a middle level, the main feature of which was a long conveyor belt. This belt fed an industrial furnace that sat on the third and bottommost level alongside three gigantic circular vats.

These vats—their green liquid contents steaming ominously and stirred constantly by rotating steel arms—were positioned directly beneath one of the mighty vent towers. An identical set of vats lay further away, beneath the second enormous vent. Fed by a complex network of interconnected pipes, gauges and valves, the vats were the beating heart of the atmospheric device: the shimmering gas that rose from them was the combustible TEB mixture that would allow the sky to ignite.

On the northern side of the vast space, Schofield saw, of all things, a huge black train—twice the width of a normal train and made of ultra-thick reinforced steel—parked at a platform that opened directly onto the gasworks via a broad ramp. Judging from the direction of its tracks, Schofield guessed the industrial-sized train had been used during the original construction of the gasworks to convey material from the submarine dock on the east coast.

The whole place stank of a foul chemical odour, the reek of TEB,

plus another rank smell that Schofield recognised with horror: burnt human flesh.

The crowd of ruffians from the Army of Thieves cheered loudly at Schofield's appearance.

It was then that Schofield saw the other prisoners.

There were four of them in total: two closer to him—their torture had already begun, inspiring the grim cheers he had heard earlier—and two further away on the balcony.

Schofield took in the nearer pair first: one was attached to a bedframe just like his. The other hung from the raised prong of a forklift in a most painful position: from his wrists, which had been handcuffed *behind* his back. His feet hovered a metre above the ground.

The man on the bedframe was Ironbark Barker: the Navy SEAL leader whose team had been shot to shit in the submarine bay and who himself had later been captured, after successfully sabotaging the TEB gas dispersal for a time.

Ironbark's face bulged with bruises and cuts, while his naked back was imprinted with a foul grid of charred burns. Schofield saw a thick industrial electrical cable at Ironbark's feet, attached by a transformer to the steel bedframe. A moment later, he noticed the small wooden bit clenched between Ironbark's bloody teeth.

The second prisoner, the one hanging from the forklift, was Jeff Hartigan, the haughty contractor who had stayed behind in Schofield's camp against Schofield's advice.

His head was bent low and he did not move at all—he could have been dead for all Schofield knew. It was hard to tell. Suspended from his cuffed wrists, Hartigan's shoulders had dislocated some time ago.

Calderon caught Schofield looking at Hartigan. 'It is a torture position known as *strappado,* or "reverse hanging". It has been used for hundreds of years, by the Medici family in Florence and the Nazis in their concentration camps, and also the North Vietnamese during the Vietnam War. It is still used today in Turkey— I know this for a fact as I instructed their torturers in its correct use.

Strappado causes excruciating pain and if left for too long in this position, the subject will suffer first, permanent ligament damage, and second, dislocation of the shoulders, and eventually full loss of use of the arms.'

Calderon smiled. 'I personally just like the look of it. The subject is at my complete mercy, with his hands pinned behind his back and his chest thrust outward so that his heart—his life force—is totally exposed.'

Schofield turned to face the other two prisoners and when he recognised them, his jaw dropped.

They were both suspended from a second forklift, one from each prong, also in the strappado position. Unlike Hartigan, however, their heads were unbowed, allowing Schofield to identify them easily.

Mother and Baba.

Like Schofield, their cold-weather outer garments had been removed—Baba hung from his swept-back wrists with his massive chest bare to the cold; it was hairy, muscled and huge. Beside him, Mother had been stripped to her trousers and grey sports bra.

Both bore bloody lips and noses, evidence of beatings already received. Schofield also noticed that a huge Army of Thieves man— it was Big Jesus—was standing nearby with a new acquisition slung across his back: Baba's massive Kord machine gun.

At the loud cheer from the crowd of thugs, Mother snapped round and saw Schofield being wheeled out on the bedframe.

'Scarecrow!' she called.

Schofield couldn't reply through his duct-taped mouth, but he locked eyes with her.

Mother yelled, 'Stay strong, boss! We got 'em just where we want 'em!'

Schofield's bedframe was erected vertically alongside Ironbark's. As he jolted to a halt, Schofield saw Ironbark look up at him—the totally exhausted gaze of a man who had been tortured to within an inch of his life. It seemed to take all of his energy just to raise his head. The smell of his burnt skin was sickening.

Calderon stood before Schofield and jerked his chin at Ironbark. 'Specialist Barker here is a fair bit further along on his journey of pain than you are. But fear not, Captain, you will catch up with him soon.'

Calderon then turned to the Army of Thieves trooper manning the electrical transformer connected to Ironbark's bedframe. He was a Sudanese fellow with studded skin and bloodshot yellow eyes; and on his back, Schofield saw, still in its holster, he wore Schofield's Maghook.

'Corporal Mobutu,' Calderon said, 'I need the electrical cable to use on Captain Schofield. Splash Mr Barker and kill him, please.'

The Sudanese torturer grabbed a nearby bucket of water and hurled its contents over Ironbark's limp body.

Calderon explained to Schofield, 'The trouble with electrocuting a human being, Captain, is that human skin, when dry, is actually quite resistant to electricity. The result is burning—you can ramp up the voltage as much as you want, but you only end up scorching the skin more. And the smell, God, it really is quite offensive. But if you *wet* the subject's skin, the skin's resistance drops and it becomes *one hundred times* more receptive to electricity. One moment, please. This is all for nothing if I don't broadcast it.'

Calderon grabbed a microphone from nearby. It was connected to a communications console on the wall. Calderon pressed the 'TALK' button and when he spoke again, his voice was magnified through every one of the many loudspeakers in the gasworks; indeed, through every loudspeaker on Dragon Island.

'*Zack Weinberg. Emma Dawson. I know you can hear me.*' Calderon's voice blared. '*Please listen to this. It is the sound of one of your comrades-in-arms dying.*'

Calderon turned to his Sudanese assistant. 'Mobutu, 10,000 volts, please.'

The Sudanese flicked a dial on the transformer and immediately the steel springs on Ironbark's bedframe flashed with blue lightning.

Ironbark's entire body shook violently as electricity coursed through him, his terrible shuddering sending droplets of water flying outwards. His teeth clenched around the wooden bit in his mouth. He grunted and strained in absolute agony, the tendons of his neck bulging, before abruptly his groans became high-pitched screams.

Calderon held the microphone close to Ironbark's mouth the whole time, broadcasting his horrific screams across the island.

Then Ironbark's screams cut off and he went completely limp,

even though the transformer was still sending the charge flowing through the bedframe.

Schofield was thunderstruck by the savagery of it.

Ironbark was dead, but this wasn't over yet.

The crowd started chanting, 'Fire! Fire!'

Calderon nodded and Ironbark's dead body was wheeled away and tipped—still attached to the bedframe—off the edge of the balcony, where it fell a short distance before landing on the conveyor belt. The slow-moving belt then carried it away. The corpse on the bedframe disappeared for about ten seconds as it passed under the broad ramp from the train platform, only to reappear again at the lip of the furnace on the far side.

Ironbark and the bedframe then tipped into the furnace where they were swallowed by the flames and the crowd of Thieves cheered with macabre, crazed delight.

In a dark corner of Dragon Island, Zack and Emma heard it all over a nearby loudspeaker.

They looked at each other in horror.

'Oh my God . . .' Emma whispered. 'Oh my God . . .'

In the gasworks, Calderon stepped over to the figure of Jeff Hartigan, suspended strappado-style from the forklift.

He slapped Hartigan's face and the executive stirred, groaning. He was alive.

Calderon turned theatrically to the crowd. 'What do you say? Rat time?'

The crowd of Thieves roared with delight.

'Mobutu,' Calderon said. 'Bring in the rats.'

Mobutu disappeared into a side room, returning a few moments later with a large wire-framed crate inside of which were six rats.

Schofield's eyes went wide.

They were of various sizes, from small and scurrying to fat and huge. They all had black furry backs, long hairless tails and frightening buck teeth. They snapped at each other with considerable viciousness.

Calderon said, 'You know, Captain, one can't help but be impressed by vermin. Rats, cockroaches, they're so *resilient*. They will outlast us, that's for sure. These rats, for instance, have survived on this island far longer than their old Soviet masters did. Consider this a demonstration for your benefit.'

Calderon jerked his chin at Hartigan. 'Put a box on him.'

Mobutu obliged. Climbing a stepladder, he placed a large wooden box over Hartigan's bowed head. The box had solid wooden walls, save for a round hole cut into its base, which was designed to accommodate the victim's neck. Once the box was in place over Hartigan's head, Mobutu stuffed some rags around the edge of this hole, sealing the gap between the box and the skin of his neck. Hartigan now looked like the Man in the Iron Mask.

There was also a hinged panel on the top side of the box—and when Schofield saw Mobutu open this panel and pick up a particularly large rat by the tail with his spare hand and hold it above the opening, every ounce of blood in his veins turned to ice.

'Oh, Lord, no . . .' he breathed.

Calderon saw this. 'I imagine a man as learned as you, Captain, is familiar with Orwell's beautiful novel, *1984*. In it, a similar form

of rat torture is used on the protagonist, Winston Smith. But there the rat torture is only employed as a threat to break Smith's will; it is not actually *used*. Know this about me, Captain: I do not bother with threats. Mobutu, do it.'

Mobutu dropped the rat into the box, and then quickly added a second one, a smaller one, before he shut the upper panel.

As he did this, Calderon raised his microphone again: 'Zack. Emma. You remember your campmate, Mr Jeffrey Hartigan. This is him, being eaten alive by rats.'

Until that instant, Jeff Hartigan's body had been practically motionless as it hung suspended from the forklift's prong. But then with alarming suddenness, Hartigan started screaming like a madman. His legs kicked frantically, lashing and thrashing, his arms strained at their bonds, but there was no escape.

Schofield couldn't see what was happening inside the wooden box covering Hartigan's head, but he could imagine it and it made him nauseous with horror.

The rats were eating Hartigan's defenceless face.

Soon they would eat through his eyes and burrow into his brain, eating that too, and only then would death come. It was a cruel and painful way to die.

Hartigan's screams filled the air, hideous shrieks of agony that were only barely muffled by the box. Through it all, Calderon held up the microphone to catch every cry.

After thirty seconds of this, mercifully, death came.

Hartigan's body abruptly went still, although the box on his head continued to shake, jostled from within by the movement of the rats.

Again, the crowd cheered. Again, Calderon smiled.

Mother and Baba both stared, open-mouthed, in disbelief.

Schofield did the same.

'Jesus Christ in Heaven, save us,' he breathed.

Calderon came up to him, still the picture of casual calm.

He looked straight at Schofield as he spoke into his microphone.

'Zack? Emma? Are you still there? You can stop this, you know, simply by revealing yourselves. That's all you have to do. Or else I can continue on sergeants Newman and Huguenot and Captain Schofield here.'

Calderon shrugged, addressed Schofield. 'While we wait for them, Captain, let's talk. Now, I understand from reading your file that you had a fractured relationship with your father. You defended your mother from his beatings and I wonder if this laid the foundations for your somewhat heroic adulthood. But even heroes suffer loss. Forgive me for opening an old wound, but I'm led to believe that your girlfriend, Ms Elizabeth Gant, was beheaded by a rather nasty fellow named Jonathan Killian. For a heroic type like you, being helpless to save the woman you loved must have been a most painful thing. As I understand it, you weren't there when she was killed, were you?'

Schofield stared straight ahead, said nothing.

Calderon said, 'To see or hear a loved one being subjected to torture is, in my experience, *the* most motivating thing for a human being. It is by far the best way to get information from a captive. Those masters of torture, the Japanese in World War II, used such methods regularly both during the war and before it during their infamous sack of Nanking.

'Right now, you have nothing that I want, but Zack and Emma do. My torture of you is solely for the purpose of drawing them out.'

Calderon leaned close and whispered in Schofield's ear: 'I will take you within an inch of death and you *will* beg me to kill you, but I'm not going to do that right now. As I said, I want to break your mind before I kill you. Mobutu, put the bit between his teeth.'

The Sudanese stepped forward and with a leering gap-toothed grin, ripped off the duct tape and made to jam the wooden bit into Schofield's mouth.

Schofield took the opportunity to call out: 'Mother! When I'm gone, you keep fighting, you hear!' but then Mobutu wedged the bit between his teeth and he could shout no more.

Mother's and Schofield's eyes met, matching gazes of helplessness.

Mother called across the space, 'I will, Scarecrow! You bet I fucking will!'

Calderon said, 'Captain, the device you are strapped to is known as a *parrilla*, a torture device used widely in Chile during the reign of the Pinochet regime. The word parrilla translates roughly as "barbecue". It is a form of electric shock torture, with the current shot through the metal frame to which the victim is strapped. I have found that old military-barracks bedframes, with their steel springs and thin crossbars, distribute the electric current to maximum effect while also leaving a unique burn pattern on the back of the victim that never goes away. Mobutu, a taste for the captain: 2,000 volts please.'

Mobutu turned the dial on the transformer.

Schofield convulsed violently.

White light flooded his field of vision and excruciating—*excruciating*—pain shot through his entire body. He wanted to arch his back, stretch out the vertebrae, but he couldn't, he was pinned down too tightly. His teeth clamped down on the bit and he grunted, trying to scream.

As he did this, Calderon held the microphone up close to Schofield's mouth, broadcasting his pained grunts and stifled screams across the island.

'Zack and Emma,' Calderon commentated, 'what you are hearing is the sound of the brave Captain Schofield being electrocuted.'

Then, through the blinding pain, Schofield smelt it.

The smell of skin burning. His own skin burning.

He screamed again.

Mother strained at her bonds. 'You motherfucker!' she yelled at Calderon. 'I am gonna rip your fucking head off!'

Calderon nodded to Mobutu and the Sudanese flicked off the dial and Schofield slumped against the bedframe, spent, exhausted, sweating, gasping. His head fell forward as he tried to suck in oxygen.

Calderon smiled. 'That was but a mere 2,000 volts against your dry skin, Captain. As you saw with your SEAL friend, Mr Barker, when the skin is wet, its conductivity increases one-hundredfold. Soon I will have Mobutu douse you in water and turn that dial to a much higher voltage. Then the current won't burn your skin—it will flow directly through your heart and kill you.'

Calderon nodded at Mobutu and the Sudanese again grabbed the nearby bucket and hurled its remaining contents over Schofield's body. Schofield hung there on the bedframe, dripping with water.

Calderon threw a sideways glance at Mobutu.

Schofield, despite his overwhelming exhaustion, felt his heart skip—this was it, this was the end—but Calderon suddenly laughed.

'Oh, no, not yet, Captain,' he said, with a torturer's relish. 'I *told* you I was going to break you before I killed you. You didn't witness Elizabeth Gant's death, but trust me, you will see your loyal friend, Mother Newman, die before your very eyes.'

Despite his own pain, Schofield shot a look at Mother.

'Really, Scarecrow. To lose *one* loved one is tragic. To lose a second is simply careless. What if it happened again: your closest friend horribly executed, dying in extreme pain, *right in front of your eyes*? That would break a man.'

Schofield's face went pale, draining of blood.

Calderon smiled.

'Mobutu. Put the box on her and insert the rats.'

What followed was more than Schofield—weakened, pinned down, helpless—could bear.

The original rat box was lifted off Hartigan's head and Schofield saw the gruesome remains of Hartigan's face. It was beyond disgusting.

Both of Hartigan's eyes had been *chewed out* and were now just empty bloody sockets, dangling with ragged flesh. Schofield stifled the urge to vomit as he saw the smaller of the two rats scurry *in through* Hartigan's left eye socket and then race out his gaping mouth.

Hartigan's corpse was unceremoniously tossed onto the conveyor belt, and to the chants of the crowd of Thieves—'Fire! Fire!'—it disappeared into the furnace.

Mobutu walked with the box over to Mother's forklift and Schofield's heart sank.

He couldn't handle this. First Gant, now Mother. His mind reeled at the thought of what was about to happen.

Abruptly, Calderon called, 'Let's make this a double feature! Bring out a second box! For her French friend!'

The crowd loved this. They cheered as a second, identical box was brought out.

The veins in Schofield's forehead bulged as he tried with what little energy he had left to yell through the bit in his mouth.

Mobutu used his stepladder to reach up and place Hartigan's grisly box over Mother's head. As this happened, for the briefest of instants, Schofield caught Mother's eye . . .

She was looking directly at him.

The look on her face was one of the most profound sadness, of longstanding friendship and deep affection. She mouthed the word 'Goodbye' just as the box came down over her head and cut off Schofield's view of her face.

Schofield strained against his bonds, but it was useless. He slumped against the bedframe, out of energy, out of determination and finally, completely, out of options.

There was nothing he could do to stop this. All he could do was watch as his closest friend in the world died a foul death at the hands of Marius Calderon.

Calderon saw this.

Shane Schofield was beaten, his mind, his spirit broken.

The second box came down over Baba's head and as its neck hole was stuffed with rags, Schofield thought he heard Mother say something to Baba. It was muffled, so he couldn't hear what she said, but it was short, just a few final words.

Then, grinning with delight at the show he was putting on for his cohorts, Mobutu mounted his stepladder between Mother and Baba, opened the top panels of both boxes and held a rat in each hand poised above the boxes, ready to be dropped.

The crowd cried for him to put them in, but Mobutu waited for the signal from Calderon.

Calderon held up his microphone. 'Zack. Emma. Me again. If you're out there, this is the sound of Gunnery Sergeant Newman and her French friend, Master Sergeant Huguenot, having their faces eaten by rats.'

He nodded to Mobutu.

Mobutu dropped the rats, one into each box.

The crowd cheered.

A second rat for each box quickly followed, then Mobutu flipped the panels shut.

Schofield watched helplessly.

Then the kicking, thrashing and screaming began.

☼

It was exactly as it had been with Hartigan.

As Calderon held up his microphone, both Mother and Baba started shrieking in pain, bobbling from their suspended arms, their bound legs trying to lash out.

Hideous noises came from their headboxes—screaming, grunting, crunching sounds.

As with Hartigan, the terrible scene lasted about thirty seconds before first Mother, then Baba, went limp and they both just hung there, strappado-style, hands behind their backs, their heads bent and still.

Tears began to form in Schofield's eyes.

Calderon said sadly, 'You, Captain, are a dangerous man to know. I honestly can't fathom how you live with yourself. Of course, from what I hear, you struggle to do even that: I know you tried killing yourself once—like your father, aren't you?—but the plucky Sergeant Newman stopped you. The question is *who will stop you now?*'

Schofield clenched his teeth around his bit, tears pouring down his face.

Calderon grinned callously, his grey eyes alive. 'Captain Shane Schofield: son to a brutal father, lover to a doomed woman, and now witness to the death of his truest friend. Consider yourself broken. Which means now it is time for you to die—'

'Sir!' a voice called from the exit doorway.

Both Calderon and Schofield turned to see a Thief standing by the door.

'What?' Calderon called.

'We got 'em! The two civilians with the spheres! Bad Willy just caught 'em! He's bringing 'em in now!'

In the end, the capture of Zack and Emma had come about almost exactly as Calderon had planned.

After separating from Mother at the quarry-mine, Zack and Emma had searched desperately for a place to hide with the two spheres.

Upon crossing the river, they'd arrived back at the base's runway, where they found a cluster of barracks structures: superlong halls that had once been living quarters for the substantial Soviet force stationed at Dragon Island.

Zack thought they'd be perfect: dusty and abandoned, and presumably filled with bunk beds, trunks and footlockers, plus locker rooms, toilets and shower rooms that would offer many places to hide.

Zack and Emma had come to the first barracks and cautiously peered inside it—

A long-legged woman in fishnet stockings, high heels and black lace lingerie walked by, casually smoking a cigarette.

Zack frowned. 'What the hell—?'

Emma hushed him. 'Look. There's another one.'

Sure enough, a second, similarly dressed woman joined the first, also smoking a cigarette as they stood beneath a glowing wall-mounted heater. In addition to the sexy underwear, both women, Zack and Emma now saw, wore garish make-up; they started talking, in a drawling Eastern European tongue.

Emma realised it first. 'They're prostitutes . . .'

Zack said, 'Six weeks in the Arctic is a long tour, especially for an army of hooligans. They have needs. Their boss thought of everything. Come on, let's check out the next barracks.'

Unfortunately, the second barracks building wasn't any better: it, too, was clearly being used by the Army of Thieves. While currently empty, its long hall was filled with row upon row of slept-in bunk beds and half-open footlockers. They couldn't hide there.

Zack and Emma hurried past the second barracks, came to one of the hangars adjoining the runway, and ducked inside it.

An enormous Antonov cargo plane filled the space. It was identical to the one that Schofield had driven into the river, another An-12.

Zack peered in through its open rear ramp: plenty of crates, some large objects covered in tarps and netting.

Emma said, 'They have *another* plane?'

'With a lot of stuff in it to hide behind,' Zack said. 'Inside, now!'

He guided Emma into the big plane's hold and they huddled behind some crates piled up in a dark corner.

It was from here that they heard the torture over the base's loudspeakers: first, Ironbark's, then Hartigan's.

But it was Schofield's electric shock treatment on the parrilla that betrayed their location.

Ever since he had spotted Zack's Nike bootprints in the mud earlier, Bad Willy had smelt blood.

Unlike Zack and Emma's desperate stumbling flight, his movement had been slow and methodical: he and his men had been progressing steadily, patiently, searching for and ultimately finding a new Nike print in the snow or mud; until they stopped at one muddy print that had been left on the concrete doorstep of the hangar containing the second Antonov cargo plane.

Bad Willy and his men had stalked quietly through the dark hangar as Hartigan's shrill screams had come blaring in over the loudspeakers.

Every so often, Bad Willy would command his men to silence and hold up a wand-shaped listening device and listen intently through its headphones.

When Schofield's electric shock torture began, Bad Willy had been holding the wand pointed at the open rear hold of the Antonov and as Schofield had screamed through his wooden bit, Willy heard it in his headphones.

A woman's soft gasp.

His men stormed the plane and found Zack and Emma huddled behind a tarp-covered mound with their Samsonite case.

Zack and Emma were shoved into the gasworks by Bad Willy and his triumphant team.

Mother and Baba's rat torture had only just finished and the two new arrivals took in the grim scene: Schofield strung up on his vertical bedframe, connected to the transformer; Mother and Baba hanging strappado-style, their heads covered by the wooden boxes, both deathly still.

Bad Willy carried the Samsonite case over to Calderon who opened it and beheld the two small maroon spheres inside.

'Thank you, Willy,' he said. 'Thank you. You have done well.' He nodded at Emma. 'You may have as your reward this delightful young lady, who will no doubt be somewhat *fresher* than our current crop of female companions. She's yours to do with as you wish.'

Willy leaned forward. '*All* mine?'

'All yours. Men! Let it be known that this woman is Bad Willy's, to keep as his own, or to share and rent out at any price he names. She is his property, a reward for duties well performed!'

'Thank you, sir.' Bad Willy bowed obsequiously. 'You are too kind.' He gripped Emma by the arm and took her over to the edge of the balcony.

'No!' Zack yelled, but he was backhanded by a Thief standing nearby and he fell to the floor, bleeding from the mouth, while the other Thieves laughed cruelly.

Calderon handed one of the spheres to Typhon. 'Colonel Typhon. Take this to the missile battery and fire it off into the gas cloud, taking into account the empty section of gas closer to this island. Set the sky on fire.'

Typhon hurried out the door with the sphere.

Fatigued beyond measure, his body aching, Schofield watched the awful scene play out.

Things couldn't get any worse: Mother and Baba were dead, Emma was about to become way-too-intimately acquainted with a member of the Army of Thieves, and Typhon was about to launch a missile into the contaminated atmosphere and incinerate all of China, most of India, and much of the rest of the northern hemisphere in an act that had been conceived, planned and executed by one of the Central Intelligence Agency's best minds.

Only then it got worse.

Calderon came over to him, smiling his smug torturer's grin. When he spoke, he spoke softly, so that only Schofield could hear:

'Congratulations, Captain, you have served your purpose. Alas, you are of no further use to me, which means you will not see the spectacular end of the world as we know it. I have no more speeches for you and no more torture either. Now you must simply die.'

He lifted Schofield's reflective glasses off his head and appraised them like a jeweller examining a diamond. They bore many nicks and scratches, including the mark from the bullet that had sliced across them earlier.

Calderon said, 'I like to keep a souvenir from the men I defeat, trophies that remind me of past victories. These glasses will be my reminder of the day I beat the Scarecrow.'

He pulled out a knife and scratched a deep A-in-a-circle into the wraparound lens of the Oakleys and then held the glasses aloft for the crowd to see.

They roared their approval.

Slipping the glasses into his jacket, Calderon stepped away from Schofield. 'Mobutu, attach an extra electrode to his heart and apply

10,000 volts. Sorry, Captain, it was nice knowing you. You were a worthy adversary, but America needs me more than it needs you.'

Mobutu attached an extra electrode to the wet skin over Schofield's heart and resumed his position by the transformer.

Calderon nodded once.

Mobutu turned the dial.

And Schofield jolted more violently than ever before.

Naked sparks flew off the bedframe this time.

Schofield spasmed terribly, his back arching as far as his bonds would allow. He head was thrown backwards and his eyes rolled up into his head and in an instant, it was over.

His body fell completely limp.

It hung from the steel bedframe, unmoving.

Mobutu flicked off the dial and as the Army of Thieves waited tensely, Calderon himself checked Schofield's pulse.

And found nothing.

Calderon turned . . . and smiled.

He didn't have to say anything. The crowd roared.

Shane Schofield was dead.

SIXTH PHASE
THE END OF THE WORLD

DRAGON ISLAND
4 APRIL, 1255 HOURS
T-PLUS 1:55 HOURS AFTER DEADLINE

We shall never surrender.

—Winston Churchill

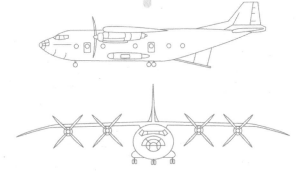

Dave Fairfax sped through the streets of Washington, D.C. with Marianne Retter by his side in a little Toyota Prius.

After they had opened Marius Calderon's classified CIA plan to use Russia to destroy China—appropriately named Operation 'Dragon-slayer'—they had given away their position and so had had to run.

Which was why they were now driving in the Prius. It was actually part of the Zipcar network—an eco-friendly car-sharing network that Dave belonged to; Zipcars were parked at various sites around the city and if you had a Zipcard, you could access them. Dave guessed—correctly—that not long after he used his swipecard to access the car, someone somewhere would detect the ensuing deduction on his credit card and flag the car for immediate detention by the D.C. police. But it was worth the risk, because he didn't plan on being in the car for long.

'Where are we going?' Retter asked.

Dave looked determinedly forward. 'There's only one place we *can* go: the one place they don't want you to go.'

They swung onto the north-west arm of Pennsylvania Avenue and beheld the famous mansion at the other end, lit up by flood-lights, glowing in the night.

'We have to get you to your appointment at the White House,' Dave said.

⏻

'The CIA will be watching it for sure,' Retter said as they cruised down Pennsylvania Avenue with the gentle flow of night-time traffic. 'They'll have people stationed all around it.'

'I imagine they will,' Dave said, 'so we're gonna need a little luck.'

They came to the corner of Pennsylvania and West Executive Avenue, the road that gave access to the West Wing Entrance. They turned onto West Executive Avenue.

Dave's eyes fell on the West Wing Entrance and its boomgated guardhouse.

Retter scanned the wider area, searching for CIA agents. Lafayette Square was filled with the usual crowd: tourists, cops and . . . four pairs of men in suits positioned at strategic points, several of whom were touching their ears and whispering into their cuffs as they surveyed the area.

'You see 'em?' Dave said.

Retter said, 'They could just be Secret Service—'

Suddenly one of the men pointed at their Prius and started running.

'Shit!' Retter said. 'We're made!'

Dave snapped to look at the West Wing Entrance.

'Aw, fuck it,' he said as he floored the gas pedal and yanked left on the steering wheel.

The little Prius squealed as it swung off the road, jumped the kerb and sped towards the West Wing Entrance!

As Dave had expected, uniformed Secret Service guardsmen in the gatehouse opened fire on the little car immediately—although he didn't think many terrorists charged toward the White House in hybrids. He and Retter ducked as their windshield shattered.

The Prius veered wildly and smashed into a reinforced gatepost, coming to a crunching halt. Its bonnet crumpled and Dave and Retter were flung forward in their seats as the car's airbags inflated with a sudden *whoosh!*

Hissing steam, the little car was quickly surrounded by no fewer than six Secret Service guards, all with their pistols raised.

The CIA men in the park who had briefly given chase on foot hung back—Dave and Retter were now in the Secret Service's jurisdiction and when it came to the security of the White House, the Service guarded their turf jealously. They didn't hand over anyone to anyone until they had done their own investigation.

'Get out of the vehicle with your hands up!' the lead Secret Service agent yelled furiously.

Dave and Retter exited the vehicle as instructed, and were promptly shoved to the ground, faces rammed into the dirt. They were then handcuffed while the car was searched.

'No devices in or under the car,' a guard reported.

The lead guard shook his head. 'Check their IDs.' He lifted Dave to his feet. 'You just landed yourself in big trouble, buddy.'

As he came to his feet, Dave said in a loud voice that every guard could hear, 'Sir, my name is David Fairfax, Defense Intelligence Agency. This is Marianne Retter, also DIA. Please check your visitor's log. You'll find that Ms Retter has an urgent appointment with the President.'

It took twenty minutes—time which Dave and Marianne spent in the back of a prison van parked just inside the West Wing Entrance—but eventually word came through.

The senior Secret Service guard opened the van himself. With him was a presidential aide in a suit.

'Turns out the lady does have an appointment,' the senior guard said. 'And you, Mr Fairfax, have a distinguished record. I've been told that if the lady wants you with her, you may accompany her inside.'

Retter said, 'You bet I do.'

'Next time,' the guard said, 'just stop at the gate and wait your turn.'

'Sorry,' Dave said. 'Couldn't do that. This place was surrounded by people who wanted to prevent us getting in. If we'd stopped,

we'd have been dead.' He gave the guard a weak smile. 'Sorry about your gate.'

And with those words, Dave Fairfax and Marianne Retter hurried inside the White House.

 **DRAGON ISLAND GASWORKS
4 APRIL, 1255 HOURS**

Like Ironbark and Hartigan before him, Schofield's body—still attached to the metal bedframe—was immediately and unceremoniously disposed of: it was tossed off the balcony.

The whole cruel contraption, bedframe and corpse, landed on the long industrial conveyor belt on the level below and commenced its journey toward the furnace fifty yards away. Before it reached the furnace, Schofield's body would pass underneath the broad ramp that stretched out from the railway platform into the gasworks.

Because of this, Schofield's corpse would be out of sight from the Army of Thieves men on the balcony for perhaps ten seconds.

Schofield's immobile body passed under the ramp, disappearing from view.

'*Fire! Fire!*' the crowd chanted furiously, eager to see their enemy's leader fall into the furnace.

Their eyes were glued to the conveyor belt on the other side of the ramp, waiting for Schofield's body to reappear.

Marius Calderon also watched, keen to see Schofield destroyed forever.

It was he who frowned first when Schofield's body *didn't* reappear as it should have.

The conveyor belt kept rolling by, but in the spot where Schofield's body and the bedframe should have been, it was bare, empty.

Calderon blinked, confused. Had something happened to Schofield's body under the ramp? He sent two men down to check on it—only to hear a brief spray of gunfire from down there shortly after. When the two men didn't return, Calderon started toward some steel stairs leading down to the lower level—

At which moment Schofield reappeared.

Only he wasn't cuffed to the bedframe . . .

. . . and he wasn't dead anymore either.

Shane Schofield stepped up onto the balcony, having climbed the steel stairs from the level below.

Calderon couldn't believe it. And for the first few moments, neither could anyone else in the gathered group of Thieves.

Schofield stood there, stock still, looking like something out of a horror movie: bare-chested and barefoot, he was covered in sweat and water and foul scorch-marks, bloody scratches and open wounds. His jaw was clenched tight and his bloodshot, scarred eyes glared at Calderon with murderous rage.

Not only had he returned from the grave, he had returned from it armed: he held a Steyr TMP machine pistol in one hand and a SIG Sauer P226 pistol in the other.

As he'd stepped up from the stairs he had placed something on the floor beside him, before taking the SIG Sauer from its back. It now stood there next to him like a loyal dog.

A little silver robot.

If anything could be said about Bertie, it was that he was a damned determined little robot.

After being blasted out of the cable car terminal earlier, he had plummeted three hundred feet before landing in the freezing waters of the bay.

Of course, the landing hadn't harmed him and he automatically inflated his buoyancy balloons and floated to the surface, bobbing there like a funny-looking mechanical duck.

Then his acquisition program kicked in: he searched for a buddy to follow.

His wheels spinning in the water, he made his way slowly but determinedly to the outer edge of the bay, where he saw to the west a point of access to Dragon Island: the abandoned whaling village.

It took him almost an hour to get there, but get there he did, and sure enough, shortly after he arrived, he saw his secondary buddy, Captain Shane M. Schofield, turn up with Veronique Champion.

When Schofield and Champion had been observed entering the whaling village, it had been Bertie doing the observing.

The little robot had hurried to catch up with Schofield, but Schofield had dashed away too quickly, to be outsmarted by Typhon at the roadblock and taken away.

Bertie could only watch in robotic dismay as this had happened.

But then, from out of nowhere, a woman's voice had said to him, 'Bonjour, little one.'

'*Bertie must reacquire his secondary buddy, Captain Shane M. Schofield,*' Bertie had said earnestly.

'Oui, he must. And when you find him, I want you to give him a few things from me,' Champion had said.

Getting past the roadblock had been a team effort: Champion had shot Schofield's two smoke grenades—still lying near the road-block, having been thrown to the ground by Typhon—and in the smoky haze that followed, Bertie had been brutal.

Guided by a thermal imager that could see through the smoke as if it wasn't even there, his cannon had annihilated the roadblock team, ripped them to shreds, and within a minute, Bertie was whiz-zing up the steep road on his chunky little tyres, heading doggedly into Dragon Island in search of his secondary buddy.

Champion, wounded and unable to be of any more help, watched him go.

But she had given him one more instruction: follow the fresh tyre tracks of the jeep that had taken Schofield away from the roadblock. By following them diligently, Bertie had come to the gasworks.

There he scurried in through a side door and arrived underneath the ramp just in time to see Schofield's body land with a thud on the conveyor belt right in front of him.

Recognising his secondary buddy, Bertie had whizzed forward and using his little robotic arms, pulled Schofield and the bedframe off the belt. A quick scan had revealed that Schofield had no pulse, so Bertie had unfolded his defibrillator and applied it according to his CPR programming.

Whack. Whack.

Schofield's body jolted twice . . .

. . . before his eyes flew open and he gasped, sucking in deep rasping breaths to fill his lungs.

As Schofield recovered his breath, Bertie used his blowtorch to cut through his handcuffs and leg rope.

Thanks to the tough little robot, Schofield was alive and free again. Indeed, the only way for him to escape from Marius Calderon and the Army of Thieves had been to die.

He snatched Bertie's first-aid pack, grabbed an AP-6 needle from it and jabbed himself with the painkiller/stimulant. His breathing evened out; he began to feel stronger.

It was then that he saw the three items sitting on Bertie's back: Champion's Steyr TMP, her SIG Sauer P226 pistol and a Magneteux.

He stood and nodded at Bertie. 'Thanks, little buddy. You're good to have around. Before we go, access your friend and foe memory bank, please.'

'*Memory bank accessed*,' Bertie said.

'Delete Lance Corporal Vittorio Puzo from friend list.'

'*Entry deleted*.'

'Good. Now, come with me. It's time to do some fucking damage.'

Facing off against Marius Calderon and his Army of Thieves in the gasworks—two against forty—Schofield and Bertie opened fire together.

Bertie blazed away with his cannon on full auto, sending forth a three-foot-long tongue of fire from the muzzle of his gunbarrel. His wave of heavy-calibre bullets cut into the crowd of Thieves, scything across them, and in the first burst alone, sixteen men fell, practically cut in half, bloody fountains spurting everywhere.

Schofield was more precise with his fire, but no less deadly.

The first man he took aim at was Calderon, but the Lord of Anarchy was quick. As Schofield fired, Calderon yanked Mobutu in front of him and Mobutu was hit twice in the chest while Calderon dived through the nearby exit door, disappearing outside, followed by Mario.

Next, Schofield took down the two men holding Zack, dropping them with one shot each before yelling, 'Zack, lie down and stay down!' Zack immediately dropped to his belly and covered his head with his hands.

Schofield then took rapid aim at the Thief holding Emma—a wiry bald man with a silver chain stretched between two facial piercings—but as Schofield fired, the man dropped down a ladder behind him, yanking Emma with him. Schofield wasn't sure if he'd hit the man or not, but he didn't have time to check, because right then a horizontal finger of fire rushed past him at very close range and he had to dive away.

It had actually been aimed at Bertie. The little robot had been doing so much damage that a Thief with a flamethrowing unit

slung from a harness over his shoulders had unleashed a lance of fire at him. The flames washed over Bertie, engulfing him completely, but the little robot just rolled out of them, his rubber tyres alight, and shot the flamethrowing Thief right between the eyes.

But then a far more dangerous attack came: the Caucasian officer known as Mako snatched up an RPG from the floor and fired it at Bertie.

The grenade shot across the wide space and hit Bertie square in the lower body.

Bertie blew apart.

His already-flaming tyres went flying out in four different directions while shards of titanium sprayed wildly outward. The little robot disappeared in a cloud of smoke.

Schofield saw it happen and his heart sank, but he couldn't stop shooting. He was now alone in this fight, which meant he had to finish it quickly.

And so, in the single minute that followed, Shane Schofield, the Scarecrow, unleashed all of his fearsome skills as a warrior on the remaining twenty members of the crowd of Thieves.

He killed like a force of nature.

His face was blank, devoid of emotion. He just marched forward, firing coolly and calmly, without a single wasted bullet, an unstoppable, relentless, merciless Marine rifleman.

He nailed every man in sight.

The few members of the crowd who managed to raise a weapon in defence went down in sprays of blood, thrown off their feet by Schofield's powerful fire. After firing the RPG, Mako used one of his own men as a human shield and took aim at Schofield but Schofield dropped them both with the same volley from his Steyr, firing it *through* the first man's chest so that the same bullets lodged in Mako's heart, too.

Schofield then saw Big Jesus and took aim at him, but the big

Chilean lieutenant was smart and he dived out the exit door, shutting it behind him—and those who fled for the door after him found that he had *locked* it behind him, sealing them in with Schofield.

They looked back in horror at the grim face of the man whose torture they had cheered only a short while ago.

Schofield shot them where they stood until there was no member of the Army of Thieves left alive on the balcony.

His enemies dead, Schofield raced to Mother's side.

As he arrived at her body, hanging motionless from the forklift, to his great surprise, he saw her head move slightly, as if cocking to one side.

'Mother?' he said, unsure. It could have been a post-death reflex.

'Scarecrow?' Her voice was muffled by the wooden box over it. 'No way. Was all that gunfire yours?'

Schofield hurriedly lowered the forklift, bringing Mother and Baba down to the floor, where he quickly shot open their handcuffs and hastily removed the boxes from their heads.

Mother's box came off first.

Two dead rats tumbled out of it . . . *headless*. Their necks ended in ragged bloody stumps. Their heads had been wrenched off.

Mother's teeth, Schofield saw, were bloody.

'Oh, Mother . . .' he said, clutching her in a firm embrace.

'Ozzy fucking Osbourne's got nothing on me,' she said, hugging him back. 'Anyone can bite the head off a bat onstage. Try biting the heads off two wild fucking rats while they're trying to get at you! Now that takes balls.'

Zack came over and removed Baba's box and, just like Mother's, out of it dropped two headless rats.

The Frenchman spat out some tiny rat bones. 'Eugh! The fur gets between your teeth!'

'That was your plan?' Schofield said to Mother. 'Fake your death and maybe make a move when they dumped your body?'

'Hey. Last I saw, you'd been crispy-fried and told me to fight on after your death. A girl's gotta do what a girl's gotta do.'

'Nice plan, actually.'

Mother shrugged. 'When they put those boxes on our heads, I said to Baba, "Do what Ozzy Osbourne would do and then play dead." Luckily, Baba is a man of fine musical taste and understood what that meant.'

Schofield smiled. 'I love you to death, Mother. And you're growing on me, too, Baba.'

Baba nodded at Schofield's weapons. 'And I know those guns, monsieur. A fine woman owns them. Is she alive?'

'For now, yes, but we can talk about that later. This resurrection isn't over yet. We gotta stop those bastards firing another missile.'

As he turned to move, Schofield saw Zack crouching a short distance away. He was bent over the remains of Bertie.

Schofield came over.

Bertie lay on the floor, horrifically mutilated. His entire lower half—his wheels and motor—had been blown apart by the grenade blast. It was now a tangled mess. His upper half was still intact and his internal battery was evidently still working, too: both his cannon and his stalk-mounted lens kept roving around, searching bravely for enemies even though he could no longer move.

'How is he?' Schofield asked.

'He wants to keep fighting, but he isn't going anywhere anymore.'

Schofield looked down at the little robot. 'That little guy brought me back from the dead. He stays with me.'

Schofield quickly grabbed an object off the nearby corpse of an Army of Thieves man. Then he picked up Bertie—what was left of him—and did something that made Zack smile.

'Hey, nice . . .' Zack said.

Last of all, Schofield went over to Mobutu's body and took his Maghook back. When he had it, he nodded at the exit door. 'This way.'

They all hurried for the door.

Mother and Baba were at the rear of the group. They crouched to grab an AK-47 each from a couple of dead Thieves, plus some spare clips and also an earpiece radio each.

As she hurried after Schofield, Mother looked back at the carnage behind them: nearly forty bloody corpses.

'Mental note,' she said softly to Baba. 'Never *ever* make the Scarecrow angry.'

Flanked by Mother, Baba and Zack, Schofield blew the lock on the exterior door of the gasworks and peered outside—in time to see Calderon, flanked by Big Jesus and half a dozen men, striding off toward the missile battery.

A short distance ahead of them was Typhon, carrying the Samsonite case with the spheres in it. He was about to cross the high bridge that gave access to the missile battery.

Without warning, Calderon turned and saw Scarecrow and at his shout, his men opened fire on Schofield and his people, trying to keep them at bay long enough for Typhon to get to the missile battery with the spheres.

Schofield immediately saw that he was too late.

He couldn't overcome Calderon's men *and* stop Typhon.

'Damn it,' he said. 'There's no way we can—'

He cut himself off as he saw the tiny figure in the distance, seemingly sitting at the far end of the high bridge that Typhon was now in the process of crossing, a figure Schofield recognised.

He never finished his sentence, for it was at that exact moment that the explosion came and the missile battery blew sky high.

The entire missile battery went up in a great billowing fireball, right in front of Typhon.

A rolling series of explosions went off as, one after the other, the six transport erector launchers on the flat-topped rocky mount blew apart, their gas tanks rupturing, the missiles on their backs either shattering to pieces or being flung off the mount by the force of the blasts.

The only explanation Schofield had for the blast was the tiny figure he'd glimpsed sitting at the end of the road bridge.

It had been the Kid, just sitting there on the roadway. The blast, when it went off, had consumed him and now he was nowhere to be seen.

Schofield recalled seeing Mario earlier, before his torture. Betraying his team and siding with Calderon, Mario claimed he had shot the Kid in the head.

Schofield couldn't know for sure, but he suspected that Mario— more mechanic than rifleman and a low-level hoodlum to boot—had made the mistake of many a criminal thug: he had shot the Kid in the forehead and walked away.

The thing was, contrary to popular belief, a forehead shot is the most *unlikely* headshot to kill someone. Through millennia of evolution, the bone of the forehead, the brain's primary protective barrier, is the thickest and strongest part of the human skull. Experienced criminal killers always fire *two* shots into the *back* of the head, where the skull is much softer: the so-called execution-style killing. Snipers will aim for the temple or, if they can, the eye. But with a shot to the forehead, if the victim can get to a hospital in a reasonable time, the wound is actually very survivable.

The Kid had evidently survived.

Long enough to complete his mission, if slowly.

Schofield pictured him, bleeding from the forehead and moving with difficulty, planting his grenades around the missile site, placing them on gas tanks for maximum effect, and then when it was done, slumping on his ass on the roadway, waiting for the end to come.

It had come in spectacular fashion.

When Marius Calderon saw his missile battery go up in flames, his mouth fell open.

He shook the shock away. He hadn't come this far without contingency plans and he still had a few of those.

'Big Jesus!' he yelled, handing the burly Thief one of the spheres. 'Get to the train! Roll it out and use its mobile missile launcher to ignite the atmosphere! Typhon! Come with me!'

'Yes, sir!' Big Jesus hurried back toward the gasworks, unslinging the Kord, accompanied by six other Thieves, their AK-47s raking Schofield's door, keeping him and his people pinned down inside.

But they didn't try to enter the gasworks. Big Jesus and his team ran right past the door—pummelling it with gunfire—and hurried around the northern corner of the gasworks.

They were heading for the railway platform's outer entrance.

After they were gone, Schofield cracked open his door and saw Calderon.

The CIA man was leaping into a jeep—with Typhon, Mario and the other sphere. He sped off in the opposite direction, heading along the road that led around the disc tower toward the runway on the other side.

'Now where is he going?' Mother said.

'He's hedging his bets,' Schofield said. 'He sent those assholes to the train to fire off a sphere on a carriage-mounted missile. If they succeed, he wins. But if they fail, he still has one sphere left, and if he has another plane he can use—'

'He does,' Zack said. 'In one of the hangars. Emma and I were hiding in it when we were caught. It looked just like the one you drove off the waterfall. Had a whole lot of stuff in the hold, all covered up.'

'Did it now?' Schofield paused, thinking. 'I'm guessing that apart from the missiles on that train, he's all out of missiles. The only other choice he has left is flying that last sphere directly into the gas cloud and releasing it like a bomb. What the—'

As he said this, Schofield had been peering out through the doorway, watching Calderon's jeep.

To his surprise, the jeep skidded to a halt beside the cable car terminal overlooking the islets to the north. Typhon leapt out of the jeep and ran inside, appearing a minute later on the *roof* of the terminal.

Schofield watched him intently. 'No . . . no way . . .'

On the roof of the terminal, partially hidden behind a low wall, Typhon crouched for a few seconds and then rose holding something in his hands: a compact and very modern black satellite dish.

The curved dish was square in shape and made of a metal mesh.

Typhon didn't waste any time. Moments later, he appeared on the ground level again, leapt back into Calderon's jeep and the jeep sped off.

Schofield's eyes narrowed.

His mind was whirring now, connecting dots. Things were moving way too quickly and he was struggling to keep everything clear in his head, when suddenly he saw it, saw it all.

'I think I just figured out what Calderon's exit strategy is,' he said.

'I thought you already figured that out? It's his second plane,' Mother said.

'No, the exit strategy *for his entire plan*, a secret CIA plan that's been in operation for over twenty years,' Schofield said. 'It's his final exit strategy, one that leaves *no trace* of the Army of Thieves and thus no witnesses.'

Schofield gritted his teeth, looked around for a nearby vehicle, and spotted one, a jeep. 'I have to stop him taking off in that plane or else this whole island and everyone on it is history.'

'What!' Mother said.

'Are you serious?' Baba said.

'Trust me. There's no time to explain. Right now, I need you two to take care of that train. Do whatever you have to do to stop them launching a missile from it. I'll take Zack and go after Calderon and his plane. Zack—'

He turned.

Zack was nowhere to be seen.

He was gone.

'Now where the hell did he go?' Mother said.

Schofield gazed back into the gasworks and thought of Emma. 'I have an idea, but that's Zack's fight. I wish we could help him, but if we don't stop Calderon now, a whole lot more people will die. Now go. You take the train. I'll take the plane.'

And with those words, they split up—Mother and Baba dashed back inside the gasworks, heading for the railway platform, while Schofield leapt onto the nearby jeep and gunned it off the mark, speeding as fast as he could in the direction of the runway in a last desperate attempt to stop Marius Calderon.

Zack crept silently across the bottom level of the gasworks, wending his way through the maze of industrial-sized piping. He passed hissing valves and vats of steaming liquids. On the sides of all the vats were warning labels written in Russian. The only text he recognised was on one huge vat marked 'TEB' followed by a warning in bold red letters.

He was following Bad Willy.

As he'd stood with Schofield, Mother and Baba at the exit door, he had glanced back inside the gasworks—and glimpsed Willy, with Emma, down on the bottom level.

During the mayhem of Schofield's resurrection, Zack had hit the ground and covered his head with his hands. He hadn't seen where Bad Willy had gone with Emma.

But now he knew.

When Schofield and Bertie had started firing, Bad Willy must have dived with Emma—his hard-earned prize—down a nearby ladder and hidden with her down on the lower level.

As soon as he'd seen them in the gasworks, Zack had taken off after them, not even bothering to tell Schofield and the others where he was going. Nothing they could have said would have stopped him anyway. They could save the world, but it would mean nothing to Zack if Emma was defiled by Bad Willy before then.

And so he'd grabbed a pistol from beside the corpse of an Army of Thieves man and hurried down to the lower level and commenced his pursuit.

☾

Mother and Baba raced through a different section of the gas-works, the uppermost level, heading for the massive train parked at the railway siding on the northern side of the vast space.

As she ran, Mother saw the megatrain start to move. Big Jesus and his six-man team were all over it, AKs in hand.

The train was only five cars long, but each car was huge, oversized in the extreme. There was an armoured locomotive at each end, then a double-levelled cargo carriage—capable of conveying jeeps, trucks and other large loads—then in the middle, a long flatbed car on which sat two huge SS-23 intermediate-range ballistic missiles, currently lying horizontally side-by-side on big hydraulic risers.

'The Russians built many train-launched missile systems,' Baba said as he ran. 'But the train needs to be stationary in order to fire the missile, otherwise it will misfire.'

Mother said, 'So they need to drive the train out of this building *and then stop it* to fire the missile?'

'Correct.'

Mother pursed her lips again. 'Think, Mother. What would Scarecrow do?'

'What?'

'Never mind,' she said, as it hit her. 'He wouldn't let them stop the train. He'd keep it *moving*. Come on, Baba. We gotta get aboard, seize control of the lead locomotive and keep that train moving.'

Schofield sped along in his stolen jeep, skirting the massive moat surrounding the disc tower, heading toward the runway.

With him was Bertie, but in a most unusual configuration—the configuration that had made Zack smile.

Bertie was mounted on Schofield's back, clipped securely to it by virtue of the flamethrower harness Schofield had taken from the dead Army of Thieves man in the gasworks. The harness's four main carabiner clips—usually used to hold a tank on the user's back—had clipped perfectly to points on Bertie's metal exoskeleton so that now he sat on Schofield's back, piggyback style.

Bertie's stalk-mounted eye looked out eagerly over Schofield's right shoulder, panning left and right, while his M249 cannon poked out over Schofield's left shoulder.

Schofield drove hard.

He saw Calderon's jeep heading round the wide circular moat, making for the steep road that led to the runway.

There hadn't been time to tell the others about the significance of Calderon's short stop at the cable car terminal.

The satellite dish that Typhon had grabbed was the uplink— the satellite uplink keeping Dragon Island safe from Russian and American nuclear missile strikes.

When he had first arrived on Dragon via that very same cable car terminal, Schofield had scanned the area for the uplink in the hope of disabling or destroying it, but it had been hidden, as it turned out, right above his head.

Typhon's recent snatching of the uplink, however, had terrible ramifications.

Calderon and his key lieutenant were getting away from Dragon Island, leaving their fake terrorist army behind. Presumably, the Army of Thieves believed he would come back for them once the sky was alight.

But he wouldn't be coming back at all, Schofield realised.

No. Watching from his escape plane, as soon as his men on the train launched their missile—or if he got away and ignited the sky with *his* sphere—Calderon would then simply switch off the uplink.

Russian Missile Command, still monitoring Dragon with their own satellites, would immediately detect that the defensive uplink was down and, enraged at Calderon's previous reversal of one of their nuclear missiles, immediately fire a nuke on Dragon.

Calderon would destroy China, while he would get away with his small leadership group and his fake terrorist Army would be annihilated by the Russian nuclear missile. The world would be irrevocably changed, the blame would be laid on the mysterious terrorist group, and Calderon would make a clean getaway, unconnected to any of it.

Mission accomplished.

Which was why Schofield had to stop Calderon's plane. If he could keep Calderon on Dragon Island, Calderon wouldn't switch off the uplink, as it would mean condemning himself to death—

Gunfire hit Scarecrow's jeep.

Schofield spun to see an Army of Thieves troop truck thundering along behind him, with men hanging off it, firing.

'Bertie! Take them out!'

'*Yes, Captain Schofield.*'

As Schofield kept looking forward, driving hard, weaving and swerving, Bertie swivelled both his eye and his cannon around and loosed two booming shots.

The first shot hit the truck's grille, puncturing the radiator, causing it to release a hissing plume of steam; the second hit its front left tyre, causing the truck to wobble, then fishtail, then skid out of control before it tumbled onto its side, spilling men everywhere.

Schofield smiled grimly. While deafening, it was like having eyes—and a gun—in the back of your head.

'Good robot,' he said.

Up ahead, he saw Calderon's car take the left-hand fork and shoot down the steep road leading to the airfield. He made to follow, but some Army of Thieves sentries quickly stepped out onto the road there and unleashed a heavy rain of gunfire. One man had a flamethrower and sent forth a blazing tongue of fire.

Schofield swore. He couldn't run that blockade.

So, without any loss of speed, he yanked his steering wheel right and took off up the right-hand fork. He could still reach the runway by going the long way, around the higher ground to the north.

It would take time and he wasn't sure if he had enough of that.

But he had to try. With Bertie on his back covering him, Schofield floored the jeep.

Zack heard them before he saw them.

He heard Emma struggling. 'No! *No!* Leave me alone!'

A sharp slapping sound followed.

'Shut up, bitch!' Bad Willy's voice echoed through the tangle of pipes, tanks and vats. 'No knights in shining armour left to save you now.'

Zack rounded the corner and beheld the scene: Emma on the ground with Bad Willy standing over her.

'There's still one left,' he said loudly.

They both snapped around. Emma's face lit up with both hope and horror. Bad Willy's face transformed from surprise to wicked glee.

'Zacky-boy,' he grinned. 'Who'da thunk it? The weedy little poindexter coming to save the girl from the nasty fucking rapist?'

Zack raised his pistol.

Bad Willy said, 'I don't have a gun, Zacky. You'd shoot me in cold blood?'

'Yes.'

'Don't miss.'

His jaw clenched, Zack fired. Twice.

And missed high with both shots. They sparked off a large pipe behind Willy's head.

He pulled the trigger again, several times: *click-click-click*.

Bad Willy grinned more darkly. 'I am going to kick the fucking shit out of you, you little pansy-assed dandy, and then I'm going to do every *kind* of nastiness to your woman here.'

Willy shoved Emma into a nearby storage cage and snapped its bolt home, locking it.

Emma shook the gate, but it was no use, she was trapped there, trapped to watch what was to come: a fight between Bad Willy of the Army of Thieves and Zack Weinberg of DARPA.

Willy lunged at Zack, teeth bared, fists flying.

Zack ducked beneath Willy's first two blows, bobbed up, and managed to land a killer punch on Willy's face. Willy froze in mid-stride.

Zack paused. Had he—?

Willy started laughing.

'Is that it? Is that the best you've got? Oh, this is not fair. Not fair at all.'

Quick as a rattlesnake, Willy hit Zack in the face and Zack dropped to the ground, nose bleeding.

Then Bad Willy grabbed him by the collar and headbutted him, dropping him again.

Emma screamed.

As he stood over Zack, Bad Willy called back to her: 'Keep doing that, honey. Keep screaming. I *love* screams, feed off 'em.'

He lifted Zack and rammed him up against a thick round pipe, narrowly missing a pressure valve sticking out of it.

Dizzy and in considerable pain, Zack's vision was becoming blurred. He felt ill. He was about to pass out, and if he passed out, this was all over. Willy would kill him and then take Emma and—

Through his blurred vision, Zack saw something on the valve beside his head. Letters that gradually came into focus: T . . . E . . .

Suddenly Willy was right in his face.

'You blasted my ear off, you little fuck,' Willy growled. 'To pay you back for that, I'm gonna hack off both your ears and make you eat 'em. Then I'm gonna slash your fucking throat and drink your blood.'

Willy unsheathed a long-bladed hunting knife and held it up to Zack's eyes.

Zack gasped, coughing.

Willy said, 'Got something to say, eh?'

Zack whispered something.

'Speak up! I can't hear you!'

'I said . . .' Zack began as, with his last ounce of strength, he quickly reached up and yanked hard on the lever on the gas valve beside his head, the valve whose label read 'TEB'.

The valve opened and a high-pressure spray of green liquid came blasting out of it, directly into Bad Willy's eyes.

Willy wailed as the searing-hot liquid gushed into his face. He dropped his knife and clutched at his eyes as the skin on his forehead, cheeks and chin immediately began to *melt*.

His wails became shrieks as the searing explosive fuel mixture— the undiluted raw concentrate that was the basis of the combustible gas in the sky—ate through the skin of his face.

Willy clawed at his cheeks, but this only served to pull away the melting skin, revealing flesh and bone. Then his hands came away and Zack saw that Willy's *eyes* were melting, too. The whites of his eyeballs dribbled down his melted-away cheeks and stuck to his fingertips.

Willy shrieked a hideous, inhuman scream.

He lunged at Zack, clutching at him with his disgusting hands, but Zack kicked him hard in the chest, pushing him away and Bad Willy fell to the ground, whimpering.

Moments later, the acid ate into his brain and Bad Willy lay still, dead.

Zack ran to the cage, threw it open, and Emma leapt into his arms and sobbed as he held her.

As the megatrain left the siding, Mother and Baba ran up alongside it and leapt onto its last carriage, a backward-facing armoured locomotive.

The train lumbered forward. It was truly a Soviet monster, double-sized in every way: two storeys high, two train-widths wide and riding on two sets of train tracks.

But it wasn't designed for speed. It had been designed for heavy cargo freight, to carry the building materials for Dragon Island from the north-east dock—now reconfigured as a submarine dock—to the central complex, which meant it was a relatively slow beast.

Today, however, it only had to clear the station and stop in a firing position to launch one of its missiles.

'We have to get to the forward locomotive,' Mother called to Baba, 'to keep this train moving!'

Blocking their way, though, was the Chilean lieutenant, Big Jesus, and his six-man team. While two men drove, Big Jesus and the other four had established a defensive position around the central missile carriage—where Big Jesus was currently busy bent over the missile, inserting the uranium sphere into its warhead.

Mother assessed the situation. They had to get past that missile car.

'Okay, handsome,' she said to Baba. 'You're gonna lay down a shitload of fire on those cocksuckers from here while I go forward and take the locomotive. Then you come and join me.'

'I beg your pardon, but how are you going to get past them?' Baba asked.

'Not going past them,' Mother said. 'Going *under* them. Now, gimme some hot lead, baby.'

'With pleasure.'

Baba hefted his AK-47 and started firing at Big Jesus and his men, while Mother jumped off the slow-moving train and crouch-ran under it.

Big Jesus returned fire at Baba . . . with Baba's own Kord machine gun. Its mighty rounds clanged loudly off the rear locomotive's armour, forcing Baba to take cover.

'Merde!' Baba growled to nobody. 'Fired on by my own beautiful gun.'

He returned fire as best he could with the puny AK-47.

By doing so, however, he captured the full attention of Big Jesus and his men, distracting them from the figure running underneath the rumbling carriages of the megatrain: Mother.

The train was only moving at about five miles an hour and its immense size meant that Mother could run bent over along the tracks underneath it. She hurried forward under the first cargo car, then—careful not to be seen by Big Jesus and his men—under the missile car.

When she crossed the gap between the missile car and the second cargo car, she was briefly exposed and found herself standing *in daylight*. The first half of the train had cleared the siding! Once its missile carriage was fully outside, it would be ready to fire.

Huffing and puffing, she pushed on and was halfway along the second cargo car with the lead locomotive in sight when she realised the train was slowing.

It was already coming to a halt, coming into a firing position.

'Outta time, must run faster,' she said to herself, ducking out from under the cargo car and running at full stride alongside it.

Behind her, she could hear Baba exchanging fire with the men on the missile car, still taking the attention from her.

Mother came to the forward locomotive, bounded up onto a running board mounted on its side and just as the train's wheels

were squealing, announcing its impending halt, she swung up into its cab, leading with her gun.

The two Army of Thieves men driving the megatrain turned from its controls, eyes wide, and reached for their weapons.

Blam! Blam!

Starbursts of blood splattered the forward windshield behind their heads. Both men fell.

Mother hurried to the controls and just as the train was about to come to a stop, she pushed forward on the throttle and the train lurched, accelerating.

On the missile car, Big Jesus felt the lurch and spun.

'They've taken the engine car!' he called to the four men with him. To two of them, he said, 'You two, stay here, keep the missile safe and hold that big fellow where he is!' He nodded to the other pair: 'You two, come with me. We must stop this train!'

With that pair at his side, Big Jesus hurried forward, leading with the Kord, going after Mother in the lead locomotive.

Mother saw them coming. 'Uh-oh . . .'

She snapped round, peered out the forward windshield.

The entrance to the submarine dock was about a kilometre away, at the end of a flat plain of open, barren ground. It looked like a tunnel, with the megatrain's tracks burrowing down into the ground near the coastal cliffs. Plenty of time to stop the megatrain and fire the missile.

I can't let them stop us, Mother thought desperately. *But how can I make sure of that?*

The solution struck her immediately.

And as the first massive round from the Kord clanged against the steel roof above her head, Mother jammed the throttle all the way forward, causing the megatrain to pick up speed alarmingly.

Then she left the lever, scooping up her AK-47, and rejoined the battle.

She was now defending the lead locomotive alone, one against three, and woefully outgunned. In her heart of hearts, Mother knew she couldn't win this battle, but if she could hold out long enough, she might just win the war.

The megatrain thundered across the barren north-eastern plain of Dragon Island, picking up speed.

The tiny figures of Big Jesus and his two comrades could be seen advancing along the roof of the second carriage, the cargo car, firing on the lead locomotive, while the muzzle flashes of a lone figure could be seen firing back at them through the open rear window of the locomotive's driver's compartment.

There was, however, no longer any sign of a gunbattle at the rear of the train.

On the roof of the train, Big Jesus and his men leapfrogged forward in perfect formation. They weren't amateurs and they knew they had the edge on Mother both in numbers and firepower. Soon they were up near the locomotive, firing at her at close range and suddenly Mother recoiled, hit in the right shoulder.

She was flung backwards and they rushed the driver's compartment, covering her.

Big Jesus reached for the control lever and had gripped it when out of the corner of his eye, he glimpsed a figure thump down onto the flat bonnet of the locomotive right in front of him.

Big Jesus looked up and that figure took form, the form of a big bearded Frenchman lying on his belly on the locomotive's bonnet, taking aim at Big Jesus's face with a pistol.

Baba fired once through the glass.

The bullet came slamming through the windshield and into Big Jesus's left eye before it exploded out the back of his head. He collapsed where he stood, dropping the Kord.

Two more shots and the other two Thieves also went down.

Baba swung in through the shattered windshield and crouched by Mother's side.

'Nice entrance,' Mother groaned, pressing a hand to the wound on her shoulder.

'I am French,' Baba said simply. 'I was born with a certain je ne sais quoi.'

Mother smiled despite herself. 'You're one bad-ass dude, I know that. You didn't stay at the back of the train like I told you to, did you?'

'I couldn't.' Baba nodded at the rest of the train. 'They sent reinforcements.'

Mother followed his gaze.

Another *two dozen* Army of Thieves men were now boarding the megatrain, clambering onto it from two troop trucks, one on either side of the train.

'I had to come here,' he said. 'So I came the same way you did, running underneath the train.'

A bullet slammed into the roof above them. Then another. Then a *wave* of them.

Mother and Baba ducked. Mother hefted her AK-47. Baba grabbed his beloved Kord from the floor.

'Come!' Baba called as he dragged her out through the shattered forward windshield. 'Out onto the bonnet! If we are to make a last stand, it is the best place!'

'Our own private Alamo . . .' Mother said as she arrived on the bonnet beside Baba.

Then, facing back down the length of the rumbling train, they opened fire together on the advancing horde of Thieves.

The exchange of gunfire that followed was vicious in the extreme: Thieves swarmed all over the megatrain like ants at a picnic, while Mother and Baba held them off from the bonnet of the lead loco-motive, picking them off left and right.

The Thieves kept coming.

Mother and Baba kept firing.

A round sizzled past Mother's ear, slicing through her earpiece's filament microphone on the way by, nicking skin, drawing blood. Close.

Then, abruptly, in between shots, Baba called, 'Mother! You are a fine warrior and a magnificent woman. Are you spoken for? If we should survive this, I should very much like to wine you, dine you and make mad, passionate love to you for many hours. But smitten as I may be, I am a man of honour and do not court other men's wives. Are you spoken for?'

Mother paused in between shots, thinking for a moment.

She thought of Ralph, her Ralphy, and of their life together which only a week ago she had described as banal and boring—and then she looked at the Frenchman, this larger-than-life warrior called the Barbarian, Baba. He was her mirror, her male equivalent.

But he wasn't Ralphy.

'Sorry, you sexy beast!' she shouted, punching off a shot. 'But I *am* spoken for! I'm married!'

Baba loosed another shot from the Kord. 'He is a lucky man, your husband! And he must be a fine fellow to capture and hold a heart as big as yours!'

'He is!' Mother called. 'He certainly is!'

The larger force of Thieves was now leaping onto the back of the lead locomotive, their takeover of the megatrain now certain and all but complete, when Baba leaned suddenly forward and kissed Mother hard on the mouth and said, 'Live for both of us then, my friend, Mother! I shall go to my grave with the taste of your lips on my mouth!'

And with those words, he leapt up onto the roof of the locomotive—totally out in the open, totally exposed—planted his feet wide and raised his mighty Kord.

Then he opened fire.

The massive machine gun blazed to life, razing the advancing horde of Thieves with an absolute *torrent* of sizzling bullets.

They dropped everywhere—shot to pieces or simply hurled off

the moving train—but there were just too many of them for Baba to take out alone and a few managed to get off some shots that found their target: first a glancing blow to Baba's left arm, then more substantial hits to the torso and shoulders.

One, two, then three shots hit his body, but still he kept firing.

Mother watched in admiration, wonder and despair.

The train kept rushing across the plain.

It was the fourth shot that felled Baba.

He dropped to his knees, yet *still* managed to get off some more shots from the Kord.

Then a bullet struck him square in the chest and he dropped to the roof of the locomotive and Mother, still on the bonnet, wounded and unable to go to his aid, shouted, 'No!' just as the train shot into darkness, into the tunnel that led to the submarine dock.

Baba had done what he'd set out to do.

He'd bought them enough time to get to the dock.

Now it was too late to stop the train.

The megatrain thundered through the short tunnel, picking up speed as it shot down the slope, still with a dozen Thieves on its back.

It emerged with a roar inside the wide hall that was the submarine dock where—now speeding totally out of control—it exploded *straight through* the guardrail separating the end of the track from the water in the dock. The lead locomotive's pointed snowplough smashed through the wooden guardrail, blasting it into a thousand matchsticks, before the whole train just *poured* off the end of the track, diving—*driving*—into the water, one carriage after the other disappearing into the sea like a huge slithering snake. Its missile car vanished under the surface, having never been able to fire its deadly cargo.

As the locomotive had shot off the end of the tracks, Mother—still on the bonnet—had seen, of all things, the *Okhotsk*, half-sunk

in the water, right next to her, a final bizarre sight for a truly bizarre day. Shot, exhausted and despairing at Baba's heroic sacrifice, Mother felt the locomotive below her drop through the air.

A second later, it hit the water.

Her battle with the Army of Thieves had been fought and although she wouldn't come out of it alive, she would at least die knowing that she had beaten the motherfuckers.

The megatrain dived into the water and sank into the darkness, never to be seen again.

While Mother, Baba and the megatrain were heading for a watery grave, Schofield was speeding across Dragon Island's north-western plain in his jeep, angling toward the runway, now chased by two Army trucks and one motorcycle with a sidecar. Harnessed onto his back, Bertie fired back at them, while Schofield did the same, driving one-handed and firing with his Steyr TMP.

Ducking bullets, Schofield crested a hill and suddenly beheld the runway, where he saw Calderon's *second* plane—an Antonov An-12, just like the first one—emerge from its hangar, wheel around on the taxiway and start rumbling down the runway, accelerating to take-off speed.

Schofield swung his jeep onto a converging course with the plane, a course that would finish at the very end of the runway.

His plan was a desperate one: he intended to drive his jeep in front of the plane, crippling its landing gear and stopping it from taking off. There was no other option: if Calderon got away, he—

A sudden volley shattered his windshield and Schofield spun to see the enemy motorcycle—with a gun-toting passenger in its sidecar—pull alongside him.

Schofield brought up his TMP but it just clicked, empty. Fortunately, at the same time, Bertie swung around and with two blistering shots nailed both the rider and the passenger and the motorbike went tumbling away, end over end.

Schofield chucked the TMP and gunned the jeep. It swung in parallel to the runway, hurtling along at almost a hundred kilometres an hour, just ahead of the rolling Antonov.

But then the Antonov surged forward . . . powering up to take-off speed, accelerating dramatically . . .

Schofield's jeep bounced up onto the runway, speeding as fast as it could go.

The Antonov thundered down the tarmac, picking up speed. Soon it would overtake the jeep and lift off, after which it would ignite the sky, while Dragon Island and everyone left on it would be destroyed by an angry Russian missile strike.

As he sped along, Schofield glanced forward and saw the end of the runway rapidly approaching. It was dangerously close, with nothing beyond it but sheer cliffs dropping down to the ocean.

I have to get in front of that plane . . .

He made to yank left on his steering wheel when suddenly, with a roar, the Antonov came alongside his jeep, its forward wheels lifting slowly from the runway . . .

He was too late.

No!

The plane lifted off with only twenty metres of runway to spare.

The sight of the Antonov lifting off from Dragon Island's western runway would have been pretty impressive in and of itself, but its lift-off that day was special in one other way.

Had anyone been watching it from afar, they would have seen the plane soar magnificently into the air with a little jeep speeding along the ground beside it, trying valiantly to keep up. But as the plane took to the air, the keen observer would *also* have seen the man driving the jeep fire something up at the departing plane: a device with a trailing cable.

Speeding along in the jeep with the wind assaulting his face and the roar of the Antonov assailing his ears, Schofield stood and fired his Magneteux's grappling hook up at the departing plane.

The Magneteux's arrow-like head lodged in the plane's fuselage up near its nose and as the Antonov lifted off, Schofield was yanked up into the air with it, clinging to the Magneteux's cable.

As he was swept up into the air, hanging from the rising plane, his jeep went flying off the end of the runway, over the cliff, dropping in a great soaring arc into the ocean far below.

The Antonov soared skyward at a steep angle, with Shane Schofield dangling from it by his Magneteux's cable.

Schofield had already done the maths in his head: the gap in the gas cloud would be perhaps seventy kilometres wide, so the Antonov would reach it in less than ten minutes. Once there, Calderon would drop a warhead into it and ignite the gas cloud.

Schofield reeled in his cable and whizzed up it, arriving near the nose of the Antonov, which, like the other one, featured a glass spotter's dome.

Schofield swung up under the glass dome, unholstered his SIG and fired it into the glass.

He ran out of bullets after two shots, but they did enough. The dome shattered and he discarded the gun, swung himself up and clambered inside.

With freezing wind whistling all around him, Schofield stepped up into the Antonov's forward nose area—

—to find Mario standing before him, his M9 pistol aimed at Schofield's head.

Calderon and Typhon were nowhere to be seen. They must have been up in the cockpit directly above the nose cone. In the hold beyond Mario, Schofield saw a large object hidden underneath a tarpaulin and at the very back of the hold, near its closed ramp, the jeep Calderon had driven from the gasworks to get to the plane.

'Mario . . .' Schofield said, his hands spread wide. He had

discarded the empty SIG when he'd climbed up through the shattered glass dome, so he was now gunless.

'I made my choice, Scarecrow!' Mario yelled over the wind. 'And that means only one of us can go home!'

'You're a two-bit hood, Mario, unworthy of the name *Marine* . . .'

'Fuck you,' Mario shouted. 'See you in Hell!'

He made to squeeze his trigger but, to his surprise, Schofield just stood there, hands still spread wide.

Then Schofield said something and suddenly Bertie popped up over his shoulder, his machine-gun barrel unfolding quickly.

Boom!

Mario's chest exploded. He was literally blasted off his feet. His legs flew up into the air as his upper body went down. He dropped to the floor, unmoving, dead.

'Hoodlums should never pick fights with soldiers,' Schofield muttered. 'Come on, Bertie. We got work to do.'

They dashed over Mario's body, heading for the short flight of steel stairs that led up to the cockpit.

As Schofield had been hanging unseen from the Antonov's nose cone by the Magneteux's cable, Marius Calderon had been in the plane's cockpit, staring intently at a screen.

He'd attached a spectroscopic long-path analyser to one of the cockpit's side windows: it looked like a stubby horizontal aerial and it gave real-time analysis of the air quality around the plane.

Its results now appeared on the screen:

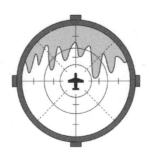

Calderon saw the gas cloud displayed as an encroaching blob at the top of the screen with his position shown at the centre. Every few seconds, the screen changed, showing the cloud getting closer as the plane advanced toward it.

They were currently 47 kilometres from the gas cloud, only four minutes' travel away.

Calderon smiled.

On the floor beside him, connected to the spectroscope by some wires, sat a Russian RS-6 nuclear warhead that had been reconfigured to accommodate a red uranium sphere. Conical in shape and covered in stencilled warnings, it was an imposing device: one capable of delivering death on a massive scale.

As soon as he'd boarded the plane, Calderon had inserted the sphere into the warhead's chamber. And now the warhead was linked to the spectroscope: once the spectroscope detected itself to be within the gas cloud, it would automatically instruct the warhead to initiate a two-minute detonation sequence, giving Calderon and Typhon time to escape before the warhead detonated.

For the explosion of the warhead would not be a small one.

It would vaporise the entire Antonov in a single fiery instant—blasting it apart as if it were made of tissue paper, before setting the gas-infused sky of the northern hemisphere alight. It was thus imperative that Calderon and Typhon be off the plane when the warhead went off, but they'd planned for that, too.

Calderon also had one last device in the cockpit: the compact black satellite dish that was the uplink. Once they were far enough away from Dragon Island, he would switch it off and leave the island to its fate.

Gunfire from the hold made him turn. 'What was that! Get down there!' he yelled to Typhon.

Calderon took the controls while Typhon dashed back into the hold.

Gun in hand, Typhon threw open the cockpit door to see the rear hold of the Antonov in turmoil: gusting Arctic wind whistled through it, causing tarps to billow and anything not tied down to swirl through the air. Making it seem even more bizarre, the hold was tilted sharply upward thanks to the ascending angle of the plane—

Someone tackled him from the side and Typhon went sprawling to the floor, dropping his gun, his attacker falling with him.

Typhon stood to see Shane Schofield rising to his feet a few yards away.

'You just keep turning up,' Typhon said as they circled each other. 'You really are something . . .'

'Where did Calderon find you?' Schofield said. 'Chile?'

'Leavenworth,' Typhon said. 'I was in the Army Rangers, but I killed a fellow Ranger who was gonna report me for an off-base incident. Calderon needed capable, patriotic men and he got me released to work for him. I brought the "Sharks" with me.'

'Great. More patriots,' Schofield said. 'Bertie!' Once again, Bertie appeared over his shoulder and—

His gunbarrel clicked, dry.

'Damn,' Schofield said as Typhon lunged at him and the two of them went thudding onto the back of the jeep in the rear of the hold, struggling and rolling.

Typhon unleashed some brutal punches, and for a short while, Schofield parried and evaded them, but he was beyond exhausted—from gunshot and torture wounds—and soon Typhon gained the ascendency, and started landing more and more blows.

Up in the cockpit of the plane, Calderon's spectroscope started beeping loudly. They had entered the gas cloud:

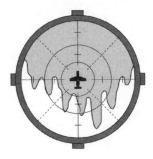

A timer on the warhead immediately started counting down.

'Time to fly,' Calderon said aloud. 'And time to say goodbye to Dragon Island. Thank you, my beloved Army. You did your job perfectly.'

With those words, he flicked a switch on the satellite uplink and every light on it went out—

—and in a room in a Russian missile launch facility in western Siberia, a console operator instantly sat upright.

'Sir!' he called. 'The satellite missile-detection shield over Dragon Island just went offline!'

His commander stared at the operator's screen for a second, then he grabbed a secure phone and relayed this information to the Russian President in Moscow.

The reply came immediately.

The missile commander hung up the phone.

'We are authorised for nuclear launch. Target is Dragon Island. Fire.'

A few moments later, an SS-18 intercontinental ballistic missile with a 500-kiloton thermonuclear warhead shot out of its silo, heading for Dragon Island. Flight time: twenty-two minutes.

All as Marius Calderon had planned.

The Antonov's hold was now a truly crazy place: tilted at a steep upward angle with a maelstrom of wind whipping through it.

Another savage blow from Typhon sent Schofield flailing onto the back of the jeep parked at the rear of the hold. In total control, Typhon straddled him and punched him again.

As Schofield recoiled from the blow, spitting blood, he suddenly became aware of a *second* source of wind in the already blustery hold.

He glanced up to see that the rear ramp was opening—a sideways look revealed that Marius Calderon had entered the hold and was at the ramp controls on the side wall.

'Why, Captain Schofield, we meet again!' he called. 'Your determination is truly admirable, but you are finally too late. We have arrived at the gas cloud and the warhead has been activated. It cannot be stopped now. Typhon! Finish him! We have to get that jeep out of the way!'

Calderon nodded at the tarp-covered object at the front end of the hold, hemmed in by the jeep.

'Yes, sir!' Typhon shouted as he gripped the weakened and battered Schofield by the throat with one hand.

He looked down at Schofield with murderous eyes. Schofield was lying defenceless on the back of the jeep, one hand hanging off it, his face dirty and bruised, his mouth dripping blood.

Typhon pulled his fist back to deliver the death blow, a blow that would drive Schofield's nose up into his brain and kill him.

His fist came rushing down, just as Schofield reached out with his free hand and pulled on a lever by the jeep's tyres.

The lever released some chains holding the jeep inside the hold and as Typhon's fist came rushing down, the jeep rolled suddenly, *straight out of the back of the steeply-rising plane* where it dropped out into the sky, with Schofield and Typhon on it!

Marius Calderon gaped at the sudden disappearance of the jeep and his right-hand man. One second they were there, the next they were gone.

'Fuck me,' he gasped.

He recovered quickly: losing Typhon was a shame but not a disaster. Typhon was an excellent second-in-command, but since he knew Calderon's real identity as a senior CIA agent, Typhon had always faced liquidation when this was all over. This had saved Calderon the effort.

As for Schofield: thank Christ. The fucking Energizer Bunny was finally gone.

Calderon kept moving. He still had a getaway to make.

The plane had just entered the gas cloud and, now flying on autopilot, it was programmed to penetrate deeper into the cloud. In less than two minutes, the warhead in the cockpit would go off.

Calderon hurried over to the tarp-covered object and threw off the tarpaulin . . .

. . . to reveal a compact mini-submarine.

It was a Russian Mir-4 Deep Submergence Rescue Vehicle, a variant of the Mir-2. Only five metres long with a curved glass bubble for its bow, it was capable of holding six crew and while it was claimed by the Russians to be used only for scientific research, the Mir-4 was actually used for submarine transfers and clandestine insertions into hostile waters. This Mir-4 had been one of two submersibles that had been on the Russian freighter, the *Okhotsk*, when it had been taken six months ago.

With the jeep now out of the way, Calderon flicked a switch and jumped aboard the sub as it was shunted by an underfloor cable to the back of the hold, ready for release. Once it reached the end of the rear ramp, it simply tipped over the edge and like the jeep before it, dropped away into the grey Arctic sky.

Unlike the jeep, however, the Mir was fitted with four parachutes, which all blossomed above it as it fell, guiding the sub and Calderon to a gentle landing in the cold waters of the Arctic Ocean.

The mini-sub landed in the ocean with a soft splash and Calderon quickly drove it under the surface, heading away to a designated retrieval location where he would be met by a CIA Sturgeon-class submarine, his years-long mission now over save for the big bang.

Calderon had taken care of everything: the gas cloud, the warhead, the destruction of Dragon Island, his own escape.

He'd only missed one thing:

The figure dangling from the underbelly of the Antonov at the end of a Maghook: Captain Shane Michael Schofield.

As Schofield's jeep had tipped out the back of the Antonov, it had dropped away toward the ocean with Typhon still on it, screaming. He had screamed all the way down.

But Schofield hadn't.

As the jeep had dropped out the back of the plane, he had called upon his trusty Maghook—small compared to the Magneteux and not nearly as sexy or strong—but it was all he had.

Leaping off the falling jeep, he'd fired the Maghook back up at the plane before he fell too far and the Maghook's bulbous magnetic head thunked against the underside of the rear ramp and held. The jeep had fallen away beneath him, but he was still in the game.

Schofield then reeled himself up using the Maghook's internal spooler, arriving under the ramp just as a submersible of some kind came rumbling out of the hold and dropped into the sky, issuing some parachutes.

'That son of a bitch,' Schofield said as he climbed back up into the blustery hold, now the doomed Antonov's only occupant. 'But this isn't over yet.'

Schofield hurried through the windblown hold and up into the empty cockpit.

He took it all in quickly: the autopilot, the spectroscope's screen showing that the plane was now *inside* the flammable gas cloud, the fearsome warhead, and *on* the warhead, a timer that currently read:

00:34 . . . 00:33 . . . 00:32 . . .

'Thirty-two seconds to the end of the world . . .' Schofield breathed. 'How do I get myself into these situations?'

He looked about himself for options, ideas, solutions.

He was basically on a flying bomb, one that would ignite a global atmospheric firestorm.

00:30 . . . 00:29 . . . 00:28 . . .

He stared at the warhead. Calderon had replaced all its exterior panels and they were all screwed shut. He'd never be able to extract the uranium sphere from it in time.

How do I stop this? How can I?

I can't.

It's too late . . .

And for the first time in his career, Schofield knew that it was true: he had finally run out of time.

Twenty-eight seconds later, the warhead detonated with all its mighty force.

The detonation of the warhead containing the red uranium sphere was devastating in its intensity. It sent out a blinding white-hot blast that expanded laterally in every direction.

Inside his Mir submersible, under the surface of the Arctic Ocean, Marius Calderon felt it. It shook his sub, even from this distance.

And then he frowned.

Deep underwater, he *shouldn't* have felt the detonation. Water was an excellent buffer against concussion waves. But he had still felt it. The only way he would feel it underwater was if . . .

'No!' Calderon shouted in the solitude of his mini-sub. '*No!*'

For the warhead had most assuredly detonated, *with* the red uranium sphere inside it. The only problem was, it had not detonated in the gas-infused sky.

As Calderon had just realised, it had detonated underwater.

It was the only thing Schofield could think to do.

Roll the warhead out of the cockpit into the hold—

00:26 . . . 00:25 . . . 00:24 . . .

Then pushing it off the back of the ramp—

00:21 . . . 00:20 . . . 00:19 . . .

The warhead tumbled end over end as it fell through the sky, its timer ticking all the way down—

Before it hit the ocean's surface with a great splash and immediately went under, sinking fast—

00:05 . . . 00:04 . . . 00:03 . . .

Where it sank and sank into the blue haze—
00:02 . . . 00:01 . . . 00:00.
Beeeeeeep!
Boom.

The explosion of the warhead under the surface of the ocean looked like the standard undersea detonation of a thermonuclear device.

After the initial white-hot blast, a great circular cloud of superheated water—packed with billions of swirling micro-bubbles—materialised and expanded, shooting out laterally before it hit the surface, sending an absolutely gargantuan geyser of water spraying up into the sky, the greatest fountain in history.

Thankfully, the warhead had sunk deep enough before it blew. The heavy weight of ocean water above it had defused its potent catalytic power and so it did not ignite the sky.

Indeed, the only person it shook was Marius Calderon.

As he climbed back into the cockpit of the Antonov and saw the great circular explosion down on the ocean's surface, Schofield breathed a huge sigh of relief.

Battered, bloody, tortured, almost overcome with exhaustion and having lost many brave people in the process, he and his team had beaten impossible odds and stopped the Army of Thieves from setting fire to the world.

It was only then that he saw the uplink dish, sitting on the cockpit's floor in front of him with all its lights extinguished.

It had been switched off.

'Oh, shit . . .' he said. 'The Russians.'

If the Russians had detected this and launched a nuke, Dragon Island and everyone on it had less than twenty minutes to live.

Schofield turned off the autopilot and swung the plane around, banking hard and fast, heading back toward Dragon Island.

FINAL PHASE

SCARECROW VS
THE ARMY OF THIEVES

DRAGON ISLAND
4 APRIL, 1400 HOURS
T-PLUS 3:00 HOURS AFTER DEADLINE

It's easy to feel when the daisies return to the battlefield that no battle was ever fought at all.
—Gretel Killeen

AIRSPACE OVER DRAGON ISLAND
4 APRIL, 1400 HOURS

Schofield's Antonov shot through the air at phenomenal speed.

On the distant northern horizon, Schofield saw the silhouette of Dragon Island: its jagged southern mountains, and on the northern plateau, the disc-shaped tower with its lone spire and the two colossal vents.

He keyed the Antonov's radio. 'American listening post, do you copy? This is Captain Shane Schofield, USMC, in distress. Is anyone out there monitoring this frequency?'

A voice immediately came on the line, jabbering in angry Russian. Then suddenly, static cut over him and an American voice came in.

'*Captain Schofield, hold for secure line,*' some clicks, then: '*Captain Schofield, this is United States Air Force Listening Post Bravo-Charlie-Six-Niner, operating out of Eareckson Air Station in the Aleutian Islands. We'd been instructed to keep an ear out for you, in case you called. Please state your service number and comm-security passcode for verification.*'

Schofield did so, adding, 'Now put me through to the White House Situation Room.'

'Patching you through now, sir.'

☉

The President's crisis team was still gathered in the White House Situation Room. With them now, however, were two extra people from the Defense Intelligence Agency: Dave Fairfax and Marianne Retter. And the CIA's representative was no longer present: when Dave and Marianne had commenced their briefing, they had requested that he leave the room.

When word came in that Scarecrow was on the line, the National Security Advisor and former Marine general, Donald Harris, jammed his finger down on the speakerphone.

'Scarecrow, Don Harris. I have the President and the crisis team here with me. Where are you and what's happened with the atmospheric device?'

'*I stopped the activation of the device, sir, but I need to know: with the uplink signal down, have the Russians launched a nuke at Dragon?*'

'Yes, they have. Three minutes ago.'

'*How long till it hits?*'

'Nineteen minutes.'

'*Shit. Can you get the Russians to self-destruct it?*'

'No. Satellite scans reveal that this missile's guidance control systems have been disabled to prevent any outside takeover, even from its own base. After what happened to the last nuke they fired at Dragon, the Russians made sure this one would hit its target. Nothing can stop that missile now.'

There was silence on the other end of the line.

'Scarecrow?' Harris asked. 'Where are you?'

'*In a plane about sixty klicks south of Dragon.*'

'Then what the hell are you thinking? Get out of there. In nineteen minutes that island is gonna be a mushroom cloud.'

'*I have people back there, sir,*' Schofield's voice said.

The President leaned forward.

'Captain Schofield, this is the President—'

'*Excuse me, sir, but by any chance did a guy named Dave Fairfax get in touch with the White House?*'

The President turned to look at Fairfax.

'Why, yes, in fact he did. He drove right through the side gate, actually. He's here now, with Ms Retter from the DIA. They were just briefing us on some CIA plan called "Dragonslayer" and an agent named Calderon.'

'*I've been doing battle with Mr Calderon all morning. Hey, Dave.*'

'Hey, Scarecrow,' Fairfax said to the speakerphone, aware of all the eyes now on him. 'How ya doin' over there?'

'*I died for a while, but I'm okay now. Thanks for everything, buddy. That info you sent made all the difference. Hope it didn't get you into too much trouble.*'

'A little,' Dave said.

'*Well, thanks. Tell the DIA director and the President that this Marine thinks you deserve a promotion. And Mr President, one more thing. I may have stopped the ignition of the atmospheric device, but Calderon got away—the bastard had an exit plan—but he'll have to turn up at Langley sometime. I may not come back from this, but I want him brought in. Can you do that for me?*'

'We'll find him,' the President said. 'You have my word on that, Captain.'

'*Thank you, sir. I've gotta go now. I just arrived back at Dragon.*'

The Antonov soared over Dragon Island.

Schofield checked the timer on his old Casio digital watch. As soon as he'd been told that the Russian nuke was nineteen minutes out, he'd started the watch's timer. It was now at:

14:41 . . . 14:40 . . . 14:39 . . .

Schofield did the calculations in his head. Another minute to land—perhaps ten to find whoever of his team was still alive: Zack, Emma, Mother, Baba and Champion—and then four to get back on the Antonov and get to MSD, minimum safe distance from the blast.

The numbers didn't look good. There wasn't nearly enough time nor did he have enough weaponry to take on the Army of Thieves. All he had was Bertie on his back—out of ammo—and a couple of pistols he'd found on the Antonov.

Either we all survive together or we all die together, he remembered his own words back at their camp.

'Fuck it,' he said.

He scanned the base as he came in for landing and saw men running every which way.

The Army of Thieves had lost not only its supreme leader but its whole command group. Now the thugs were looking for someone to tell them what was happening and what to do.

He keyed Bertie's short-range radio: 'Mother, Baba! Zack, Emma! Renard! Can any of you hear me—?'

A man's voice came in. '*I hear ya, buddy, although I sure ain't your fucking mother.*'

'*I hear ya, too,*' another reedy voice hissed. '*Calling for your mommy, eh? I think I fucked her once and she loved every minute of it.'*

There was no reply from Mother, Baba or any of the—

'*Captain, it's me,*' a softer voice came in.

It was Zack.

'*I'm alive and have E with me.*' Knowing others were listening, he was obviously being careful not to mention Emma's name.

'We gotta get everyone off this island. You've got nine minutes to meet me at the spot where Baba emptied out some diesel fuel.' Schofield didn't want to broadcast their meeting point.

'*Copy that. See you there.*'

A few seconds later, a woman's voice came in, her accent French:

'*Scarecrow, this is*'—a pained cough—'*Renard. You*'—cough—'*came back?*'

'Where are you now, Renard?'

'*Where you left me. But I have*'—Blam! A gunshot, loud and close—'*a bit of a problem here.*'

'Stay there. I'm on my way.'

Blam! Another. '*Hurry.*'

'*Ooh, aah! Yeah, stay there, Renard, we're coming, too!*' another voice mimicked Champion's over the airwaves.

14:01 . . . 14:00 . . . 13:59 . . .

As he banked over Dragon Island, Schofield tried to reach Mother and Baba, but he only got more crude replies from snarling Thieves.

Nothing from Mother or Baba.

Damn . . . he thought sadly.

Schofield brought the Antonov in for landing, shooting past the mighty vents before sweeping low over the disc-shaped tower—with one of its spires now lying on its side—and touching down on the runway. The Antonov's tyres hit the tarmac and it taxied down the length of the runway, before pulling up fifty metres short of the western cliffs.

At least twenty members of the Army of Thieves had been gathered by the airstrip's hangars when the plane had come roaring in and landed.

They immediately leapt into jeeps and charged after it, to see if their boss was on board.

Schofield leapt out of the Antonov—

13:10 . . . 13:09 . . . 13:08 . . .

—and saw it.

Saw the motorcycle-and-sidecar lying askew on the northern side of the runway, the one whose rider and gun-toting partner Bertie had shot earlier. Their dead bodies still lay beside it.

Schofield ran over to the bike-and-sidecar, lifted it upright and kickstarted it. It roared to life.

He peeled out, kicking up a spray of dirt behind him.

12:30 . . . 12:29 . . . 12:28 . . .

He couldn't believe what he was doing.

He was going *back* into Dragon Island—doomed Dragon Island, inhabited by a leaderless throng of Thieves—with only twelve minutes left to save his friends.

Schofield gunned his motorbike up the hill that lay between Dragon Island's runway and its abandoned whaling village—the same hill he'd hurtled down half an hour earlier.

11:00 . . . 10:59 . . . 10:58 . . .

He glanced back at the runway and saw four jeeps filled with Thieves arrive at his plane; saw them swarm inside it.

They emerged shortly after, looking confused and bewildered. One of them saw Schofield speeding away, pointed and opened fire. Two jeeps took off in pursuit.

Schofield reached the fork in the road at the top of the hill and swung left, heading for the whaling village as his timer passed through ten minutes.

10:00 . . . 9:59 . . . 9:58 . . .

A minute later, he came to the roadblock guarding the whaling village, the same one where Typhon had outwitted him earlier.

A single Army of Thieves jeep was still parked sideways there, but the men who had been manning it lay dead: shot by Bertie in the smoke-grenade haze that Champion had provided for him.

Schofield raced past the roadblock and skidded to a halt in front of the frost-covered village.

He leapt off the bike, gun up. 'Renard!' he called.

Movement to his left—

—a shaggy polar bear flashed between a pair of sheds and went bounding away.

Blam!-Blam!

Gunshots.

From within the village, from the direction the bear had gone.

Schofield ran that way.

He rounded a corner just as—*Blam!-Blam!-Blam!*—more gunshots rang out and he saw Veronique Champion, sitting in a corner with her back to the wall, her last remaining gun, her tiny Ruger LCP pocket pistol, extended and firing at a shaggy white bear!

That bear dropped, punctured all over with bullet wounds—and in a fleeting instant, Schofield saw three *more* dead bears lying in the snow beside it and in that instant, he saw what Champion had been dealing with in his absence: holding off a steady supply of polar bears with a very small-calibre gun.

The newly arrived bear roared as it bounded toward Champion and she fired at it, too, but after one more shot, the little Ruger went dry and she looked up in horror as the bear, furious and deranged, charged at her unhindered.

Schofield fired both his pistols and the bear went sprawling head-first into the snow, hit squarely in the back of the head, and it slid up against Champion's feet, its tongue lolling, its brains oozing out from a huge exit wound.

Champion looked up and saw Schofield and exhaled with deep relief.

He hurried over, quickly lifted her in his arms and carried her back to the motorbike.

As he carried her, Champion found herself looking directly at Bertie, peeping over Schofield's shoulder.

'*Hello*,' Bertie's electronic voice said pleasantly.

''Allo,' she replied.

'Looks like we got here just in time,' Schofield said, sliding her into the bike's sidecar.

'I still can't believe you came back *at all*.'

Schofield checked his watch.

8:01 . . . 8:00 . . . 7:59 . . .

'In eight minutes, this island is going to be wiped off the face of the Earth by a Russian nuclear missile,' he said. 'And my philosophy is simple: when it comes to my teammates, I don't leave anyone behind.'

He gunned the motorbike. 'Hang on.'

They zoomed up the hill, away from the whaling village, back up into Dragon Island.

Sixty seconds later, they arrived at the fork in the road at the top of the hill. From there they could see all the main features of Dragon Island: the airstrip, the disc-shaped tower, the northern bay.

7:01 . . . 7:00 . . . 6:59 . . .

Schofield stopped the bike, his eyes focused on the runway—

'Oh, no . . .'

He saw the Antonov, surrounded by cheering members of the Army of Thieves, being pushed slowly toward the cliffs at the end of the runway!

The plane tipped off the runway and began to roll down the short embankment separating the airstrip from the cliff-edge. Then the Antonov tumbled over the cliff and fell out of sight.

The Thieves all around it cheered.

Schofield swallowed, his eyes wide. Of all the things that might have happened, he hadn't expected that. But then, the Army of Thieves had no idea of the thermonuclear strike only six minutes away.

'What?' Champion said. 'What?'

'That plane was our escape,' Schofield said flatly. 'We are now officially stuck here.'

Schofield stared out at the spot where his Antonov had disappeared over the cliff, stunned.

Champion said, 'There *must* be another way out of this. Another plane or helicopter, or maybe some kind of bunker we can hide in—'

Gunfire sizzled over their heads from the two Army of Thieves jeeps that had just arrived from the runway.

It roused Schofield from his reverie and he snapped round to face Champion, something in his eyes. 'A bunker, yes . . . a nuclear bunker.'

Champion said, 'Ivanov said there was a special bunker-like laboratory buried under the main disc—'

'No. Not that one. We'd never reach it in time anyway. I saw another one. Earlier. But where was it . . . ?'

More bullets whistled past them.

Champion ducked. 'Can you think as we ride!'

'Right.' Schofield gunned the bike away with renewed intensity, fleeing from the jeeps.

A few seconds later, he turned to Champion. 'I just remembered where it is.'

6:00 . . . 5:59 . . . 5:58 . . .

Schofield's bike-and-sidecar skidded to a halt in front of the cable car terminal.

Schofield carried Champion toward the terminal's side garage, the door of which was suddenly hurled open from within by Zack and Emma. As requested, they'd gone to the place where Baba had released diesel fuel earlier.

Zack ushered them inside. 'What's going on?'

5:10 . . . 5:09 . . . 5:08 . . .

Schofield hurried past him, still carrying Champion. 'When they saw the uplink had been turned off, Russia fired a nuclear missile at this island. It's five minutes away.'

Zack went pale. 'Five minutes? What can we possibly do in five—?'

'We get to a nuclear bunker.' Schofield raced through the garage and entered the terminal proper. He hurried over to the cable car and looked up at its cable stretching all the way down to Acid Islet.

He recalled seeing the thick lead door in the hall on Acid Islet earlier, the one down on the bottom level with a nuclear symbol and a warning sign in Cyrillic on it. At the time, he'd thought it was a chamber for nuclear storage, but it wasn't: it was a nuclear bunker.

Of course, Dragon Island would have several fallout bunkers on it. It was a first-strike Cold War target. And placing a bunker under Acid Islet made sense: the islet was already partially protected by the cliffs of the bay, plus the seawater separating it from Dragon Island would act as an extra buffer against the concussion wave from any nuclear explosion.

'That cable car is too slow. It won't get us down fast enough,' Emma said.

'You're right, it won't.' Schofield was still looking up at the cable. It stretched steeply away from them, sweeping down to the station on Acid Islet a thousand feet away.

He turned.

'Everybody up onto the roof of the cable car. We're gonna zipline down that cable.'

4:20 . . . 4:19 . . . 4:18 . . .

They all clambered up onto the roof of the bullet-battered cable car.

The cable swooped downward, impossibly long and dizzyingly steep, ending at the islet far, far away.

Once they were all up on the roof of the cable car, Schofield said, 'Okay, Zack and Emma: use your belts. Loop them over the cable like this.'

He looped Zack's belt over the cable, then crossed its two ends so they formed an X. 'We dislodged most of the ice on the cable when we came up earlier, so the cable shouldn't be too icy. To slow yourself as you slide, pull your hands outward; that'll cause your belt to squeeze on the cable and arrest your slide. Got it? Good. Go.'

Zack went. He leapt off the cable car and with a scream of terror shot down the superlong cable. He became very tiny very quickly as he slid away.

Emma was next. She stepped tentatively to the edge of the cable car's roof.

'We're seriously out of time, Emma,' Schofield urged. 'You gotta go now.'

'Right,' she said, and with a final deep breath, she slid away down the outrageously long zipline.

That left Schofield and Champion. Schofield lashed his own belt over the cable—

3:31 . . . 3:30 . . . 3:29 . . .

—and pulled Champion into a tight embrace.

Their faces were inches apart. Her arms were wrapped tightly around his neck while his hands were stretched upward, holding his belt looped over the cable.

'Hang on tight,' he said.

And for the briefest of moments, Veronique Champion looked deep into his scarred eyes.

And to Schofield's complete surprise, she suddenly gave him a quick but passionate kiss on the lips. 'I've never met a man like you. You are special.' She pulled back from him. 'Now fly, Scarecrow! Fly!'

As she said it, five members of the Army of Thieves burst through the terminal's door, machine guns blazing.

But their bullets hit nothing, for the moment they entered the terminal, Schofield—with Champion gripping him tightly and Bertie still on his back—leapt off the cable car's roof.

The tiny figures of Schofield and Champion shot down the super-long cable that connected Dragon Island's clifftop terminal with Acid Islet's sea-level station.

They looked infinitesimally small in front of the towering cliffs behind them and the vast horseshoe-shaped bay around them—but they didn't care for the view now.

They slid fast, very fast, shooting down the long swooping cable, their enormous slide lasting a full twenty seconds.

Schofield gripped his belt tightly and as he saw the yawning square doors of the station on the islet getting closer, he pulled outward on his belt, causing it to tighten around the cable.

They slowed immediately and at first he thought he had left his braking move too late, and he pulled with all his strength on the belt and it bit against the cable, trying to slow, and they entered the lower station fast and—

—swung to a lurching halt.

Zack and Emma were already on the platform and they helped Champion down.

When she was safely down, Schofield dropped to the platform and checked his watch:

3:01 . . . 3:00 . . . 2:59 . . .

'Three minutes, folks,' he said. 'Run. Run as fast as you can.'

They bolted out of the cable car station, down the short road and into the huge hall-sized building filled with vats and tanks.

2:00 . . . 1:59 . . . 1:58 . . .

Zack and Emma ran in front, while Schofield ran with Champion draped over his shoulder, limping along as fast as she could.

1:30 . . . 1:29 . . . 1:28 . . .

Across some catwalks, zigzagging.

1:00 . . . 0:59 . . .

'One minute!' Schofield called.

Down some ladders. Champion made it awkward, slowing them down.

0:40 . . . 0:39 . . .

Schofield landed on the bottom level and saw the door he'd seen before: the superthick metal door with the nuclear symbol on it. 'There it is!'

0:30 . . . 0:29 . . .

They rushed across the floor of the hall.

0:18 . . . 0:17 . . .

Zack and Emma dashed inside the thick reinforced doorway.

0:16 . . . 0:15 . . .

Schofield, Bertie and Champion ducked in after them.

0:14 . . . 0:13 . . .

Zack and Emma swung the heavy door shut behind them. It closed with a resounding *boom*.

0:10 . . . 0:09 . . .

They all scampered down a concrete stairwell, down several levels.

0:05 . . . 0:04 . . .

Through two more thick doors.

0:03 . . . 0:02 . . .

Through a final door, which Schofield slammed shut behind them as they all dropped to the floor, backs pressed against the solid concrete wall.

0:01 . . . 0:00.

There was a moment of silence.

Then it came.

Impact.

The Russian ICBM came rocketing out of the sky like a thunderbolt, lancing down toward Dragon Island at over a thousand kilometres per hour.

The remaining members of the Army of Thieves had perhaps five seconds to admire its dazzling tailflame and smoketrail—enough time to realise with horror exactly what it was and that it brought with it their deaths.

The missile detonated.

A flash of light and an almighty boom were followed by a shockingly powerful outward-moving blast-wave that consumed Dragon Island.

The base's two gas vents—previously so huge and gigantic—were instantly ripped apart by the shockwave. They simply disintegrated to dust. The disc-shaped tower tilted and fell before also being obliterated completely by the thermonuclear flame. Some of Dragon's coastal cliffs trembled under the weight of the colossal explosion and spilled giant chunks of rock into the sea. The cable car terminal toppled off its perch, falling into the bay.

Everything was incinerated, every structure and person on the island was vaporised.

A towering mushroom cloud rose into the sky.

Dragon Island was no more.

So was the Army of Thieves.

Deep within the earth, in their nuclear bunker on Acid Islet, Schofield and the others all looked up at the deafening roar of the blast.

The concrete walls around them shook, but held. The lights flickered, but the generators continued to work.

When it was over, they all looked at each other.

'What do we do now?' Zack asked.

Schofield saw an old communications console on the wall. He walked over to it. It was connected to a generator and appeared to be in working order.

'We radio home. Then we settle in and wait for someone to come and pick us up.'

That wait, it turned out, wasn't long, only a few days.

After contacting the listening post at Eareckson Air Station again, Schofield was once again put through to the Situation Room.

An attack submarine with nuclear shielding—the USS *Seawolf*—was dispatched to pick them up. It would arrive, he was told, in three days. Until then, all they could do was wait.

During that wait, they drank what water they had sparingly and shared the few MREs that Bertie carried.

Schofield thought of Mother and Baba—especially Mother. They had apparently succeeded in stopping the launch of the megatrain's missile, but at what cost: had they been shot? Wounded? Killed? They hadn't replied to his radio calls earlier. Schofield wondered what had happened to Mother. If she had even been alive when the

Russian nuke had hit, he couldn't see how she could have survived its blast. And if she'd been killed, he hoped she had gone out the same way she had lived—all guns fucking blazing.

'Farewell, Mother,' he said softly. 'You were my loyal, loyal friend. I wish I could've been with you at the end. I'll miss you.'

When the *Seawolf* eventually arrived, it stayed under the surface of the icy waters of the bay.

The main island was a charred wasteland, a black apocalyptic hellscape.

Although partially sheltered from the primary blast, the hall on Acid Islet was now a skeleton of its former self: every single one of its many glass windows had been shattered and its roof had been wrenched away by the concussion wave. Its many vats and tanks now lay open to the sky.

Three crew members left the *Seawolf* in full biohazard suits. They carried a trunk with four more protective suits in it and a stretcher.

It took a while, but eventually everyone was transferred to the *Seawolf* in the biohazard suits. Once aboard, they would be quarantined in a radiation-proof chamber, scrubbed down and continually checked for residual radiation.

Schofield entered the *Seawolf* last, carrying the broken Bertie in one hand. In front of him walked Zack and Emma, and in front of them, two crewmen carried Champion on the stretcher. During the wait in the bunker, Schofield had cleaned and redressed her stomach wound several times, but now she needed proper medical attention.

On the way to the quarantine chamber, Champion was diverted into the sub's specially equipped infirmary—a sealed-off medical area specifically designed to treat crew members affected by a radiation leak in the sub's nuclear reactor. There she would be treated by the sub's medical officer, also in a biohazard suit.

As he handed Champion over to the medical officer, Schofield heard a muffled shouting coming from inside the sealed-off medical area. It sounded like, 'Hey! Scarecrow!'

He peered inside—and saw Mother sitting up on a bed, yelling and waving at him.

'Yeah, you! You big sexy hunk of hero stuff!' She grinned broadly. 'You fucking-A did it! You are *the man*! *The fucking man!*'

In a bed to her left, attached to a bunch of tubes and drips, and currently in a deep coma, was Baba. Beside him, a heart-rate monitor pulsed weakly; he was alive, barely.

Despite his fatigue, Schofield couldn't help but smile. Next to him, Zack's jaw just dropped.

Schofield said to Mother, 'I tried to call you on the radio but got no response. What happened on the train? How did you get away from the blast?'

Mother grinned. 'I did what you would've done: I drove that train at full fucking speed into the submarine dock's pool! The firefight was brutal and my French buddy here got shot up bad—but he held them off long enough to get us over the line. Anyway, just as the train shot into the water, I grabbed Baba and dived off the top of the locomotive, and while it went under, we landed with a splash right beside the bow of that freighter, where I'd seen a little Russian submersible.

'We were both wounded—him worse than me—so I just dragged him across to that submersible and climbed inside it, to get somewhere dry where I could check his wounds.'

Schofield looked at the still figure of Baba in the bed beside her. He had about six body wounds, including one right in the centre of his chest. Chest wounds were usually fatal unless you had some kind of haemostatic, or blood clotting, agent like Celox gel or a QuikClot sponge—and Schofield knew that Mother and Baba hadn't had either of those.

'How on Earth did you patch him up and stop him bleeding out?'

Mother grinned again, and jerked her chin at Zack. 'It was all thanks to *him*, actually. You may find this hard to believe, boss, but sometimes I do actually pay attention to techno-babble. One day back at camp, before all this started, Zack was telling me about our new MRE ration packs. He said the water filtration pills in them were chitosan-based and that chitosan is the key ingredient of Celox gel. Now, those MREs also have a crap-tasting jelly in them, and jelly is just gelatin. I figured, well, if I mixed the filtration pills with water and the jelly, I might end up with a gooey gel vaguely like Celox. So I pulled out my MRE and did exactly that. It produced a nice thick gel which I applied to his major wound. It formed a decent clot, not a perfect one, but one that was good enough to seal and contain the wound. The submersible had a first-aid kit with some bandages in it and I used them to cover it all up. Not sure how much longer it would've lasted, but it kept him alive long enough till we got picked up.'

Schofield shook his head. 'You made a clotting gel from the ingredients of your ration pack. You sound like—'

'I know!' Mother said. 'I'm fucking MacGyver!'

'You sure are. Wait a second. How did you get away, then? I tried to call you on the radio.'

Mother said, 'I heard you on the radio but my microphone got shot off during the shootout on the train and Baba's musta fallen off at some point, probably when we landed in the water; we did land pretty hard. Anyway, I could hear you but I couldn't transmit. You said we had to get off the island, pronto, so I figured some kind of serious boomtime was coming. So I fired up that submersible and drove it as deep as possible, to put as much water between us and Dragon as I could. The Mir worked fine but its radio was a half-broken piece of shit. I only managed to attract this sub's attention by pinging constantly on the active sonar.'

Schofield nodded at Baba. 'How is he?'

'He's still critical. They put him in an induced coma. The doc doesn't know if he'll pull through.'

Schofield said, 'I gotta go to quarantine and get scrubbed. I'll talk to you later.'

As he said this, Veronique Champion was placed on the bed to Mother's right.

Schofield said to Champion, 'I'll come back to check on you, too.'

Champion nodded. 'Thank you . . . again.'

Mother saw this exchange and threw a wide suggestive grin at Schofield. She raised her eyebrows. 'Take your time, Scarecrow. I got some girl talk to do with my new French chickadee here.'

OUTER BALTIMORE
24 SEPTEMBER, 1650 HOURS
(FIVE MONTHS LATER)

Shane Schofield sat in the basement office of a little townhouse in the suburbs of Baltimore.

Oddly, he wore his full dress uniform: white peaked cap, fitted blue coat with medals, gold belt buckle and pale-blue trousers with red piping. His attire looked far too formal for the little basement office, but then when he was done here he *was* going to the White House.

Across from him, behind her desk, sat Brooke Ulacco, his plain-looking, plain-spoken, sixty-bucks-an-hour suburban psychologist.

It was nearing the end of the day and Schofield had just spent the afternoon recounting his experiences at Dragon Island, including his torture at the hands of Marius Calderon.

Until that day, he hadn't been allowed to talk to Ulacco about his mission to Dragon—as it involved CIA matters, he'd been informed by his superiors that her existing TS/SCI clearance was not high enough. He'd insisted that they get her the appropriate clearance, so he could tell her everything. It had taken a few months and even more background checks but Ulacco had passed and a 'SAP'—or Special Access Program—addendum was attached to her existing Top Secret clearance. For Schofield it was well worth the wait to be able to tell her everything.

When he had finished recounting his story, Ulacco nodded slowly.

'So, how'd you do it?' she asked.

'What?'

'How did you keep your head together? This Calderon guy tortured you both physically and mentally. He taunted you about your father and about Gant's death and then, so far as you knew, he killed your closest friend, Mother, in front of you with rats in a goddamn box. As your therapist, I would have serious problems with someone doing this to you. So. How did you do it?'

Schofield leaned back in his chair.

He knew exactly how he'd done it.

'I did what you taught me,' he said.

'What I taught you?' Ulacco was rarely surprised. Her calm, cocksure, seen-it-all facial expression was not often broken. But now it was. 'What did I teach you?'

'You taught me to compartmentalise my mind,' Schofield said. 'In a memory location. Or in my case, a, ahem, memory submarine.'

Ulacco eyed him closely. 'I've often wondered about this, Shane. You chose a submarine as a memory locale because it is a perfectly sealable structure, but one with a purging option—one from which you can jettison memories. Did you jettison your memories of Libby Gant?'

Ulacco asked that question without expression, poker-faced. And even though she actually hung on the answer, she added, 'There's no right or wrong answer to this question, by the way.'

Schofield paused for a full minute, thinking long and hard.

Ulacco watched him, waiting.

Then he spoke.

'No. I didn't. I could never jettison my memories of Libby. She was an incredible woman and I loved her and to remove all the wonderful memories of her would be to remove something that makes me whole, makes me who I am, makes me *me*. During my torture—and especially when I thought Mother had been killed—I just shoved all those good memories into a compartment deep within the submarine of my mind, shut the steel door and spun the flywheel till it was sealed tight. After that, Calderon couldn't touch

Gant. Nothing he could say or do to me would reach those memories, all those great memories. And I was okay.'

'You were okay? You *died*.'

'Only for a little while.'

Ulacco cracked a wry half-smile. 'So you're telling me that a memory technique that I taught you here in my crappy basement in Baltimore kept you sane while you were being tortured by one of the world's foremost experts in breaking the human mind?'

Schofield nodded. 'Yep.'

Ulacco turned away for a second, and despite herself, actually looked a little proud. It only lasted a second, but Schofield saw it. Then her usual self kicked back in.

'And then you sorta saved the northern hemisphere from annihilation?' she said.

'Yes.'

'So you could say that by saving you, *I* actually saved the world?' she said cheekily.

Schofield returned her smile. 'I think you could say that.' And they laughed, for the first time in any of their meetings.

Ulacco stood. 'Your time's up, Captain. And you have an appointment with the President to keep.'

Schofield stood and nodded seriously. 'Thanks, Doc. Thank you for all your help. Oh, there's just one more thing.'

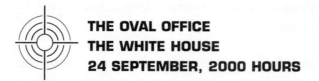

**THE OVAL OFFICE
THE WHITE HOUSE
24 SEPTEMBER, 2000 HOURS**

Shane Schofield stood to attention in the Oval Office in his full dress uniform while the President of the United States hung a medal around his neck.

Beside him stood Mother, also in her dress blues and also at attention. Beside her stood four civilians—Dave Fairfax, Marianne Retter, Zack Weinberg and Emma Dawson—and one robot.

Standing happily by Zack's side, his lower body completely rebuilt and his exoskeleton shining, was Bertie.

Watched by the Commandant of the Marine Corps, the Director of the Defense Intelligence Agency and the Director of DARPA, they had all received various medals for 'gallantry and intrepidity at the risk of their lives above and beyond the call of duty'.

Off to one side stood Brooke Ulacco, dressed in her quickly assembled Sunday best, looking a little stunned to be there. When the President stood before her, he had no medal in his hands.

'Dr Ulacco,' he said softly. 'Captain Schofield has nothing but the highest regard for you and your skills as a therapist. Being President is a pretty stressful job and I've been looking for someone to talk to about it, a therapist of sorts. Someone who'll be tough but fair, yet also discreet. And I hear you now have a substantial amount of security clearance; this would only require a few more background checks. You up for it?'

For the first time since he had met her, Schofield saw the unflappable Dr Ulacco go wide-eyed with shock.

Once the medal ceremony was over, the President had the Oval Office cleared of everyone but Schofield.

'I have someone here to talk with you, Captain,' the President said. He keyed an intercom. 'Mary, please send in the ambassador.'

A side door opened and into the Oval Office walked three figures: one of whom Schofield had never seen before and two that he had.

The man he didn't know was a tall regal-looking fellow with swept-back silver hair, a long aquiline nose and an imperious bearing; he wore an obviously expensive suit.

The other two—also wearing civilian clothes—were Veronique Champion and Baba. Champion looked fit and svelte in a tailored skirt-suit and heels. She wore perfectly applied make-up and her black hair hung down to her shoulders, having been cut for the occasion. For his part, Baba had trimmed his beard a little but he

looked very uncomfortable in a suit. He still wore one arm in a sling.

'Captain Schofield,' the President said, 'may I introduce to you the French Ambassador to the United States, Monsieur Philippe de Crespigny.'

Schofield noticed that the President had used the formal method of introduction; only when someone did that, they usually introduced the more senior person *to* the more junior person. For the President to name Schofield first was to suggest that in this room, he ranked higher than the French ambassador. Schofield was sure the ambassador didn't miss that either.

'Monsieur.' The French ambassador bowed as he shook Schofield's hand. 'I believe you know Major Champion and Master Sergeant Huguenot.'

Schofield nodded to Champion and Baba. 'I do. It's good to see them again and looking so well.'

The President said, 'The ambassador has a message to deliver to you, Captain, from *his* President.'

The ambassador stood a little taller. 'Captain Schofield,' he said stiffly, formally, 'the Republic of France sends its sincere thanks to you. Major Champion and Master Sergeant Huguenot have informed the President of France that your actions in the field, in addition to saving several other nations, saved France. It is my duty to inform you that the President has thus rescinded the standing bounty on your head. The Republic of France no longer has a grievance with you, Captain Schofield.'

Schofield's mouth fell open.

Champion smiled at him. Baba grinned.

And the President of the United States, in particular, looked very, very pleased.

A short buffet of cakes and coffee followed in the Roosevelt Room, as usually happened after a presidential audience.

Zack and Emma were showing the President Bertie's many features while Champion chatted with Brooke Ulacco.

Mother's husband, Ralph, was also there in his best suit and a truly awful tie, yet Mother looped her arm firmly through his as they chatted amiably with Baba and Schofield.

'So, Scarecrow,' Mother said. 'Did they ever find that CIA asshole, Calderon, the "Lord of Anarchy"?'

Schofield shook his head. 'No, but I'm guessing that one day I'll be called into a high-level meeting and at that meeting will be a very senior CIA asshole who will tell me that Marius Calderon has been found, dead.'

'Only he won't be dead . . .' Mother said.

'No. Calderon is one of the CIA's best and brightest. He formulated that plan for Dragon Island nearly thirty years ago and it worked perfectly—everything went as he foresaw it, except for one variable: us. If we hadn't been up there, all of China and most of the northern hemisphere would be in ashes right now. No, I wouldn't be surprised if Marius Calderon is already back in the States, back at Langley with a new face and a new name, but probably the same office.'

A few minutes later, the President quietly tapped Schofield on the shoulder. 'Captain, a word, please.' He guided him out of the room.

They went downstairs to the Situation Room, where some intelligence people waited, including the directors of the DIA and CIA.

'Captain,' the President said, 'I want you to hear this right from the source. Director.'

The Director of the Central Intelligence Agency stepped forward, looking suitably grim. Despite himself, he looked Schofield up and down before he spoke, as if assessing the man who had ruined a long-laid CIA plan.

'Mr President. Captain Schofield. We finally found Marius Calderon. He's dead. Two weeks ago, his submersible was found by a Norwegian fishing trawler, drifting in the Arctic Ocean. The submersible's oxygen supply had malfunctioned sometime after Calderon went under. He suffocated.'

Schofield looked the CIA director square in the eye.

'Thank you, Director. I never expected to hear that.'

Schofield returned to the soiree in the Roosevelt Room.

He was met at the door by Mother and Brooke Ulacco.

'Hey, Scarecrow, we were just talking with Sexy French Chick.' Mother jerked her chin over at Champion. 'Guess what? Do you know what *renard* means in English?'

'No.'

'*Renard*,' Mother said slowly, 'is French for *fox*.'

Schofield took this in. 'Is that so?'

'Uh-huh. I think there might be something in that,' Mother said. 'You know what else, she asked if you might be open to joining her for a drink after this.'

Schofield glanced over at Champion—and caught her looking at him before she turned quickly away.

He turned to Ulacco. 'Thoughts?'

Brooke Ulacco shrugged. 'It was always going to take a formidable woman to light a spark in you again. And that woman is pretty damn formidable. I say, go for it. A date would be good for you. Mother?'

'I approve,' Mother said softly as she gave Schofield a peck on the cheek. 'And I think the old Fox would, too.'

Schofield gazed at Veronique Champion—Renard, Fox—for a long moment, thinking about it.

And then he walked over to join her.

Later that night, Schofield and Champion could be seen in an all-night coffee shop a few blocks from the White House, talking, smiling and, occasionally, laughing.

They talked long into the night.

It was late, after two a.m., when Schofield returned to his temporary barracks apartment at the Marine Corps complex in Arlington.

There was something on his bed.

On the pillow.

A pair of battered wraparound reflective glasses, with an A-in-a-circle etched into them.

His glasses, last seen in the possession of Marius Calderon.

There was nothing else with them. No note. Nothing.

Scarecrow glanced uneasily around the apartment. Then he picked up the glasses and gazed at them long and hard.

THE END

ACKNOWLEDGEMENTS

I'd like to send out my thanks to all the usual suspects who make my books possible.

To my wife, Natalie, who was, once again, the first to cast her eyes over the manuscript, and thus the first to express her horror at the rat scene.

To Cate Paterson at Pan Macmillan, thank you for all of your support over the last fourteen years. I still think it's pretty fantastic that you discovered me by finding *Contest* in a bookstore. And to Jon Wood at Orion in the UK, who was a fan long before he became my UK publisher.

To Catherine Day, my erstwhile editor, who keeps me honest.

To Tracey Cheetham in publicity and Jane Hayes in marketing for the many phone calls they make and take on my behalf and for being the 'back office' that organises my books tours; and to all the sales reps for the many hours they spend on the road between bookstores: thank you for all your hard work.

To my good friends in the military both in Australia and the US, you know who you are. Thank you for all the technical advice. Any mistakes—and fictitious weapons—are mine and mine alone, and were made over their objections. I'd also like to send a special shout-out to everyone at the Australian Army's incredible 2nd Commando Regiment. Every Australian should know that the adjective 'elite' does not do our elite commandos justice; trust me, when you see them in action, their cool professionalism makes you feel very, very proud.

To the good folk at Azur resort in Queenstown, New Zealand. After being stranded in Singapore by that volcanic ash cloud in 2010, Natalie and I went to Queenstown and it was there that I sat down and, in the glorious peace of one of Azur's lovely cabins, mapped out the story of *Scarecrow and the Army of Thieves*. The little collection of *National Geographic* magazines in their library was a great research tool, too, with excellent issues about both the Arctic and the old Soviet Union.

To those wonderful people who, in exchange for making the winning bids at charity auctions in aid of some of my favourite causes, got characters in this book named after them. They include: Peter and Lenore Grzonkowski who, a few years ago, generously paid to have the names of three teenagers, Emma Dawson, Brooke Ulacco and Bryce Ulacco in this book (sorry about the wait!); Marianne and Mike Retter (they got a fun character for their donation); Linda Duncombe who bought the name William Thompson (the Kid); and Don and Margaret Harris: their donation allowed Don to become the National Security Advisor. Don, your character may have survived this book, but mark my words, if you return in another one, you will most assuredly die a gruesome death! I promise! Let me also mention the fine charitable work of my good friend Gary 'Smokey' Dawson OAM, at whose Bullant Charity Challenge Gala Dinner most of the above character names were auctioned. Gary is a fine Australian who has raised millions of dollars for charity. If you want a character named after you, get a ticket to that gala, which is usually held in November.

To my Wednesday golfing buddies, the WAGS, for keeping me sociable. They have been calling me 'Murderer' ever since I killed one of them on page 1 of *The Six Sacred Stones*.

Lastly and most importantly, my sincere thanks to all of my fans out there: to those who enjoy my books on international flights or in their homes, or who come to my book signings and speeches just to say 'Hi, I enjoy your books.' (Sometimes people hurry past the signing table and call that out from a distance!)

I make no bones about the fact that I write to entertain. That is exactly what I do. And I firmly believe that reading for enjoyment has value in our world. So thank you just for enjoying my stuff.

Matthew Reilly
Sydney, Australia
October 2011

AN INTERVIEW WITH MATTHEW REILLY

WRITING *SCARECROW AND THE ARMY OF THIEVES*

SPOILER WARNING!

[WARNING—This interview contains SPOILERS from *Scarecrow and the Army of Thieves*. Be careful if you are reading it before you read the book!]

Matthew, your last three novels have featured Jack West Jr. What made you return to Shane Schofield, a.k.a. Scarecrow, whom—apart from his special mission in Hell Island*—we haven't seen since 2003's* Scarecrow*?*

When I was on tour with *The Five Greatest Warriors*, fans would always ask me, 'When are we going to see a new Scarecrow novel?' As I said to them back then, I have always wanted to return to Schofield, but I wanted to wait for two things: first, for the world to change, and second, I wanted to wait until I was ready to write about him again.

Let me backtrack a little. I really enjoyed writing *Scarecrow*. Really enjoyed it. With that book, I wanted to take the concept of the thriller novel to the ultimate extreme: to extremes of pace, action, thrills and sheer emotional rawness. *Scarecrow* was supposed to be an ultra-intense thriller. It was intense to read (yes, I received hate mail for the guillotine scene) and it was intense to write.

It was partly because of that intensity that I wrote the Jack West series, *Seven Ancient Wonders*, *The Six Sacred Stones* and *The Five Greatest Warriors*. They are not as severe as the Scarecrow novels (Schofield's world is both harder and meaner than the one Jack

West inhabits) and thus are very different to write. I like to think the Jack West books are more 'adventure' than 'thriller', and I will often recommend them to a parent looking for reading material for a younger teenager.

The other reason is that after September 11, 2001, the world changed, with America getting embroiled in wars in Iraq and Afghanistan, and I didn't want to set a Schofield novel in either of those two countries (although he did visit Afghanistan briefly in *Scarecrow*). The Jack West books, however, are about the small countries of the world standing up to the big ones, and post-9/11, this kind of story reflected how I perceived the world from 2001 to 2008. (The Jack West books also allow me to write about the mysteries of history, a topic that I love but which doesn't quite fit in with Scarecrow's world.)

But then came the extraordinary rise of China, exemplified by the Beijing Olympics in 2008 and China's continued economic rise in the years since. This was the change I was waiting for. As you now know, having read the book, the rise of China is the basis for Calderon's decades-long plan in *Scarecrow and the Army of Thieves*. So, I waited for the world to change and finally it did, providing me with a story I could put Shane Schofield in.

And so, after writing three Jack West books, I found myself thinking about Scarecrow again. And the main thing I thought was, *How on Earth would he pull himself back together after the horrific death of Libby Gant in* Scarecrow? This would be one of the key plotlines in *Scarecrow and the Army of Thieves*.

On that topic, did you spend more time thinking about his state of mind for this book?

I really did. In fact, I went even further than that. I thought, *Who would be the worst possible villain he could face, given that he is probably still traumatised in some way?* My answer: a villain who is an expert in psychological warfare and torture. A key event in *Scarecrow and the Army of Thieves* was always going to be the torture scene, where I hope readers will really worry that Marius Calderon has broken Scarecrow's mind.

The notion of how Scarecrow fortified his mind—the idea of a *loci of memory*—was integral to this. I asked myself, *How do you defeat an expert in the art of breaking people's minds?* My answer: you create a virtual vault in your mind. The flow-on question was even more interesting: by creating such a vault with a purging option, is it possible that you might *forget* loved ones?

I thought these were all good character issues that fans of Shane Schofield would really like to see explored. If I could weave them into a full-tilt, rampaging, action-packed plot, then I just might have something.

Speaking of the plot, how did you come up with the idea of the atmospheric weapon at the heart of the story?

Given the kind of novel that I write, I am always, well, looking for new ways to destroy the world. (If the CIA is tracking my Google searches, I am in so much trouble!)

I read a lot of non-fiction and, over the years, I have read a bit about the inventor Nikola Tesla. He was an absolutely brilliant man. (For a brief look at Tesla, check out the movie *The Prestige*, in which David Bowie plays him very well; it's not a bad movie either). When I first came across the quote from Tesla in which he fears that he might ignite the atmosphere with his experiments—yes, it's a real quote—my storytelling brain started ticking: *Hmmm, ignite the atmosphere, you say . . .*

I had actually intended to use the atmospheric device as an ancient weapon in a Jack West novel, but then in 2010 I got stranded in Singapore thanks to that volcanic ash cloud from Iceland that swept across Europe. Looking at the satellite images of the ash cloud, I thought of Tesla and asked myself, *What if that ash cloud were flammable?* And, *Who would build a weapon that could ignite the northern hemisphere using such a cloud?*

Of course, the answer was obvious. The Soviet Union would! And the good thing about the Soviets is that when they did something, they did it big. The story quickly followed: what if there were a long-abandoned Soviet base up in the Arctic that housed this terrible weapon and a band of terrorists decided to seize the base and set it off?

Tell us about the origin of the Army of Thieves?

Quite simply, I didn't want my bad guys to be just a standard group of terrorists. I don't like that kind of story. It's also been done many times before.

I want twists, I want intrigue, I want deeper conspiracies. I thought the story would be a lot more interesting if this horribly violent yet very capable terrorist group might actually be part of a complex plan that originated nearly three decades ago.

I should also add that I wanted the Army of Thieves to be really, really *nasty*.

Good villains are hard to find. And when I decided to bring Scarecrow back in a new novel,* I wanted him to go up against totally impossible odds: a large, brutal and ruthless terrorist army. Even more, I wanted him to go up against this army with a group of civilians and not his usual band of battle-hardened Marines. Worse still, Scarecrow himself would be on an emotional razor's edge when it all happened.

All this is why *Scarecrow and the Army of Thieves* is rather visceral and, at times, quite violent; indeed, it is perhaps the most visceral and violent of all my books. I thought *Scarecrow* was pretty tough, but I think *Thieves* is tougher—it does, after all, have the torture scene, including the very gruesome rat torture.

But in the end, villains must be feared. Death must be feared. And death at the hands of these villains, this Army of Thieves, was always going to be really, really scary.

(*A quick note: I don't consider *Hell Island* to be a full novel, and I think my fans think the same way. For the record, in my mind *Scarecrow and the Army of Thieves* follows on directly from *Scarecrow*. As far as *Hell Island* is concerned, even though it is a very cool and action-packed Scarecrow story, it was written as part of a special government-sponsored project in Australia, and did not get a release in the rest of the world. So, to me, *Hell Island* exists as a nice side adventure for Scarecrow and Mother, and a great short book for new readers who might wish to try my work. That said, just for the fans, I did mention the plot of *Hell Island* in passing in *Scarecrow and the Army of Thieves*. And for the eagle-eyed among you, *Hell Island* does provide the only crossover character between the Scarecrow and Jack West universes: the Marine named Astro.)

Technology seems to be developing so quickly—although everyone will be glad to see the return of the Maghook! Do you enjoy keeping up with the developing weaponry available to your characters?

I love discovering new high-tech weapons. Indeed, this was exactly why I put Schofield up in the Arctic with a equipment-testing team in this book! It gave me a chance to put the latest weapons and technology in his hands.

I am constantly on the lookout for new weapons and tech. Often I find out about new stuff just by reading the newspaper (this was

how I found out about the explosive-resistant goo made by DSS; go online and check out the 'before and after' photos of a building that had the goo painted on one half of it; very cool).

Mind you, this also worked for Schofield's character and this was very important to me. After the trauma he suffered in *Scarecrow*, I figured that the natural question a reader would ask is, *Where would the Marine Corps put a Marine who might have become unstable?* The answer: you send him to the Arctic to test some new weapons and devices.

It also allowed me to create Bertie. Bertie is loosely based on existing battlefield robots like the Talon, the Packbot, the SWORDS and one anti-explosives robot I saw at a military base, but as I often do, his capabilities have been augmented. Those other bots are not—so far as I know—capable of totally independent action, whereas Bertie is, and that's what makes him a lot of fun to have around. I love the idea of this determined little robot that just never gives up.

As for the Maghook, I am its biggest fan. But I am also aware that I could easily overuse it, so I try to use it only for major moments in the story. That said, when I started writing *Thieves*, I found myself thinking that perhaps *other* armed forces might have developed their own, better, Maghooks by now, and thus we get to see the French version of it, *Le Magneteux*.

Your books keep getting bigger and faster, not to mention even more gruesome with your torture scenes! How do you keep defying expectations?

I only have one goal with each new book that I write: it must be better than the one that came before it. It must be faster or cleverer or more intense. It must, in some way, take the kind of story that I like telling to a new, never-before-seen level.

When I wrote *Scarecrow*, I set out to make it faster than anything I had read before. The Jack West books were more epic in their scale than anything I had done till then. With *Scarecrow and the Army of Thieves*, I was after a new level of pace and *intensity*—my motto was: 'Leaner, meaner, faster!'

I like to think that one of my strengths as a novelist is that I have read lots of thrillers and seen nearly every action movie known to man. This means that I know what has been done before. If I ever find myself writing a scene and saying to myself 'Oh, this was like that scene in . . .' I immediately stop and re-conceive the scene. On the other hand, I love it when I am writing and saying to myself, 'In all the many movies and books I have seen or read, I have never seen *this* before.'

That said, I do like to make references to some of my favourite 1980s action movies, and in *Thieves* I even mention one of my favourites, *Predator*. And my long-suffering wife, Natalie, will tell you that, like Mother, I think that music peaked in the 80s!

It was fantastic to see Mother again, but you also introduced us to a new character who is the male equivalent of her: Baba. Are we likely to meet with him again?

Ah, yes, Baba! I'm so pleased with how he turned out.

Part of the fun of writing a sequel is that you get to play with the characters you have a history with. Mother has been an awesome character to write about and she's fun because she breaks all the rules of conventional society. She is a favourite among the fans (readers have said they will hunt me down if I ever kill her off), and her character is well known and much loved. As I thought about the story of *Thieves*, I decided that I wanted to test Mother by making her meet her male equivalent. And thus Baba was born.

I also wanted Scarecrow to have a new, but edgier, female interest. To get that edge, I decided to make Veronique Champion and
Baba assassins working for Scarecrow's old enemy, the French, and
to also make Veronique a relative of one of the French scientists
killed in *Ice Station*, so that when she meets Schofield, all she has
is hatred of him. If she is eventually going to like him, he is going
to have his work cut out for him in winning her over.

You want to know a secret? After I delivered the manuscript for
Thieves, Baba was the subject of some serious discussions with
my editors in Australia, the UK and the US. My editors thought
he perhaps should die, given that he had been shot so thoroughly
on the megatrain, and that it might be a better story if he died
heroically (and with the taste of Mother's lips on his). I gave this
serious thought but, in the end, I decided that he was too much
fun to have around, and so I looked up blood-clotting agents and
had Mother save him. So, yes, Baba will return, still chewing the
scenery, drinking like a Viking and making love like a silverback
gorilla!

***And the rat torture. Can you take us through why and how you
wrote that scene?***

As I said earlier, I wanted *Scarecrow and the Army of Thieves* to be
very visceral and graphic. The rat scene exemplifies this.

In the end, however, that scene was all about Mother's and Baba's
characters: it's about the lengths they are prepared to go to in order
to avoid a horrible death. That turns out to be biting the heads off
live rats. Unfortunately, that did require me to *demonstrate* to the
reader just how horrible that kind of death was, and Jeff Hartigan
was the unfortunate one to suffer for it.

My thanks to Alice Cooper for the inspiration!

And you have created a great new super-villain in Marius Calderon. Will we see him make a deadly comeback anytime soon?

The creation of Calderon was actually a big thing for me. In all his other outings, including *Hell Island*, Scarecrow killed the villain of the story. Now, sure, those villains deserved what they got, but I decided that it was time for Scarecrow to have a nemesis, a villain who could come back in future adventures if only just to mess up Scarecrow's world. A Moriarty, so to speak, or a Blofeld.

This is why Calderon's past is described is such detail in *Thieves*. He's smart, he's cunning, and he's also ex-paramilitary, so he can hold his own physically, too. Having a villain like him around opens up my mind to new story possibilities. Right from the start, he was always going to survive *Thieves*, but when we see him again in a future book, he might have a totally new face.

I also loved writing that last page, where Scarecrow finds his scratched glasses on his pillow and so knows that Calderon has been *in his room*!

Any Hollywood news?

I wrote the first draft of the *Scarecrow* screenplay and now a new screenwriter has been brought in to rewrite my stuff. I'm not upset by this. It's actually standard Hollywood procedure, especially on a movie as expensive as *Scarecrow* could be.

And *Hover Car Racer* is still ticking along with Disney. I am less involved in that project than I am with *Scarecrow*, but they were talking about directors a few months back. In the end, because of their scale, my books would make very expensive movies, and when studios make expensive movies, they want to get name actors and top directors, and to get those, you need a kick-ass screenplay.

This means a bit of waiting, but I'm happy to wait . . . and keep writing new novels in the meantime.

So what is next—is it back to Jack West Jr or another Scarecrow novel?

Believe it or not, last year I actually wrote a whole new novel in secret. This book is also a little different: it's a murder-mystery thriller set in the year 1550. Imagine 'Matthew Reilly meets *The Name of the Rose*'! It may be set in the past, but it is whip-fast and definitely not for the squeamish.

Having said that, I do now find myself thinking about what to write next, and yes, that is a choice between Scarecrow and Jack. I have to admit I quite liked hanging out with Scarecrow and Mother again, and Baba is a lot of fun, too, so a new Scarecrow novel is currently looking good.

Any final words?

As always, I just hope the book took you away from the real world for a few days and showed you a good time. I hope you enjoyed Scarecrow's big return.

Matthew Reilly
Sydney, Australia
October 2011

DRAGO

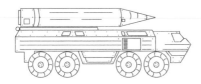

Transporter Erector Launcher

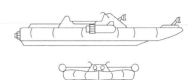

AFDV (Experimental)

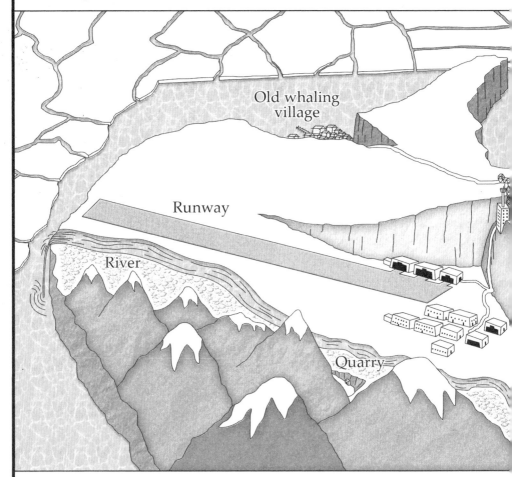

Old whaling village

Runway

River

Quarry

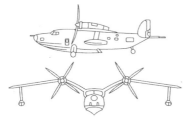

Beriev Be-12

V-22 Osprey

A Finder's Magic